Praise for

Fifth Avenue Glamour Girl

"In this captivating novel, Renée Rosen invites readers to peer behind the lovely facade of the iconic Estée Lauder, at her real origin and hardscrabble rise. This illuminating tale about ambition and friendship . . . explores the dangers inherent in embellishing the truth."

—Marie Benedict, *New York Times* bestselling coauthor of *The Personal Librarian* and author of *The Mitford Affair*

"An ode to the singular magic of chasing and catching one's wildest dreams. . . . Rosen is at the height of her storytelling prowess with this glittering novel that shines as brightly as the heroine at its center. I absolutely could not put it down."

—Kristy Woodson Harvey, *New York Times* bestselling author of *The Summer of Songbirds*

"A dazzling story of the beauty of female friendship and the dogged persistence of a cosmetics legend who knew that she—and the women around her—was meant for more."

—Stephanie Marie Thornton, *USA Today* bestselling author of *Her Lost Words*

"Renée Rosen . . . creates a heroine as timeless and remarkable as the products she introduced to women all around the world. A truly inspiring rags-to-riches tale, told by a wonderful storyteller."

—Natasha Lester, *New York Times* bestselling author of *The Three Lives of Alix St. Pierre*

"A page-turning story of resilience and self-determination. . . . An inspiration for us all."

—Lynn Cullen, national bestselling author of *The Woman with the Cure*

"An intimate and fascinating glimpse into the woman whose determination to fulfill her dream literally changed the face of American women, told with an immediacy that was captivating far beyond the final page. A must-read!"

—Shelley Noble, *New York Times* bestselling author of *Summer Island*

"This beautifully written story will be one you won't be able to put down as you cheer these women on."

—Madeline Martin, *New York Times* bestselling author of *The Librarian Spy*

"Renée Rosen's gift for creating real, fallible, and compelling characters we grow to love and cheer for shines in *Fifth Avenue Glamour Girl*. . . . A brilliant, absorbing, and emotional novel you won't want to put down!"

—Christine Wells, author of *One Woman's War*

"Readers will love this fascinating story of two women concealing the blemishes of their past while building a friendship that will carry them through the heartbreak and ambition of claiming their space at the beauty counter."

—Georgie Blalock, author of *An Indiscreet Princess*

ALSO BY RENÉE ROSEN

The Social Graces
Park Avenue Summer
Windy City Blues
White Collar Girl
What the Lady Wants
Dollface
Every Crooked Pot

Fifth Avenue Glamour Girl

RENÉE ROSEN

Berkley
New York

BERKLEY
An imprint of Penguin Random House LLC
penguinrandomhouse.com

Library of Congress Cataloging-in-Publication Data

Names: Rosen, Renée, author.
Title: Fifth Avenue glamour girl / Renée Rosen.
Description: New York : Berkley, [2023]
Identifiers: LCCN 2022032819 (print) | LCCN 2022032820 (ebook) |
ISBN 9780593335666 (trade paperback) | ISBN 9780593335673 (ebook)
Subjects: LCGFT: Novels.
Classification: LCC PS3618.O83156 F54 2023 (print) |
LCC PS3618.O83156 (ebook) | DDC 813/.6—dc23/eng/20220708
LC record available at https://lccn.loc.gov/2022032819
LC ebook record available at https://lccn.loc.gov/2022032820

First Edition: April 2023

Printed in the United States of America
3rd Printing

Book design by Alison Cnockaert

To my family, with love

Prologue

NEW YORK CITY, 1984

I CANNOT TELL A lie. Although that's not *entirely* true.

Who among us can honestly say they've never embellished a story, omitted an incriminating detail or spared someone's feelings with a well-intended fib? We are all guilty of deception in one form or another. Having spent the bulk of my career in the cosmetic industry, I know all about creating illusions, whether it's that birthmark you're concealing beneath foundation, the eyebrows you pencil in each morning, the gray roots you cover before detection or that face-lift no one knows about. The point is, none of us are completely authentic, exempt from playing with the slippery truth. But just how far we'll go, and which lines we refuse to cross, is for each of us to determine.

This is the very dilemma I'm faced with as I listen to the voice on the other end of the telephone. It sounds like a whiskey-soaked *last call* coming from a woman smoking an unfiltered cigarette. She's a writer, a fairly accomplished one, and is quick to mention that her previous book landed on the *New York Times* bestseller list. She explains that she's conducting research for a biography she's working on about a friend of mine.

"Oh? Which friend?" I am mentally scrolling through my Rolodex, thinking of the various actors, artists and businessmen I know.

"Estée," she says, mispronouncing her name, emphasizing the long *e*. "Estée Lauder."

"Oh, really?" I sound mildly curious, possibly even amused, but my nerves are already knitting together. I feel warm, prickly. Even a little nauseated. "Well, she's certainly a fascinating subject," I say. "I mean, c'mon, she's a self-made woman. She took the makeup industry by storm."

"Yeah, only that's not my angle."

"So, no overnight success story, huh?" I ask, fishing.

"Not exactly." The way she laughs at this makes my gut twist. "Actually, I think it would be better if we do this in person."

I get the feeling she's all bloodhound, that she's after something that could be damaging to both Estée and me. Even as I hear myself agreeing to meet her later that day for a drink, I feel my guard going up. Some things from the past need to stay there.

She suggests a hole-in-the-wall bar on 96th and Second Avenue, but if we do this, it's going to be on my turf. "Let's meet at the Pierre instead." I catch myself checking my watch, as if she can see me, as if I have a pressing schedule to juggle. "How's four o'clock?"

After we hang up, I grab my coat and head out to clear my mind. It's early January and everything is frosted in ice and snow. Steam rises from the manhole covers along 49th Street as I turn up my collar and stuff my hands deep inside my pockets. I'm getting cold, and since I have a good hour to kill before our meeting at the Pierre, I duck inside Saks Fifth Avenue.

The revolving door gives way to a hum of piped-in music, soft murmurings and a burst of perfume coming from the cosmetic department. As I look around, my eyes land on the Clinique, Prescriptives and Aramis counters. I see Estée's stamp everywhere in this store. Her presence is just as visible in Macy's, Bloomingdale's, Bergdorf's, Bonwit Teller, Neiman Marcus—in any department store across the country or around the world. The field is crowded with new players like Charles of the Ritz, Lancôme, Clarins, CoverGirl and dozens of others, but only one name dominates and that's Estée Lauder. She's at the top of her game. Bigger than Helena Rubinstein and Elizabeth Arden combined. It doesn't surprise me that someone would want to knock her off her pedestal, and that *someone* is waiting for me at the Pierre.

It's just a short walk from Saks, less than fifteen minutes, and as I step inside the hotel, I glance up at the rotunda ceiling, muraled with wispy clouds and a warm blue sky. In a crowded room of fashionable women with fur coats draped over their shoulders, men in tailored suits and pocket squares, I spot Lee Israel. She doesn't look like a successful author. She's slovenly, to say the least. As I get closer, I see there's cat hair clinging to her sweater, which is pilling and full of nubs. My first impulse is to tweeze her eyebrows. All I can think is that she's the most unlikely person to be writing about a cosmetic icon, which is not to say she wouldn't be a perfect candidate for a makeover. A little foundation would cover her ruddy complexion and the broken capillaries. Some blush would define her otherwise nonexistent cheekbones.

After the briefest of introductions, she asks what I'm drinking and jumps right in. "I can't remember if I mentioned this on the phone or not, but this is an *unauthorized* biography. You should know up front that Estée's already refused to talk to me. Same for the rest of her family. But I'm writing this book anyway, without her consent. And without her input."

I get the impression that she's expecting me to come clean and tell her everything I know. And I do know *everything*. I also know that I can't talk about Estée without revealing my own story, the two are so entwined. Regardless of what Lee Israel wants to ask me, the only real question is, will I tell the truth, or will I lie?

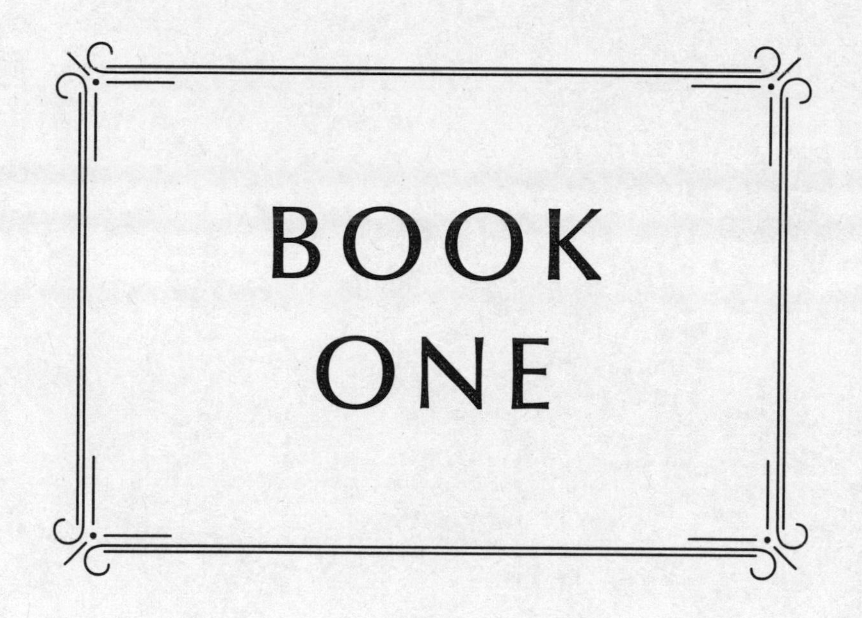

BOOK ONE

1

NEW YORK CITY, 1938

I WOULD NEVER FORGET the first words Estée Lauder said to me: "That's the wrong shade of lipstick for your coloring."

She'd crossed the room and was standing beside me, her advice unsolicited and, frankly, unwanted. I was getting my hair cut and dyed at Darlene's Palace of Beauty on 75th and Broadway. I'd gone there on an impulse as soon as they opened. I was their first customer that day, seeking refuge after the Hermitage Hotel for Men ousted me. I was twenty-one and no better equipped to face adulthood than a newborn left outside a firehouse, a baby bird fallen from the nest.

Darlene, the owner, picked up her scissors for some last-minute snips. She was a stout, gruff redhead with three pin curls across her forehead and a constellation of acne scars along her left cheek. While exhaling cigarette smoke from the corner of her mouth, she pumped the hydraulic foot pedal on the base of the chair. She bumped me *up, up, up* until I was eye level with a petite blonde who introduced herself as Estée—which came out sounding like *Est-Stay*—Lauder. She had luminous skin, not one pore visible on her face. She was pretty, but not extraordinarily so. You wouldn't have looked twice at her until you got to know her and then, well, then, you couldn't take your eyes off her. She had what I called creeping charisma, in that it snuck up on you. Despite sometimes being pushy, her charms were cumulative. She was not short on opinions, but still, she had the ability to draw people to her and could get away with saying and doing things that no one else dared. If someone had told me then that Estée and I would have become the closest of friends, I never would have believed them.

I assumed we were about the same age but later on learned that she was seven years my senior. Later still, I'd discovered that she was actually nine years older. For someone trying to portray herself as nearly a decade younger than she was, she certainly didn't dress the part. The woman standing before me wore a boxy beige town suit with the jacket buttoned to her throat. The tiny little beige hat, tilted just so, seemed affixed to her blonde marcelled hair. Even my mother wouldn't have worn such an outfit. Yes, the quality was good, and I knew how to spot finely made clothes, but the style was that of a middle-aged woman trying to hide figure flaws.

"I'm sorry," she said. "I didn't catch your name." She spoke like a blue blood, with the affected speech pattern of someone who spent her summers on Martha's Vineyard.

"Gloria. Gloria Downing." The name still sounded foreign to me. It even tasted funny on my tongue. I'd taken it from a box of matches still in my pocketbook: *Downing Brothers Safety Match Co.* Estée didn't notice the strange hitch in my voice because she was too busy looking at my dress. I'd been wearing the same one for three days now. It was wrinkled and smelled faintly of the gin I'd spilled on it the night before.

That dress was one of only a handful I'd held on to. The rest of my extensive and rather expensive wardrobe had been auctioned off, along with just about everything else inside our Fifth Avenue penthouse, including the penthouse itself. Even my Cord 812 and the other family automobiles had all been sold, the proceeds going to pay my father's legal fees, fines and restitution. Not that I would have worn those dresses or driven that car ever again. They were as good as stolen. Before we were forced out of our home, I'd stuffed what was left of my life into a single suitcase that was now stowed behind the front desk at Darlene's Palace of Beauty.

For the past six weeks, I'd been secretly living at a bachelor's hotel near Times Square. For obvious reasons, I knew that was never going to be a long-term solution. In fact, that very morning, my breasts and I had been escorted off the property. So now, on top of everything else, I had no place to live.

"And can I just say one more thing?" Estée was asking. There was something distinctly feminine and delicate about her. *Frilly* was the word that came to mind. She had a way of holding her hands just so, pinkies out, like she was having tea with the queen. "May I?" she asked again.

I turned my eyes to an article about Carole Lombard and Clark Gable in a back issue of *Photoplay*. Estée got the message and retreated. When she was gone, I looked at myself in the mirror. Of course she was right about the lipstick. It didn't work with my new hair color at all.

I had just gone from being a platinum blonde to a brunette—and I was a natural blonde, mind you. My hair had always been my trademark. The shade I picked from Darlene's puny selection was Dark Brown #1. It was not a particularly flattering choice. My skin tone was much too cool for a brunette. I'm not even sure a different shade would have helped. The style—Darlene had lopped off eight inches, leaving me with a chin-length cut and a thick row of bangs—was not exactly becoming, either.

Basically, I'd made a mess of my appearance, which seemed apropos, seeing as my father had made a mess of my life. And the lives of so many other people: longtime family friends, relatives, government officials—no one was spared. Not Tommy or his family, either. Not even our housekeeper or the doorman who had entrusted their entire life savings to my father. So, in the grand scheme of things, ruining my looks didn't matter. Actually, that had been the reason for my impromptu visit to Darlene's Palace of Beauty. It was all part of my disguise, my attempt to put my past behind me.

I had assumed that would have been the last I'd see of Darlene and Estée, but I could not have been more wrong. As I was about to retrieve my suitcase and pay the bill, Darlene fired her one and only shampoo girl, who had apparently been tying up the telephone line all day.

"I'm trying to run a business here . . ." Darlene said, with a cigarette parked in her mouth. "I can't have you yapping on the phone when you should be doing shampoos . . ."

I listened to her berate the girl before ordering her out of the shop. With the doorbell chimes still ringing, Darlene shoved the cash register drawer shut with her hip and lit a new cigarette off the one she was about to grind out.

While she muttered about needing to hire a new shampoo girl, I heard my brother's voice sounding off inside my head: *Get yourself a job, Gloria*. What little money I had left was dwindling fast, and I'd just dropped $5.50 on my hair. Glenn was still chattering in my ear, reminding me that I was no longer a rich girl, that I had to find a way to support myself.

"I—I can do it. I can shampoo hair." The words escaped like a sneeze I hadn't felt coming on.

"You?" Darlene's eyebrows tickled her pin curls. "After what you just did to your own hair?" She released a sharp, curt laugh.

"Listen," I said, "you need help and I need work. Just give me a chance."

And that's how I got a job. My first job. *Ever.* I was a shampoo girl and an occasional sweeper of floors. Not that either task—

shampooing or sweeping—sounded difficult, but keep in mind that the only hair I'd ever shampooed was my own and the only floor I'd ever swept would have been none. We had a housekeeper for that. Until we didn't.

Immediately after hiring me—an act of desperation on both our parts—Darlene handed me a pink smock that drooped down my shoulders and hung on me like a sack.

"I'll need this in a smaller size," I said, tugging on the sleeve.

She glared at me. "What do you think this is, Bergdorf's?"

I wanted to quit on the spot.

Ten minutes after that, I wanted to quit again. While waiting for my first shampoo to arrive, I stopped halfheartedly pushing a broom around and made the grave mistake of taking a bathroom break without asking permission.

Darlene was waiting for me outside the restroom. Drawing on her cigarette, which was approaching an inch-long ash, she said, "If you need to *go* and you can't *hold it* till your break, you need to ask me first."

Well, everything inside me bristled at this. I hadn't asked if I could go to the bathroom since grammar school. I was unaccustomed to being told what to do, when and how to do it. But catching a glimpse of my suitcase, containing all my worldly possessions, triggered alarms inside me. I had no home, no place to rest my head. I needed this job. I needed the money.

After choking out as sincere an apology as I could muster for my bathroom blunder, I set out to shampoo my first head, quickly realizing that I had underestimated the task at hand.

"That water's ice-cold," the woman said, scowling up at me. I cranked the knob the other way and she shrieked, loud enough to capture everyone's attention. "Good God, now it's scalding." Before I got the temperature to her liking, I'd accidently shot a stream of water down her back. Needless to say, she didn't bother tipping me.

I'd barely gotten rid of her when another head appeared in my bowl. Bored and sinking fast, I escaped into the jaunty rhythm of "It's De-Lovely" coming over the radio. At the first refrain, a hair dryer kicked on and drowned out the music. Thankfully Bernice, the manicurist, rolled across the room on her stool and turned up the radio at the front desk. I noticed that Bernice never walked anywhere. With a push off her heels, she rolled to answer the phone, schedule appointments, fetch a magazine for a customer.

With the music back, I began humming along, tapping my foot. I could never resist the urge to dance. At parties, I was the first one on the dance floor and loved pulling people—especially the wallflowers—out there with me. I had a soft spot in my heart for the shyer girls. I could hardly enjoy myself knowing they were off to the side, sullen and self-conscious. So I'd get them on their feet and make sure they were having a swell time.

"It's De-Lovely" had me momentarily forgetting about my troubles as well as the woman's head in the bowl. It wasn't until she cried out that I saw I'd gotten shampoo in her eyes.

Thirty minutes and four customers later, I had unintentionally sprayed another young lady in the face and made a middle-aged woman moan so loudly I thought I was hurting her. When I apologized, she grabbed my wrist, panting, "Don't. Don't stop. Please don't stop."

I watched the wall clock inch from twelve to one with no break in the action. I ended up working through lunch, thinking I needed the tip money more than food. I was about to shampoo an elderly woman when Estée waltzed over. All morning I'd been trying to figure out exactly what she did at Darlene's. She wasn't a beautician, she wasn't a manicurist or even the receptionist. What's more, she wore a wedding ring, and where I came from, married women didn't work. Turned out that she was renting a small corner of the shop where she set up a little concession stand to sell cold creams and lotions she made in the kitchen of her Upper West Side apartment. She made the stuff and she hawked it. Oh boy, did she ever.

Estée came up and leaned over the woman I was shampooing. "I have something that would look perfect on you, madam," she said. "May I show you how to apply it? It will only take five minutes and I promise when I'm done, your skin will glow."

I highly doubted this was possible. The woman's face reminded me of a speckled egg, peppered with liver spots. But damn if Estée didn't end up selling her a jar anyway.

Estée swooped in on my next customer, too, using her same spiel: "I have something that would look perfect on you . . ."

"Oh no, thank you," said the woman. She had tiny red bumps along her rosy cheeks. "My skin's too sensitive."

But Estée had already uncapped a jar and reached for the woman's hand. And once Estée had hold of her, there was no retreat. She rubbed circles around and over all protests while doling out beauty advice: *Sleeping in mascara will destroy your lashes. Wash your face twice a day just like you'd brush your teeth. Never pick at blemishes* and *don't sleep on your stomach or side unless you want wrinkles.* As one who often slept both *in* my mascara and *on* my stomach, I was tempted to douse her with the water nozzle.

By three o'clock, things had slowed a bit and my hands were red and raw from shampooing. I grabbed an emery board off Bernice's cart, plopped down in a chair and began filing my nails until Darlene came over and thrust a broom at me. I got the hint and went about sweeping the floor, collecting clumps of hair blowing across the pink and black tiles like tumbleweed. Every few strokes I paused and ran my palms down the front of my smock before cradling my chapped fingers.

Estée came up to me with one of her jars, untwisting the cap. "I have something that would—"

"Spare me the sales pitch," I said, leaning in on the tip of my boom handle.

"But I have a wonderful cream for your hands. I promise they'll feel soft and supple."

"No, thank you." My hands were throbbing and stinging, hurting the way hands that have never been asked to do a day's work would hurt. She was trying to help but I didn't want her touching me, rubbing her miracle cream into my skin and expecting me to buy a jar.

We were in a standoff, or at least I was, trying to look as mean and scary as possible. She wasn't biting. Instead, Estée smiled in an easy, amused sort of way, like she found my ire entertaining, which I found infuriating.

"Hey, Gloria," Darlene called over, pointing toward the shampoo bowl with her chin. "Customer." It came out in three syllables: *Cus-to-mer.*

"*Com-ming!*" I leaned the broom against the wall and headed over to the bowl.

"Good afternoon," I said to the woman. She gave me a look: *How dare you keep me waiting?* I twisted the hot knob full blast and let her have it.

"Whoa—eek!" she shrieked, pulling away.

I adjusted the water and tried again, resenting the way this woman treated me. Of course, I'd forgotten about the numerous shampoo girls who'd been all but invisible to me through the years. I never asked their names, asked how their days were going, if they'd read any good books lately. I was always a generous tipper, though, dropping an extra quarter or two into their open palms. Until I stood on the other side of the bowl, I thought the tip was all that mattered. But now, less than one day into this job, I understood. The women who came into Darlene's didn't see me as a living, breathing person—a person who just a few months ago was one of them, only richer. I told myself that if I ever got back on my feet, I would never again think anyone was beneath me.

The afternoon dragged on and I didn't know how I was going to make it through the day. It was ungodly hot inside the beauty parlor. And pink. I'd never seen so many variations of pink, everything from the Pepto-Bismol wallpaper that curled in the corners to the cotton candy chairs. Even the hair dryers looked like giant pink Easter eggs. The only thing in there that wasn't pink was Estée: head-to-toe beige. The shop even smelled pink, a noxious combination of setting lotion, nail polish and perfume. Already I could feel a headache coming on.

Sweat trickled down my back as the oscillating fan moved the hot air from side to side. I kept pushing my damp bangs aside with the backs of my soapy wrists. One of the hair dryers kicked on, and after Bernice rolled over to raise the volume on the radio, the announcer's voice crackled over the little mesh speaker. First came the weather report followed by "*. . . Later today, Gustaw Dowaziac—*"

My ears stood at attention and my skin prickled up. Dowaziac was not a common name. At least it hadn't been until three months ago, when it landed on the front page of every New York City newspaper and was reiterated—with great disdain—over every radio station. That's when I'd adopted Downing as my last name. Prior to that, if I had a nickel for every time I had to spell "Doe-ah-zee-ack. D-o-w-a-z-i-a-c"—well, I would have been rich in my own right and would never have ended up in such dire straits.

"*. . . Dowaziac will be transferred from the Manhattan Criminal Courts Building jail to the Sing Sing maximum-security prison, where he will begin serving his twenty-five-year sentence. Fifty-two-year-old*

Dowaziac pleaded guilty to nine federal felonies, including mail fraud, making false statements and making false filings with the Securities and Exchange Commission, tax evasion and . . ."

The announcer was still going on and I imagined everyone in the beauty shop had connected the dots and was staring at me. My lungs were stuck together and I couldn't take a deep breath.

And then came that dreaded high-pitched ping in my right ear. The first sign of a vertigo bout coming on. *Not here. Not now, please, God!* The side of my face was already growing numb as the room took off in a nauseating whirl. My legs turned to jelly and I held on, gripping the side of the shampoo bowl. Staring at a stationary object always helped while waiting for the spinning to stop, so I locked eyes on a bottle of Drene shampoo, concentrating on the wavy, water-rippled label. As I stared at the *d*, desperate thoughts of Tommy seeped in, thick and inky. I couldn't make it without him. I wouldn't survive on my own. He had to take me back, marry me, take care of me . . .

That was the last thing I remembered before the floor tiles tilted up and met my face, my head missing the corner of the counter by less than an inch.

2

WHEN I CAME to, Estée was kneeling next to me, laying a cool pink compress across my forehead. I tried to get up, but the room whirled again. I wondered if I had a concussion.

"Easy now," she said, gently coaxing me back down. "Just stay still for a moment."

I was aware of Count Basie on the radio and a circle of faces staring down at me, their worried expressions kaleidoscoping.

Bernice asked Darlene if I was *in trouble.*

"I dunno." Darlene lit a cigarette and asked me point-blank: "Well, are you? Are you *in trouble*?"

Oh, I was in trouble, all right, but not the kind of trouble she was expecting of a twenty-one-year-old unmarried woman. I was in trouble because my father was a despicable human being. When he was arrested back on April 1st—which turned out not to be an April Fool's joke at all—I was as stunned as everyone else. All I knew was that we Dowaziacs lived quite well indeed—even during the Great Depression. But that was only because we were living well on other people's money—money my father was supposed to have been investing on their behalf.

I didn't even understand how my father's scam worked, but there was a lot of talk about forged statements and robbing Peter to pay Paul. What I did understand, though, was that every major historical event had a villain. The Great Chicago Fire had Mrs. O'Leary's cow, and Prohibition had Al Capone. While some blamed the Great Depression on President Hoover, to me, Gustaw "Gus" Dowaziac was the man who poured salt on the wounds of those already bleeding financially.

I was the youngest and the only member of my family who saw my father for the monster he was. While I kept asking how he could have done such a thing, my mother, sister and brother took a different tack. They insisted that the judge had been unfair, that my father hadn't meant to steal from anyone and that if only the stock market hadn't crashed his clients would have seen a big return on their money. It was like we'd all purchased a ticket for the same movie, only I ended up watching an entirely different show.

It was rare for me to stand apart from them. As the youngest, I was accustomed to being moved about like a chess piece, never voicing my own views since no one in my family listened to me anyway. But this time I couldn't buy into their baloney about the judge, the stock market and everything else because Tommy Cavendish and his parents were among my father's victims, which meant I was a victim, too.

Mr. and Mrs. Cavendish never cared for me to begin with. It was bad enough that I was Catholic and new money—new money that would turn dirty—but after my father robbed them blind, Tommy broke all ties with me and broke my heart. His $25,000 and his parents' $75,000 meant more to my father than my future happiness, and for that, I could never forgive him. I shook my head to clear the thoughts, which only stirred up the vertigo.

"Come on now," I heard Estée saying to the others. "Don't crowd her." She sounded protective of me as she waved them back, and despite my disliking her, I could not fight my need to be comforted. Even by her.

I was light-headed, shaky and scared. I'd had plenty of vertigo bouts, but I had never fainted from one before. The vertigo began a few years ago, around the time my mother started pouring chardonnay in her coffee cup and my father's insomnia kept him pacing, his slippers slapping the hardwood floors until three or four in the morning. I think the vertigo was my system picking up on something lurking beneath the surface, like a metal detector scouring the beach. The doctors were baffled, and with no remedy, I learned to manage the bouts as best I could. Sometimes they were mild and passed so quickly no one noticed I'd even had one.

When my equilibrium returned, Estée helped me up. "Let's get you some fresh air. Are you hungry?"

I placed my hand on my stomach. It felt hollow. I was starving, the kind of hunger that borders on nausea. I definitely needed food. That had to have been why I'd fainted. No dinner last night. No breakfast or lunch. It was four o'clock and I couldn't remember the last time I'd eaten anything that hadn't come from a vending machine.

A blast of hot summer air hit me as we stepped outside. I could feel the sidewalk sizzling beneath my shoes as we walked over to the Broadway Luncheonette three doors down. We sat at the counter and Estée ordered two iced teas and a club sandwich for me.

After I gobbled that down, she said, "Can I just say something?"

As if I could have stopped her. I dabbed the napkin to my mouth and waited.

"Let me give you some advice." She did a quarter turn on her stool and looked me in the eye. "You need to lose that chip on your shoulder."

"I beg your pardon?" Despite her having helped me after my fainting spell, I was winding up to let her have it.

"I'm sorry if the truth hurts," said Estée, "but you have a lousy work ethic."

"A lousy work ethic?" I wanted to laugh. I had no work ethic at all. I pushed my empty plate aside and tossed my napkin on top.

"You're going to get yourself fired if you don't shape up. I've been watching you all day and I'm only saying this for your own good. You're lazy. You were walking around in there today like a prima donna, acting like it's an inconvenience to do your job."

That was *exactly* how I felt. The fact that she'd figured me out was impressive but also annoying.

"Darlene won't think twice about firing you," she said. "You saw what happened to the last girl. Jobs are hard to come by right now. You can't afford to lose yours. And if you don't mind my saying, you really need to take a little pride in what you do."

"Oh, please, I'm a shampoo girl, for Christ's sake."

"Maybe you're a shampoo girl today, but if you change your attitude, you might be able to make something of yourself. Don't forget that we become the people we *think* we are. It's true." She nodded in response to my doubtful expression. "You have to first picture what you want to happen in your mind. If you want to be successful, you have to imagine you already *are* successful. Get it? You can do anything you set your mind to. Anything at all. It all starts up here." She smiled as she tapped her temple.

"Good God, do you hear yourself?" I forced a laughed. I wanted to say something clever, something about her naïveté, but *that word*—I was never sure if it was pronounced *ni-e-va-tay* or *ni-ev-ity*, so I sidestepped it: "Are you always such a Pollyanna?"

"Are you always such a goddamn sourpuss?"

I hadn't expected her to fire back at me like that. I was stunned. Something about her—Miss Prim and Proper—saying that struck me as . . . well, as hilarious. I started to laugh, which in turn got her laughing. Another surprise: Estée had a sense of humor.

"I'm serious," she pressed on, trying to recover. "Now see, the way I do it is I approach each customer like they're someone who could help me in the future."

"Help you? How?"

"You know, help me launch my business. All it takes is one movie star to endorse your face creams and you've got it made."

"Somehow I don't see a lot of movie stars coming into Darlene's *Palace of Pinkness.*"

"No, but someone who comes to me for a facial could be a budding actress or know a famous actress. Or someone even more important." Estée's eyes went wide and I could tell she was getting all revved up. "Why, just the other day a woman came in who is Mary Pickford's second cousin, and she promised to tell her all about me." Estée smiled, relishing the possibilities. "The point is, you just never know. Anyone who comes through the door could be connected to someone who knows someone. Do you see what I'm getting at?"

"Yeah. You're telling me you're just a social-climbing opportunist."

"Oh." She laughed again, playfully swatting at my hand. "You are a miserable little mope, aren't you?"

"Touché!" I raised my iced tea to her. Snapping open my pocketbook, I pulled out my gold cigarette case—one of the few luxury items I'd held on to because it hadn't been *stolen*.

"Fancy," she said. "Where'd you get that?"

"It was a gift."

"A gift, huh? From who?"

God, she was nosy. "A secret admirer." I couldn't bring myself to say *ex-boyfriend*, and *my would-be fiancé* sounded even worse. The truth was, Tommy's mother disapproved of me, so for nearly a year we were secretly pre-engaged—which, unlike being a little pregnant, resulted in nothing.

"Lucky you. A rich suitor."

I sighed, breaking apart inside. I had no rich suitor anymore. It was over with Tommy. Despite all my hoping and wishing, I knew deep down that he was never coming back to me.

"I'll bet he's handsome."

"It's really none of your business."

"For crying out loud, Gloria! What is wrong with you? You're young. You're beautiful. You've got someone buying you expensive presents." She tapped her lacquered nails on the cigarette case. "What have you got to be so angry about?"

I took a sip of my iced tea, stalling, thinking, *What haven't I got to be angry about?*

"Well?" She was waiting for an explanation.

Just as I was about to tell her I was a vagabond, I remembered my suitcase. "Oh God, all my stuff. My suit—"

"Don't worry. It'll be fine at Darlene's. You can get it later. Do you have a train to catch, is that it?"

"Jesus, no! I don't have a train to catch—I have no place to live!"

She pulled back, her face a little pinched. "What do you mean? Where's your family?"

"I have no family!" I blurted—a full-blown lie that came out with the force of a cork shooting off a bottle of champagne.

"No family? At all?" Estée leaned in closer, her elbows on the counter.

This was a pivotal moment, but I wasn't prepared for it. Never saw it coming. So all that came out was a meek reflexive croak: "My family's gone." This was not a total lie. My mother was temporarily living with her cousin on Long Island, where I wasn't welcome unless I was willing to forgive my father. My sister, Gail, and I never got along, and she'd barely said goodbye before moving her family to Boston, where my brother, Glenn, was also living now. And my father, well, he was certainly gone, locked away for so long, he'd probably die behind bars. So, yes, in a sense they were all gone. I had no family.

"Oh, Gloria." Estée's shoulders dropped, her expression turned tender and full of concern. "You poor thing, you. I just can't imagine . . ." She let her words ring out like the tone of a bell growing ever fainter. "Where have you been living up until now?"

"At a hotel. But I'm running out of money and I don't know what I'm going to do and . . ."

She reached over for my hand. "It's okay. Calm down."

I jerked from her touch, the panic escalating. My nerves felt raw, exposed live wires. I didn't know why this was all registering in my brain just then. Wouldn't the time to have panicked been hours before, when I was kicked out of the hotel? I believed this was what you called a delayed reaction. I seemed to have been prone to them.

"It's okay," Estée repeated. "Just take a breath. Together we'll figure this out."

Together? As in the two of us? She was going to help me? I can't begin to explain what a calming effect her words had on me. You see, I'd never had a real problem before because someone else had always stepped in and solved it before I had a chance to fret about it. Someone—usually my father or Tommy—always took care of it for me. They were gone and now here was Estée, my new savior.

She brought a glossy red fingernail to her mouth, bit down and then, as if thinking better of it, dropped her hand to her lap. "I'd have you come stay with us for a while, but there's barely enough room for Joe and me. Let alone our son."

"You have a son?" There was no masking my surprise. Married *with* a child and still working?

"Leonard's five."

I was still stunned. If I'd married Tommy, I would have stayed home and raised his babies.

"Let me just think here." Estée drummed her nails along the

Formica, and after several rounds of thrumming she said, "I might know of a place you can stay. That is, if you're not too picky. A friend of Joe's was renting a room in a house up on West Eighty-First Street. He just moved out. His room may still be available." She pulled a pen from her pocketbook and reached for a napkin, scribbling down an address. "Here—" She slid the napkin over to me.

The Millers 163 W. 81st. Between Amsterdam and Columbus. A room in a stranger's house? Was she crazy? I couldn't picture myself doing that in a million years. But then again, I couldn't have pictured myself being a shampoo girl, either. I folded the napkin and tucked it inside my pocketbook.

"You're welcome," she said.

"Sorry. I just never expected to be in this position."

"Join the club. My family lost *everything* in the crash. *Everything.* The big house in Flushing. The cars, the chauffeur—I tell you, we lost it all. Times are hard right now, Gloria. Everybody's struggling."

This was my first inkling that Estée and I had anything in common. Part of me desperately wanted to confide in her. But I caught myself because our circumstances were not the same. She lost everything in the stock market crash. I lost everything because my father was a crook.

When the bill came, she reached for it. "You can get it the next time."

Next time? There was going to be a next time? I looked at her and asked, "Why?"

"Why what?"

"Why are you being so nice to me? I've been horrid to you. Absolutely horrid."

"Well, I'm beginning to think that's part of your charm." She smiled, pinched open her change purse and took out a few coins and a dollar bill. "I knew you didn't like me at first. For all I know you *still* don't like me. I'm not used to people *not* liking me, Gloria.

You're a challenge"—she waved her finger at me—"and I have to admit, I do like a challenge. I guess you could say I wanted to see if I could win you over."

She sounded a bit like my father, a man so charismatic he could make anyone fall under his spell. I looked at Estée, and despite all she'd done for me that day, I was still on the fence about her: Did I admire her or resent her? She was charming, but then again, so was my father. And yet she was compassionate. She oozed compassion.

"So, what do you say, Gloria Downing?" Estée extended her hand to me. "Truce?"

I reached for her like you would a lifeline. "Truce."

3

THANKS TO ESTÉE, I ended up renting that room in the Millers' brownstone on the Upper West Side. Also thanks to Estée, one week later, I was still fretting about that chip on my shoulder. Everyone who knew me—*really knew me*—had the right to say I was lazy, spoiled, coddled all my life. But Estée had picked up on that right after meeting me. *Was I that transparent?* She'd touched a nerve and now I felt the need to prove myself to her. And to myself. I wanted to show her I had developed a good work ethic. Maybe even an excellent work ethic, at that.

I became more engaged in my chores at Darlene's Palace of Beauty, which was in and of itself something of a miracle. I got lost in the rhythm of the busy shop and it made the time go faster. Stationed at the shampoo bowl, I took extra care to greet each client, asking about their day while I tucked the towel inside their cape so no water would rush down their necks. I gently eased head after head into the bowl and checked the water temperature against my wrist, like a baby's bottle. I massaged every scalp with care. I didn't even balk—did not say a single word—when one customer covered up her gray roots with black shoe polish. *Oh, the lengths to which women would go to extend the life of their hair dye!* I gently scrubbed until my cuticles were black and two inches of white hair flanked her part. In between shampoos, I swept the floor and took it upon myself to uncrate new cases of shampoo and organize the shelves in the back room. Darlene would have to remind me to take my breaks.

I remember the swell in my chest when she thanked me for cleaning the combs and brushes, for bringing her a stack of fresh towels, and I got a smile out of Estée when she saw me straightening the magazines on the front table. I was no more than a sapling and each droplet of encouragement caused me to bloom and thirst for more. In short order and much to my surprise, I discovered that there was genuine satisfaction to be found in doing one's job well. This may sound obvious to others, but I was not exactly a well-adjusted twenty-one-year-old back then, so the rewards of working were quite a revelation to me.

One afternoon, while looking for something productive to do, I met Estée's husband. Joe Lauder came into Darlene's holding five-year-old Leonard in one hand, and in the other, a white paper bag with a sandwich inside for Estée. Joe was a good-looking man, not too tall, not too short, with a solid build and lots of curly brown hair. Leonard broke away from him and made a beeline for Bernice, the two of them rolling across the floor on her stool. While Estée dabbed cream on her client's face, Joe introduced himself.

"I can't believe you bring your wife lunch," I said, shaking his hand. "Do you have a brother?"

He laughed, setting the paper bag on Estée's counter. "What can I do?" He shrugged. "She forgets to eat otherwise."

"Oh, Joe," Estée called over, "that's her. That's Gloria. The new girl I was telling you about."

I smiled at him. "I can only imagine what she had to say about me."

"Not a thing to worry about," he assured me. "She likes you. Thinks of you as a little sister."

I knew this was meant to be a compliment, but I already had one big sister and she didn't like me.

Half an hour later, I was in the supply room on my break when Bernice rolled in. "Oh, that Leonard," she said, sorting through a tray of nail polishes, "I could just eat him up."

"The father's not too bad, either," I said. "I still can't believe he brings her lunch."

"Oh, Joe is a prince. And why not? He married an honest-to-goodness princess. Estée comes from a royal family, you know."

"I did *not* know that." *A married princess working at Darlene's?* I had my doubts.

"Oh yeah, sure. Her father was a king or a prince or something in Venice or Vienna, someplace like that," she said, waving the particulars aside. "She's used to being waited on hand and foot, so she married the right guy—I'll tell you that much." She plucked a bottle of lacquer off the rack and rolled back out to her station.

I still had ten minutes left of my break, so I smoked a cigarette while trying to compose a letter in my head to Tommy that I knew I'd never write much less send. He wouldn't respond and I couldn't handle another rejection.

"Oh shoot, shoot, shoot," Estée said, rushing past me toward a gunmetal gray washbasin, the type found in janitors' closets. She frantically wiped the front of her jacket, knocking the buttons to and fro while a yellow stain grew deeper and wider. "My sandwich—it slipped right out of my hands—and look—"

"It's only mustard. It'll come out." I crushed my cigarette in the ashtray.

"And what if it doesn't?"

"Then it's a good excuse to get rid of that thing."

Estée's eyes landed on me hard. "Well, that's a lousy thing to say." She was working the buttons free on her jacket. "I love this outfit."

"All I'm saying is, you have a swell figure. Why not show it off a little?"

"Because there's a time and place for that sort of thing." She twisted out of her jacket, revealing a beige blouse underneath, also buttoned to the top.

Buttoned-up. That pretty much described Estée back then. It wasn't that she was uptight but, rather, disciplined. Everything she did was purposeful, helping her leap from one lily pad to the next.

"This is my place of business." Estée continued blotting at the stain. "I need to look professional. Proper."

"Proper is one thing. Dowdy is another." I walked her over to the mirror and placed my hands on her shoulders. "Let me just show you something. Undo those top buttons."

"What? Why?"

"Trust me." She resisted so I reached around and unfastened them myself. "There." I spread her collar open. "See how much better this looks? It shows off your neck. And honestly, you don't even need the jacket at all."

Estée pulled away from me and buttoned herself back up.

"If you're that modest, put a scarf around your neck."

"I'm not *that* modest."

"Frankly, you could use a burst of color. Everything you own is either beige or brown or gray." How ironic that I should be pointing this out, given that she'd once corrected my shade of lipstick.

"Are you done insulting me?"

"Is that what you think I'm doing?"

The corners of her mouth turned down.

"Aw, no, no," I said sincerely. "I'm only trying to help."

"Well, it's not helpful. It's insulting." She left her jacket on a hook to dry and went back out to her counter.

Estée hardly said two words to me the rest of the day. She was the closest thing I had to a friend and I couldn't afford to lose her. After the last customer left and Darlene was getting ready to lock up, I dared to approach Estée.

"I'm sorry I hurt your feelings earlier," I said. "Really I am. Let me make it up to you. Let me take you for a drink." I'd gotten some nice tips that day and was ready for a splurge. Besides, there wasn't a bartender in town that I couldn't charm a few free drinks out of. All it took was a lingering glance, a smile or a compliment about their aftershave.

Estée gave me a skeptical look but didn't say anything. The more she resisted, the more determined I became. "Please?"

She consulted her appointment book, the edges curling from all the page flipping. I glanced over her shoulder and saw that every minute of every day was accounted for. She scheduled everything—from bathing to coffee breaks, to giving facials and makeup demonstrations, right down to telephoning her mother.

"Oh, c'mon," I said. "Call your husband. Tell him you'll be a little late and let's go."

"Well"—she reached for her pen—"how long will it take?"

"It's a drink, Estée. It'll take however long it takes." I pulled the pen away, slapped it on the counter and tugged her arm. "Now c'mon."

Despite her protests, we hopped on the Broadway streetcar and rode it down to 52nd Street.

"Where are you taking me?" she asked.

"Trust me."

We passed a slew of jazz clubs, the music blaring out from behind closed doors as we made our way down the sidewalk before ending up at the Onyx Club. It took my eyes a moment to adjust to the darkness as we entered the club's cavernous, smoky world. People were sitting shoulder to shoulder at the long mahogany bar, stools angled toward the stage in back, empty save for the upright bass, a couple of microphones and music stands.

Estée and I tucked into a tiny round table off to the side. I ordered a martini and Estée asked for a cup of coffee.

"Coffee?" I turned to the waiter. "No, no, no. She'll have a martini, too."

Estée was so serious back then. In that respect she reminded me of Tommy when we'd first met. I figured that if I'd managed to loosen up Thomas Cavendish III, Estée Lauder would be a breeze.

And she was.

Two sips into that martini, she started talking. "I love Joe, I do, but . . ." Her thoughts trailed off.

Anytime someone finishes a sentence with a qualifier like that you know there's more to the story.

"He seems like a terrific fella," I said.

"Oh, he is. He really is, but— It's just that, well . . ."

Here it comes.

"Some men have a head for business and others—like my poor Joe—they just don't have what it takes. He had a textile company down on Schmatta Row in the Garment District but it went out of business."

"Oh, I'm sorry to hear that."

"And then he opened a cafeteria and that went bankrupt, too. He's been picking up odd jobs here and there, but it's not enough. I'm the only one keeping us afloat." She swirled the olive around her glass. "It wasn't supposed to be like this," she said. "I mean it—I'm not kidding. I wasn't raised to live this way."

"Bernice was telling me you're a member of some royal family in Venice?"

"Vienna, not Venice. And Bernice tends to exaggerate. We're *aristocrats*, not royals."

I shot her a look.

"It's true," she said with great nonchalance. "I was born into a very old, highly regarded aristocratic family."

Not just anyone could say that. I raised my glass to her, finding this bit of information dutifully impressive.

"We moved to the States when I was a baby," she continued. "My family was very well-off, very prominent. We had an enormous house on Long Island with chauffeurs and servants—the whole bit. My father's idea of work was taking care of his horses." She laughed and took another sip from her martini. "When I was younger my parents entertained a lot of important people, even famous people, from all around the world. If the stock market hadn't crashed"—she shook her head—"I wouldn't have to work to support my husband and child."

It occurred to me that had it not been for the market crash, Estée and I could have very well crossed paths. The fact that we were here now, two girls fallen from privileged grace, convinced me that we were destined to have been in each other's lives no matter what.

"Usually, I never drink during the week," she said as she finished her martini. "Shall we get another?" She was already signaling for the waiter.

After round two arrived she began to babble: ". . . I'm exhausted. Up at six in the morning. All day long I'm working at the beauty parlor. Or giving facials or consultations. Oh, but"—her mood shifted upward—"I found out where Claudette Colbert is staying while she's in town. I'm going to wait in her hotel lobby and—"

"And then what?" I laughed, thinking she was joking.

"I'm going to introduce myself and tell her about my cold creams and lotions."

"You really think that's a good idea?" This is what fascinated me about Estée: it never occurred to her that someone—especially someone like Claudette Colbert—wouldn't be interested in her products.

"Oh, Gloria, I can feel it. I'm *this* close"—her fingers pinched together—"to landing a big, big star to get behind my skincare line. You wait and see, I'm going to be a huge success." She smiled, but a second later it vanished and she looked concerned. "Tell me the truth." She reached for my wrist. "You don't *really* hate the way I dress, do you?"

"The truth? Yes. But"—I raised my finger—"you're not without hope. Luckily for you, I have a real eye for fashion."

"*You* have an eye for fashion?" Her skepticism was insulting but I let it go.

After draining her glass, Estée tossed her napkin on the table. "I'm going to powder my nose," she said, struggling to get up from her chair. "Let's have another round. It's on me."

I glanced about the room and for a split instant I thought the man at the bar was my father. I felt compelled to walk over to him and ask, *How could you have done it?* Of course, it wasn't him. My father was behind bars, not drinking at one.

By the time Estée returned to the table, I had paid the bill with my tip money and given the bartender a wink for the round he picked up.

"Where's our drinks?" Estée asked, nearly backing into the table behind her.

"I think that's enough cocktails for tonight," I said, getting up, guiding her out of the Onyx Club.

She was a little unsteady, so I accompanied her home, to an

eighteen-story residential hotel on Broadway and 78th. While I was helping her fit the key into the lock, Joe opened the door.

"Oh my goodness," he said, laughing, helping her inside. "Look at you. You're a mess, Blondie."

I smiled, loving that he called her Blondie. Loving that he was amused by her intoxication rather than annoyed. "It's my fault," I said.

"Yes." Estée nodded, leaning into Joe. "It's all her fault."

"Well, come in," he said, surprising me with an encouraging wave. "Let me at least catch up with you." He set Estée down on the sofa, letting her slump against the cushions while he went to the liquor cabinet. He poured two glasses of bourbon, one for him, one for me. By the time he sat down next to Estée, her eyes were closed.

"I shouldn't have let her have that second martini," I said.

"She's a cheap date, isn't she?" He smiled.

"She wanted to order a third, but I stopped her."

"Well, thank goodness for that."

Estée let out a snore and Joe and I laughed.

Cupping her face, he said, "What am I going to do with you, Blondie?"

"I really am sorry about this."

"Ah, it's good for her once in a while. She works too hard. I'm glad you were able to get her out for a little fun."

Estée roused a bit just then. "She hates the way I dress," she mumbled, and again Joe and I both laughed.

After finishing my bourbon, I thanked Joe for the drink, and as I was leaving, he said, "Don't be a stranger. Come, you'll have dinner with us Sunday night. I'm making a pot roast."

That would be the first of many Sunday-night dinners I had with Estée and Joe. He did the cooking and afterward I attempted to help with the dishes while Estée sat at a little desk, planning her appointments for the week ahead, filling up every inch of her engagement book. It was like family night. Sometimes we'd play bridge, if we could find a fourth—Joe's clever way of introducing me to his friends. Other times we'd listen to our favorite 78s or radio programs, or else just sit around the table talking. I looked forward to those Sunday nights more than the two of them ever could have imagined.

4

IT DIDN'T TAKE long for Estée and me to fall into the habit of walking home together after work. We'd start heading up Broadway and I'd drop her off at 78th Street and keep going until I hit the Millers' on 81st.

On one hot July evening while we were walking home, Estée prattled on while I worried the tips inside my pocket. I was trying to calculate my earnings, rotating the nickels and dimes, the occasional quarter that customers had dropped into my pocket like I was a piggy bank.

". . . She's very influential, you know," Estée was saying now, referring to her last client that day. "She's going to introduce me to Bette Davis."

"And you believed her?" I would have bet every coin in my pocket that Estée's client didn't know Bette Davis from Shinola.

"I'm not kidding," Estée said. "She knows someone who *knows* someone who knows Bette Davis's social secretary."

"Ah, the ole knows-someone-who-knows-someone trick."

"Go ahead and laugh but I'm telling you, I'm going to make Bette Davis a spokesman for my products."

"And just how do you plan on doing that?"

"I'm putting together a special basket for her of creams and lotions along with a note from me. I'm going to give it to my client to give to her friend to give to the secretary to give to Bette Davis."

"How much you want to bet that basket never makes it to Bette Davis?"

"What do you mean?"

"There's three *someones* who might help themselves to that basket of goodies before they reach their final destination."

"No one would do that," she insisted, and then a beat later: "Would they? Who would do a thing like that?"

My mother. She wouldn't have thought twice about it. In her own way, she was as unscrupulous as my father.

"Well, I don't care what you say, I'm still doing it. And, you know, once Bette Davis starts using my products, well, that puts me—Estée Lauder—on the map . . ."

I didn't want to encourage or discourage her, so I changed the subject and asked what she thought of the new curtains Darlene put up in the shop.

Estée groaned. "Just when you thought there wasn't enough pink in that place."

"I don't suppose she'd consider another color. Maybe white or even ivory?"

"You'd have an easier time getting her to quit smoking."

We were laughing when we came to a red light and Estée noticed the woman standing next to her. Jabbing me in the ribs, she said, "Now there's a woman who could use my Creme Packs."

"Estée, shush, she'll hear you."

"It's just such a shame. Every woman can be beautiful. They just need someone like me to show them how."

I willed the traffic light to change.

BY THE TIME I made it back to the Millers' that day, I was exhausted. The humidity and heat clung to my dress like wet gauze, and the balls of my feet were burning. I found Mrs. Miller in the living room, sitting in one of two mismatched chairs, separated by a little rickety table. An upright piano was off to the side, with an accordion parked in the corner.

"Hello, hello—" Mrs. Miller's customary greeting was always two back-to-back *hello*s.

"Hello, Mrs. Miller."

After the market crashed, she and her husband had begun taking in boarders to help make ends meet. Sylvia and Richard Miller were in their fifties, an old vaudeville couple. They had a song and dance routine, along with a comedy bit, which they had resurrected for me the day I'd moved in.

When Mrs. Miller introduced me to her husband she'd said, "I've been in love with the same man for thirty-five years. If my husband ever finds out, he'll kill me."

To which Mr. Miller had retorted: "Sylvia and I always hold hands. If I let go, she goes shopping."

"And how was your day, Gloria?" Mrs. Miller asked, closing her copy of *Variety*.

"Long. Tiring," I said, stepping away.

Mrs. Miller uncrossed her ex-dancer legs riddled with veins to rival rivers on a map. Those legs seemed too thin to hold her up along with that thick braided coil of gray hair atop her head. "It sure is hot out there, isn't it? I don't remember it being this humid in July. August, yes, but never in July. Except for one year, maybe in '34 or '35 . . ."

Small talk. I wasn't up for it. "If you don't mind"—I gestured toward the kitchen—"I'm gonna get a glass of water and go upstairs and lie down."

"Well, that's just fine. You do that, dear," she said as I pushed through the swinging door.

I could tell Mrs. Miller's kitchen had been put to good use through the years. It wasn't that it was dirty, for Mrs. Miller was a stickler for cleanliness, but it did have that aged, broken-in feel about it, right down to the loose checkerboard tiles at the base of the stove. The copper pots and pans had oxidized, patinaed along their bottoms.

When I first turned on the tap, it choked out a burst of cloudy water before running clear. I was parched and gulped down a glass before refilling it and heading for the stairs.

"Did you remember to turn the light off in there this time?" Mr. Miller asked, having appeared out of nowhere in an undershirt, his suspenders off his shoulders, hanging down to his thighs. "I'm sure Mr. Edison appreciates your business, but I, however, do not."

I went back into the kitchen, turned off the light and assured Mr. Miller I would be more careful in the future. Heading up the staircase, I passed a series of photographs on the wall. There were pictures of a little boy, maybe six or seven years old, along with photos of the Millers back in their heyday, posing with a variety of stars—Al Jolson, Eddie Cantor, Mae West and Fanny Brice. Back then, Richard and Sylvia Miller had been a sensational-looking couple. He was all chiseled and she was the definition of voluptuous with nonstop legs. Amazing the toll time takes on the human body.

"Hey, Gloria—" Bobbi called to me.

Her bedroom door at the top of the stairs was ajar. Bobbi Koerner was another tenant at the Millers'. She was about my age, an eccentric artist type who fancied herself a bohemian, always wearing scarfs about her head like a Gypsy. I discovered I rather liked her company one night as we'd sat at the wobbly kitchen table, keeping it steady with our elbows while we drank whiskey and smoked cigarettes.

"C'mere," she said, "I want to show you what I'm working on."

Slipping out of my shoes, I hung my heels off two fingers and inched inside her room. Bobbi was sitting on the edge of her bed across from an easel. She had a kitchen knife in one hand, a pot of glue in the other and a pile of banana peels on the floor, resting on some old newspapers.

"Well?" she said. "What do you think?"

I peered at the easel. The canvas displayed a mountaintop, snow covered, with a skier coming down the slope.

"You like it?"

I cocked my head, sizing it up. "Actually, yes. Believe it or not, yes, I do."

"Well, don't sound so surprised."

"Sorry. It's just, c'mon, I mean, you made that out of bananas."

When we first met, Bobbi introduced herself as a banana artist. I thought she was joking. But no, Bobbi Koerner did indeed make art out of bananas. She took the peels, scraped away the pulp and trimmed them into fine strips that turned brown and black as they dried, looking more like strands of leather or suede. When she deemed them ready, she sculpted those tendrils into various shapes and objects. Some of her pieces were shockingly good. And complicated. She'd created birds in trees out of banana peels, women's bodies out of banana peels, a big-wheel bicycle out of banana peels—she'd even done a self-portrait, her long dark hair hanging to her waist in spiky points. If she hadn't told me, I never would have guessed that her medium of choice was the banana. You might have expected her room to smell of rotting fruit, but no. I smelled nothing but her Charbert perfume. Though she hadn't sold a single piece when I met her, in years to come, Bobbi would insist that she was to the banana what Jackson Pollock was to paint splatter.

I left Bobbi and headed to my room at the far end of the hall. There was a sorry-looking New York Giants pennant on the wall, faded by years of sunlight. I was certain that pennant, along with the football stickers on the closet door, had once belonged to the little boy in the photographs along the staircase.

When I'd first moved into this room four weeks ago, everything had been so pristine, but it hadn't taken long for me to undo all that. Left on my own, everything went south. The bedspread was bunched up on one side, dirty clothes were heaped on the floor, shoes kicked off here and there, the wastebasket was overflowing with previously tear-soaked tissues and crumpled-up cigarette packs.

The Millers' bedroom was next to mine, and at night I could hear their radio playing through the thin walls. While most stations ended their broadcasts at midnight, the Millers listened to a station that went all night, from their bedroom and therefore into mine, until four o'clock in the morning.

Physically and emotionally, I was depleted. So tired and overtired that my bones throbbed and my eyes burned. I hadn't really had a decent night's sleep since my father's arrest. Even after he pleaded guilty, I couldn't believe it. Forget that he had torpedoed my love life, the real question was, who was this person and what had he done with my father? What happened to the man who'd told uproarious stories that left everyone mopping tears from their eyes? The man who'd paid every medical bill when his secretary's son came down with scarlet fever? The man who'd grown prizeworthy tomatoes on our city terrace? The man who used to sometimes take me out of school so the two of us could go bowling? The man who'd taught me right from wrong? Maybe my mother and siblings could turn a blind eye to what he'd done, but I didn't have that luxury.

I plopped down on the bed and shifted my thoughts to Tommy. Thoughts of my father and Tommy were constantly running in the background of my mind, like a song you can't get out of your head. I was the only one who called Thomas Cavendish III *Tommy*. He came from a proper Presbyterian family and was set to follow in his father's footsteps of becoming an award-winning author until I sent his well-plotted future off course. When we met, Tommy had been engaged to someone else. Lana Chadwick was everything his family could have hoped for in a daughter-in-law: beautiful, poised, with a Seven Sisters' degree. It was all set until I laid eyes on their son. I wanted him. And I got him. We were introduced by mutual friends at a barbecue in Locust Valley and it was bye-bye, Lana. As soon as his parents got over losing Lana, Tommy and I planned to marry. Then my father killed any chance of that happening.

I knew Tommy loved me, but the problem was, he feared his mother more. One of the reasons he'd fallen for me was my levity. I added fun to his oh-so-serious, preordained life. The first night we met I shocked him out of his very proper posture, ruffling up his hair as I cooed and started calling him Tommy. I taught him to do the East Coast Swing and I made him laugh, which had been nearly impossible in the beginning. He'd let only one eyebrow hike up and then possibly the corner of his lovely mouth. With subsequent tries he'd finally give in and laugh full on.

Well, he wasn't laughing when my father got arrested and he and his parents realized they'd been wiped out. Tommy felt especially responsible, since he'd convinced his parents to invest with my father based on Gus Dowaziac's impeccable reputation and track record. All of which had been a lie, which made me a by-product of that lie. I was left with nothing but uncertainty. Who and what was I supposed to believe in now? Did the sun really rise in the east and set in the west? I was left to question everything about myself and the world around me.

There was no safe place for my mind to rest. Thinking of the past tormented me, and the future, unknown and uncharted, filled me with the kind of anxiety that made my skin crawl. My only escape was in those split-second openings between past and future, grabbing hold of the present moment as best I could, taking stock of what I had right here and now: a roof over my head, food in my belly, a handful of clothes in the closet, a job of sorts . . . Glenn hadn't said anything about my mother getting any more death threats, and since I'd become a brunette, no one had recognized and harassed me on the street. My heart was still beating, my lungs still breathing . . .

Eventually I must have dozed off because I woke sometime later that night, still in my clothes, the sound of Kate Smith singing "God Bless America" coming from the radio next door. I looked at the clock. It was just past midnight. I grabbed my toothbrush and headed to the bathroom we all shared at the end of the hall, next to Waller's room.

Waller Weston—a stage name if ever I'd heard one—was another tenant, an aspiring actor who was quite possibly the most handsome man I'd ever set eyes on. I hoped he wasn't home yet, as I had realized, to my horror, that if I could hear the Millers' radio through my wall, then Waller could hear *everything* happening in that bathroom through his.

I looked in the mirror, fogged with tarnished edges, thinking how disappointed Estée would be in me for not removing my makeup. I was just too tired and couldn't be bothered. I cleaned up as best I could and remembered to turn off the light, yanking the chain hanging from the medicine cabinet. I opened the door and there was Waller, loosening his necktie, releasing the top three buttons on his shirt.

I nearly dropped my toothbrush as I did a clumsy side step, shoulders to the wall, trying to get out of his way. "Oh, sorry—hi, sorry."

"You're up late," he said casually, raking a hand through his luscious dark hair. "I didn't know you were a night owl."

"Yeah, I guess. No, not really. Couldn't sleep." God, I sounded like a ninny.

"Well, good night."

"Yeah, good night. Sleep tight." *Sleep tight?* The old me, Gloria Dowaziac, would have flirted circles around that man, but Gloria Downing, broke and brokenhearted, had lost her confidence. I turned into a babbling schoolgirl around Waller, but I couldn't help myself. He made Valentino look like Greta Garbo's sloppy seconds. Really, you couldn't stop staring at Waller and the thing was, he knew it. But not in a conceited way. He just knew that he made the world around him a little more beautiful. And it wasn't just his face with its perfect Roman nose, the strong chin and dark eyes. He was tall, fit, and moved with a swagger.

Back in my room, I stepped over a clump of clothes to get to the bed. As ridiculous as it sounded, I'd kept waiting, half expecting Mrs. Miller to come in and clean up, vacuum the area rug, empty the ashtray and change the sheets. Obviously, I wasn't ready to fully accept that the upkeep of my room—like everything else in my life—was now my responsibility. I promised myself that one of these days I would get around to cleaning. But until then, I was a walking disaster, a helpless slob.

I knew Estée didn't live like this. Her drawers were probably organized, her shoes lined up, side by side in neat rows next to Joe's, her closets tidy and orderly. She was the sort of person who sent thank-you notes and birthday cards that arrived on time. She was the antithesis of me.

I'm not sure why I felt compelled to compare myself to her. It wasn't fair. Not to me, anyway. A very deep part of me was so fractured, and she seemed so together. I envied those irritatingly perfect little teacup hands, her flawless skin, her sunny disposition. Maybe if I stayed close to her some of what she had would rub off on me.

I rolled over and flipped my pillow to the cool side, where I lay sleepless until my alarm went off and it was time to get up and face this uncertain world all over again.

5

ABOUT A WEEK later I found Estée in the back room of Darlene's, sitting on a wooden crate, bawling into a pink towel, hoping to muffle the sound. A pile of dirty smocks lay on the floor in the corner, waiting for me to take them to the laundry around the corner. Well, they would have to wait a little longer. I pulled up another crate and sat next to her.

"What is it? What's wrong?"

With her face still buried in the towel I heard her say, "Bette Davis is in California for the rest of the year. She never even got my basket."

"Come on now." I draped my arm over her shoulder. "You knew that was a long shot."

She lifted her face, her eyes more red than hazel. "Oh, please, this isn't just about Bette Davis. It's everything. I'm sick of this." She gestured around the stockroom. "I can't make a living giving treatments in this place." She dropped her face back into the towel and howled. All I could do was stroke her shoulders and wait for her to compose herself.

Eventually she sat up, puffy-eyed, her face blotchy. One of her clip-on earrings landed in her lap and she yanked off the other one, throwing them against the wall like she was playing craps. "I need to catch a break. A real break," she groaned, and dragged her hands over her face.

I remember thinking it was one of the only times I'd ever seen Estée touch her face. Everyone else's, yes, but never her own. It clogged pores and promoted wrinkles, she'd said. In the midst of all this, I also noticed that she wasn't wearing her jacket and that the top two buttons of her blouse had been released from captivity.

"I put $30 worth of products in that basket. $30 gone—just like that."

I didn't say *I told you so*, and handed her a fresh tissue.

"Well"—she shrugged, dabbing her eyes—"I guess it's time to come up with a new plan."

"What kind of new plan?"

"I'm not sure yet." She looked as though she was about to cry again but stopped, and I could see the struggle on her face. She didn't like feeling defeated. It was as if she were stuffed inside a box, using her elbows and knees, using everything she had, trying to find a way out. "I can't settle for this." She indicated her station in life with a flutter of her hands. "From the time I was a little girl I've known that I was supposed to be famous. And wealthy. It's in my blood. I'm Estée Lauder," she proclaimed. "I can't settle for mediocrity. I can't be *average*."

Her posture and expression began to shift, her back straightening. "I come from a long line of famous and very well-respected people," she said. "You go to the social register and you'll see my father, my aunts and uncles, too. My uncle John is *very* famous. He lives here now, but back in Vienna, John Schotz is a renowned skincare specialist. He taught me everything. And you know," she said with an air of pride, "my creams and lotions really are the best."

"I think they're terrific," I said in all honesty. When I used them, I did notice a difference.

"They really are, aren't they?" Her eyes were pleading. I had no idea why she needed me to acknowledge this, but she did. I nodded and she kept going. "They're far better than anything you'll find in the department stores. My Creme Packs and my Super Rich All-Purpose Creme are ten times better than what Helena Rubinstein or Elizabeth Arden sell at their spas." She sniffed. "And you know I'm an ace when it comes to sales. Everyone says so."

"That you are." She could turn a short subway ride, seated next to a perfect stranger, into a face cream sale. She always carried samples around with her, and even if the women were offended—and I'm sure several were—they still took the free products. And somewhere down the line, maybe the next day, the next week or the following month, they tracked her down and bought more.

We both sat for a moment. And then I saw it—a spark, a pinprick of hope in her hazel eyes. It was as if something deep inside her had just been accessed.

"You know what I'm going to do, Gloria? I'm going to open up more concessions. All over the city. In every beauty parlor I can find. What's to stop me? I'll make sure every woman on the Upper West Side, the Upper East Side, too, knows who Estée Lauder is."

And right there, in that back room at Darlene's Palace of Beauty, I watched the magic of Estée appear before my eyes. Word by word, sentence by sentence, she was climbing her way out of a deep, dark hole and constructing a bridge from where she was to where she wanted to be.

AFTER THAT, ESTÉE put all her energy into selling, selling and yet more selling.

One Friday right around closing time, Bobbi came to pick me up at the shop. We were going to a gallery opening that night and she appeared in the doorway wearing a sheer, billowy shapeless dress, long dangling necklaces to her waist and a scarf tied about her forehead, hanging down the side of her arm.

Well, Estée took one look at Bobbi in all her bohemian beauty, grabbed hold of her hands and said, "What a pleasure to meet you. Gloria's told me so much about you."

If Estée couldn't touch you within three minutes of meeting you, something was wrong.

Bobbi was gracious, if not a bit overwhelmed by Estée's greeting. Turning to me, Bobbi said, "So, you ready to go, Glor—"

"Oh, wait—" Estée inserted herself between us. "I have something that would look perfect on you. May I show you how to apply it?"

Bobbi gestured to an imaginary wristwatch. "We're heading downtown and—"

"I promise it will only take five minutes. And you'll want to look your best tonight now, won't you?" She had taken hold of Bobbi's arm and was leading her to a chair. "I promise you won't be sorry." Estée was already tucking Bobbi's enormous pile of hair inside a terry cloth turban. "You have such beautiful skin and those eyes—simply gorgeous! You should play them up. May I?" She held up a pair of tweezers. "Your eyebrows frame your face," Estée said as she plucked away. "They're your most expressive feature, did you know that?"

Actually, she was right about that, and after she'd finished and smoothed Bobbi's brows back in place, I was amazed by the difference. Yes, the skin was red, but her eyes—they popped, wide and bright.

Next came the Cleansing Oil, followed by a thick slathering of her Super Rich All-Purpose Creme. "This is going to make your skin glow. You'll see." Estée finished Bobbi off with a touch of rouge, some turquoise eyeshadow, red lipstick and a light dusting of face powder.

"Ta-dah!" She turned Bobbi around to face the mirror.

Bobbi gazed at herself, bringing her fingertips to her cheeks. She was still Bobbi, but now her lips were quite luscious-looking, and her skin did absolutely glow.

"Well?" Estée hunched down, her arm wrapped about Bobbi's shoulder, her face also appearing in the mirror. "What do you think?"

It took a moment before Bobbi's top lip curved upward ever so slightly. "Wow," she said in barely a whisper, moving her fingertips from her cheek to her cherry red lips. She liked it. How could she not?

"See?" Estée said as she stood up straight. "I always say, there are no homely women, just lazy ones."

I thought Bobbi was going to slug her. I know I would have. But much to my relief, Bobbi began to laugh.

She was still laughing about it several hours later when we left a bar near the art gallery, sloshed up on martinis, our arms draped over each other's shoulders.

Fortified on gin we turned down Waverly Place when I spotted something on the ground. A banana peel. Until I met Bobbi, I didn't realize how many discarded banana peels there were lying around the city. They were everywhere: tossed onto the sidewalk, hanging over the lip of a garbage can, run over in the middle of the street. And it was always bananas. Never orange peels or an apple core, nary a mango in the land—just bananas.

To my surprise and immense horror, Bobbi picked it up.

"Ugh, Bobbi"—I winced—"that's filthy. You have no idea where that's been. It's full of germs."

"I'll wash it off," she said, gently folding it up and tucking it into her pocketbook, which made me nearly gag. One person's trash was truly another's treasure.

Bobbi turned to me and, imitating Estée, she said for the umpteenth time, "There are no homely women, just lazy ones."

We both burst out laughing all over again.

"Don't take it personally," I said. "That's just Estée. When it comes to beautifying women, she can't help herself. She thinks it's her mission or something, like it's up to her to make every woman look as good as she can." It was true. Estée never stopped selling, never stopped giving out samples of her products. She'd even invite perfect strangers into her home for free facials. Wherever she saw an opportunity, she seized it.

I thought she was nuts, but word about Estée was slowly getting out. That following Monday a smartly dressed woman with half a dozen chiming bracelets came into Darlene's looking for Estée. She was Florence Morris, the owner of another beauty parlor, House of the Ash Blondes—brunettes need not apply. She'd heard about Estée from some of her clients and was interested in setting up a cosmetic concession inside her shop. And so, Estée began spending her days going back and forth between Darlene's on 75th and Broadway and House of the Ash Blondes on 72nd and Columbus Avenue.

Tired as Estée was, it was worth it. After she cleared her rent for both shops and paid the extra salesgirl she'd hired and trained, she took home about $10 a day. That used to be pocket change for Gloria Dowaziac, but for Gloria Downing—and during the Depression—$10 was a fortune. And to think Estée was making this money on her own, through nothing more than honest hard work and her stubborn determination.

6

BY AUGUST, THOSE who could afford it had emptied out of the city and headed for the beaches and the cooler breezes of their second homes in the Hamptons. My family once had a shingled manor with a view of the water, and I'd spent my summers lunching on crab salads, playing tennis and golf, sunbathing and shopping—buying whatever caught my eye simply because I could. Not a care in the world.

Now those days were soured memories, and with New York being dead, business at Darlene's was equally dead. Mostly we sat around smoking cigarettes, flipping through back issues of *McCall's* and *Life*. We did our nails and I took advantage of the downtime to change my hair color again. It was a good thing I worked at a beauty parlor because my hair grew fast and within just a few weeks I could see the hint of my blonde roots shimmering through. This time I went with a shade called Golden Auburn. It was a little lighter and looked a bit better but not by much.

I was still gazing in the mirror, getting used to this latest version of myself, when Darlene called me into the back room.

"I hate to do this," she said as she lit a cigarette. "And believe me, it's not because of you. I just can't afford to keep you on."

"What are you saying? You're firing me?"

"I've got no choice. And I'm not happy about it—now I'm gonna have to do shampoos myself."

Any inkling of confidence and a sense of independence that had been propping me up these past two months had just been knocked out from under me. I leaned against one of the storage shelves to steady myself. I was staring at my hands and then the floor.

"Besides," Darlene said, "let's face it, you're not a shampoo girl. This isn't what you should be doing with yourself. You're too capable for a job like this."

I looked up, skeptical. I'd been called many a thing before, but *capable* was not one of them.

"I mean it. You're smarter than you give yourself credit for." She drew down hard on her cigarette and fingered one of the pin curls resting on her forehead. "You might not think so now, but I'm doing you a favor. There's a big bold world waiting for you—it's time you get out there and make something of yourself."

After Darlene was done talking, I turned and busied myself with items on a shelf, mindlessly stacking and unstacking boxes of permanent wave solution, watching them blur together. I could hardly believe I was on the verge of tears. Despite all the kind things that Darlene had said, I glommed on to only one fact: I'd failed. My first shot at being self-reliant and I hadn't been able to cut it. Feeling already small and shrinking fast, what I thought of as my remaining positive traits had just been erased. What difference did it make if my girlfriends—who no longer returned my calls and had scratched me off their guest lists—would have been hard-pressed to find a more loyal, devoted friend? So what if I was a good listener and had spent hours engrossed in their heartaches, their triumphs? Even

Darlene had confided in me about her lazy son-in-law, her penny-pinching landlord. None of it seemed to matter now, and when I caught a glimpse of myself in the mirror, all I saw was a loser.

I hung my pink smock up in the back, grabbed my pocketbook and quickly said my goodbyes to Darlene, Bernice and Estée.

I was halfway out the door when Estée called after me. "Wait—I'm coming with you."

Standing outside the shop with Estée, I relayed my conversation with Darlene.

"C'mon." She grabbed hold of my arm. "Let's get a drink."

I could hardly believe it—Estée was being spontaneous, abandoning her appointment book for me. I was touched. I vaguely remember getting on the Broadway streetcar. I wasn't sure where we were heading, but Estée seemed to have someplace in mind.

As we closed in on Midtown, I still couldn't believe I'd lost the only job I'd ever had. And it was a lousy job at that. *What now? How was I going to support myself? How was I going to afford rent at the Millers'?* I was scared of the future in a way that rich girls never were.

It was moments like this when I missed my father the most. Yes, he'd made bad things happen, but he also knew how to make bad things go away—a spider in my bedroom, a math teacher I didn't like after he persuaded the principal to move me to a different classroom. My father got me out of both my speeding tickets, and when my bicycle was stolen, he'd bought me a new one, a better one. One night a bat flew in through our open balcony door and he went after it, first with a tennis racket and then a fishing net. He'd always been there to set things right, and it went against my nature to turn my back on him, but what he did had destroyed my loyalty, if not my love for him. And I did still love my father, which made it hurt all the more.

Estée and I got off at 52nd Street and I realized we were heading back to the Onyx Club. We grabbed the same table we'd sat at before and ordered our cocktails.

After I rehashed what Darlene said, Estée paused for a sip of her gimlet and said, "She's right, you know. It *is* a big bold world out there. You really are capable of doing so much more."

There was that word again—*capable.* "Yeah? Like what?"

"Like anything you set your mind to."

"Oh, please. Don't start with the mind stuff again." I reached inside my pocketbook for a cigarette. "That seeing-it-all-in-your-head-first nonsense may work for you, but not me."

"That's because you're always so negative and you pooh-pooh it."

It sounded like a bunch of hooey to me, but she was right about one thing: I had to be more positive, but that didn't come naturally to me. Any good thought that floated my way was as fragile as a soap bubble. It burst the instant I tried to grab hold of it.

Estée folded her hands on the tabletop and gave me a disapproving look. "Well," she sighed, "don't worry. Something will turn up."

"It'd better turn up soon. I'm broke."

"What about that fella, Tommy?" She pointed to my gold cigarette case. "Couldn't he loan you a little money, just until you find something else?"

The gin nearly sloshed out of my coupe and I had to set it down with both hands.

"Obviously he's got money," she said. "I'm sure he wouldn't mind."

I shook my head and laughed. The sound came out small and sad. "I can't go to Tommy. I don't even speak to him anymore." The words split me down the center. It had been five months and it still stung like a fresh cut.

The band went back onstage, and while they played, I continued to worry about my future. I had a few dollars set aside from my last paycheck, supplemented by tips, but that was barely enough to cover next week's groceries and my rent. Half the city was out of work. Even Joe couldn't find a job. I supposed if worse came to worst, I could ask my brother for a loan, but God, I didn't want to resort to that. He'd tell my sister and I'd never hear the end of it.

Estée ordered another round of drinks and a plate of olives, cheese and crackers, which I ate as if it were the last meal I'd ever have. By the time I finished my martini, the panic was beginning to recede. My thinking was a bit more reasonable. I was pretty sure the Millers wouldn't throw me out on the street, and so what if Glenn told my sister I needed to borrow money? Did I really care what Gail thought of me? Well, yes, actually I did.

Gail and I had a long-running rivalry. My sister took after my father in the looks department: dark brown hair and a hefty build. She was forever battling her weight and resented that I'd inherited my mother's lightning-fast metabolism along with her platinum blonde locks. It was also no secret that I was my father's favorite and he'd been mine. In each other's eyes we could do no wrong. The pedestal we'd placed each other on reached to the clouds, and the higher up you are, the harder the fall.

The band finished their set and I applauded and helped myself to the last olive. It was quiet enough now that Estée and I could hear ourselves talk. She was telling me about an idea she had.

". . . Miami Beach," she said triumphantly.

"Vacation?" I asked, sucking the salt off the olive stone.

"Hardly. I've just been thinking lately that Miami is where I need to set up some concession stands. That's where the rich and famous women go for the winter."

She was right about that. My family always went to Miami Beach for Christmas. Sometimes Easter, too.

"Isn't it a marvelous idea?"

"When would you go?" I asked.

"I'm thinking right after Labor Day."

"That soon?"

"I'll need to get the lay of the land and make some connections so I can be set up by the time the in-season guests start arriving for winter."

"So you'd be down there for the whole winter?" I dropped the olive pit on my plate.

"Not the *whole* winter." She sounded slightly defensive. "But I'll go back down for a few weeks here and there—maybe I'd stay a month or so." She lifted her empty glass, set it back down and raised her hand to get the waiter's attention.

"But what about your business up here? Who's going to oversee that? And what about Joe? Can he get away for that long?"

"He's staying here in New York."

"Joe's *not* going with you?"

She looked around, ignoring my question.

"Estée, what's going on?"

"Where is he?" She was still trying to flag down the waiter. "You want another?" she asked.

"When *don't* I want another?"

After the waiter sauntered over and took our order, Estée tried changing the subject, but I yanked her back in. "Estée, what is going on with you and Joe?"

She sighed. "I just need to get away for a bit. Besides, he can't very well look for work up here if he's down in Florida." She sighed again, harder this time. "Oh, let's face it. I'm not happy. Joe's not happy. We've been at each other's throats for weeks. I think the break will do us both some good."

"I'm so sorry. I didn't know—"

"I wish you'd quit looking at me like that."

I couldn't help it. I was truly surprised. I'd never suspected they were having problems. I thought about our dinner at their place just that past Sunday. I never heard a cross word, a snide remark, never saw an angry glance between them. Nothing. Now she was shattering my faith in the perfect couple. They'd always given me hope that maybe—just maybe—there was still a chance for me, that there was such a thing as being happily married.

The waiter came back with our drinks.

Estée took a big sip, set her glass down and anxiously ran her fingers along the stem. "We just need a little time apart from each other, that's all," she said. "Really, it's for the best. We've already discussed it. He's staying here to look for work and to give us both a little breathing room."

"What about your son?"

"Leonard will come with me."

"But won't he be starting school in September?"

"Jesus, Gloria, why are you bombarding me with questions? I thought you'd be happy for me."

"I'm not *bombarding* you. And I'm certainly not happy to hear that you and Joe feel the need to take a break from each other."

"Joe and I will be fine," she said. "Right now I need to focus on making money."

"But you need to be realistic."

"I don't *believe* in being realistic. If I were being realistic, I wouldn't have tried to start my own business in the first place. So don't talk to me about being realistic. That's one of those words that's right up there with *impossible.* They're not part of my vocabulary."

"But I think you need to prepare yourself for the fact that it's not going to be as easy as you—"

"I'm not interested in what's easy."

"I just don't want you to get your hopes up. You could be setting yourself up for a big disappointment."

"Leave it to you to try and burst my bubble. Do you *always* have to tell me *exactly* what you think?"

"I'm not going to just tell you what you want to hear. And can I just remind you that you had *no* problem telling me when you thought I had a lousy work ethic?"

"Oh, would you let that go already?"

"You asked me what I thought, Estée, and I'm telling you the truth."

"Okay, all right, I—I get it. Just stop." She spread her hands out on the table and drew a deep breath. We glared at each other until she blinked and shook her head. "Truce?"

I nodded. "Truce."

In the weeks and months to come, this would become our way of settling arguments, of agreeing to disagree. But just then, we sat in silence, still stewing, before we both burst out laughing.

7

I ARRIVED HOME LATER that day, greeted by Mrs. Miller's jovial, "Hello, hello!"

"Hello, hello, to you, too." I was still tipsy from my cocktails with Estée and decided to call my brother before I sobered up and lost my nerve.

I lumbered up the staircase and went to the telephone extension resting on a stand in the alcove at the end of the hall. I dialed the operator and read Glenn's number off a piece of paper tucked inside my pocketbook. Unlike Gail, Glenn and I had always been pals. Maybe because we were closer in age, maybe because he was just a better human being. He was the only member of my family I couldn't give up on. While waiting for the operator to place the call, my mind wandered back to the last time I'd seen my brother, a little over five months ago. We were in his hotel room. He'd stuffed $100 into my clenched fist and told me to grow up.

When my world fell apart and I was left with no home and no money of my own, Glenn had smuggled me into the Hermitage Hotel for Men, where he was living at the time. It was a bachelors' hotel, hence the smuggling part. Glenn warned me that the management was very strict about unescorted women on the premises and instructed me not to leave the room without him. So, while Glenn went to his accounting job each day, I stared at the bad artwork on the walls and listened to my father being desecrated over the radio while waiting for someone to come rescue me. Oh, if ever there was a damsel in distress, it was me.

One day Glenn came back to the hotel in the middle of the afternoon and my world shattered once again.

"What are you doing home so early?" I'd asked.

"Get your things together. C'mon, get packed."

"Why? What's going on?"

He'd taken his suitcase down from the top shelf in the closet and started frantically pulling clothes off hangers. "I just got fired."

"What? Why?"

"My boss didn't think it was wise for an accounting firm to employ a CPA with the last name Dowaziac. You and me—we're pariahs in this town. All of us are. Mom's been getting hate mail—even death threats. Somehow they tracked her down at Cousin Marta's. We can't stay here. C'mon—we're going to Boston to stay with Gail."

"No—wait a minute—I can't." Staying with my sister was not an option.

"Well, you do what you want, but I'm leaving. I can't stay in New York."

The thought of losing Glenn had amplified all that I'd already lost. I began to crumble to a new low. "Don't go. Please don't leave me here alone." I dropped onto the bed, crying.

"I can't stay here and take care of you. I can't even show my face in public anymore. They spit on me, Gloria. My co-workers actually *spit* in my face." He'd winced and that's when I saw the bruise on his cheek and realized they'd done more than that. I could only imagine my father, a former amateur boxer, scolding Glenn for not fighting back: *Shoulda decked 'em all.*

"If you won't come to Gail's," Glenn had said, "you need to find a way to take care of yourself."

"But how?"

"Oh, for God's sake, Gloria—figure it out. Go to secretarial school. Take a typing class or something. Get some skills so you can get a job. And stop crying."

That, of course, had only made me cry harder.

"Here." He reached for his wallet and shoved a wad of cash into my fist. "This is all the money I've got on me—be smart with it."

I clutched the bills to my chest.

"I've paid the rent here through the end of the week. And whatever you do, don't go wandering around the hotel. They'll throw you out. I gotta get going. I'm on the 5:20 train."

"Glenn, no. Please don't go."

"I say this with all the love in my heart, Gloria, it's time for you to grow up."

After Glenn left, I died a little right there in his hotel room. Eventually I found my way to the gin bottle and left the room, looking for someone to help me. I wandered the halls, even knocked on a few strangers' doors. A bellhop finally found me sobbing, crumpled on the floor in the hallway. Next thing I knew, I was out on the street with my suitcase. And that's when I finally got it. No one was going to save me. My survival was up to me. *Everything* was up to me. This had been something of a seismic shift in my existence.

The operator's voice cut into my thoughts. "Collect call from Gloria. Will you accept the charges?"

The first thing Glenn said when he came on the line was: "You could have at least waited for the long-distance rates to drop."

"Oh . . ." I was already sobering up. I had no idea what time it was. "Sorry."

"I'm kidding. I'm joking. It's good to hear from you."

I asked how he was getting along in Boston, and after he'd filled me in on the CPA firm he'd started working for, he gave me an update on my mother. "Not that you really care," he said, "but she's all settled in at the new place."

Glenn and Gail had moved my mother from her cousin's in Long Island into an efficiency in Poughkeepsie to spare her from more hate mail and so she could be closer to my father in Sing Sing. My siblings had done all this without any help from me, financially or otherwise. Not that any of them expected anything from me, the baby of the family.

"How is she?" I asked, certain that I knew the answer.

"You know," he said, "she's Mom."

"Enough said."

My mother was the ultimate hypochondriac. Headaches threatened to become brain tumors, stiff backs could be ruptured discs, sore joints were surely the signs of rheumatoid arthritis, just as gas was appendicitis. She lived in her own little world filled with imaginary ailments and convoluted thinking. Her husband was locked away for twenty-five years, but to her it was only a temporary setback. Soon they'd return to Manhattan, she was sure of it. And until then, she would defend him even in the face of damning evidence to the contrary.

"So," Glenn said, "I know you didn't call to talk about Mom. What's really going on? How are you? How's the shampoo shop going?"

"Well, actually, it's not *going* anymore. I was fired. But it wasn't my fault. Business is slow."

"You should have gone to secretarial school. Didn't I tell you that?" I could picture him turning out his lower lip. "Now what are you gonna do?"

"Find another job, I guess."

"You guess, huh? Doing what? What are you qualified to do? Did you manage to put any money aside from the shampoo shop? Remember what Dad always said about *paying yourself first.*"

"Well, he certainly did that, didn't he?"

"Don't start with that, Gloria. Dad didn't set out to harm anyone. It was just bad timing. And the judge went hard on him, used him as an example."

Now I was completely sober. Glenn sounded like my mother. And my sister, too. They swore my father started out with the best intentions. And maybe that was true, maybe the first or second time he transgressed he promised himself, *Never again. I'll put the money back and none will be the wiser.* I could have forgiven him for that. But he hadn't stopped there. Taking money from our housekeeper, the doorman, from Tommy and his parents, had been intentional and no one could have convinced me otherwise.

"Just tell me," Glenn said, "did you at least manage to save any money?"

"Well, that was something I wanted to ask you about."

"Uh-huh." His voice had that flat *I knew it* tone. "Let me guess, you need money, right?"

"I'll pay you back."

"How much do you need?"

"I don't know." I pulled back the curtain and looked out the dormer window, avoiding my reflection in the glass. "Maybe $20 or $30 . . ."

"Oh, Gloria." Now he sounded even more annoyed. "That won't last you until you find a new job. Be realistic. Listen, I'll put a check in the mail for you, but I want you to consider moving up here. I spoke with Gail and—"

"Oh God, no—"

"I spoke with Gail and she said you can come live with her."

"What? I don't want to live with her."

"She has an extra room. But—and she was adamant about this—she expects you to help out with the housework. And the kids. You'll have to earn your keep."

"I—I can't. There's no way in hell that I can live with Gail. We'd kill each other."

ONE WEEK LATER, still hopelessly unemployed, a letter arrived from my brother with a check enclosed for $100. All his note said was:

Spend this wisely.

Love Glenn
P.S. Happy Birthday.

It was August 23rd and there I was, celebrating my twenty-second birthday with a tin of graham crackers and a glass of milk. I dipped a corner of my cracker into the milk and watched paisley swirls of cinnamon and oil swim along the surface. I brought the cracker to my mouth, sucking the milk from it before it went soft and collapsed against my tongue. I did this over and over again, like when I was a little girl.

I was sure that if I'd told anyone—Bobbi, Estée, the Millers, maybe even Darlene and Bernice—they would have helped me celebrate my birthday. But I was playing the martyr, having not heard a peep from my mother or sister. Or Tommy, not that I expected to. So I was all alone, out of work and feeling good and sorry for myself.

I'd celebrated my twenty-first birthday at the Plaza Hotel. Tommy was there, along with all my friends and my parents' friends, too. More than 200 guests with a lavish six-course dinner, a band and hours of dancing. No expense had been spared. A table was piled high with gifts, and in a teary-eyed toast to his youngest, my father handed me the keys to a brand-new 1938 fire-engine red Cord 812, an automobile that for all intents and purposes had been stolen. Stolen from my father's clients.

But the night of my party, I didn't know anything about his Ponzi scheme and all was right in my world. Everyone sang "Happy Birthday" as they wheeled out an enormous sheet cake.

"C'mon now, make a wish!" my mother had said, hovering over my shoulder. I could smell the booze coming off her breath, leaching from her pores.

I closed my eyes and thought for a moment. Everything had still been possible for me at that point and there were so many things I wanted. I wanted to marry Tommy. I wanted his family to finally accept me. I wanted a big engagement ring. I wanted an apartment overlooking the park. With so many wants, I couldn't pick just one to wish upon. And because I was superstitious enough to believe that it was bad luck if you didn't blow out *all* the candles—twenty-two, including one *to grow on*—I was feeling pressured.

"C'mon now, before you burn down the whole place!" my mother had said.

She was rushing me and I had wanted that moment to myself, to properly formulate my request. I could feel her breath along the back of my neck. Finally, I decided on the one thing I'd wanted more than anything else. I wanted to be Mrs. Thomas Cavendish III. Just as I closed my eyes and was about to make my wish, my mother said, "Well, we haven't got all night." And with that, she swooped in and blew out my candles.

When she did that, I think she jinxed my dream of marriage.

And when Tommy had broken off all contact with me, my mother—being the superlative role model that she was—offered me this sage advice: "Tell him you're pregnant. That way he'll have to marry you."

"You want me to *lie* to him?"

"Why not? Women do it all the time."

Well, not *this* woman. I couldn't have done it.

I wiped up the graham cracker crumbs, rinsed out the glass, setting it on the drainboard, and decided to top off my birthday by doing a load of laundry. It was that or buy new underwear, which I couldn't afford.

I stripped the bed and scouted the floor for my dirty clothes, remembering to separate the dark colors from the lights. Mrs. Miller had taken pity on me and given me a laundry lesson after I'd turned an entire load pink—the culprit being a sweater that should have been washed by hand anyway.

With my sheets, a set of towels and several weeks' worth of underwear gathered in my arms, I went down to the unfinished cellar, which had an old washing machine and a clothesline that ran the length of the room, sporting Mr. Miller's boxers and Mrs. Miller's girdle and foundation garments, which she referred to as her *gotchkees.* The washer was in the corner, next to the furnace, next to Mr. Miller's workshop space.

He did small home repairs, not because he loved doing handiwork and not because he was especially good at it but because he refused to pay someone for anything he believed he could fix himself. This explained all the half-finished projects throughout the house: doors not hung properly, missing sections of crown molding, windows that didn't seal, the reversed hot and cold water controls in the upstairs bathroom sink. Clearly, Mr. Miller was a better entertainer than a carpenter. And he always had leftover scraps of materials, so wherever you looked you'd find bits of lumber and metal rods tucked up in the rafters on the ceiling, slid behind the door. It looked as if the entire house were shimmed together like a collection of pick-up sticks. You'd pull one out and the whole place might have fallen down.

I heard the floorboard overhead squeaking; someone was in the kitchen. A moment later the telephone rang, followed by Mrs. Miller calling for me. "Gloria? Gloria, are you down there? Telephone, dear. It's your friend Estée. She says it's important."

I went back upstairs and took the call on the extension in the front hallway. "Estée? Is everything okay?"

"Oh yes, never better." She sounded chipper. "Joe and I were talking tonight and, well, I have a marvelous idea for you."

"For me?"

"Actually, it was Joe's idea, but I still think it's just marvelous." She cupped the phone and shushed Leonard. I could almost picture him tugging on her arm, vying for her attention. "Gloria," she said, "why don't you come down to Miami with me?"

"Yeah, right." I laughed.

"No, I'm serious. You could help me with Leonard. I was going to hire a babysitter anyway. I'd rather give you the money. It won't be much, but I'll pick up the hotel room, all our meals. It'll be fun."

"You're serious about this?"

"Of course I'm serious. You need a job and I need help. We can go down right after Labor Day. What do you say?"

I leaned against the wall, the phone cradled between my ear and shoulder, the cord twisted around my index finger. An all-expenses-paid trip to Miami Beach did sound inviting. And it wasn't as if I had a new job lined up here.

"What's the matter? You have a better offer?" she asked teasingly. "Well, what do you say?"

I smiled, gripping the receiver. "I say, look out, Miami, here we come."

8

I ASSUMED WE WERE traveling by train because it was cheaper than taking a plane. And that was certainly part of it. But as we were boarding the Vacationer line to Florida, Estée confessed that we were taking a forty-three-hour train ride because she was afraid of heights and terrified of flying.

"No foolin'," I said, getting situated in my seat across the aisle from her. Estée always struck me as fearless, and it was strange being the brave one for once. "You're really afraid of heights?" I asked.

"Oh yes, I'm scared to death," she said, looking over at Leonard next to her, his face pressed to the glass of the window seat. "It's a terrible problem for me. I can't use ladders. Not even a stepladder. Joe has to get everything down from the top shelves for me. I hate elevators, and even escalators make me sweat. And whenever we drive over a bridge, someone else has to be behind the wheel because I keep my eyes closed the whole time."

"Well, you're going to have to get over all that if you plan on taking the world by storm."

She frowned.

"But it's true, you know."

"Let me take Miami by storm first and then I'll worry about the rest of the world."

The porter came down the aisle, making his last boarding call. We were seated in coach and I felt the engine rumbling beneath me. Leonard clapped and cheered as we chugged off, shimmying from side to side, the train's horn blasting.

In order to stick to her daily budget, Estée brought along a snack of cheese and crackers for our lunch and a peanut butter and jelly sandwich for Leonard. By six o'clock that night, I was starving. Leonard was, too. We made our way to the dining car, and after nine hours of sitting, it felt good to stand up and stretch my legs, give my rear end a break from the coach springs.

The dining car was handsomely decorated in dark wood paneling, gold wall sconces, linen tablecloths and plush chairs. Leonard sat beside his mother, his little legs swinging back and forth while he marveled at his surroundings.

"You wouldn't believe what they charge you just to *sit* in here," Estée said, shaking her head as she glanced at the menu. "And would you look at the prices." She blew out an incredulous breath.

I knew Estée was worried about money, so I ordered the tomato soup and a sandwich. Leonard didn't take such mercy on his mother, saying he wanted the shrimp cocktail and a steak.

"That's some expensive taste for a young man," I said.

"You can have the fish sticks," Estée told him.

"Daddy always lets me have shrimp cocktail."

"Well, Daddy isn't here right now and he's not paying for this."

Leonard pushed out his bottom lip and folded his arms across his chest.

Estée looked at him and folded, too. "Oh, okay, all right, you can have the shrimp cocktail. But no steak. You can have a hamburger instead."

It seemed like a good compromise to Leonard, who returned to smiling and swinging his legs.

Ten hours into our travels, the more fortunate passengers were in their luxury Pullman sleepers. Leonard had conked out from all the excitement, while Estée and I stayed up playing gin rummy until we could barely keep our eyes open.

I tried to sleep but it was no use—my seat was uncomfortable and people moving up and down the aisle kept bumping my armrest. I glanced over at Estée, who was still awake. She had her makeup case open on her lap and was meticulously removing her eyeshadow, applying her Cleansing Oil and Super Rich All-Purpose Creme, her full routine. It was the first time I'd ever seen her without makeup. Her eyes and lips seemed smaller, but her skin was positively luminous.

I must have dozed off eventually because when I opened my eyes again, it was morning. Estée was having a cup of coffee and had already put her face on. I dared to look at myself in my compact. I had mascara smeared beneath my eyes, along with dark circles.

By the time we arrived in Miami, I was exhausted. Estée had to have been, too, but you wouldn't have known it to look at her. She stepped off that train just as fresh and flawless as she'd been when we boarded back in New York.

ESTÉE'S FRIEND ARLENE Forester picked us up at the train station. Though Estée was broke, she retained her rich, fancy friends who'd somehow dodged the effects of the Depression, holding on to their second homes in Miami and Palm Beach. Estée rubbed elbows and face creams with anyone who had money, and I sometimes worried that she might know some people from my past.

"Arlene," said Estée, grabbing hold of both our hands, pulling us toward each other, "I want you to meet someone very special. This is Gloria. Leonard's nanny."

Leonard's nanny? I tugged my hand free, though Estée didn't seem to notice. Yes, I was there to look after her son, but I'd thought I was also there in the capacity of her friend, not the hired help.

Arlene was pleasant enough and coiffed to perfection in a sleeveless shift that showed off her toned, suntanned arms. With her lovely white sandals and matching pocketbook, she was the epitome of Miami Beach. She had already done some hotel scouting for Estée, who'd specified that wherever we stayed, it had to be clean and affordable. Soon we arrived at the Colonial Inn on Collins Avenue. It had a little black stagecoach in front and a pool in the back, and the lobby was nicely decorated with overstuffed chairs in the lounge.

"Oh, this is going to be perfect," Estée said, thanking Arlene profusely before she left us to unpack and settle in.

While Estée finished checking in at the front desk, I took Leonard to our room: a double with an adjoining door. I was to take the one room and Estée and Leonard would take the other. Leonard was delighted, jumping up and down on the double bed while I worried he was going to fall or break something. That was the first time I'd been alone with him, just the two of us, and up until then, I hadn't really pondered the enormous responsibility of looking after someone's child. What if he hurt himself? What if he ran off or wouldn't mind me? He was so rambunctious, and I was desperate to calm him down before Estée came back. I slipped a penny into the little machine on the nightstand so he could try the bed massager. Well, he thought this was just dandy, especially when I convinced him to lie down. He stretched out on his back, giggling; his cheeks jiggled as the bed joggled him about.

When Estée came into the room, I gestured toward Leonard and said, "I think someone approves of this hotel."

"Well, don't get too comfortable here."

I noticed the deep lines burrowed across her forehead. "What is it? What's wrong?"

"We're checking out in the morning. They want $115 a week for this place. What was Arlene thinking? I said 'affordable.' I can't afford this."

The next day, we went looking for a new hotel with our suitcases in hand—one of which was filled with jars of creams and lotions. Before we left New York, Estée had made extra batches of all her products and there hadn't been an inch of open counter space left in their apartment. Even the dining room table had been covered. Joe ended up storing the groceries in the front hall closet. She had given him explicit directions on which labels went with which products, and he was on the ready to send down more bottles and jars as soon as needed.

In the meantime, we wandered the city until we wound up at the Admiral Hotel, some eight or nine blocks west of Collins Avenue. The lobby was sparse, with a vending machine in the corner next to a plastic plant in need of dusting. A few elderly couples shuffled across the tiled floor, the men in swimming trunks riding up within an inch of their armpits, the women with fruit baskets for hats and oversize sunglasses. Estée, Leonard and I shared one room this time: twin beds for Estée and me and a cot for Leonard.

I snapped open my suitcase only to find my clothes in a jumble. "Think this will hang out?" I asked, holding up one of my dresses that was to cotton what raisins were to grapes.

"Oh no. Oh, Gloria." She looked at the mess inside my suitcase. "Who taught you to pack?"

"Who taught *you*?" It had never occurred to me that this was something taught, passed down from generation to generation, from mother to daughter. I watched as she demonstrated how to roll whatever items I could, and instructed me to turn other things inside out. Our housekeeper did all our packing and I imagined Estée's family had a housekeeper, too, but perhaps that was before she was old enough to travel.

Later that night, I woke up and found Estée seated by the window, counting her money: crumpled bills, one on top of the other like dried leaves, and stacks of coins down to the pennies.

"This is all I have," she said, scooping the bills in one hand, the loose change in the other. The moonlight coming through the drapes illuminated the tears in her eyes. "I'm sorry but this has to hold us until I can start selling."

I was beginning to question this arrangement I had with her. Estée was supposed to pay me $4.50 a day to watch Leonard and I felt certain that I wasn't going to see a dime of that until she got her business up and running down there. What little money I had was dwindling. I feared having to ask Glenn for another loan to tide me over until I got a real job.

A real job. That had been nagging at me ever since I'd been introduced as *the nanny.* Babysitting Leonard may have bought me a little time, but as soon as I got back to New York, I was going to have to find a job. My biggest hurdle was that I didn't know what I wanted to do, never mind that I wasn't qualified to do anything. I asked myself, *What would Estée do?* God, how I admired her ability to chart a course. I willed myself to think like her, but I wasn't as strong as Estée and it all collapsed on me. A small voice inside kept telling me to swallow my pride and move to Boston. It was just easier. But if so, why was every cell in my body resisting it? I felt sick each time the thought crossed my mind.

Neither Estée nor I could sleep that night and so we stayed up talking, whispering really, so as not to wake Leonard.

"I miss Joe," she said, peeling back the curtain, letting in a wider wedge of moonlight that revealed our view of the parking lot. "I really do." She let go of the curtain and the room went three shades darker. "Don't you ever get lonely?" she asked.

I had to laugh. "Of course I do."

"So how come you never date?"

"Oh, I date. I went out with that guy, Lawrence. Remember?"

"Once."

"Twice, actually," I corrected her.

"So, what happened? Why did you stop seeing him?"

I reached for a cigarette and lit it, extinguishing the flame so she couldn't see my face. Lawrence was a tall, handsome man who was the editor of *Christianity Today*. He attended mass every Sunday and on our second date said that honesty was the most important quality in a relationship. Well, I never could have been honest with him. There was no way he would have knowingly entered into a relationship with Gus Dowaziac's daughter. He needed to find himself a nice girl. A good girl. I ended our date early, and when Lawrence went to kiss me, I placed my fingertips over his lovely mouth and said, "Don't."

"Don't?"

I'll never forget the look on his face when I shook my head. "No. Don't. I can't." And with that I'd hurried up the front steps and disappeared inside the Millers' house.

"So?" Estée was waiting. "What happened with him?"

"Ah"—I wrinkled my nose, shook my head—"we weren't right for each other."

"In what way?" She pushed.

And I pushed back. "In the way that people aren't right for each other."

"So you're not going to tell me about it, are you?"

"There's nothing to tell." I wanted to tell her every detail, but I was too guarded. So afraid that sharing even a little would lead to sharing more and that before I knew it, I would be confessing *every-*

thing about my past. I hated lying to Estée, but I had no choice. When I met her, news about my father was still raw. I feared if she knew I was a Dowaziac, she never would have befriended me. Darlene never would have hired me. The Millers would not have rented a room to me. I would have been a leper. I'd swapped Dowaziac with Downing out of sheer preservation. Now the lie was out there and the more time that passed, the thicker and more entangled grew the roots. Maybe some people wouldn't have held it against me, but I wasn't willing to take that chance. I had to keep a tight seal on anything too personal.

"And there hasn't been anyone else since?" Estée asked.

"Not really." There was a man I met on the subway, Aaron something or other. We had coffee. That was it. I had a few other dates here and there, but nothing ever came of them because I wouldn't allow it.

"Well," she said, somewhat exasperated, "it doesn't seem to me like you're even looking."

"Because I'm not."

How could I explain to her that I'd been abandoned by all the men in my life, starting with my father, Tommy, even my brother? I could never trust another man not to up and leave me.

9

BY SEVEN O'CLOCK the following morning, Estée hit the ground running. On next to no sleep, she was up and dressed in a smart-looking lemony yellow suit that I'd found for her on the clearance rack at Lord & Taylor. She didn't want to try it on until I told her it was marked down forty percent. It looked terrific on her and made her the best-dressed guest at the Admiral Hotel. Not that *that* was saying much, but still, no one would have imagined that she had less than $5 to her name.

So with great panache, Estée went into battle. I had to hand it to her. She knew what she wanted and she wasn't afraid to fight for it. I was envious of her drive and determination to see her dream through. My only dream had been to marry Tommy and have his children. But now I couldn't even think about getting married to *anyone*. Who would marry the daughter of a convicted felon? Yes, I was hiding behind the shield of a phony last name, but what if I was found out? I saw what had happened to my brother. He'd gotten fired, roughed up and harassed for being a Dowaziac. My mother had been constantly barraged, too. Gail escaped all this because she was married, and no one knew Mrs. Nathan Baker was really Gus Dowaziac's daughter.

I was growing ever more aware of how often people asked for your full name, first and last. Even on this trip the hotel register required it so I could get a second key to our room, on the sign-out sheet for towels at the swimming pool, and to retrieve mail and any packages from the front desk. Thankfully no one asked for proof, as my driver's license would have surely given me away.

Still, this business of my name was becoming increasingly messy. I did, however, take some solace in being down in Florida, since the farther away from New York you got, the less potent was Gus Dowaziac's stink.

So while Estée was out knocking on beauty parlor doors, I put on my swimsuit and took Leonard down to the hotel pool, clasping his little hand in mine so he wouldn't run ahead of me. I recognized the elderly couples from the lobby the day before. The women were sunning themselves on the plastic pool chairs, the markings waffled on the backs of their legs when they got up to dangle their feet in the water. Men with suntan oil matting down the hair on their shoulders and backs played cards off to the side. Next to Leonard, I was the youngest person there. Not exactly what I had envisioned as my all-expenses-paid trip to Florida. But it was sunny and seventy-eight degrees in September, and according to the papers, it was barely fifty and raining back home.

Leonard couldn't wait to get in the water, a kidney-shaped pool too shallow for a diving board. Even so, I worried he would drown on my watch, so I sat on the edge, surprised by how cold the water was.

"Aw, come in, Miss Downing. Come in the pool, please?"

Miss Downing. There it was again. That name. Hearing it come from Leonard, I felt like I was lying to this innocent child. "Call me Gloria and maybe I will."

"Gloria!" he shouted, seemingly delighted to be referring to an adult by her first name. It was quite empowering for him and he chanted, "*Gloria-Gloria-Gloria*," begging me to get in the water.

Finally, I gave in and joined him, up on my tiptoes, my skin turning to gooseflesh.

"Challenge you to a handstand contest." He dipped up and down.

"It's cold," I said, my fingertips skimming the water's surface. "Aren't you cold?"

"Nope." He disappeared underwater and I panicked, trying to reach for him just before he shot back up, soaking me with a forceful spray.

"Leonard! That wasn't nice." I hoisted myself out of the pool and he sulked while I toweled off.

Eventually he found other ways to amuse himself, splashing around in the shallow end until his fingers and toes pruned up. When it was time for lunch, I called him over to the side of the pool, holding out a towel, which he converted into a cape. I reached inside my tote, fished out a sandwich for him and said he'd have to wait a full hour before going back into the water.

Sitting at the foot of my chaise, he impatiently picked at the plastic slats and tugged on his towel. "I miss my dad," he said out of nowhere, suddenly looking like he was on the verge of tears.

I felt a stab to my heart because in many ways, I missed my dad, too. Or the man I thought he'd been. I remembered our family vacations to Miami Beach. My mother would sit beneath an umbrellaed chaise, passed out after her second gin and tonic, while Glenn and I played in the hotel pool with our father. Gail, too self-conscious to remove her cover-up, stayed on the sidelines while my father splashed her, shouting, *Get in here, my plump little dumpling*, which didn't exactly help Gail's self-image. My father was a burly man, his arms thick and muscular. He'd take turns hoisting Glenn and me into the air before tossing us back into the water. He'd wait for us in the deep end while we climbed up to the high dive. Glenn was terrified and I remembered how my father would taunt him: *C'mon,* Glenda. *Your little sister's not afraid.* Oh, but I was, only I wouldn't show it. I stood stoic on that diving board, toes scrunched together, hands outstretched, arms close to my ears, so determined to prove to my father how brave I was. I lived for his applause and cheers when I sprang up through the water.

My father loved the sun and never tired of it. He could bake in its rays from early morning until late afternoon. And I was struck with a sharp pang of sadness: he might never see the sun again, much less Miami Beach.

I looked at Leonard and then at the rusted clock above the snack bar. It had been almost fifty minutes. What good were ten more minutes going to do? I got up and jumped into the pool. "Wanna race?" I called out to him.

Leonard squealed with delight and jumped in after me.

We swam from one end to the other and back again. Three times. When we'd had our fill of that, Leonard wanted to see who could hold their breath the longest, which I let him win within seconds, still worried that he might drown on me. After half an hour, I'd had enough but Leonard stayed in the water.

"Gloria? Gloria, watch me! Watch this!" Leonard shouted as I toweled off. He was floating on his back, his skinny arms out to his sides.

"What a good little swimmer he is," the woman next to me said. Her name was Mrs. Saltzman and she reminded me of Mrs. Miller. She and her husband were from Staten Island and had been coming to the Admiral for as long as she could remember.

"Who needs all the tumult of Collins Avenue?" she said.

I did. I needed the tumult and excitement of Collins Avenue.

Mrs. Saltzman introduced me to the other ladies, and I made

small talk with them. By four o'clock, I'd had enough sun and Leonard looked like he could use a nap. As could I. Playing lifeguard all day, in addition to Leonard's need for constant attention, had left me exhausted. After bidding Mrs. Saltzman and the others adieu, I packed up our things and we went back to the room to rest and get cleaned up, waiting for Estée to return.

This was the basic routine the three of us fell into. Every day for the next two weeks, Estée would be out the door by the time Leonard tugged me awake. We put on our swimsuits and went to the lobby for the free buffet, which consisted of bagels and cold cereal. Estée told me to put a Hershey's Kiss in the bottom of his milk so he'd drink the whole glass. After breakfast we'd go outside and he'd challenge me to races and all kinds of water games. We had lunch followed by more swimming. One day when it rained, we stayed in the room and he showed me his postcard collection, which he'd brought from home, stored inside an old shoebox. Leonard displayed them one by one and told me all the places he wanted to visit. He was entertaining and my constant companion until his mother came home. I admit, I felt a pang of jealousy whenever he'd leave my side and run into her arms.

Estée's shoes came off the moment she got inside the hotel room, and sitting on the side of the bed, rubbing the balls of her feet, she'd tell me about her day and the prospective clients she'd met. I could tell Miami was wearing on her. And yet, no matter how exhausted and discouraged she was, she mustered the energy that Leonard demanded of her. Whether it was going through the postcards or playing checkers or reading him a bedtime story, she gave that little boy her all. She was wonderful with him.

One day, as she slipped out of her shoes and Leonard slipped into her arms, she kissed the crown of his head and said to me, "Believe it or not, I think I'm starting to get somewhere in this town. I finally got a beauty parlor to take an order."

"Really? Estée, that's fantastic."

"It's a small order. But it's a start."

"What's a small order?"

"They took a dozen Creme Packs and a half dozen bottles of Cleansing Oil."

"And what do those sell for again?"

"Let's see . . ." She glanced toward the ceiling and clucked her tongue. "The Creme Packs are $3.95 each and the oils are $1.98."

My mouth dropped open. "My God, Estée, that's over $500."

She laughed. "You really are bad at math, aren't you? It's actually $59.28."

"Oh." I let that sink in, but my excitement rebounded. "But still, Estée, this is great news. We have to celebrate."

"We don't have enough money to celebrate."

"We don't need money. We just need to do something special to mark this occasion. That way you'll always remember where you were and what you did when you got your first big break down here."

That night, Estée, Leonard and I snuck out to the pool and went for a nighttime swim. It was still hot, even after the sun had gone down—eighty-five degrees according to the thermometer on the side of the snack bar. It was the first time Estée had even ventured into the little kidney-shaped pool, and as she inched down the steps in the shallow end, I watched her tiny teacup hands skim the surface. The lights on the side of the pool were illuminating the ripples in the water.

"Ah," she said, "it's like bathwater." She plunged down to her shoulders. "The last time I went swimming at night, Joe and I were skinny-dipping."

"What's skinny-dipping?" asked Leonard.

"Never mind," I said, playfully dunking him under. I knew skinny-dipping had to have been Joe's idea. He coaxed that playful side out of Estée in much the same way I did. I couldn't think of anyone else in her life, besides Leonard, of course, who gave her permission to have a little fun.

We must have stayed in the pool for close to an hour, and after toweling off, we scampered into the lobby and raided the vending machine: Necco Wafers, Milk Duds, Chuckles and three bottles of Coca-Cola. Back in our room we had a picnic on the floor. Leonard was having the time of his life and was so worn-out he slept until nine the next morning.

BY THE END of our second week, things had really begun picking up for Estée. Arlene came through, sending some wealthy women Estée's way, and while I was at the pool with Leonard, Estée was giving facials in our hotel room. Soon after, word started to spread. The women who received their facials and complimentary samples told their friends, who told their friends, and so on and so on.

For the next three weeks, Joe was sending down boxes of creams with envelopes full of black and white ESTÉE LAUDER labels that Leonard applied, rather enjoying the taste of the stickum as he licked the back of each one.

And I got paid, finally. Estée gave me $29—all in small bills and a dollar in change. She owed me more, but that was all she could spare at the time. I tried to be gracious, but even though playing with Leonard all day didn't seem like work, the bills in my hand were underwhelming. On my day off, after inspecting my blonde roots, I went to a beauty parlor Estée recommended and dropped $4.75 on a new color: Mahogany Suede.

On my way back to the hotel, I passed a souvenir shop and plucked two postcards off the stand: one for Leonard and one for my brother. *Greetings from Miami, Glenn*, I started to write but stopped, the pen growing so heavy in my hand that I had to set it down.

What would come next? *I'm vacationing down here on the money you gave me. Geez, look at me—I got a job. I'm a goddamn nanny, but I can't quite make ends meet—please send more money . . .*

Who was I kidding? This wasn't a job. There was no future in this. I couldn't live on $29 dribbles coming in here and there. I felt paralyzed by my own helplessness. Darlene said I was *capable*. Capable of what? I didn't know how to do anything other than shop and shampoo hair. How was I ever going to land a real job? That voice in my head sounded off, almost deafening—*You can't make it on your own. You're still a Dowaziac. Pack up and move to Boston.*

10

ON WEEK SIX, the last week of our Florida adventure, Estée was invited to a party at Arlene Forester's second home, in Palm Beach. Babe Cushing, the fashion editor of *Vogue*, was going to be there, and Estée thought if she could just get a mention in the magazine, her business would be on its way.

Three days before the party, Estée, fresh from bathing, stood before her closet, wrapped in a towel, her hair up in a turban. She wanted my help in planning her outfit for the party. I stood next to her, looking at the dresses she'd brought along, and nothing was really suitable.

"But what about this one?" She held the hanger beneath her chin, displaying a simple slip dress.

I reached over, running the coral fabric between my fingers. "It's not bad," I said, releasing the dress, "but we're talking Palm Beach. If you want to make an impression on those folks, you need to up your ante."

Estée flung the dress onto the bed and pressed her fingertips to her temples.

"C'mon now," I said, "you've made some money down here. I

think buying a good dress—just one good dress—would be a smart investment."

Well, she liked that idea and the next morning presented me with a shopping itinerary she'd created on a sheet of Admiral Hotel stationery. Setting my coffee aside, I glanced at the paper:

9:30–10:15 Morris Brothers
10:15–10:45 Nelson's
10:45–11:00 Richards

"See," she said, "this way we can hit three stores right down on Washington and Española Way."

I shook my head. "Estée, trust me, you are not going to find the dress you want at Richards."

"That's why I only allotted fifteen minutes there. See? Just enough time to take a quick look—you never know. We might get lucky."

I scanned farther down the list. She had scheduled a whole twenty minutes for lunch at McCrory's snack bar. I looked at her and scrunched the list up in my fist.

"What are you doing?"

"This is not the way you go shopping."

"But—but—" She reached for the wad of paper, trying to flatten it out.

"Forget the itinerary. Let's just go and have some fun."

We left Leonard with Mrs. Saltzman and headed straight for Burdines. I pulled a number of dresses for Estée and said, "Don't look at the price tags. Just try them on."

She slipped into the fitting room and came out, modeling each one, twirling before a three-way mirror, swishing the fabric back and forth. She really did have a terrific figure when she showed it off. And those bright colors brought out the hazel in her eyes, the creaminess of her skin. Every dress she tried on looked better than the one before, but the ultimate was a royal blue satin dress with puff sleeves, a cinched waist and pleats all around. We both fell in love with it until Estée looked at the price.

"It's $51!" She splayed a hand across her chest. "I can't—"

"Oh yes, you can. You need this dress. You can't afford *not* to have it. Just sell some extra Creme Packs and you've got it made."

After hemming and hawing, she took the dress. It was almost two in the afternoon and by then Estée had abandoned her notion of sticking to her schedule. And apparently her budget, too. We had a leisurely lunch at a charming little outdoor café, enjoying crab salads and iced tea—her treat, which was good because I couldn't have afforded any of it.

"Oh, I wish you could come with me to the party," she said as we lingered over coffee and a shared slice of key lime pie. "I don't want to go alone. This is a tough crowd. You don't know what these people are like," she said.

Oh, but I did.

"Will you come with me? Please? Arlene said I could invite anyone I wanted."

Me? Walk into the lion's den? Into a Palm Beach party where I might know people? Was she crazy? "What about Leonard? I have to watch him."

"No, no. We'll ask Mrs. Saltzman to watch him for the night."

Mrs. Saltzman adored Leonard. She would have jumped at the chance, so I went for another excuse. "I don't have anything to wear."

"You can borrow one of my dresses."

I cocked an eyebrow. "One of your dresses that wasn't good enough for you to wear in the first place?"

"Oh, please, Gloria. This is important. I need you there with me. Babe Cushing is going to be there," she reminded me.

In the end she wore me down. Just as I knew she would. Mrs. Saltzman was thrilled to watch Leonard so I could accompany Estée. I didn't really care about meeting Babe Cushing, but the prospect of an open bar was inviting.

ARLENE'S HOME WAS right on the beach and it was beautiful, with a sweeping southern exposure and rich, lustrous marble floors covered with plush area rugs. You never would have known that we were in the midst of the Depression—not with this crowd. White-gloved, tuxedoed waiters weaved throughout the partygoers with silver trays of champagne. The women were dressed in flowing satin; the men were in elegant double-breasted suits and silk pocket squares. I felt terribly underdressed, as I knew I would, wearing one of Estée's rejects, which could have benefited from a strand of pearls. Estée had also loaned me a velvet beaded evening bag filled with tiny jars of face cream.

"I tucked a few things inside"—she'd winked—"just in case."

I should have known. She never went anywhere without her samples. And that's when I got it. I wasn't her safety net, there for moral support and reassurance; I was her attendant, her courier. As Estée and I moved deeper into the party, I heard the delicate clinking of those jars jostling around inside my evening bag.

Swirls of cigarette and cigar smoke mixed in the air along with heavy doses of expensive perfume. A jazz combo was playing Cab Calloway songs. The various rooms were crowded and one or two faces looked familiar, or maybe that was just my nerves trying to get the better of me. As far as I could tell, no one posed a threat.

Estée and I stuck close together, sipping our drinks, nibbling on canapés and skewered shrimp. Naturally, the very moment I began to relax, just as we were heading out to the terrace, I did indeed glimpse someone who nearly made me gasp aloud. In fact, I wasn't sure that I hadn't. There she was: Alexandria Spencer. *Why her, of all people?* Alexandria was barely four feet, eleven inches tall, and like many other little angry creatures, she was a Tasmanian devil of a gal. She had once been a dear friend, but I couldn't keep up with her shifting moods; one minute she'd be kind as a kitten, the next she'd have her claws out. Alexandria caught my eye, and before I could head outside, she made a beeline for me. Estée perked up, assuming Alexandria was coming up to her.

But I knew better. This was my moment of reckoning. I was about to be exposed. Bracing myself, I decided I would explain to Estée why I'd lied about my name and my parents being dead. And then I'd beg for forgiveness. That was my plan, but as soon as Alexandria opened her mouth, I knew I couldn't let *her* be the cause of my downfall. I couldn't give her the satisfaction.

"Well, if it isn't Gloria Dow—"

"What a surprise," I said, cutting her off.

"Oh my"—a bejeweled hand rested on her chest—"look at you."

My shoulders tensed up. Something hot and unsettling began blistering beneath my skin, and a high-pitched ping sounded off inside my ear. *Oh no. Not a vertigo bout. Just hold on, hold on.*

"How are you, Alexandria?" I managed to say, my eyes locked on to her forehead as the side of my face began to tingle.

"I see you changed your hair."

I'm not sure what I said in response. I was too preoccupied, anticipating the room about to spin. I waited. Waited some more. And thankfully the bout passed. A mild one, gone undetected. But now it was my fear that was whirling.

"Did you hear that Thomas is engaged?" She laughed at my flattened expression, knowing she'd just gutted me. "He and Lana got back together right after he stopped seeing you. Of course his family's thrilled. They always loved Lana." She smiled cruelly. "You're not married yet, are you?"

Typical Alexandria. She knew perfectly well I wouldn't have met someone and gotten married in under six months. She just wanted to hear me say it out loud, as if being single was the worst thing that could happen to a girl. "Nope," I said. "Not married yet." I stared at the part in her hair. She was the size of a high-top table—I could have rested my drink on her head.

Alexandria blew a plume of smoke up at me. "Well, if you'll excuse me, I need to get some air. It suddenly got a bit too stuffy in here for me." She gave off a haughty snort and walked away.

"You *know* her?" Estée looked at me, stunned, clearly impressed. "How do you know her?"

"Long story," I said, trying to wave it away with my hand. I could tell Estée was about to press for details but thankfully something else grabbed her attention: two potential customers, well within reach.

"My, what a beautiful brooch that is," Estée said to the woman standing closest. "I have one similar to that. From *Austria*. I was born there," she said, which landed like a brick at their feet.

The two women turned toward Estée, taking her in for the first time. The taller of the two did look familiar, though I couldn't recall her name. They were chilly, to say the least. The one gave Estée a less-than-encouraging glance, but Estée took it as an invitation to elaborate.

"Yes, in Vienna." She smiled. "My father was a close personal friend of the emperor."

This raised an eyebrow. Perhaps she was a bit more interesting than they'd thought.

Still reeling from the news about Tommy, I went in search of more champagne. When I returned, Estée was talking to the same two women about the importance of a good moisturizer. I should not have been surprised. There wasn't a conversation—not one about where in the world was Amelia Earhart, or King Edward

VIII giving up the throne, or the outbreak of grasshoppers in Nebraska—that Estée couldn't steer into a discussion on skincare and beauty products.

I was about to take a sip from my coupe when she pulled me close to her side. "Oh, and I want you both to meet my top salesgirl."

Top salesgirl? I supposed that sounded better than *the nanny*, but why couldn't she have just said I was her friend? Again, I came face-to-face with the fact that I was nothing more than the hired help.

"This is C.Z. Guest and Simone Taylor," said Estée.

Ah yes, C.Z. That was her name. I had met her at a horse show when I was still with Tommy. Thank God she didn't remember or else didn't recognize me. But then again, how could she have—the woman barely glanced my way when Estée made the introductions. I was invisible now, not even worthy of a polite greeting from people who had once been my peers.

Outcasts like me needed to snag rich husbands to garner any respect, only that wasn't likely to happen with a father in federal prison. So what would become of me now? I'd taken this strong-independent-woman routine about as far as I could. Much as I hated to admit it, everything was pushing me toward Boston.

"You know," Estée continued, "I have something that would be perfect for your complexions. May I tell you both about it?" She was already opening her evening bag, taking out a small jar of cream.

I cringed, embarrassed for her, but the women seemed genuinely interested. Certainly more so than they had been about her Austrian heritage.

Later that evening, Estée was finally introduced to Babe Cushing. Babe was quite elegant, with a choker of pearls and a velvet black-and-white off-the-shoulder gown.

"How is everything going at *Vogue*?" Estée asked, as if they were old friends.

"Fine, fine," she said. "Have you met Nancy yet?"

Nancy was a model. She also looked familiar, and not because she'd recently posed for the cover of *Harper's*. Years after Arlene's party, Nancy would reemerge as Slim Keith, but at the moment, she was still Nancy, and I was certain we'd met somewhere before. While they continued chatting, I glanced around for Alexandria but thankfully didn't see her again for the rest of the evening.

When Estée went into her spiel about cosmetics and pulled out another sample jar of cream, I wanted to slink away, pretend I didn't know her. But Babe and Nancy were captivated while Estée smoothed the cream onto the backs of their hands, talking about the importance of moisturizing twice daily. Soon half a dozen other women had circled around Estée while she demonstrated her Super Rich All-Purpose Crème and I polished off my drink.

I watched the women take their little samples and move on, but it wasn't long before Estée was surrounded by a new group. This time, it was all men. She was an excellent flirt, and you could tell she loved the attention. One of them couldn't remember our names and had taken to calling us Salt and Pepper on account of Estée being a blonde and me being a brunette.

Estée laughed and smiled, and playfully touched one man's hand as he lit her cigarette. I thought she was going to get herself into trouble, the way she was trifling with them all, but she deftly shifted the conversation.

"So, tell me, gentlemen, are your wives here with you tonight?" she asked.

"I'm not married," the one said, holding out his hand as if wedding bands couldn't come off.

"What about your girlfriend—is she here?"

"No girlfriend, either."

"I bet Sally wouldn't agree with that," said his buddy, nudging him in the ribs.

"Oh, do bring Sally over," said Estée. "Please? I'd love to meet her."

And in the meantime, Estée handed them each her business card and told them to send their wives, girlfriends, sisters and mothers to her for a free facial and consultation at one of her salons back in New York. She was the only woman I'd ever known who carried a business card.

Soon Sally came over, a pert little thing with silky blonde hair. Estée took hold of both her hands and smiled. "Why, you're absolutely beautiful. You know, I have something that would be just perfect for you. May I?" She reached for my evening bag and pulled out a little jar of cream.

By the time we left the party, Estée had handed out all but two of her business cards and all her little sample jars of cream—emptying both our evening bags.

"Oh, wasn't that fun!" she said as we were waiting out front for the valet to bring around our rental car.

"Are you kidding me?" I looked at her, exasperated. I was exhausted. "All you did was work the whole time."

"Oh, I know." She was giddy. "Wasn't it fun!"

IT WAS OUR last day in Miami, and while Leonard splashed about in the pool, I lay back on my chaise, letting the sun's rays beat down on me. I was still contemplating a move to Boston but only because I feared that I'd never find a job back in New York and I had nowhere else to go.

Boston seemed like the easy way out, but I knew Gail would make me pay dearly for putting a roof over my head. She'd saddle me with her kids and the housework. She'd relish the thought of me on my hands and knees, scrubbing the bathroom floor, doing laundry, making beds and washing dishes . . . Who was I kidding? I wouldn't last a week at my sister's, and Glenn didn't have room for me at his studio apartment. In the end, I'd still have to find a job and a place of my own in Boston. I'd still have to learn how to take care of myself. It would be no different than if I stayed in New York.

If Estée were with me right then, she would have told me to think positively, to ask myself what I truly wanted, to make a decision and not look back. I could hear her now: *You can do anything you set your mind to.* My eyes flashed open, and staring into the sun's blinding rays, I saw it all so clearly. I'd just walked myself in a complete circle. There was only one answer to the question of what to do with Gloria Downing. It was obvious and very simple, though certainly not easy. But at least now I knew what I had to do.

11

WHEN WE RETURNED to Manhattan, it was the middle of October and I was galvanized, determined to make a fresh start. The first thing I did was legally change my name. What surprised me most was not how easy it was to do but the tug in my heart of breaking that final tie to my family. I was truly leaving them behind. Especially my father, who I knew would take it as a slap in the face. But Gus Dowaziac was behind bars now; he couldn't help me anymore. The time had come for me to stand on my own two feet.

As I left the New York City courthouse that day, I headed down Centre Street with my paperwork—*Order Granting Leave to Change Name*—tucked inside my pocketbook. My every step was lighter, easier, like I'd left some heavy burden back in that courtroom. It was fall, overcast and chilly, but I had that happy, first-day-of-spring feeling, where everything was coming back to life, where anything was possible.

Emboldened by all this, I set out to find a job. Every morning I picked up the *New York Times* and the *Post*. I scoured the classified ads and took to the streets looking for anyone who would hire me. The diner on the corner turned me down for a waitress position; so did the ice cream parlor across the street. The five-and-dime next door wouldn't bring me on as a cashier because I had no prior experience. I tried half a dozen different beauty shops and couldn't get hired as a shampoo girl, either. It was soon obvious that I couldn't even get a job I *didn't* want.

Meanwhile, as the weeks stretched on, Thanksgiving was just around the corner and another check arrived from Glenn with a note saying how disappointed he was about me changing my name. He also warned that if I didn't find some kind of work soon, I would have to move to Boston.

While I was barely scraping by, Estée's business was beginning to grow. Before leaving Florida, she had successfully opened a concession inside the Hotel Charles in Miami Beach and had hired and trained a salesgirl who was willing to work on straight commission. Estée was also in the process of opening another concession at a beauty parlor in Midtown. I was hoping she'd hire me to work at her new stand, but she never said a word.

One afternoon I ran into her at Darlene's. I was getting my roots touched up, which Darlene, thankfully, did free of charge. After Estée asked how the job hunt was going, I came right out and asked her to hire me.

"Oh, Gloria," she said, not letting her eyes meet mine, "if only you'd said something sooner."

"What do you mean, *sooner*? You know I've been looking. For weeks now."

"Well, if you must know, I just hired a new girl." She busied herself with a jar, her little teacup hands pretending to tighten the lid so she wouldn't have to see the hurt expression on my face.

This stung more than I could have imagined. "Thanks a lot," I said. She obviously didn't think I could do the job, and that put

Estée in the same camp with everyone else from my past who believed I was incapable of being a responsible adult.

"Well, don't get so upset," she said. "What did you expect—you've never been a salesgirl before."

"Oh, but I sure was at that party in Palm Beach, wasn't I? 'Here everyone—*meet my top salesgirl*.'"

Estée's cheeks went dark as she pulled me into the back room. "Marjorie's worked in cosmetic sales before," she said with a shoulder roll. "She has experience."

I was angry when I left Estée at Darlene's, and to soothe myself, I headed downtown, where I stood on the sidewalk, gazing at the window displays at Bergdorf Goodman. Behind that glass was a world of splendor. My distress over Estée was replaced by deep yearning. I longed to feel those satin fabrics draped across the mannequins, to touch the elaborate beading at their necklines. I couldn't bring myself to go inside, for the temptation would have been too great and I was all too aware of the extra money Glenn had sent, pulsing inside my pocketbook. The old me would have said *to hell with it* and blown it all on a scarf or a pair of shoes, consequences be damned. But I was officially Gloria Downing now, and I had to be responsible for this new person I'd declared myself to be.

Reluctantly I moved on. It was cold that day, the season's first flurries floating through the crisp air. I buttoned my coat to my collar and plunged my hands inside my pockets. As I approached 50th and Fifth, I contemplated whether to pray for God's help at St. Patrick's or sulk in a bar around the corner. It was in that very moment that I passed a tiny sign nestled in the bottom of a plate glass window at Saks Fifth Avenue: NOW HIRING SHOPGIRLS. INQUIRE WITHIN.

Inquire I did, and once I stepped inside that store, as I took in the bronze sculpted decor, the fluted pilasters, the marble floors and crystal chandeliers, something inside me came alive. Though I'd shopped at Saks countless times before, I now saw the store anew. I couldn't explain it, but I felt like for once I was in the right place at the right time.

I was given an interview on the spot and had been rather strategic when I met with the floor manager, Mrs. Coopers. I complimented her on the pin she was wearing: a yellow-gold leaf studded in jade and pearls. She smiled and touched it, as if confirming it was still there.

Leading me into the stockroom on the ninth floor she said, "New merchandise arrives every day. It needs to be tagged properly and sent to the precise department."

I looked around and was downright tickled to be in that room, surrounded by racks and racks of clothes, hatboxes and shoeboxes stacked floor to ceiling that had just arrived, straight from the designers. A blue satin dress caught my eye. I ran my hand over the sleeve like you would a lover's arm.

"This is a beautiful Vionnet gown," I said.

Mrs. Coopers looked at me as if to say, *You know Madeleine Vionnet?* Did I ever. I'd once owned several pieces of Vionnet couture, along with Jacques Heim, Chanel and even a couple Schiaparellis. I used to shop at Saks Fifth Avenue all the time. I even had my very own Saks Fifth Avenue charge plate up until my father's fiasco deemed it invalid. My mother, sister and I passed the scissors as we cut our cards in half. But that aside, I knew the labels, knew a good woolen blend and good tailoring when I saw it. We moved on to the next rack and I commented on the use of the bias cut in another dress. Well, Mrs. Coopers was dutifully impressed, and I was offered the job immediately. I felt a burst of pride unlike anything I'd ever experienced before: *And what do you do, Gloria? Why, I'm a shopgirl at Saks Fifth Avenue, thank you very much!*

Mrs. Coopers escorted me to the back room on the seventh floor, where I was seated behind a large wooden desk and given all kinds of very official-looking forms to complete. As I wrote out my name, I felt justified in legally changing it. Still, I was nervous about someone from my past waltzing into Saks and recognizing me. In bold moments I thought, *So what if they did?* It wasn't like I ran the Ponzi scheme. I didn't steal from anyone. I reminded myself I had nothing to feel guilty about, but I could never hold that argument for very long. I would always come back to feeling inexplicably responsible for my father's actions. I feared that one of his victims would accost me like they had Glenn and my mother. They could do it here in the store, out on the street, in a restaurant, on a crowded subway train. I was a woman, so I doubted anyone would rough me up like they had Glenn, but the shame, the humiliation of it all, loomed over me like a thundercloud.

I figured that if anyone came into Saks and tried to make trouble, I could talk my way out of it—a case of mistaken identity or someone bearing a grudge. Really, though, what were the odds that someone would try to get me fired? I figured slim to none, and seeing as I had no other employment options, it was a risk I was willing to take.

MRS. COOPERS QUICKLY became something of a mentor to me. She was a middle-aged woman with no ankles to speak of. She favored cropped buttonless jackets in bright colors and thick chunky shoes with two-inch heels. Her hair was another matter altogether. Held in place by a couple of tortoiseshell combs, it was nearly white, towering above her head like stiff egg whites. She was a strict floor manager and had lots of little expressions, little pearls of wisdom. The one that still sticks with me was the talk she gave me on my very first day about tigers, elephants and slugs.

"You must always remember," Mrs. Coopers told me, "there are three types of employees. Only three. Do you know what they are?"

I had no idea, but I had already been around Mrs. Coopers long enough to understand that she was a fan of the rhetorical question. All that was required in terms of a response was maintaining proper eye contact.

"Well, I'll tell you," said Mrs. Coopers. "The three types of employees are"—she started on her index finger—"tigers"—up went the next finger—"elephants and"—the ring finger—"slugs." She nodded. "Tigers, elephants and slugs. Do you know the difference between the three?"

Again, I waited for her explanation, my eyes trained on hers.

"Tigers are the ones with the smarts. They're smart and assertive. They're the ones who take control, take the initiative. Tigers are the stars. The ones groomed for advancement. The elephants are the hard workers. They're very necessary and do exactly as they're told but nothing more. And lastly, we have the slugs. They are dead weight. Lazy and always looking to cut corners. They never last long and are expunged upon detection." *Expunged upon detection.* She actually spoke that way. Then she clasped both my hands and narrowed her eyes. "Be a tiger, Gloria Downing. Be a tiger and you will go far."

Though I'd been raised to be a slug, I refused to be controlled by my past. Each morning when I arrived at work, I took in the floor. This was a crucial time of day for me. A reckoning of sorts. When the glass counters glistened and the floors, freshly polished overnight, were at their most brilliant and all was peaceful, I knew I had a choice to make. I could dwell on the fact that I *had* to work and could no longer afford the items I sold. I could focus on all that I'd lost, or I could take pride in how far I'd come. It was a battle every day and I never knew what was going to tip the scale one way or the other.

Now I did not start off as a tiger. Instead, I was a *floater*, which involved moving from department to department, depending on the store's needs. One day I was in jewelry, the next they'd put me in handbags and shoes, fine dresses another day, cosmetics or lingerie the day after that.

What surprised me most about this job at Saks Fifth Avenue was that it didn't seem like a *job*. Not at all. I was astonished by how much I liked working. Actually, I didn't just *like* working. I *loved* it. I knew quality and I had excellent taste. I thought of it not as persuading someone to buy a particular item, but rather as helping a friend put together the perfect outfit. If I'd stopped to think about it as selling, I probably would have choked.

Considering my very brief work experience, never before in my life had I been given an opportunity to be so useful. So productive. At Darlene's I was often ignored by the hoity-toity clients and I felt subordinate to Estée as Leonard's babysitter, but being at Saks Fifth Avenue was altogether different. It's not that I didn't wait on my share of snooty customers, but for the most part, I was respected for my knowledge, my abilities. I was a problem solver. Even I could see that I had great potential, that I could indeed be a tiger.

When Mr. So-and-So needed a special anniversary gift for his wife, I sold him a Bulova wristwatch filled with rose gold and a lovely salmon dial. I sold an elegant pair of Cartier cufflinks to a harried housewife in need of a last-minute birthday present for her husband. Another woman had been sent to procure an emergency necktie to replace the one her boss had spilled a martini on at lunch. When a bored wealthy woman was looking for something to brighten her day, I sold her a black silk faille cocktail dress with a cream fichu. I knew how to talk to these women. They were me in my former life. I did especially well in the jewelry department and women's dresses.

Mrs. Coopers was very pleased with my performance. "You're doing an excellent job, my little tiger," she'd say. "Just excellent."

The only drawback to being at Saks Fifth Avenue was that, yes, from time to time I did see a familiar face. But the thing about snobby people was that they could be standing two feet in front of you and never make eye contact, never say a word. So while thankfully I never waited on someone from my past, I did see them milling about, and with my new hair color—Chestnut Roast #5—they paid me no mind. I was safe for the time being, but I was constantly looking over my shoulder.

Shortly after I started working, I became acquainted with a Saks Fifth Avenue legend, Mrs. William Hutt. I remember I had been assigned to the jewelry department that day and noticed a very stylish woman who looked like Park Avenue itself in her close-fitting slouch hat made of the most luxurious-looking champagne silk. She was admiring a pendant display that I had arranged just that morning, showcasing two designers: Otto Prutscher and Josef Hoffmann.

"May I help you?"

"No, no," she said with a sweet smile. "I'm just looking. That's all. They're so beautiful."

"If I can show you anything, please let me know."

I went about looking for my next tiger-like task and from the corner of my eye I just so happened to see that sweet woman slipping a Hoffman pendant into her pocket. I was stunned. And offended. She was stealing, and I was reminded that even people who looked wealthy could be criminals—my father, case in point. I had to right the situation. I knew I wasn't allowed to leave my counter, and by the time I finally managed to flag down Mrs. Coopers, the woman had moved on, disappearing deeper into the store.

"I just saw someone steal one of the Hoffman pendants," I said.

Mrs. Coopers's eyes flashed with alarm as she looked about the floor.

"It was a woman," I said, "about forty, maybe forty-five. She was wearing a hat and—oh, wait, there she is! That's her." I pointed to a necktie display.

"Oh"—Mrs. Coopers smiled—"that's Mrs. Hutt."

"Quick," I said, "before she gets away."

"Oh, I should have told you about her. Mrs. Hutt does that from time to time. Helps herself to this and that." Mrs. Coopers fluttered her fingers, no big deal. "We simply tally up whatever she takes and provide her husband with a total at the end of the month. It's really quite harmless. She's actually a very good customer, so we mustn't do anything to embarrass her."

In the coming weeks and months, I would witness Mrs. Hutt slip a 25¢ barrette into her pocketbook and a $250 humidor inside a shopping bag, and of course there was the $18.25 Sunbeam kitchen mixer that she'd wrapped in an Hermès scarf—which she had also helped herself to—before carrying both out of the store like a newborn baby.

And so there you have it. We had a prolific kleptomaniac in our midst. Eventually, I became rather friendly with Mrs. Hutt and would call her attention to any new arrivals in order to boost my sales.

"Good afternoon, Mrs. Hutt," I'd say. "Did you see these gorgeous new cashmere sweaters? Here's one in your size."

An hour later, that sweater would be gone, and I'd reap the rewards of a nice sale.

12

BY EARLY DECEMBER, Saks Fifth Avenue was already in the Christmas spirit. Each day when I arrived, I felt as though I were stepping inside a winter wonderland. Greeted by the carolers near the main entrance, I was delighted by the decorations: sparkling snowflakes in the front windows, wreaths on the doors, sprigs of holly tucked inside the display cases, garlands and giant red velvet bows everywhere. The eight-foot Norway spruce dazzled with enormous red and green ornaments, tinsel, and twinkling lights.

Estée came into Saks all the time, in part to see me but mostly to keep tabs on the cosmetic department. She would hover near the Max Factor counter, inspecting each item, examining the bottles, taking out a little notebook and jotting down a few things. She'd move on to Elizabeth Arden and Helena Rubinstein and Revlon. She'd study the way customers browsed and how the shopgirls stood back, politely waiting to ring up a purchase.

Though I loved my job at Saks, I was still sore at Estée for not hiring me.

"Gosh," she said with a sigh, "I would give *anything* to have my skincare products in a store like this someday. I can't believe what they charge for Arden's face cream," she said, inspecting a satin slip. "My creams are far better."

"I've never tried Arden's cream," I said dismissively, folding a stack of nightgowns that had arrived that morning. Mrs. Coopers had just taught me the proper folding technique: one sleeve at a time, smoothed straight across the back and then the sides, before folding from the bottom up. I took such pride in that perfectly symmetrical pile I'd created.

"My dream is to get my products into Saks Fifth Avenue," said Estée. "You know what they say, 'You're not really in business until you're in Saks.'" She tapped her lacquered nails on the counter, so I knew there was more coming. This was the drumroll. I concentrated on the next nightgown, avoiding all eye contact. "How about you introduce me to the buyers?"

I smoothed my hand over a folded sleeve, unwilling to look at her. She had some nerve. Asking me for a favor like this after refusing to hire me. I had the power now and I was irked, but I wasn't about to get into it with her on the sales floor.

"Well"—her nails were still clacking against the countertop—"what do you say?"

"I don't even know who the buyers are, Estée. And even if I did, it wouldn't do you any good."

Her hand froze in place. She didn't like that answer. Nor did she like it when I explained how precious counter space was for cosmetics.

"It's really hard to come by. From what I've heard, it's even tough for Elizabeth Arden, Helena Rubinstein and Revlon to get more space, so I highly doubt they'd make room for a newcomer like you that no one's ever heard of."

That didn't go over very well, either. Estée left that day and refused to return any of my telephone calls. She ended up not speaking to me for the next three days.

I was upset and complained about Estée to Bobbi. The two of us were at Mr. Foster's, our favorite neighborhood tavern, named after the owner's dog, a lovable mangy hound who drooled all over the window bay where he kept an eye on the rest of us. That day, Mr. Foster had a droopy Santa's hat perched between his ears.

While waiting for our cocktails, I turned to the bartender. "How've ya been, Marty? I missed you the last time we were in." I smiled as he said something about taking a day off. "Well, you know this place just isn't the same without you."

"What's going on?" Bobbi whispered. "Do you have a thing for Marty now?"

"No, I have a *thing* for free drinks."

Marty slid the cocktails before us. "On the house."

"Oh, Marty? Really? Are you sure? You're the best."

"Well done," said Bobbi as we took our martinis to a table up front. In the light coming through the window I could see that Bobbi's appearance had reverted back to her pre-Estée-makeover days. She hadn't kept up with tweezing her brows or applying the eyeshadow and lipstick prescribed, confirming Estée's belief that there really were no homely women, just lazy ones.

"So tell me again what Estée did?" she asked.

"It's just that she acts like I owe her something," I said, fiddling with my cigarette case. "And for what? My so-called *all-expenses-paid* vacation to Miami?"

"Yeah, chasing after her little brat."

"Leonard's not a brat," I said a little defensively. Leonard had been the best part of the whole trip. "But you should have seen her," I said, turning the conversation back around. "She just waltzed into Saks like she owned the place. And she's so pushy sometimes."

"And selfish," Bobbi said, fishing a cigarette from my case. "She's *really* selfish. And full of herself. And I don't know why. She's nothing special. She's a huckster. And the biggest name dropper I've ever met. If you ask me, she's just a social climber."

When Bobbi started in on her like that, my first instinct was to protect Estée. It was one thing for me to criticize Estée and another for Bobbi to do it. Yes, I admit it was annoying the way Estée would wax on about her lunches and cocktail parties with C.Z. and Babe Cushing or some other Palm Beach socialites, but I didn't dwell on that.

"I don't know why you put up with her."

Why? Because I loved Estée, because I admired her. I drew strength and courage from her. I needed her in my life. To me, Estée was a sterling example of how to get ahead on pure determination and honest hard work. My father had failed me in that respect, but Estée, well, Estée was my role model, even if I couldn't always follow her advice.

Sitting in that tavern, I'd just wanted to vent and get a few things off my chest, but Bobbi wanted to do a character assassination. Bobbi didn't care for Estée. I knew that. And at times I felt my loyalties stretched between the two of them.

THE NEXT DAY, while working again in the lingerie department, I noticed a mother and daughter walking through the store. Every few feet they would stop to admire a dressing gown or a silk pajama set. Seeing them pinched at my heart, reminding me of the many shopping sprees I'd had with my mother. We'd end the day with heaps of packages and a big gooey sundae when I was little, replaced by cocktails when I was older.

Not long after the mother and daughter vanished into the store, I spotted a couple of girls I'd gone to school with. And what's more, they spotted me, too. Jennifer and Joan saw me behind the counter. A name tag on my chest, a cloth in my hand. I was caught. Even my dark hair hadn't thrown them off. My heart pulsed loudly in my ears; my skin grew clammy.

"Gloria Dowaziac?" Joan cackled. "You—you *work* here?"

"Selling girdles!" Jennifer snickered, holding up an all-in-one Corselette.

I cleared my throat and squared my shoulders. "Is there something I can help you with?"

The two giggled and after a painful moment Jennifer pointed to a French lace peignoir set on a display mannequin. "I'd like to see that."

I should have told them we didn't have it in her size. But that was the last one in stock and I knew it would fit her perfectly. Instead, I turned to Jennifer and said, "Forget it. I'm not waiting on you."

"I beg your pardon?" She gave me an indignant look.

"You heard me." I folded my arms and narrowed my eyes in one fluid motion. "Just get out of here."

Jennifer folded her arms right back at me. "Unless you want me to report you, I suggest you do as I say."

"Well, don't just stand there," said Joan. "Get it off that thing so she can see it. Chop-chop."

The only thing harder than dressing a mannequin was undressing it. They weighed a ton and each time you moved them you were bound to have some casualties—an arm popped out of the shoulder, a hand fell free from its wrist screws. Joan and Jennifer must have been quite amused watching me wrestle with that negligee, trying not to tear the delicate lace. I was sweating by the time I'd finished, and when I presented the peignoir to Jennifer, she felt the fabric and wrinkled her nose.

"Aw, never mind," she said. "I don't feel like trying it on anymore."

They were still chortling as they walked away.

WHEN I GOT home that night Estée telephoned and asked if I had time for lunch on my day off. She'd made a reservation at Longchamps in the Empire State Building. It was an upscale restaurant that she knew I couldn't afford. That right there should have been my first clue that she hadn't really forgiven me. But I agreed to meet her there anyway because I missed her terribly. Also, I felt guilty not doing whatever I could to get her into Saks.

The restaurant was packed, and we were led down the mirrored staircase to a table in the lower level, equally crowded and artfully decorated in Longchamps' signature cinnabar red and gold colors.

As soon as we were seated, Estée scrutinized my face as only she could, her eyes traveling from my forehead to my chin. "You're not moisturizing twice a day, are you?"

"Guilty as charged."

"I'm not kidding. If you don't take care of your skin now, you're going to look like a prune by the time you're forty." She placed her napkin in her lap. "Promise me you'll do a Creme Pack treatment tonight."

"I promise." She gave me a doubtful look, so I added a two-finger salute. "Scout's honor."

While perusing the menu, Estée began telling me about her newest concession stand in the city. "Honestly, I don't know what I'd do without Marjorie. She's doing a fabulous job." Estée eyed my expression, looking to see if she'd nicked my pride.

And she had. Marjorie was the salesgirl Estée had hired instead of me.

"She sold $25 worth of Creme Packs just yesterday alone," Estée said as she closed her menu.

"I'm so glad that you and Marjorie are keeping the women of Manhattan well moisturized. We wouldn't want a lot of prunes running around the city, now would we?" I said, scanning the menu to see what I could afford.

The waiter came by for our orders. Estée went for broiled shad roe on toast for $3.15, while I decided on the onion soup au gratin for 90¢.

After the waiter left, I could not resist the urge to follow up her Marjorie jab with one of my own. "You'll never guess who came into Saks yesterday? Wallis Simpson. That's right, the Duchess of Windsor." I watched Estée's eyes widen, the green in her hazel irises showing through.

"Did you *wait* on her?"

Such a strategic question on Estée's part. She genuinely wanted to know, but she also had to get in that inglorious, subservient *wait on her*. "No, but I did say, 'Good afternoon, Duchess,' and she smiled right back and said, 'Good afternoon.'"

Just knowing that I'd seen the duchess, let alone spoken to her, filled Estée with such envy that all she could do was fire back by telling me that she was giving Marjorie a raise.

"$8.50 a day," she said, needle-nosing her napkin to dab the corners of her mouth.

That was $1.25 more than I was making. I squeezed out a smile.

All through lunch and even over a slice of lemon chiffon pie that we shared along with a pot of demitasse, we were taking turns one-upping each other, shadowboxing. We'd easily gone ten rounds and it was exhausting.

When the bill came, I reached for it out of spite.

"Oh no," said Estée, grasping for it, which was her nature. Those little teacup hands were fast, always quick to reach for a check even when she didn't have the money.

"No, I insist." I tugged back harder, knowing that the staggering $6.75 meant I'd either be skipping lunch or bringing a sandwich from home for the rest of the week.

"I said I'd get it." Estée grabbed it back.

It was on the third or fourth tug when the bill tore in half. We both stared at the tattered check, silent.

"Well, that settles it," said Estée, "we'll just split it."

And with that, we both started laughing.

"You know," she said after leaving the restaurant, as we walked down 34th Street, "Marjorie is a terrific salesgirl. She really is, but"—she looped her arm through mine—"sometimes I really do regret not hiring you when I had the chance."

13

ON CHRISTMAS MORNING I came downstairs for coffee and found a gift waiting for me: *The Settlement Cook Book: The Way to a Man's Heart.* Even before I opened the card, I knew it was from the Millers—well, from Mrs. Miller, that is. She had scratched out the message on the front where it said *Get Well Soon* and written: *Merry Christmas.*

Mrs. Miller had a drawer full of greeting cards, some new, some used. She collected them like trading stamps, and whenever an occasion arose, she'd reach for one. Didn't matter if someone else had already signed it, she just crossed out whatever was there and treated it like new.

Even though they were Jewish, the Millers celebrated Christmas, which struck me as odd. With no other plans for the day—Bobbi was going to her parents', Darlene was at her sister-in-law's, Bernice was upstate and Estée and Joe were spending the day with her family in Queens—I accepted an invitation to join the Millers for their annual open house. Their guests began arriving around four o'clock, and soon the place was filled with old vaudeville friends.

Mr. Henry, a ventriloquist, brought his dummy, Irwin, along

and seemed to be onstage as soon as he stepped inside. "And who is this pretty little number?" the dummy said when I was introduced. "I'd sure like to unwrap her for Christmas."

"Now don't be rude, Irwin," Mr. Henry scolded the dummy.

I didn't know what to say. I hadn't planned on being part of his act.

But it went on that way, everyone taking turns, dusting off their old comedy and musical bits. A man they called Freddy juggled dinner rolls. His wife tap-danced. There was joke telling, singing and more dancing. Mrs. Miller took up her accordion and Mr. Miller accompanied her on the piano while they did a routine, interrupting each other with one-liners and playful quips.

At one point Waller joined the festivities, which surprised me. Waller Weston—Mr. Man About Town? I would have thought he'd had dozens of invitations for Christmas. I wondered why he chose to celebrate at the Millers'.

After many glasses of spiked eggnog followed by goblets of red wine, I watched Mr. Miller playing piano while another man joined in on his clarinet. Waller was dancing with Mrs. Pryn, who smiled and laughed as Waller swished her to the left, spun her to the right.

Though we'd been roommates for months now, Waller and I were practically strangers. Each time I saw him, it was as if I were seeing that gorgeous face for the first time. The eyes, his jaw, the smile, it all drew me in—there was no fighting it. I didn't even realize I'd been staring at him until he traded Mrs. Pryn off to her husband and headed toward me, his hand extended.

I had just enough alcohol in me to accept his offer. It was a jazzy number, and I shouldn't have been surprised that Waller was a supremely smooth dancer or that his dime-store Pinaud Clubman smelled wonderful on him; hints of bergamot and something woodsy delighted me. We finished that dance and then the music changed tempo, a slow number.

I was about to return to my chair when Waller said, "Hey, where you going?"

I smiled, couldn't think of a word to say as he pulled me close. His arms felt strong and sturdy in a different kind of way than Tommy's embrace had felt. It was different but nice. Very nice. I wondered if he could feel my heart beating, pounding against his chest while I stared into his shoulder, afraid of making eye contact. I was so focused on trying to act nonchalant, doing my best to conceal the heat building up inside me, that I never heard the telephone ringing or someone calling my name. All I remember was Mrs. Miller tapping me on the shoulder. "It's for you, dear," she said. "I think it's your friend Estée."

ESTÉE HAD BEEN hysterical on the telephone, her voice wheezy, each word gasping for air. She was still crying when I arrived at her apartment some twenty minutes later.

"It's all my fault," she said as she answered the door, her eyes puffy, her nose red.

"I got here as soon as I could," I said, shrugging off my coat and scarf. "What is going on?"

"Poor Joe. What have I done?"

"Is he okay? Where is he?"

"I don't know." She clasped both sides of her head and began to sob even harder. I'd seen Estée break down before, but this was such a gut-wrenching ache that I felt my own chest tighten.

"Okay, all right, just take a deep breath." I tried coaxing her over to the sofa, but she twisted away and started pacing with a kind of rudderless aim. "Okay, just—just start at the beginning and tell me what happened."

"We were on our way back, driving home from my family's," she said, dabbing her eyes. "Joe and I got into a big fight about me going back down to Florida after New Year's. And well"—she paused before the window, pulled back the drapes and looked out—"one thing led to another and I told him"—she was off pacing again—"I told him I want a divorce."

"What?" I dropped down on the sofa.

She shook her head as if she herself couldn't believe she'd said it, either. "I know, I know. But I was just so angry."

"You don't want to divorce Joe. Do you?"

"No." She let the sound of that sink in and added, "Oh, I don't know." She plopped down beside me, her shoulders slumped forward. "Do you think Elizabeth Arden or Helena Rubinstein did it all on their own? Look at the men they married—they married royal princes who were millionaires."

"Is *that* what this is about? You want to divorce Joe so you can marry a rich prince?"

She cringed, rightfully so, hearing her own words thrown back at her. "I just want—I want a certain lifestyle. I thought Joe wanted that, too, but he's not willing to go out there and work for it. And he resents that I am. I told him," she said, barreling on, "'If you'd get out there and make a decent living, I wouldn't have to work so hard. I wouldn't be going down to Florida all the time.'"

She sniffled and shook her head. "I feel trapped. I love Joe and I love my son, but being a wife and mother is not enough for me. I know you're not supposed to say that, but it's the way I feel." She shook her head again and blew her nose. "And did I tell you Joe wants another baby? We can't afford another child right now. You see how we live."

I knew she'd been born into an aristocratic family and I knew that, like me, she'd been accustomed to the finer things in life, but we were in the middle of the Depression. And given that, I thought she had a nice enough two-bedroom apartment. Yes, her kitchen was small, packed to the gills with jars and ingredients for her beauty products, and yes, her icebox sounded like a freight train, but she had a parlor and a dining room. I was tempted to remind her that all I had was a bedroom next to the Millers and their blaring radio.

"Oh God, what have I done?" Her mood had changed from self-righteous anger to pure remorse. She began rocking.

I put my arm around her shoulders, but she refused to sit still.

"I can't lose him, Gloria. I just can't. Why did I have to open my big mouth? Maybe he's right. Maybe I shouldn't go down to Florida and—"

We heard the key in the door and in walked Joe, his eyes rimmed red, cheeks flushed. Estée jumped off the couch and ran into his arms. I quietly collected my pocketbook, coat and scarf and showed myself out.

Merry Christmas to all and to all a good night.

14

1939

RIGHT AFTER THE holidays were over, the decorations started coming down and Saks Fifth Avenue was returned to its pristine, preholiday splendor, the crystal chandeliers glinting off the display cases and the marble floors. I had just said good morning to Mrs. Hutt, who'd helped herself to a gold compact mirror, and was finishing up with a customer in the jewelry department when I looked up and saw Tommy—my Tommy—with his new wife, Lana.

My heart turned to brittle, crumbling bit by bit. I could barely bring myself to look at him. Instead, all my attention went to Lana. I'd never met her before and was stunned to see that she had *my* platinum hair, *my* blue eyes. I got the sick feeling that all I'd ever been was a stand-in for her, a mere carbon copy but with a better sense of humor and looser morals. I'd have bet dollars to doughnuts that Lana hadn't slept with him before their wedding night.

From behind the counter I watched as he placed his hand on the small of her back, steering her toward a hat display. I remembered the feel of that hand on my spine, always navigating. I could tell that Lana had good taste. Expensive taste. The first hat she went for was a velvet turban with a feather and a black veil that covered her eyes.

She smiled at him through the mirror, but Tommy instead handed her a navy blue saucer hat with a lacy brim. She modeled it for him before reaching for a lovely burgundy fascinator with satin bows along the top. His bottom lip turned down, and after trying on a few more styles, they bought the navy blue saucer hat. He never noticed me standing behind the counter, but I saw the two of them all too clearly. While he handed his Saks charge plate to the shopgirl, I saw Lana glance back longingly at the velvet turban hat.

I was mesmerized, my eyes glued on them until they disappeared down the main aisle, dissolving into the wash of shoppers. Once they were gone it struck me—*That could have been me.* The mere thought rolled over me, flattening me out like a cartoon character. I never wanted to be a woman like Lana, beholden to anyone, especially a man. I wanted to be in a position to buy whatever damn hat I pleased.

That day I set a new record for the highest jewelry sales at Saks Fifth Avenue.

IT WAS A Saturday night and I ended up working late. Estée and Joe were at a party and Bobbi was at an art show. But I was a tiger and rather than sitting home alone, I'd volunteered to stay late and help with inventory. Afterward, a handful of us stopped off for a few drinks at the Hickory House on 52nd and Seventh Avenue. I was drinking manhattans and playfully feeding cherries to my co-worker Paul, who performed for them like a pet seal.

It was almost eleven o'clock when I made it back to the Millers' house. In my drunken haze, I flipped on the overhead light in the foyer and saw Waller in the living room, sitting in Mr. Miller's chair, a glass of amber liquor in his hand.

"Oh, sorry." I quickly snapped off the light. "I didn't know you were in here."

"That's okay."

I was fumbling my way toward the staircase when he called to me. "Hey, don't rush off. Come"—he waved me over—"come, have a drink with me."

The last thing I needed was another drink. *Oh, but just look at him.* Yes, suddenly another drink sounded like an excellent idea and so I joined Waller, taking over Mrs. Miller's chair. I'd never sat there before; it was sort of like her throne, off-limits to the rest of us. It was surprisingly uncomfortable and made me question how she could sit there day after day, night after night.

This was the first time Waller and I had ever really been alone together, and after the cocktails I'd had earlier, not to mention the two fingers of Scotch I was having just then with Waller, I can't exactly remember what we talked about. I do remember him telling me that he didn't get the role in a play he'd auditioned for and that he once had the room I was staying in upstairs.

"You did? How long have you lived here?" I asked.

"Oh God, forever." He refilled my glass.

I started to take a sip and stopped. "Wait—why would you give up that room and move next to the bathroom?"

"You kidding me? I got sick of hearing the radio all night long."

I nodded. "*All night long* is right."

We were both laughing and then something shifted, and our discussion took a turn. I asked what he was doing home on a Saturday night. I knew I was drunk when I followed up that question with: "A good-looking fella like you—I would have thought for sure you'd have a date tonight."

"So, you're saying you think I'm good-looking, huh?"

"No, I'm saying—objectively speaking—you're a good-looking man. That is not the same as me saying *I* think you're good-looking."

"I see . . ." He smiled.

We were both sitting side by side, leaning forward, our faces less than a foot apart. He reached over and ran his fingers along the tips of my hair. He looked at my lips, my eyes and then my lips again and I thought, *Oh my God, we're going to kiss.*

And we did. This was the first man I'd kissed since Tommy and I can't explain what a revelation it was for me to discover that someone else could kiss not only as well as Tommy but maybe even a tad bit better. That right there restored my faith in men and in mankind.

Waller and I kissed, tumbling drunkenly out of our chairs and onto the living room floor. One of us—I think it was Waller—had the good sense to get out of there before Bobbi or the Millers walked in on us. The next thing I knew we were upstairs. In his room. In his bed.

THE FOLLOWING MORNING, I rolled over and there was Waller. I lifted the bedsheet and looked underneath the covers. *Oh, good God!* My head about split open. Both of us were naked. What had I done? I stole another glance at Waller, who still managed to look handsome even with his hair rumpled as he lay on his back, lips slightly parted, chest rising rhythmically.

Still drunk, I studied the clock on his nightstand. It was twenty past eight and it took a moment before I realized it was Sunday and I didn't have to rush off to work. But at the same time, I knew I couldn't linger in Waller's bed.

After gathering my clothes, I crept down the hall and collapsed in my own bed. Each time I closed my eyes, I saw flashes of the night before. *Waller!* I couldn't recall the details, so maybe he wouldn't be able to, either? Maybe he wouldn't remember any of it. There was always that hope. And in the meantime, I began to justify my actions. I had already given myself so purely and innocently to Tommy, believing I was still a good girl because we were going to be married. Until we weren't . . .

I finally dozed off and slept until half past noon. I got up, threw on some clothes and went downstairs in search of coffee and aspirin. And naturally, as I was heading into the kitchen, I ran smack into Waller. He was coming up from the basement with an armful of laundry. His boxer shorts on top were hard to miss and I felt ridiculously embarrassed for him.

"Oh." He said this in such a neutral way, it was impossible to interpret. Was that an *Oh, I'm happy to see you* or an *Oh, where did you run off to?* or was it an *Oh, good God, not you*?

"Oh, hi." I sounded like a lovesick girl when, in fact, I was nothing of the sort. While I may have been attracted to him—how could you not be?—I was most certainly not in love or in danger of falling for him. And I couldn't tell you why that was so. Maybe it was precisely because he was too good-looking. It had been my experience that those too-good-looking types were more trouble than they were worth.

"Just doing some laundry," Waller volunteered as if I hadn't figured that out for myself. He hefted the bundle up in his arms and his boxers fell to the floor.

I had no choice but to bend down and pick them up. "These look familiar," I said with a raised eyebrow.

He smiled his perfect smile and said, "So, ah, what are you doing later?"

That was all it took. We spent the rest of the afternoon in his bed and several times he had to cover my mouth with his hand to muffle me.

Afterward he lit a cigarette, took a drag and passed it to me. *Don't say a word. Wait for him to speak first. Why isn't he saying anything?* "So," I said, "how's the acting going?"

He shot me an odd look. "You *really* want to talk about that? *Now?*"

"Yeah, sure. Why not? How's it going?"

He sighed, held out his hand, and I passed his cigarette back over.

"It's—I don't know." He took a drag and blew the smoke out the corner of his mouth. With his free hand, he ran his fingers through his hair. "I'm up for a few parts. We'll see what happens. It's a tough road, you know. Acting is—well, it's just so damn hard to catch a break."

"Are you any good?"

"What kind of a question is that?" he asked, choking as he inhaled.

"Sorry. I didn't mean that the way it sounded. I just mean, are you good *enough*? Do you have something to fall back on, just in case . . ."

"Acting's all I know. That and bartending. But hey—no one makes a better cocktail in this town than me." He gave off a sad laugh. "Can we talk about something else?"

I don't recall what topic we moved on to. All I could be certain of was that Waller and I never discussed what happened the night before or that following day. We didn't even talk about it when it happened for a third time, either. And that was kind of the beauty of it. By our fourth encounter, we knew exactly what we were doing, and we were both perfectly fine with it. It was unspoken and understood. So, from time to time, whenever we were feeling low, or just plain randy, we sought each other out. Sometimes Waller would knock on my bedroom door at two in the morning when he got off work and he'd summon me back down to his room.

"Why don't we just stay in here?" I asked one night.

"Your room is a mess. Besides, we don't want to wake the Millers. And you, my dear, can be quite noisy."

15

IN THE SPRING of that year, I got my first raise and was able to move out of the Millers' house and into my own apartment. I'd found a small one-bedroom in a fourth-floor walk-up on the Upper West Side, at 79th and Amsterdam. It was tiny and dark, not the sort of place Gloria Dowaziac would have ever stepped foot in, but I wasn't her anymore, and I had the proof on my new driver's license, which I often stared at endlessly, like a lover's photograph.

Leaving the Millers' had been harder than expected. Sylvia Miller was more of a mother figure to me than my own mother had ever been. *The Settlement Cook Book* she got me for Christmas was on a shelf in my kitchen along with a set of her old dishes and a dented pot she'd given me. Mr. Miller and a boy from the neighborhood carried a secondhand couch, a bed and a chair up the four flights of stairs. Mr. Miller even fixed the toilet, which kept running, and got my windows unstuck.

Other than the usual street traffic, the sound of water running through the pipes and the radiator clanking when the furnace kicked on, my new place was quiet. Too quiet. I didn't know what to do with myself.

Bobbi had a new boyfriend, a painter, who was one of those rare men with acne scars that gave him a rugged, almost sexy look. And like all new loves, Bobbi spent every free moment with him. I hadn't met any of my neighbors yet and I was feeling lonely, so lonely that I put a call in to Waller for a little Sunday-afternoon romp. Thankfully he obliged, and in no time we had sufficiently ravished each other.

"I was surprised to hear from you so soon," he said, reaching for his trousers bunched up on the floor.

"Disappointed?" I asked.

"Not a chance."

"Actually, I was surprised you agreed to it," I said, reaching for a cigarette and my lighter. "I thought you were seeing somebody. What's her name? Sharon, Sheryl?"

"Sherri. And not anymore." He hoisted up his trousers, zipped his fly and grabbed his shirt off the floor. "She was getting too clingy. She wanted a relationship."

"How dare she!" I laughed.

He smiled but there was something sad behind his eyes. While he sat on the edge of the bed, tying his shoes, he told me how he'd come close to landing a role. "I got a callback and everything but"—he shook his head—"they went with the other guy. It's *always* the other guy they want."

"Hang in there." I gave his shoulder a pat. "Your turn's coming."

"That's what they keep telling me. That and 'Change your name.'" He sighed, helped himself to a puff of my cigarette before passing it back.

"Your name? What's wrong with Waller Weston?"

"Everybody's okay with the Weston part, but they think Waller is too *obtuse*."

"What does that even *mean*?"

"You tell me. I haven't a clue. But I find it hard to believe that my name is what's holding me back."

"Well, what's your real name?"

He laughed. "Oh no. Not telling."

"That bad, is it?"

"I don't know what my parents were thinking."

I didn't press the matter only because I was using something of a stage name myself. "Well, if it helps, I think Waller Weston suits you."

He eased up off the bed, kissing my cheek before rising to full height. "See ya later, alligator."

After he left, I plopped back on the pillows and drew a deep, satisfying drag off my cigarette. I knew I should have felt like a tramp for being so casual about having sex with Waller. But as I saw it, my wholesomeness had been snuffed out by Tommy. I no longer had my virtue to protect, and besides, Waller was safe. He wasn't a boyfriend—he couldn't break my heart. He was a no-strings-attached lover, and I felt very modern about that.

My downstairs buzzer rang, and I wrapped the top sheet about my naked body, hobbled over to the intercom and pressed the button. "Did you forget something?" I scanned the room looking for Waller's house keys, maybe his wallet or belt . . .

"Gloria, buzz me up." It was Estée. "I need to talk to you."

While she climbed the stairs, I hunted down my garter belt and stockings and had just enough time to shimmy back into my dress, which was pooled on the floor. My hair was a mess. I hastily tried patting it into place as I let Estée in.

"Are you okay?" I asked, shocked by the dark circles beneath her eyes, the hard expression on her face.

"Oh, Gloria, I can't do this anymore. I'm exhausted." She pushed past me, yanking off her hat and gloves. "I can't keep doing this to Joe. It's not fair to him. Or to me."

I thought she meant the shuttling back and forth between Florida and New York. She traveled all the time, two or three weeks down there, two weeks back home, and I knew it was taking its toll on her. She usually had Leonard with her so that Joe could stay back in New York and focus on his job hunt. Every morning he put on his suit and tie and went down to the Garment District. We were in the thick of the Depression; no one was hiring. I was still somewhat amazed that I'd been able to land such a great job at Saks. The best Joe could do was pick up some odd part-time work selling buttons, bolts of fabrics, but nothing that paid the kind of money he needed and, more importantly, the kind of money Estée craved.

"I've been giving this a lot of thought," she said, pacing by the windows. "I mean *a lot*, a lot of thought." She suddenly stopped and pivoted toward me. "Do you have anything to drink here?"

"Estée, what's going on?" I asked as I retrieved a bottle of whiskey from the kitchen and poured her a glass.

She took a sip and winced. "I've decided I'm going back to Miami. And I'm taking Leonard with me. And"—she took another sip—"I'm going to divorce Joe."

"What? Oh, Estée, no."

"I have to. I know in my heart it's the right thing to do."

"But why? How can you do this to him?"

"To him? What about me? Why do you always take his side?"

"*Sides?* You think this is about me taking sides? You're my friends. I want what's best for both of you. I just don't understand why you're doing this." I wanted to take her, shake her. What other husband would do for Estée what Joe did? I'd never seen a man be so supportive of his wife, acting as her true partner. He looked after Leonard, getting him dressed and off to school each day. It was Joe who was there when Leonard came home and Joe who fed and bathed him. He read his son bedtime stories each night so that Estée could make more products in the kitchen or attend a party, hoping to meet the right clientele. Estée never had to worry about housecleaning or laundry or making sure the icebox was full. She leaned on Joe for the most basic things at home, right down to retrieving anything she couldn't reach on the top shelves. I wondered if she realized that in every respect Joe was truly her ladder for success.

"You don't understand. I have to do this. I just have to."

"Why?"

"Because I've, oh God, I've"—she looked at me and squeezed her eyes shut—"I've met someone."

On that, I poured myself a glass, too. I took a long pull before I could bring myself to ask for details. "Who is he?"

"It just happened. Well, actually nothing's happened yet. I told him I couldn't until I talked to Joe. But oh, Gloria, I think I'm falling in love with this other man. That's why I have to tell Joe right away. I can't start something with Charles until I end things with Joe. But it's not all because of Charles. That's not why I want to divorce—"

"Wait, slow down. Who is this Charles guy?"

"Charles Moskowitz." She sighed like a lovestruck schoolgirl. "He's on the board of directors at Metro-Goldwyn-Mayer."

"Oh, Estée, are you sure about this? Is it just the Hollywood thing?"

She looked offended, but I had to ask.

"It has nothing to do with that," said Estée. "Charles makes me feel—well, I've never felt this way with Joe."

"But you love Joe. I know you do."

"Of course I do. I'll always love Joe but that doesn't mean he's the man I'm supposed to be married to. Now I just have to work up the nerve to tell him I want a divorce."

"This is going to devastate him."

"I know." Her eyes instantly filled with tears.

"And it's going to break your heart, too. I can see it." I could tell that she really didn't want to hurt Joe, but she was going to do it anyway. I knew her and at the end of the day, Estée did whatever she had to do to get what she wanted. "Estée—"

She held up her hand and stopped me as if she knew I was about to tell her she was making a mistake. "I'm leaving for Miami tomorrow," she said. "Leonard's coming with me. Will you do me a favor? Take care of Joe?"

THE LAST PLACE I wanted to be was in the middle of Estée and Joe's marriage and subsequent divorce. But Estée had asked me to keep an eye on him, which I did.

A few days after she left him, I met Joe on my lunch break at the Horn & Hardart Automat at 57th and Sixth Avenue. It was about a ten-minute walk from Saks and I hadn't been able to get away from my last customer until about five past noon.

Despite the steady drizzle and his not having an umbrella, Joe was waiting for me outside, tucked in beneath the dripping awning. He looked like he hadn't slept in days. Foolishly, I asked how he was holding up, as if I couldn't see for myself that he was broken.

Joe shook his head as he held the door for me and we stepped inside the busy dining room, lined wall to wall with sleek vending machines displaying hot food and cold sandwiches and pies of every variety. Other than thanking me for meeting him, Joe hadn't said a word until we'd selected our food, dropping our coins into the slots and turning the polished knobs: mac and cheese with a side of creamed spinach for him, an egg salad sandwich and tomato soup for me, fresh brewed coffee for both. My heels clacked across the marble floor as we made our way to a little table in the corner.

"Mental cruelty," he said, bewildered as he spread a napkin across his lap. "She's suing me for divorce on the grounds of *mental cruelty*."

"Jesus, Joe." I planted my elbows on the table and leaned into my hands.

"Tell me, when have I ever . . ." He couldn't finish the sentence.

I looked up at him just as puzzled. Joe was a teddy bear, a kind and gentle soul.

"I suppose she had to come up with a reason," he said. "But why *that*, of all things?"

"I'm so sorry, Joe. Really, I am. You didn't deserve that."

"And who is this Charles fellow?"

I stared into my soup.

"Is it serious?" he asked, and then answered his own question. "It can't be serious. She hardly knows this man. Just because he's some big muckety-muck with Metro-Goldwyn. Let's face it, she left me because I'm a nobody and—"

"Joe, no, that's not—"

His hand flew up to stop me. "I'm a nobody and I'm broke. But I got news for you, I could have been making a million dollars and it wouldn't have been enough for her. Estée wants— No"—he stubbed his finger to the table—"she *needs* to be in the limelight. I know my Blondie. Estée wants to be famous. And rich. That's what she's *always* wanted."

I didn't want to say that I'd thought the same thing. Instead, I stalled, peeled back the top slice of bread and sprinkled pepper onto my egg salad.

"I think she met this guy and decided he'd open doors for her. And that's something I can't do. You should have heard her going on and on about how Charles knows Spencer Tracy and Bette Davis and Gary Cooper." Joe kept talking and picked at his food before pushing his plate aside. "She just loves rubbing elbows with those movie stars. And she thinks if she can get just one of them to use her creams, they'll help make her a household name." He crumpled his napkin. "She's got stardust in her eyes—that's all this is. Sooner or later, she'll come to her senses. She'll come running back to me."

Joe seemed so confident, but I was struggling with my own loss. Estée wasn't just my friend. Both she and Joe were like family to me.

Because of them, I always knew I had somewhere to go on Sunday nights. At least I did when Estée was in town. I treasured those evenings, sitting around their dining room table, coffee cups and dessert plates replaced with after-dinner drinks and full ashtrays, our laughter threatening to wake Leonard, asleep down the hall. I knew it sounded absurd and selfish, but I felt like Estée had walked out on me, too. I feared that she'd no longer confide in me the way she once did. I worried that her letters and postcards from Florida would taper off. I was heartsick thinking that she was moving on, leaving me behind.

I wasn't as strong as Joe, not as convinced that she'd come back to either one of us.

16

1984

THE COCKTAIL WAITRESS at the Pierre sets down a manhattan on the rocks for me and takes Lee Israel's empty glass, replacing it with a fresh Jameson, neat. I wonder if that's her second or possibly her third.

After searching inside her Strand tote bag, she pulls out a pocket-size spiral notebook and a ballpoint pen, its cap engraved with teeth marks. While she makes some notes, I take in the hotel bar. It's wonderfully ornate, all bursting in rococo style: brilliant chandeliers, soft muted colors in the murals gracing the walls. For a split second I almost forget why I'm here.

After a long pull from her drink, Lee Israel says, "I'm hoping you can shed some light on a few things for me."

"I'll try. If I can."

"Well, for starters—and I find this interesting," she says, leafing through the pages, "no one seems to actually know when Estée Lauder was born."

"Oh." I laugh. "I'd chalk that up to vanity."

"Maybe." She shrugs. "But what she claims in her interviews isn't squaring with the hospital or the census records. Must drive the fact-checkers crazy."

I don't respond to this. Already I'm regretting that I agreed to this meeting.

She jots something down in her notebook. I look but can't make out her handwriting. I'm not surprised that she found discrepancies in Estée's birth date. For years she's been claiming she's younger than she is. I'm not even sure Joe ever knew her real age.

Lee Israel turns to a clean sheet of paper and asks, "Are you still in touch with Harriet Allen?"

"Now that's a name from the past. How do you know about Harriet Allen?"

"Because"—she cocks her head—"I'm damn good at what I do."

"I see that. So, ah, tell me, what got you interested in writing?" I ask, trying to derail her.

She ignores my question, takes out a pack of Marlboros. "You still in touch with Harriet Allen?" she asks as she lights up.

"Harriet Allen?" I glance around the bar. Two elegantly dressed women at a nearby table are there for tea. A delicate three-tiered china stand displays watercress finger sandwiches, scones and petits fours. "It's been ages since I've even thought of Harriet, let alone spoken to her."

"Do you know if she's still in the city?"

"Sorry." I take a sip from my drink. "Can't help you there."

"What about Charles Moskowitz?"

I almost drop my glass. She's not kidding she's good at what she does. How in the hell is she digging up all these names from the past? I haven't smoked in years, but those Marlboros look tempting.

"Did Charles break up Estée's marriage to Joseph?"

"No, not exactly."

"Can you be more specific?"

"It was so long ago," I say. "I honestly don't remember." Which is a flat-out lie.

"Okay, then." She slips on a pair of thick-framed glasses with a smudge in the center of the left lens. "Why don't we go for something nice and easy? Tell me what you know about Arnold"—she pauses to consult her notes—"Arnold Louis van Ameringen."

Good God. There was nothing easy about Arnold Louis van Ameringen. I gesture toward her Marlboros. "May I?"

She nudges the pack closer to me. "Where did she meet him?"

I stall and take my time lighting my cigarette. Already, I can see this is going to get messy.

"Well?" Her heavy brows rise, clearing the rim of her eyeglasses. "Do you know what happened between them?"

Yes, I knew. I toy with a book of hotel matches, turning them over and over in my hand.

"Well?" she asks again, moving her head to the side until she's directly in my sight line.

I exhale toward the ceiling. "I'm sorry, but I'm not really at liberty to say."

She scratches down a few more notes and I will myself not to fidget, not to let her see me squirm.

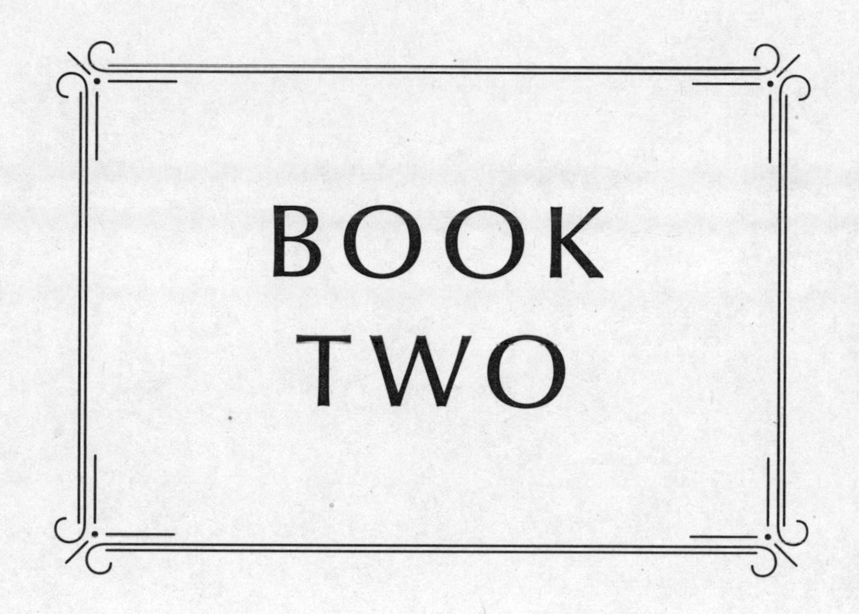

BOOK TWO

17

1939

ESTÉE WASTED NO time getting on with her life. Six weeks later, by the middle of May, her marriage was over. And so was her affair with Charles Moskowitz.

She was back in New York, sitting on my sofa, surrounded by clumps of damp tissues and a half-empty bottle of wine. "He just couldn't make room for me in his life," she said. "He's always busy. Busy, busy, *busy.* Always working. Working, working, *working.* And when he's not working, he's on the arm of some starlet. I couldn't open a newspaper or magazine without seeing him with another woman. A different girl in every photograph. He says it's just publicity for them, but I don't buy it. I don't buy it for a single second. He promised to introduce me to Greta Garbo—never happened. He said he'd send a basket of my face creams and lotions to Irene Dunne, and that never happened, either. He took me to a party with a bunch of movie people in Miami, and five minutes after we arrived, he left me standing there by myself. I was alone for half the night."

I didn't want to point out that she'd done the very same thing to

Joe. And me, too. The three of us had gone to a party several months ago. Neither Joe nor I wanted to go. Joe, because he didn't like parties or being introduced as Mr. Estée Lauder, and me, because I feared running into people I knew. Still, Estée had begged, saying she needed us there. We gave in, and before we'd even gotten our coats off, she had abandoned us.

"And those people—those movie types—unless you're a *somebody*, they won't give you the time of day."

I had never known a room that Estée couldn't work, a crowd she couldn't charm. But apparently, she was out of her league in those Hollywood circles. Not that she ever made it to Hollywood on account of her fear of flying.

"Charles kept saying, 'Come out to California.' He said he wanted me by his side for some premiere or a gala, but it was always at the last minute and he knew perfectly well that by the time I'd get there by train, the whole thing would be over." Her eyes misted up. "I thought this was *it*, you know? I thought everything in my life was leading me to this man. I was so sure Charles was my destiny. I thought he loved me. I—I—" She cut herself off and looked at me, suddenly horrified. "I divorced Joe for this—for nothing."

The biggest tears I'd ever seen poured down Estée's face. These were tears from her very core, the wettest, the saddest of them all. The same kind of tears I'd shed over Tommy. Over my father, too. I handed her a fresh tissue and wrapped my arms around her. While I was sorry to see her in such pain, selfishly I was grateful to have my friend back.

Eventually she composed herself and though her eyes were still dewy, she smiled weakly and said, "I'm such a fool. I've made a mess of everything. What do I do now?"

"You do what you do best," I said. "You find a way to turn this ugly mess into something beautiful."

ESTÉE'S BIRTHDAY WAS just around the corner, on July 1: her thirty-third, according to Joe; her twenty-eighth, according to her.

I remember Joe had met me after work a few days before, saying he wanted to do something special to help her celebrate. The two of us were walking from Saks Fifth Avenue to a little outdoor café on Madison and 53rd. The city was fully steeped in summer's heat. My hair was sticking to the nape of my neck.

About half a block away, he said, "It's just that she's been so down lately. You know, over the whole thing with Charles. I thought she could use some cheering up. I really want her to have a nice birthday."

I paused on the sidewalk, because this moment needed to be acknowledged. This right here summed up Joe's unwavering love for Estée. Even after she'd kicked him in the teeth, after she'd divorced him and taken up with another man, he still wanted her to be happy. And he wanted to be the one to make her happy. He took absolutely no pleasure in seeing her heart ripped apart, just as his had been. His loyalty to Estée was admirable. Short of her committing murder—and perhaps even that would not have dissuaded him—Joe Lauder would defend and root for his Blondie no matter what.

He reminded me a little of my mother in that way, still blindly devoted to my father. Sadly, I'd lost that kind of faith in the people closest to me. According to Glenn, the rest of my family made regular visits to Sing Sing and kept up a steady stream of letters and telephone calls. But I couldn't get myself there. The only reason I'd ever want to speak to my father again was because I desperately wanted to look him in the eye and ask, *Why? Why did you do it?* Part of me was afraid of how he'd answer that question, but more than that, I knew if I went to see him, he'd rope me back in. I was all too aware of his power over me. One look and Gloria Downing would dissolve back into the helpless Gloria Dowaziac, Daddy's little girl. For as long as I could remember, I'd been defined by his larger-than-life personality. I was just now starting to discover who I was on my own without him. Sometimes I even liked this new me. But even so, I wasn't strong enough to hold my ground against him and I saw no path to forgiveness or redemption. It left me standing at the corner of independence and indentured.

"I thought I'd make a reservation for dinner at the Stork Club," Joe said after we'd arrived at the café and taken our seats, surrounded by flower boxes filled with red geraniums.

"Wow, that's a splurge. I'm sure she'll love that." I pulled a cigarette from my gold case and leaned in while Joe struck a match for me. "You know, though, it's pretty tough to get a table there."

"If I have to, I'll grease the maître d'. You think $5 would do it?"

"I'm sure it wouldn't hurt."

"Estée's always wanted to go there." He blew out the match, dropped it into the ashtray. "And you have to come with us, okay?"

I exhaled, shaking my head. "Oh no. Joe, I can't go with the two of—"

"Otherwise she'll think it's a date and she won't go."

I knew Estée talked to Joe nearly every day, but she insisted she wasn't looking to reunite with him and she certainly wasn't trying to lead him on. I thought for a moment. "What if we invite Mac?" Mac Steiner was a remnant salesman whom Joe had recently introduced me to.

"No." Joe shook his head. "You can't bring Mac. That's a double date and Estée won't go."

He was probably right about that. "But . . ." I was still thinking of a way out.

"Please, Gloria? I need you there."

I could hear it in his voice, see it in his eyes. He truly did need me there. I couldn't find it in me to say no to him any more than I could ever say no to Estée.

And so, that Saturday night, I joined the two of them for Estée's birthday celebration at the Stork Club on East 51st Street. Even in my best dress, which I'd purchased on sale with my employee discount, I felt terribly underdressed. Estée, however, looked spectacular in a red satin gown with a matching bolero cape, a gift from Charles that she'd worn to a party for some movie people vacationing in Palm Beach. Joe also cut a dashing figure in his evening jacket and bow tie. After confirming our reservation, the doorman unlatched the fourteen-karat-gold chain that kept the interlopers out and far away from the showgirls, Broadway actors and movie stars dining within.

Neither Joe nor Estée had been to the Stork Club before. She of course had been too young for a restaurant like this when her family had money. I, however, had been to the Stork Club numerous times; with my family, with friends, with Tommy. Various tables held the ghosts of happier days for me, a life barely recognizable now. Estée couldn't stop looking around, practically squealing when she spotted Barbara Stanwyck dining with Robert Taylor.

Joe was more taken with Estée than the room's fanfare. "Blondie," he said, "you've never looked lovelier."

"Do you really think so?"

"I do." He nodded and kissed the back of her hand. "I really, *really* do."

He was so smitten, and so was she. The two of them were gazing into each other's eyes and the love between them was palpable. I know Joe didn't want this to feel like a date, but it was a date, all right. I shouldn't have been there, but I did love seeing the two of them together like this again: smiling, laughing, finding every excuse to reach over and graze the other's hand or arm. I was sure Estée was wondering how she could have ever let this man go.

The tuxedoed waiter came by for our drink orders and Estée said, "What about champagne? Oh, I'd just love a glass of champagne."

"All right then," Joe said to the waiter, "a glass of champagne for the birthday girl and for you, Gloria?"

I was going to go easy on him and order the Stork Club cocktail when Estée said, "Oh, let's get a bottle. We're celebrating tonight."

I saw Joe crack his menu, eyes darting down at the wine list, a subtle grimace streaking his face. What choice did he have? He wanted only to please her so he ordered a $7.50 bottle of Pol Roger. And that was just the beginning. Estée wanted the pâté, followed by the vichyssoise and the broiled lamb chops for her entrée. I could almost hear Joe mentally tallying up the bill inside his head. I was reminded of how Estée couldn't deny Leonard his shrimp cocktail on the train when we were heading to Florida. Joe and I both opted for the dinner special: minute steak, a baked potato and salad for $5.75.

The Stork Club was obviously beyond Joe's means. He was still struggling, filling in with part-time work whenever he could find it. But he was proud and doing his best not to appear shocked by the outrageous prices. Oh, how I wished Estée could see the lengths to which he was willing to go to win her back. I took a sip of champagne and watched Estée sparkle as she looked around the room, her thoughts telegraphing—one day she was going to be the one at the table that everyone was stealing glances at. This was where she wanted to be, where she felt she belonged.

By the time the salads and pâté were served, Joe had relaxed, probably resigned to the fact that dinner was going to cost more than he'd anticipated. The three of us talked about Estée's business, about Leonard and about Mac Steiner.

I'd been out with Mac twice now and we'd had a good time. He'd taken me to the Capitol Theatre to see *Calling Dr. Kildare.* After the show we'd shared a burger and a pitcher of beer. One week later we went to dinner and ended up sitting on the front stoop of my building for an hour, talking, mostly about Joe and Estée and how much they still loved each other.

Even before Mac kissed me, I sensed he wanted to see more of me. Part of me wouldn't have minded. After all, Mac Steiner was a good man, not immediately handsome, but the combination of his light brown hair and olive complexion was growing on me. Plus, he was Joe's friend. But because of my past, I was keeping Mac at arm's length while keeping Waller—whom no one, not even Estée, knew about—close by, close enough to touch.

Estée, Joe and I lingered at the Stork Club over coffees and dessert. We were all having such a wonderful evening until poor Joe got hit with two bombs—the first was the bill. The second came as a shock to me as well.

Estée smoothed her napkin down on the table and announced that she was leaving town in the morning. "I'm going back to Palm Beach."

18

1940

NOTHING LIKE A damp, slushy March in Manhattan to make a girl crave a little warmth and sunshine. All Estée had to do was ask me to come visit her in Florida, and I was on a flight bound for Palm Beach. I had a week off from Saks Fifth Avenue and I intended to make the most of it.

Leonard was back in New York staying with Joe and that meant Estée was free. Boy, was she ever. She was light and airy, up for anything, fully enjoying life as a single girl again. She told me about all the various men she'd had dinners and drinks with. One was a buyer for Marshall Field's who was in town from Chicago. Another was a public relations director for Coty. Another worked in research and development for Max Factor. She'd also gone dancing with a salesman for Pond's. Somehow they were all connected to *the business* and of course that was not a coincidence. Estée never stopped working. For her there was no distinction between work and play.

The day I arrived, Estée said we were meeting C.Z. Guest at the Palm Beach Country Club for cocktails later. That clubhouse was a breeding ground of potential exposure for me, and I was dreading the awkward introductions, possibly followed by more lies and vague explanations. I couldn't bear it. I decided that if anyone recognized me, I would just break down and tell Estée the truth and pray she wouldn't send me back to New York on the next plane. That was my plan, but fortunately C.Z. telephoned, full of apologies at having to cancel. I was relieved and the knots in my stomach finally loosened for the first time since hearing we were going there.

"Oh, phooey," Estée said, hanging up the phone. "I really wanted you to see the clubhouse. I was just there the week before and it was spectacular. C.Z. and I played golf and had the most wonderful lunch . . ." Her shoulders slumped forward. She seemed truly crestfallen.

To pull Estée out of her slump, I convinced her to spend the rest of the afternoon by the pool, her disappointment fading along with my anxiety. Later that night, after a modest dinner—two pastramis on rye and chocolate phosphates at a nearby deli counter, we went back to the hotel and got gussied up for a night on the town.

Estée was debating between two pairs of shoes. "What do you think?" she asked, standing before me while I brushed my teeth, a white sandal on her left foot, a navy slingback on the right.

"The navy," I garbled with a mouthful of toothpaste. "Shows off your ankles more."

She consulted again with the mirror. "Hmmm. I think the white's better."

"Then why did you ask me?"

"Because the heel's scuffed on the white and I thought I could get away with the navy."

"But I just told you the navy was better."

"But I like the white better."

"So why did you ask me?" I said again. This was so typical of Estée. She always knew what she was going to do but still we went through the dance, going round and round.

"Give me your toothpaste," she said, hand extended.

"What are you doing?" I asked as she squirted out a ribbon of Colgate onto her sandal.

"I'm getting rid of the scuff."

"With toothpaste?"

"You'd be surprised what you can do with this little tube." She took a washcloth and began buffing away. "Once Leonard drew all over the dining room wall with crayons, and this"—she held up the toothpaste—"took it right out." She wiped off the excess and held up her shoe. "Ta-dah."

My God, she was right. It worked. Another one of Estée's little tricks.

That night she wore those white sandals with a stunning low-cut royal blue dress that put my pale green frock to shame. The Estée I first met never would have worn such a revealing outfit and I was pleased, knowing that I'd had some influence over her fashion sense.

We finished getting ready and headed straight for the Seafood Bar at The Breakers. It brought back memories, which I washed away with my first gimlet.

Estée and I made quite a pair and a group of men had soon circled around us, offering to buy us drinks and oysters and pressing their business cards into our hands. Before long, Estée had saddled up to one of them, Arnold Louis van Ameringen, whom everyone called Van. He'd caught her attention earlier when he was performing magic tricks at the bar, making cigarettes disappear in the palm of his hand and pulling a quarter from behind someone's ear. He was older, nearly twenty years Estée's senior, and not the most attractive man in the room, though he was unquestionably the most stylish. He had a certain something despite the thinning hair, graying at the temples, and the leathery complexion that comes from having baked on the beach too long. He spoke with a subtle accent, probably Dutch, and peered intently at you with pale blue eyes from behind his pince-nez. I would come to learn that he was a powerful businessman with all kinds of connections to the fragrance industry. He also had a wedding band.

The evening pressed on and I thought Estée was just going to get his business card and we'd move on, but she showed no signs of budging. Not that it really mattered to me. I was having a marvelous time; men with nice manicures and expensive cufflinks lit my cigarettes and told me I smelled heavenly. I was right in my element—just like old times—and it felt good to flex my atrophied flirting muscles. Only now, my approach was slightly altered. I was no longer the rich, sought-after Dowaziac heiress. Instead, I was a young, fashionable career girl working at Saks Fifth Avenue, no less. I hadn't felt this good about myself in ages.

Estée eventually broke away from Van and pulled me aside. Pinching open her evening clutch, she took out her hotel room key. "Do you think you can see yourself home?" she asked, handing it over to me.

"Ah, sure. I guess."

"Van's getting a room here at The Breakers."

"And you're *staying* with him? Estée, he's married."

"You're sure you can get back to the hotel by yourself? I bet one of the fellas here will gladly drive you back."

She'd completely ignored my disapproval. And if she thought I'd get into an automobile with one of these men after a night of drinking, she had another think coming. "Yeah, sure," I said. "I'll get a taxicab." And with a warning look, I added, "Just be careful."

I was perturbed and not because she was abandoning me among a room full of strangers. What perturbed me was that Van was a married man. Even the amount of flirting between them had a stink to it. Now he was getting a room and Estée was spending the night with him. Surely this was something that Mrs. Van would not have approved of.

Estée leaned in and pressed a kiss to both my cheeks. "I'll see you in the morning."

Well, morning turned out to be the following afternoon. That was when she finally appeared, looking sheepish but still coiffed as ever as I let her into the room.

"Thank God there's coffee." She headed toward the pot I'd ordered up from room service, walking as if she were Frankenstein's monster.

"How was your night?" I asked.

She looked at me and grinned, clutching her hands to her chest.

THE NEXT DAY, we drove down to Miami Beach and Estée took me to the Roney Plaza Hotel at the corner of 22nd Street and Collins Avenue. I didn't know how Estée pulled it off, but amazingly enough, she had managed to set up a concession in the corner of the hotel's posh lobby. It was just a little table, draped in a velvet cloth. On top was an easel-backed frame holding a tastefully engraved card that said EUROPEAN SKINCARE TREATMENTS BY ESTÉE LAUDER. She'd even hired a young girl with high cheekbones and a French accent to look after the stand in Estée's absence. It was quite impressive, and when I asked how she'd been able to swing it, Estée said she worked the hotel staff night and day until they finally agreed to lease the space to her.

"And you wouldn't believe some of the clientele that comes through this lobby," she said. "I saw Henry Fonda, Vivien Leigh and Gary Cooper just the other day. Come"—she gestured—"I want to show you around."

She gave me a guided tour of the hotel, pointing out various paintings and tapestries on the walls, a vase that once belonged to some empress I'd never heard of. We went out to the gardens, where flamingos posed on one leg while pecking at the fountain, letting the water cascade down their long, slender necks.

When our tour was over Estée glanced at her wristwatch and said, "It's still early. Why don't we go have a drink out by the pool? Van should be here soon."

Van? I had no idea he'd be joining us.

It was a beautiful day, in the low seventies with just the right amount of breeze to stir the palms stationed around the pool. We sat at a big umbrellaed table while sunbathers stretched out on their chaises. The pool was peppered with swimmers and I could see the cabanas along the beach with yet more sunbathers, more swimmers bobbing up and down in the waves. A waitress on roller skates, going table to table, made her way to ours, took our order and *whoosh*, off she went.

Halfway into our martinis, Van arrived, looking crisp and stylish in a pair of white linen trousers and a navy blue jacket, an ascot at his neck. He ordered a martini and caught up to us with three long pulls. He regaled us with stories about the hotel while the sun glinted off his Rolex watch and wedding band. His overwhelming presence and the way he commanded the attention of every room he entered reminded me of my father, which was one more strike against him. I was certain Van couldn't be trusted. But Estée, well, she soaked in his every word.

As she shook the last bit of gin off her toothpicked olive and was about to pop it into her mouth, Van stopped her. "Remember what I told you about garnishes"—he raised a reprimanding finger—"for decoration only."

Since when did cocktail olives count as garnishes? I'd already eaten mine.

Estée smiled, her cheeks growing red as she set the olive back in her glass.

Her ego may have been nicked but she got over it as soon as we moved into the Bamboo Room for dinner. She'd heard that the Duke and Duchess of Windsor were expected to dine there that night. Estée was looking around the room, all wide-eyed, hoping for a glimpse of them.

When it was time to order our entrées, Estée couldn't decide. "Gloria, why don't you go ahead?"

Van plucked her menu from those teacup hands. "Allow me." Turning to the waiter he said, "She'd like the rack of lamb. Medium rare."

Van seemed to delight in this sort of thing. He was something of a Svengali for Estée. Though he was very charismatic and entertaining, I still found him tedious and pretentious. Estée, however, was as obedient as a well-trained pup. This was a side of her I'd never seen before.

By the end of the evening, I could tell that something beyond their tryst at The Breakers had started. My skin wanted to blister up each time he reached for her hand or I saw Estée lean in closer to him. The whole thing agitated me in a way I had not expected.

19

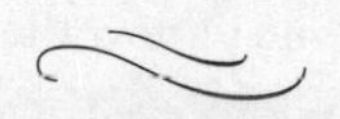

FOR THE REST of my time in Palm Beach, Van was inescapable. He was what we talked about over coffee first thing in the morning. And at lunch. It was Van whom we'd made our plans around, waiting in the hotel room because Estée didn't want to miss his call. I didn't like him and I was having a hard time keeping my feelings to myself.

One afternoon, at my insistence, Estée told the front desk to come get her by the pool if he telephoned.

As we relaxed on our chaises, she said in a lazy drawl, "Van's the sort of man I should have married."

"Except for the fact that he's already married."

"Very funny." She sighed, stretched her arms overhead. "Isn't he divine?"

"Divine?" I lifted my sunglasses, propping them on my head. "All I know is that he's *mar-ried*."

"Oh, Gloria, please don't rain on my parade." She got up and went to the side of the pool, dangling her feet over the edge.

I followed and eased into the water, up on my tiptoes to ward off the shock of cold, my arms out to my sides. "Seriously," I said, "what are you doing with him? He's not good for you. You don't need him."

"You don't know what I need," she snapped. "And don't criticize things you don't understand. You've never been married. You don't know how hard it is. You don't know the first thing about having a relationship. My Lord, you don't even *date*."

Well, now this was true. Sort of. Yes, I'd never been married, but I did date. Here and there. And of course I had Waller on the side. But I wasn't going to mention any of that now.

"And besides," she said, "you have no idea what a lousy marriage he's in. Van's wife is no saint. Believe me. She's humiliated that man. He's not doing anything that she hasn't done to him first. And for your information, she knows all about me."

"Well, if she didn't before, she will now after the way you're gallivanting all over town with him."

"For God's sake, Gloria, what is the matter with you?"

"What about Joe?"

"What about him?"

"What am I supposed to tell him? You know he's going to ask me how you're doing."

"You tell him I'm fine."

"But what if he wants specifics? You're putting me in an impossible position."

"We're divorced, Gloria. Relax."

"I won't lie for you."

"I'm not asking you to lie for me. And frankly, this is none of your business." Without another word, she got up from the side of the pool, gathered her things and went back to the hotel room.

She was right, it was none of my business, but I couldn't help the way I felt. Because of my father, I was overly sensitive to anything that smacked of dishonesty, of betrayal. My antennae went up right along with my ire and indignation. I figured the more outrage I showed over other people's moral lapses, the more distance I could put between myself and my father. I didn't want to be like him, living under a cloud of deception, and yet that was exactly what I was doing. And herein lies the crux of hypocrisy. Or at least of *my* hypocrisy.

I couldn't figure out which side of the line I belonged on, alternating between harshly judging others for their infringements while simultaneously internalizing the shame of what they'd done. In the case of Estée and Van, it felt as if it were *me* betraying Joe. As if *I* were betraying Van's wife, too.

Later that night, Estée was barely speaking to me, and while she had dinner with Van, I stayed back at the hotel, obsessing over the whole thing. Estée and I had a complicated, almost sister-like relationship. We'd take cheap shots at each other and bicker from time to time, but this was the first real fight Estée and I had ever had. And I'd ignited it. Estée had always been my anchor. My best friend. I couldn't afford to lose her.

After she went to meet Van, I realized I'd gone too far with her. I hardly slept that night and developed a terrible vertigo bout that lasted nearly a record ten minutes and left me drained. Sitting in the dark I began thinking, which was never a good idea for me. I lacked Estée's ability to think constructively, to map out the future inside my mind, to focus on what I wanted rather than on what I feared. I had an overactive imagination and, like my mother, I spun tales of worst-case scenarios. All thoughts led to me being alone and penniless, living on the streets of Manhattan.

Aside from Van, seeing what Estée had accomplished down in Florida made me question my own ambitions or lack thereof. And it wasn't that I was lazy—far from it. No one was more shocked than me to discover what a hard worker I was. Even Mrs. Coopers acknowledged that. But there had to be something more for me in this world than being a shopgirl—even if it was a shopgirl at Saks Fifth Avenue.

The next morning I fixed Estée a cup of coffee from the room service tray, handing it to her as an olive branch.

"I'm sorry about yesterday," I said.

She tugged her bathrobe closed, set the coffee aside and plopped down on the rumpled bedsheets. "I just don't understand why you can't be happy for me."

"I'm trying to be. Really I am. I'll try harder. I promise."

Two days later, when I left Palm Beach, things between us were still strained, though we tried to pretend all was normal. She hugged me goodbye, promising to get together when she arrived back in New York. I was still rattled on the flight home, wondering if I'd done some irreversible damage. The only thing I knew was that Estée was a grown woman. She didn't need or want my advice about her relationships, but it was easier to look at her mistakes than face my own. It was at 30,000 feet that I decided to stop investing so much time and energy in Estée and start focusing on my own future.

JOE WAS WAITING for me at the Newark airport. He'd offered to pick me up, not only to help with my luggage but to pump me for information about Estée. I braced myself as I stepped off the plane.

Before we'd reached his car, he asked, "So how's my Blondie? Tell me everything. Is she happy? How's business going down there?" And then the inevitable: "Is she seeing anyone? She's not, is she?"

I stopped walking and swallowed hard.

"Well?" He turned back and looked at me, his face blanching on the spot.

This right here was the very predicament I didn't want to find myself in, but there I was, in the middle. Again. Joe told me everything. Estée told me everything. And I felt I had some moral obligation to come clean with them both. I couldn't bear keeping any more secrets, harboring any more lies. I was buckling beneath the weight of my own deceptions as it was.

I opened my mouth, and as soon as I mentioned Van's name, Joe and I headed to a nearby cocktail lounge, tucked my suitcase in with the coat check and ordered two martinis.

"Is it serious?" he asked, tapping his speared olive exactly as Estée had done before Van corrected her etiquette.

"I don't like him," I said. "And she knows it."

"I talk to her all the time. Almost every day. I get letters and long-distance calls. And by the way, *she's* the one who calls *me.* She never said a word about this Van fellow."

"She just met him. Maybe she's waiting to see where it goes before she—"

"But is it serious?" he asked again, sliding the olive off the toothpick with his teeth. Van would not have approved.

"I think it's more infatuation than anything."

He went quiet and I said nothing to fill the silence while he pulled a cigarette from the pack of Lucky Strikes and lit it. "Did she tell you I got a job?"

"Joe, that's wonderful. Congratulations."

"Yeah, I'm selling zippers—"

"Zippers?"

"You wouldn't believe how many people need zippers nowadays. It's a strong market," he said, despite sounding crestfallen. "Buttons are a thing of the past. Zippers are what's in. And the money's not half bad." He sounded like he was trying to convince himself. "Didn't Estée tell you about it?"

I shook my head, watching him deflate before my eyes. I refrained from saying she'd hardly mentioned him, other than when I'd brought him up during our fight.

"This Van fellow, I'll bet he's rich, isn't he?"

I nodded and wrestled with whether or not to mention that he was also married.

Joe scrubbed a hand over his face. "You know what? I don't care who this guy is. I know Estée still loves me."

"Deep down she knows it, too."

"Let her go have her fun with Van and anyone else she wants. I don't care—it's only temporary. What Blondie and I have is special. It's not something you can put a price tag on." He ground out his cigarette with a bit too much force. "Goddamn Van."

20

I HADN'T HEARD A word from Estée since I'd been back in New York. Usually while she was down in Florida, she'd send me letters or postcards all the time. I'd even broken down and sent her a quick note, all general and cheery, not a word about the way we'd left off. She never responded and I told myself she was busy and not to take it personally.

But my theory was blown to bits one afternoon in May. A full seven weeks after I returned from Palm Beach, I went to Darlene's for a much-needed trim and a new hair color. I was now officially a redhead, which I rather liked, and I had decided to let my hair grow out. It nearly reached my shoulders. I looked over at Estée's concession stand. She had a new girl working there who was giving someone a facial. As Darlene was finishing up my hair, I casually asked if she'd heard anything from Estée lately.

"Estée?" Darlene propped her cigarette between her lips. "You just missed her."

"You mean she's back?" I caught my reflection in the mirror. There was no hiding my surprise. Or my hurt.

"Oh yeah. She stopped by to say hello, check in on her stand."

"I see." I brushed my fingers through my hair, in need of a casual gesture. "She must have just gotten back to town."

"Yeah, she's been back for—let's see"—Darlene drew down on her cigarette—"probably a week, maybe ten days. Something like that. And she brought the new boyfriend back with her . . ."

Darlene was still talking, but I wasn't hearing her. *Estée was back in town, and she hadn't bothered to contact me . . .*

I left Darlene's Palace of Beauty and headed toward work, passing a wash of strangers on the sidewalk. I thought I saw my father crossing an intersection, something about the man's gait and the tilt of his fedora. Part of me wanted to chase after him, but of course, it was just my eyes playing tricks on me. That man on the street got me thinking about my mother, too. On April 1st, the anniversary of my father's arrest, I'd fought with myself about calling her, but I knew she'd only speak to me if I was willing to forgive my father, which I wasn't able to do.

Usually, I loved New York in the springtime but my mood was tarnished. I wasn't taking in the budding flower boxes along Fifth Avenue, the smell of hot dogs roasting or the sunlight coming down from between the buildings. I was back to sulking about Estée. I didn't think our relationship was that fragile, but apparently it was. I couldn't shake the feeling that our friendship was over.

LATER THAT DAY, Mrs. Coopers stopped by my counter in the lingerie department, where I was unpacking a new shipment of foundation garments. Glancing up from her clipboard she said, "I see you changed your hair color again, Miss Downing."

I could tell this was simply an observation and not a compliment. Clearly, she didn't care for Chestnut Red #2A.

"By the way," she said, "I have some good news for you. We're going to be moving you over to cosmetics. Permanently."

"You are?" A small flutter in my core began expanding. "Is this a promotion?"

"One of the girls is getting married. Her last day is Friday and we'll start training you as early as tomorrow. Congratulations."

"So this *is* a promotion."

"If you wish to call it that, I suppose you may. You'll be taking on more responsibility but I'm afraid there'll be no increase in your monetary compensation. I always told you the tigers are the ones who advance." And with that, she turned and left me to unpack boxes of brassieres, girdles and ladies' fine underwear.

No increase in your monetary compensation . . . That was what she'd said, but still, I was getting promoted. All my hard work appeared to be paying off. The excitement in my belly mushroomed ever more. I was so proud and my first thought was, *I can't wait to tell Estée.* Then I remembered there was no Estée.

The day progressed, and while I was showing a customer a garter girdle, I noticed Mrs. Hutt coming down the escalator and lazily drifting over toward the hanging rack of silk slips.

"Now you can see how lightweight this is," I said to the customer. "It has front, back and side panels along with four garters." While the woman examined the garment, I greeted Mrs. Hutt and watched as she ran her gloved fingertips along the display case.

I went back to my customer and Mrs. Hutt went back to the slips and gingerly folded one up and tucked it into her pocketbook.

"Have a wonderful day, Mrs. Hutt," I called after her.

I finished ringing up the girdle sale, jotted down Mrs. Hutt's new *purchase* and brought out a white cloth, which I used to buff away the fingerprints along the glass case. Just then Estée came sweeping in and my day got even better. She was wearing a belted green dress with rickrack stitching along the collar and cuffed sleeves. I smiled, so excited to see her, to tell her my news, but the look on her face stopped me. I could tell she was still angry with me.

"Well, look at you," she said drily. "So you're a redhead now." Before I could say anything, she added, "Just thought I'd come by and see what the competition is up to."

But the competition was down on the main floor and I took comfort in knowing that she'd at least come looking for me. "Speaking of the competition," I said, unable to keep it in, "I just got a promotion. I'm going to be working in the cosmetic department. Full-time."

"Well, good for you," she said kindly. "So, what else is going on?"

In a flash she dismissed my news, pretending indifference, but I saw the flicker in her eyes. She was already processing how my promotion could open doors for her here at Saks Fifth Avenue.

"When did you get back in town?" I asked pointedly.

"Oh, not too long ago." She was being intentionally vague and nonchalant. She picked up a silk slip, the same one Mrs. Hutt *bought*, and ran her fingers over the fabric before making a subtle disapproving face.

"And how are things with you?" I asked.

She set the slip aside. "You mean, how are things with Van?"

"Among other things. How's business? How's Leonard?"

She looked at me, and despite her best efforts to fight it, the corner of her mouth inched upward, giving way to a full-blown smile. "I'll tell you what, why don't you come by my place when you get off work—I have a new cleansing cream I'm working on—you can be my guinea pig and I'll tell you all about everything. Leonard'll be at Joe's so it'll give us a chance to catch up."

After work that day, I stopped by a flower stand and picked up a bouquet of peonies, daffodils and lilies and went to Estée's apartment. Not long after the divorce, she had moved to a new place on the corner of 78th and West End Avenue that had a Hungarian restaurant on the ground floor. She must have been doing okay financially because it was a very nice apartment, costing her a whopping $125 a month for five rooms.

I handed her the flowers when she answered the door, the stems having soaked through the wrapping paper, turning it pulpy.

"You didn't have to do that," she said.

"I know. But I wanted to."

"Why?" She set the flowers aside, as if she'd get to them later.

"Why? Because I thought you'd like them. And because I've missed you. I'm glad you're back."

"Uh-huh, I see." She turned and headed into the kitchen.

"Are you still mad at me?" I asked, trailing behind her.

"I'm not mad at you," she said, though she didn't sound *not mad* at me. "Why would I be mad at you?"

"Obviously you're still upset about what happened when I was down in Florida."

"Don't be ridiculous. It's not that."

"Well, then, what is it?"

She didn't say anything and I followed her back out to the living room.

Finally, she sighed, dropping a hand to her hip. "It's just that, well, you're one of my dearest friends and sometimes, honestly, sometimes I feel like I don't even know who you are. You never let me in."

"Estée, I'm—"

She raised her hand, stopping me. "You're so guarded all the time."

I froze. I had no idea where she was going but wherever it was, it was too close to the edge for me.

"You won't tell me a damn thing about yourself. The first mention of anything remotely personal and you change the subject. I ask about your family and you won't say a thing. I ask how you know

Alexandria Spencer and you say, *It's a long story.* You're a vault. Makes me wonder what you're hiding and why you don't trust me."

That landed heavy on me. My insides collapsed. "I'm a private person, is all," I croaked out, and then added, "What do you want to know about me?"

"You never talk about your past, or about what happened with your parents."

"Because it's painful," I screeched reflexively. And it was. The truth was excruciating. "I don't want to rehash what happened." And I didn't. That part was absolutcly truc. "I'm sorry if that offends you."

"Okay, all right." The same hand that stopped me moments before was now surrendering. "It's just that I tell you *everything*."

I wanted to point out that Estée liked talking about *Estée*. Next to talking about cosmetics, her favorite subject was herself. I wasn't like that. I never had been. Even before I had things to hide, I was never all that forthcoming.

"I tell you *everything*," she said again, "and you don't tell me a damn thing."

Keeping everything inside was exhausting. If only she knew how many times I'd come close to telling her about my past. I'd worked up a million different ways to apologize and justify not telling her the truth all along. But now, seeing how she'd reacted to my disapproval of Van, I found it hard to believe that she could have overlooked my lies. As I saw it, I had to protect my past for fear she would no longer be my friend. And I needed her in my life. Estée was my strong shoulder to lean on; she gave me tough love when I needed it and inspired me to push myself, to better myself. Not divulging the truth was a testament to how much she meant to me.

"You don't confide in me about anything, and when I confide in you—well, you're very quick to pass judgment on me."

"So this *is* about what happened in Florida. I'm sorry, but you know how I am. I'm not going to just tell you what you want to hear."

"Then maybe you shouldn't say anything at all."

"Maybe I shouldn't. Maybe I should just stand back and watch you throw away a man that I *know* you still love. He's not going to wait around forever, you know. He's still a man, after all. He has needs."

"Don't say that."

"But it's true. You know it is."

Estée pressed her fingertips to her forehead, squeezing her eyes shut, and her voice cracked. "I'm so confused."

And with that, I softened, too. "I know you are. Don't you see? That's why it's hard for me to keep my big mouth shut."

For a long moment, neither one of us said anything, and then Estée broke the silence. "Truce?"

I nodded. "Truce."

She came over and hugged me with a fiercely tight grip. We both mopped our eyes and she put a Bing Crosby 78 on the Zenith, which also had a built-in shortwave radio. "Stormy Weather" played out, with a little scratchy hiss here and there.

While she fixed us both a gimlet, she lightened up the mood, telling a funny story about one of her clients down in Palm Beach. "So, she always likes to have a few extra jars of my Super Rich All-Purpose Creme on hand and because it's so darn hot down there, I told her to store them in the refrigerator. Well, Mrs. Nevins—that's her name—well, she was having a luncheon and her cook mistook the face cream for mayonnaise. Can you believe it?"

"Oh my goodness."

"She accidentally mixed my face cream into the salad dressing."

"Oh God! Did anyone get sick?"

"Not a one." She smiled, proud. "That's the beauty of it. My Super Rich All-Purpose Creme is one hundred percent natural—

you can actually eat it right out of the jar. Mrs. Nevins even said it didn't taste half bad."

We had a good laugh over that and I was reassured that our friendship was back on track or at least heading there. She turned the record over, dragged a kitchen chair into the living room and patted the seat.

"I've been working on this new cleansing cream," she said, draping a towel over my shoulders. She held my chin and tilted my face up to the light and frowned. "You haven't been using your Creme Pack treatments twice a week, have you?"

"Not every week, no," I confessed. Sometimes I was so dog-tired I didn't even remove my makeup but I didn't dare tell her that. She would have been horrified if she knew that some mornings when I was in a rush, I'd touch up yesterday's mascara with a fresh coat.

"You have to train yourself to care for your skin. Every day. It's a must."

"Yes, ma'am."

"Now this is a new cleansing regimen I've been working on." She saturated a piece of cotton and dabbed the lotion across my brow and cheeks. It tingled and had a pleasant scent.

"So, in case you were wondering," she said, "Van came back to New York with me."

"So I heard. Darlene told me." I tried to keep my voice neutral.

"He has some business to tend to here in the city."

"Where's he staying? Not here, is he?"

"No," she said, a little annoyed. "He keeps an apartment in town. On Park Avenue. It's lovely."

"I'll bet it is." I managed this without any bitterness.

"Oh, and while he's here in town, he's going to make some introductions to the head buyers at Bonwit Teller and Gimbels. He says it's time for me to start thinking bigger. 'Get into the department stores,' he says."

For once I found myself agreeing with him. "I think he's right."

"Oh, so do I." She swirled a solution over my face in small, deliberate circles. "And I think it's no accident that you've been promoted to the cosmetic counter."

"You didn't seem all that excited when I told you earlier." I couldn't help myself—it just came out.

"Well, of course I was. I'm very happy for you."

"I'm not getting a raise, though," I said, shaking my head. "Don't you think that's kinda lousy?"

"You know," she said, skipping over my lament, "Saks Fifth Avenue is the one department store that would really put me on the map. I need to get my products in there. And I'll tell you what I really like about Saks—"

"What's that?"

"Their charge plate. It makes all the difference. Women can just charge whatever they want there. They don't have to worry about not having enough cash in their pocketbooks. And their husbands won't know how much they spent until later, after the bill comes in. That gives Saks Fifth Avenue a real edge. I could make so much more money if I was in there." She looked at me—the rest unspoken.

I didn't know what to say. Did she really think I had any pull there at all? Part of me was flattered. "I wish I could help you"—I shrugged a heap of guilt off my shoulders—"but I don't even know the buyers." "It's Only a Paper Moon" was playing, the record popping and hissing, scratching along. "Doesn't Van know anyone at Saks?"

"Unfortunately, they're not the people I need to get to. But—and now this is interesting"—she shook a bottle of white lotion—"Van says I need a fragrance. He says if I add a fragrance to my line it will help. He says it will really draw the women in. What do you think?"

"Hmmm, I'm not sure."

"Why not?" She was challenging me, unable to fathom that the great Van could be wrong about anything.

"Well," I explained, "it's just that you almost never see a woman come into Saks and buy perfume for herself. Usually, it's a husband buying for his wife, or a boyfriend for his girlfriend, someone maybe buying it for their mother. Occasionally a woman comes in looking for a gift for a friend or someone else, but otherwise—no, they won't buy perfume for *themselves*."

We'd reached the end of the record. There was no more Bing but I still heard a hissing, scratching noise.

Estée frowned. "I have a nose, you know. My uncle even said so and he—" Suddenly her eyes flashed wide right before she let out an earsplitting screech that made my heart jump. "Oh my God— Oh my God—" She leaped onto the sofa, pointing. "It's a—a mouse!"

"What? Where?"

She pointed and we both screamed as it ran behind the music console. I rushed onto the couch with her, the two of us holding on to each other, stomping our bare feet on the cushions.

"What do we do? What should I do?"

"Well, I'm not going to kill it," I said, keeping my eye on the tail still sticking out. We'd probably scared the mouse more than it scared us.

Still standing on the couch, Estée bent down and reached for the telephone on the side table. She yanked on the cord, straining for the receiver. I assumed she was calling the building's super.

Instead, she telephoned Joe.

He was there fifteen minutes later with a mouse trap and Leonard at his side. I found it so curious that the person she called for help was not Van but Joe. Good ole Joe, her unsung hero.

21

WORKING IN THE cosmetic department required a bit more preparation on my part. I was required to wear a certain amount of makeup each day, which included eyeshadow, eyeliner, mascara, rouge and red lipstick—the brighter, the better. I was also expected to wear nail polish and a fragrance.

The other salesgirls were as territorial as cats and did not exactly roll out the red carpet for me. A colleague named Vivian moved in on one of my customers, claiming *I saw her first.* I let it go, didn't say a word, mostly because I was afraid of her. She reminded me of my sister. There was a passing resemblance, but mainly it was because she was just as bossy as Gail and downright mean.

Like Vivian, Gail had resented my arrival from day one. Rather than embracing her new role of big sister, she mourned no longer being the lone daughter, the center of attention, and took solace in boxes of animal crackers. When I was two, she attempted to flush me down the toilet. Another time she poured black pepper on my cereal, promising me it tasted sweeter than sugar. She shaved off my eyebrows and occasionally locked me inside closets. Each time I looked at Vivian, that trauma came echoing back. I was not about to mess with her. If she wanted the sale, I'd give it to her and find other ways to make my quotas.

Amid this sea of hostility, there was one shopgirl who befriended me. Harriet Allen. She was a year younger and had long dark hair, large doe-like eyes and a slight pout even when she smiled. Harriet was my only ally in the cosmetic department. She was always eager to lend a hand, helping balance my cash drawer at the end of the day, fetching shopping bags when I was down to my last few. She'd even help close a sale by complimenting a lipstick or rouge I'd recommended to a customer.

One day while Harriet was helping me clean up a nail polish spill, Joe stumbled in, hoping to buy me a cup of coffee. This of course was code for *I need to talk to you about Estée.* I still had fifteen minutes until my break, and in those few minutes, while I was tending to the polish stain, Harriet made her move.

Honestly, I had nothing to do with Joe taking Harriet's telephone number that day, or his asking her out for dinner the following week. Still, Estée blamed me.

We were at Schrafft's on 82nd and Broadway, having their famous lamb hash, when she dropped her fork with a loud clank. "How long were you planning on sitting there before you told me about this Harriet woman? Apparently, Joe had a date with her—no, I'm sorry, make that *two dates* with her."

"He told you about her?" I dabbed my mouth with my napkin.

"And it's a good thing he did because clearly, you weren't going to say anything to me. How in the hell could you set him up with your co-worker?"

I explained how the two had met, how I'd been only an innocent bystander, but Estée couldn't hear me. She stirred her coffee so hard, it sloshed over the lip of her cup and into her saucer before she just shoved the whole thing aside.

"Just calm down." I was aware of people at the next table looking our way.

"Calm down! He's been out with her *twice* this week. *Twice!*"

"I tried to warn you about this. You can't expect him to just sit home night after night. You're divorced. You're with Van. And Joe is still a man—and a very attractive man. What did you think was going to happen?"

Estée fiddled with her bracelet and then her earrings. I could feel her leg bobbing up and down beneath the table. "He can't be serious about this girl," she said, sounding exactly like Joe had sounded when he'd found out about Van.

"I think he's lonely. You can't fault him for that. And you can't blame me because of Harriet."

"Is she pretty?"

"I'm not doing this with you, Estée."

"Ooh, I just wish he wasn't going out with her."

"That's funny because I know Joe wishes you weren't going out with Van."

IT WAS A cold December morning and I awoke before my alarm, thinking of my mother. It was her birthday and I contemplated calling her. She was a mess, but she was still my mother and from time to time I missed hearing her laughter, missed her illogical approach to life: how she thought dishes from the bottom of a stack were somehow cleaner than the ones on top, how she thought she could strengthen her eyesight by refusing to wear her glasses, how Friday the 13ths were actually good-luck days.

Last year, in a weak moment, I'd asked Glenn for her telephone number, and he'd given it to me but warned not to call her. "I mean it," he'd said. "She's still angry with you. And not just because of

Dad. She's furious that you changed your name." Well, I was *furious* at him for telling her that, but I kept quiet. I almost never voiced my anger to him or anyone else in my family because they still saw me as a little girl, the baby, and dismissed my protests as silly temper tantrums.

The alarm went off and I slid out from under the covers and went into the bathroom. My stockings were draped over the shower rod, dry now, and when I turned on the fan they swayed back and forth like eels. The longer I was awake, the less compelled I felt to reach out to my mother, and by the time I'd made it to work, the urge had vanished, like a fine mist absorbed into the atmosphere.

I was working the first shift that day and had arrived at Saks before the store opened. That week the Christmas decorations had gone up—the sparkling snowflakes and wreaths, the garlands and red velvet bows I'd seen the year before—and the usual piped-in music that played all day had switched over to Christmas songs. I couldn't get "Good King Wenceslas" out of my head and each time "Silent Night" came on, I found myself growing overly sentimental, beating back tears.

I was not relishing another Christmas season designed for festive family gatherings. Every Christmas morning—it didn't matter if we were in New York or in Miami Beach—my father woke us to watch the sunrise on our respective balconies. Whether the sun was shining or the snow was falling, he'd stretch his arms out, trying to embrace us all in one big hug, saying that this moment was the greatest gift he could ask for. After we'd scramble inside and open our presents, he made us renew our promise to always come home for Christmas. He wanted to be able to look around the room and see his family all together, all under one roof. My vision blurred a little on that and I had to blink to clear the threat of more tears.

Something else that made this time of year painful was being surrounded by happy couples. Joe was seeing Harriet, Waller was dating an impossibly long-legged actress, Bobbi also had a new beau and of course Estée was heading to Palm Beach to be with Van. Not that I begrudged any of them, but I admit I was feeling good and sorry for myself. I had accepted an invitation to the Millers' open house, but aside from that, I had no plans. I was going to be all alone. Standing behind the Elizabeth Arden counter with that thought looming large was enough to make my eyes well up once again.

Thankfully, my tears were interrupted by Mrs. Coopers. "How are you set with the Arden cream?" she asked, peering at me from over her eyeglasses.

I always checked my inventory at the start of each shift, so I knew this off the top of my head. "I only have eighteen tubes left," I said.

"*Only?*" She adjusted her spectacles.

"It's our most popular seller." Elizabeth Arden's Eight Hour Cream was flying off the shelves.

"I'll go ahead and put in for another dozen," she said, nodding, jotting it down on her clipboard.

"If I were you, I'd make that two."

"Oh, would you now?" Her tone was somewhere between amused and annoyed at my telling her how to do her job.

"I know I can move them," I said. "They won't gather dust, I assure you." After once making the grave mistake of running out of a popular product, I now made sure to get my requests in early. Plus, I'd picked up a tip from Estée and kept copious notes on my regular customers. I wrote down the date they bought certain items and sent them reminders whenever it was time to replenish. When we introduced a new cream, rouge or lipstick, I would call and tell them all about it.

"Very well then, two dozen." Mrs. Coopers made a notation and asked to see my tally sheet from the day before. "Well, well, well," she said, smiling. "Excellent, Miss Downing. Excellent. Keep up the good work. I knew you were a tiger when I hired you."

Vivian rolled her eyes and Mrs. Coopers moved on to the Max Factor counter while I sorted through the receipts and notes that Harriet had left for me when she closed the night before.

At nine o'clock the doors opened, and the first customers trickled in. Santa already had a line of children waiting for him behind a velvet rope, and the live mannequins were strolling about, modeling the latest gowns, fur stoles and jewelry. I spotted Mrs. Hutt, who, for no apparent reason, had just helped herself to an ornament hanging off a Christmas tree display.

Thanks to a string of customers, the morning flew by and I had just returned from my lunch break when that dreaded, familiar ping in my ear sounded off. *Oh, good God, no. Not now.* I'd never had a vertigo bout at work. My last one had been over a month ago and had been mild. But judging by how numb my face was growing, I didn't think I'd be as lucky this time.

Right before the whirling started, I heard a man asking if I was okay.

"I'll—I'll be with you in just a minute," I managed to say as my eyes locked in place on his ring. The only way to keep myself upright was to focus on something and not move my eyes or my head until the spinning stopped. I concentrated on every detail of his ring. It was a gold signet ring that reminded me of a sealing wax stamp. Truly, it was one of the ugliest rings I'd ever seen but I continued staring at it. I could see now that it featured a pyramid with an eye in the center, watching me.

"Are you okay?" I heard him ask again.

"Yes. Yes, I'm sorry. Just a little dizzy. It'll pass. I'm fine. Really. I apologize."

"Can I get you some water? Do you need to sit down?"

"No, no," I said. "It'll pass. I just can't move my eyes until it does."

I think he asked if I could talk without moving my eyes. I don't remember if I answered him. I thought he would have gone to another counter, sought out another shopgirl, but instead, he waited and I was barely hanging on, his ring still serving as my focal point. After a few minutes, I dared to shift my vision; a test, to see if the bout was passing. Once I could move my eyes, I slowly moved my head. Finally, I looked up and that's when I saw the man's face. It was not the face I'd been expecting, especially given that ring. In an instant I forgot all about the vertigo.

He was handsome, but handsome men came into Saks all the time. Honestly, I didn't know what it was about him. I couldn't have told you what color his eyes were, or whether his nose was long or short, his lips full or thin. It was like looking at a mosaic, and when you added up all his features, the cumulative impact was, well, very enticing.

"I've never had *that* effect on a woman before," he said, grinning, knowing perfectly well that he always had *some sort of effect* on women.

I laughed. "It's not you. Trust me."

"You're sure you're okay?" He tilted his head to the side. He was definitely attractive. Not Waller attractive but then again, how many men were? I decided he was more sexy than handsome. Sultry and sensual, strapping with an edge that called to you like a red button that said *Don't touch.* He had captured the attention of the other salesgirls, too. Especially Vivian, who couldn't stop staring.

"Yes. I'm much better. Thank you." I cleared my throat. "So, is there something I can help you with?"

Setting his fedora on the counter, he revealed a full head of wavy brown hair, the kind that I would have liked to run my fingers through. But he took all temptation off the table when he smiled slyly and said he was looking for perfume. "It's for someone *very special.*"

I cleared my throat again and shifted gears, becoming the ultimate professional. "Do you know if she likes floral scents? Citrus? Maybe something spicy?"

"Ah, no." He shook his head. "I'm afraid I don't."

"Well, what fragrance is she currently wearing?"

"I'm afraid I don't know that, either." He smiled apologetically, yet full of swagger. "Tell me"—his eyes suggestively moved down my neck, searching for my name tag—"what's *your* favorite perfume, Gloria?"

"Well"—I paused, feeling my body going flush—"Shalimar is lovely," I managed. "Le Jade is also quite nice."

He smiled, stroked a finger across his chiseled jaw. "And what would you suggest if I really wanted to impress this girl?"

"Well, in that case, Chanel No. 5. You can never go wrong with Chanel."

"Well, in *that* case, Gloria"—he winked—"I'll take it."

What an outrageous flirt. Winking at me while buying Chanel for *someone very special*. I refused to even look at him as I rang up his sale, gently wrapping the perfume box in tissue paper and placing it inside a bag.

"Thank you, Gloria. I appreciate your help. Oh—and take care of yourself."

I looked up again only to see the other women watching him ride up the escalator, disappearing in the upper floors. I gathered my wits, took out a white cloth and wiped his fingerprints off my counter.

ESTÉE SHOWED UP not long after that, bursting through the front doors with her pocketbook swinging off one wrist, a shopping bag dangling off the other. She was catching the train for Palm Beach the following morning and had come to say goodbye.

"But I thought you weren't leaving until next week," I said.

"Well, I was but then Van said it would be better if I came down early."

"Uh-huh." I clucked my tongue and busied myself with a stack of receipts.

"And it's not like I'm going to be seeing much of Joe while I'm here in town anyway." She looked around and dropped her voice to a whisper. "Which one is she?"

"It's Harriet's day off." I delivered this flat as a pancake.

Estée pursed her lips. "Well, that explains why I couldn't find Joe this morning. Does he talk to you about her?"

"No. He talks to me about *you*."

She smiled, satisfied, and went back to discussing Van. "I'm a little worried about how he's going to split his time while I'm there. You know, with the holidays and all. Do you think he'll spend Christmas with me? Or with *her*?"

"With her," I said, tucking the receipts inside the cash drawer. I knew that was going to hurt but I hated the way Estée acted around him, desperate and needy. It was like she'd surrendered to him and had no say in their relationship, in what she wanted. That wasn't the Estée I knew and loved.

"What about Christmas Eve? And New Year's—you don't think he'll be with *her* on New Year's Eve, do you?" She said this with great alarm, as if the possibility had just occurred to her.

"Of course he's going to be with her." I got that last jab in because I was annoyed. When she first left Joe, Estée needed me. Especially after her breakup with Charles. *Oh, Gloria, come meet me for a drink. Oh, Gloria, I'm so lonely, I can't even get out of bed. Oh, Gloria, I think I'm having a nervous breakdown.* I always dropped whatever I was doing and ran to her rescue. Now she had what she wanted, and she was abandoning me. I'd been replaced by Van, who was asking her to play second-best. It killed me that Estée couldn't even see that she was the other woman.

"Van could still decide to spend Christmas and New Year's with me."

"That's not the way *these things* work."

"What do you mean, 'these things'?"

"You're the mistress. Remember?"

"Well, merry Christmas to you, too." Estée turned to leave, grabbing her pocketbook and sliding it across the counter.

"Estée, wait—I'm sorry."

She stopped. "Just once, couldn't you *just once* tell me what I want to hear?"

"Not my style," I said. "You know that."

"I know. It's one of the things I love about you and it's one of the things I hate about you."

"Truce?"

She nodded, trying to fight off a smile. "Truce."

"Merry Christmas, Estée. We'll celebrate when you're back in town."

I was somber watching her walk away. When she reached the revolving doors, she turned around, as if she knew I was still looking, and blew me a kiss.

After Estée left, I had to explain to an irate customer that we no longer carried Gouraud's Oriental Cream.

"But why not? Saks Fifth Avenue has always carried Gouraud's."

She reminded me a bit of my mother, the same blonde hair that curled and bounced at her shoulders, the one-too-many chunky gold bracelets. I even thought I detected a whisper of wine on her breath, but that could have been my imagination.

"Well," she said, "I'll just have to buy it elsewhere."

"I'm afraid you won't find it anywhere else, either. The FDA took it off the market."

"The FDA? Why?"

"Because women were developing mercury poisoning after using that cream—it was turning their gums black, making their teeth fall out." The woman's eyes grew wide, horrified. "But don't worry. Have you tried Elizabeth Arden's Eight Hour Cream?"

I ended up selling her the Arden cream along with some dusting powder and Max Factor's pancake makeup, rounding out another nice day of sales, much to Vivian's and the other shopgirls' ire.

At the end of my shift Mrs. Coopers examined my sales total and nodded. "Excellent, Miss Downing. Excellent." She started to walk away but stopped. "Oh, I almost forgot. Someone dropped this off for you earlier today." She set a box on the counter, gift wrapped in the Saks Fifth Avenue special Christmas paper. It was adorned with a delicate red bow and had a tiny card attached.

Estée. I should have known. The sun rose up inside me. She never would have forgotten about me for Christmas. Had I known she was going to leave town early, I would have insisted we open our gifts ahead of time. I'd already bought her present, a leather-bound appointment book for the new year. I waited until after Mrs. Coopers moved on to the next counter before I opened the card.

Surprisingly it was not from Estée. Instead, it read: *Have dinner with me, Gloria. Edward Clifford* and his exchange: *RIV side 0570.* Who was Edward Clifford? I didn't know anyone by that name.

I unwrapped the box and my heart about burst. I looked around the store, unable to stop smiling as I pressed the bottle of Chanel No. 5 to my chest.

22

LATER THAT WEEK, Edward and I were seated side by side at a candlelit banquette in an Italian restaurant draped with garlands and holly berries. He confessed that he'd seen me the moment he stepped inside Saks.

"What can I say, I'm a sucker for redheads. I knew I had to find a reason to go over and talk to you." He was confident without being cocky.

We were turned toward each other, managing to keep a respectable distance apart, but that was no easy task. We were magnets, fighting the force to lock together. There was just something about him that pulled me in. There was never an awkward silence or a lull in the conversation, though I later wouldn't have been able to recall what we talked about. I did, however, remember liking the way he listened when I spoke, how he laughed at all the right places. And I liked his eyes. They were blue and lovely, the irises unusually large and sultry. So penetrating was his gaze, I couldn't have looked away even if I'd wanted to.

I knew he wanted to kiss me, and I most definitely wanted to kiss him, too. Waiting for that first kiss was electrifying. And about the sexiest thing I'd ever experienced. Neither of us was able to hold out much longer, and before I knew it, we were sitting closer and closer still, until we just started necking right there at the banquette. And I didn't give a goddamn who saw us.

Edward offered to walk me home and we left the restaurant, arm in arm, stopping every few feet to neck some more, undeterred by the cold, biting wind. I still hated his signet ring, but oh, I did love his kisses.

As we approached my apartment building, I knew exactly what would happen if I let him upstairs. And what did it say about me that I was seriously considering it? Then again, what was the point of denying myself? It wasn't as if I was a virgin anymore. Plus, I was a Dowaziac, no longer the kind of girl you took home to Mother. I think that had a lot to do with why I'd started having sex with Waller in the first place. I had nothing to lose.

We paused outside my building, just beneath a streetlamp. I could feel the heat coming off him, waves of it radiating toward me. I looked into his eyes, and in that light, gazing right at him, I believed that I was capable of having the same sort of detached tryst with Edward that I'd been having with Waller. I was never going to fall for Edward—a man who wore that god-awful signet ring.

"Would you like to come up?"

After we got inside and flung off our coats, I kicked the front door shut while my hands loosened his necktie and I worked my fingers down his shirt buttons. I don't remember him unzipping my dress but it was off me, pooled around my ankles. We knocked over a lampshade as he backed me up against the wall and hoisted me onto his hips. We were both a little drunk and a lot clumsy. It was all hunger and urgency, and when it was over, I slid down his body and rested my head against his chest, his heart beating in my ear, both of us laughing at our abandon.

If it ended right then and there, in the middle of my living room floor, maybe I could have walked away from him or let him walk away from me. But we both went back for more. After a cigarette and some more laughs, we moved to my bedroom, into my bed, and that was where everything slowed way, way down and I discovered just how much my body liked his and how much I could like this man. I hadn't felt this way about anyone since Tommy. Edward and I never took our eyes off each other as we laced our fingers together, gripping onto each other, tighter and tighter the whole time.

Afterward, with the moonlight peeking in from the parting in the drapes, he propped himself up on his elbow while we shared a cigarette.

"So, Eddie"—I reached over and rumpled up his hair—"what are you—"

"Eddie? Whoa—" He stopped my hand. "No"—he shook his head, smiling—"no one calls me Eddie."

"Oh"—I laughed coquettishly—"but I can, right? Can't I?"

"Not if you expect me to answer. Eddie's the name of a two-year-old."

I took my hand away. I must have liked Edward more than I realized and I felt foolish, having caught myself trying to duplicate the magic of when I'd met Tommy. It was like trying to force an old shoe onto the wrong foot.

Edward ground out the cigarette, pulled me in close, and we kissed and touched and explored each other once again. Even more slowly this time. I don't think he missed one inch of my body. And the way he caressed me with his fingers, his lips, the way he tasted all of me—this was a man who knew what he was doing and he knew *exactly* what he was doing to me. Afterward we talked and tumbled about the bed, our limbs twisted up in each other and the sheets. In reality, being with Edward was nothing like it had been with Tommy. Or Waller. This was something altogether different. Something I couldn't explain and couldn't understand.

As Edward drifted off to sleep, with his arms wrapped around me, I caught myself already thinking about when I might see him again.

Would he want to come to the gallery opening the following weekend with Bobbi and her new boyfriend? Maybe we could have dinner beforehand, or better yet, maybe the two of us could have dinner earlier in the week? I wondered if he liked galleries. Plays? Movies? What about dancing? Did Edward like to dance? Waller was a good dancer . . . Edward seemed like he'd be a reader. I could picture him lying on my couch on a lazy Sunday afternoon with an Agatha Christie novel. Or no—wait—he was probably more the biography type . . .

While Edward lay beside me, sleeping, I was wide-awake, thinking and overthinking, giving him all kinds of attributes until a sinking feeling began to settle in my gut. *Who exactly is this man in my bed anyway?* Over dinner he'd said he was a lawyer and that he grew up in Kansas City. Other than that, I didn't know a thing about him. For all intents and purposes, Edward Clifford was a stranger. My own father had lied to me, so why should I have believed anything this guy said? Never mind that I hadn't told him the truth about myself, dodging every personal question he'd asked.

The next morning, I was cold to Edward, already wrapped in my bathrobe, and when he reached for me, I pulled away in every sense of the word.

"I should get ready for work," I said.

"What time do you have to be there?"

"Noon."

He leaned over, consulting my alarm clock. "It's only eight o'clock." He laughed. "Come back to bed."

"I need coffee." I scampered off toward the kitchen.

"Hey—"

I stopped in the doorway, looking over my shoulder while he propped a pillow up behind him and leaned against the headboard. "Did I do something wrong?"

"No. It's nothing. I just—I had too much to drink last night. We shouldn't have . . ." My words petered out as I headed to the kitchen.

"Gloria—"

I listened to the bed springs wheeze as he got up and padded into the living room. I heard his belt buckle hitting the floor as he stepped into his trousers.

"I'm sorry," I said, losing count of the number of coffee grounds I'd scooped into the percolator, "this is all just—it's happening too fast."

Hoisting his pants on his hips, he came and stood next to me. "So," he said, resting his hands on my shoulders, "if it's happening too fast, we'll slow it down."

He was saying all the right things and I hated him for it.

IT HAD BEEN a week since Edward gathered his clothes off my living room floor and left my apartment. I hadn't heard a word from him since. I'd blown it. And while I initially felt relieved, as the hours and days stretched on, I found myself deeply regretting how I'd played the whole thing.

I went to work that next Saturday, waited on customers, took my thirty-minute break in the back room, pushing a scoop of tuna salad around my plate while letting my coffee turn cold.

"Why so glum?" Harriet asked, taking a seat across from me at a long table, pulling a sandwich out of a brown paper bag: bologna on white bread, wrapped in wax paper.

"I thought I met someone," I said, letting a dollop of tuna drop from my fork onto the plate. "But, well . . ."

"You mean that fella with the perfume?" She pushed her sandwich aside and settled in for a story, elbows on the table, chin resting on her knuckles. "What happened?"

"It's over. I ruined it."

"What'd you do?"

I shook my head, not wanting to reveal that I was a dirty whore who invited this man back to my apartment. "Eh, I'm okay," I said, trying to sound convincing. "I'll get over it."

Harriet eased her elbows off the table and reached for her sandwich. We both grew quiet for a moment until she brought up Joe. "Did you know that he still talks to his ex-wife? Every day?"

"Well, they're still friends—and don't forget they have a child."

"Yeah, but *every single day*? Is that normal?"

"Who's to say what's normal between two people? I guess it's normal for them."

"They even talk every day when she's down in Florida. And you know how expensive long-distance calls are. The whole thing just makes me so mad," she said. "I don't know what to do. I think I'm falling in love with him. I really do."

"Oh, Harriet, do not fall in love with Joe. He's fresh out of a divorce. A divorce he didn't want in the first place."

"Don't say that." She contemplated her sandwich and set it back down. "You don't know what it's like when we're together."

I sat back, weighing what she'd said. Harriet and Joe *were* spending a fair amount of time together, but I knew he was still in love with Estée.

Now it was Harriet who'd grown glum, finishing her sandwich, fisting up the wax paper into an angry ball. Honestly, I didn't know which one of us had it worse.

At closing time that day, I didn't want to go home to an empty apartment. Bobbi and Waller were busy with their respective romances, so I walked around the city, past a blur of Christmas window displays and twinkling lights. I had the sensation that something was missing. It was sharp and jarring, that feeling you get when you think you've misplaced your pocketbook. I knew what it was, too. It was *him*. I was missing Edward. But that was absurd. How could I be missing someone I hardly knew?

23

THE FOLLOWING MONDAY while at work, taking inventory of Christmas bags, Christmas boxes, red bows and wrapping paper, I looked up and there he was, standing at my counter. Sparks ignited inside me, shooting off in all directions, fireflies taking flight.

"Is this slow enough for you?" Edward asked.

That was all it took for him to be back in my life. And just in time for Christmas. Together we bought a tree, some tinsel and one ornament—a red and gold tree topper. Since I didn't have any lights or bulbs, we strung popcorn and cranberries and made do with what we had. He stood behind me, his arms circled about my waist, my head leaning back against his chest, admiring our work.

"That is one sorry-looking tree," I said, laughing.

"C'mon, it's our first tree. Have a little faith. Next year we'll have a better one. Loaded with ornaments, lights—the whole bit."

I drew a deep, satisfied breath. He was already thinking of next Christmas. So much for us taking it slow. I smiled and rested my hands atop his and glanced down at his ring. That creepy all-seeing eye was looking directly at me.

"So, what's the story with this?" I asked, tapping his finger.

"Oh, this?" He held his hand out. "It's my Freemason ring."

I twisted about to face him, my brow wrinkled.

"I'm a Mason," he said with a puff of pride. "A thirty-third-degree Mason." *Puff, puff.*

"What exactly is that?"

"You've never heard of the Freemasons? It's a secret society."

The word *secret* jumped out, hanging in the air before me. "Ooh," I teased to cover my reaction, "that sounds serious."

"Oh, it is," he said mockingly. "We have a secret handshake and everything."

"Show me the handshake." I slipped out of his embrace and reached for his hand.

"Nope. Can't do it."

"Why not?"

"I told you, it's a secret."

I thought he was joking. "Oh, come on now. I won't tell anyone."

"I'm serious. I can't show you. It really is a secret. I took an oath."

"Well, okay then." I didn't say another word about the Freemasons but something about it got under my skin, like a splinter. "I'll go fix the eggnog."

"I'll help."

"No, no." I waved him off. "I'll do it. You stay there and enjoy your tree."

I stood in the kitchen, feeling agitated, though I couldn't say why. I took down a bottle of Bacardí and slammed the cupboard shut. He had a secret handshake. *A freakin' secret handshake.* That was the *big* secret he was keeping from me, while I was keeping an enormous secret from him. How could this relationship possibly work? Telling someone you legally changed your name wasn't the sort of thing you casually dropped into conversation. Plus, it begged the question *why?* And if *I* couldn't get past what my father had done, how could I expect anyone else to? I was certain that those closest to me—Estée and Joe, Bobbi and the Millers—would cut me out of their lives, just as I'd cut my father out of mine. Edward had a strong moral compass. He'd never be able to accept this flaw in my character. I poured more rum than was needed into the eggnog and went back out to the living room. I was prepared to drink up and send him on his way, feigning a headache or sudden sore throat. That was the plan.

But when I saw him crouched down in the corner, flipping through my minuscule 78 collection, mostly purchased from a used-record store, an unexpected calmness settled over me. The world quieted down and all of life's hard edges seemed to soften. It was like he belonged there in my home. His very presence had transformed the room, making it feel warmer, safer than it ever had before. We spent the rest of the evening listening to Bing Crosby records and dancing barefoot in the living room in front of the fireplace.

It was romantic and overwhelming. I was fairly certain I could fall in love with this man and he with me. And I was terrified. This wasn't supposed to have happened, but it was happening—it had already happened. I'd been so swept away that I'd forgotten to construct the detours and roadblocks I'd put in place with other men.

I'D BEEN SEEING Edward nonstop for three days and three nights and it was over dinner, while he was telling me about a bankruptcy fraud case he was working on, that I finally connected the dots. Edward wasn't just a lawyer. No, he worked for the New York District Attorney's office. Edward prosecuted the bad guys who committed wire fraud, insurance fraud, money laundering, tax evasion and Ponzi schemes. My father's crime was exactly the sort of case he worked on. *Oh God, what if he'd been involved in* The People v. Dowaziac?

I tiptoed around that subject. "So, ah, did—did you ever work on that—that— Do you remember that Dowaziac case?" I tried making it sound as casual as possible but the tone of my words—I didn't even sound like myself. My stomach tightened to knots and I immediately wished I hadn't said anything.

He shook his head. "No, not me." Without skipping a beat, he picked up his knife and returned to his steak.

My question hadn't given him the slightest pause. He hadn't detected the queer twitch in my jaw, the odd pitch to my voice. He had already moved on, asking if I had plans for New Year's Eve. So that was it. I had just skated past my father's sins. I should have left it alone, but guilty people can never do that. Instead, I kept picking at it, tonguing the sore.

"You didn't tell me you worked at the district attorney's office," I said.

"Yes, I did."

"When?"

"Pretty sure I told you all about it on our first date."

"Well, that explains it," I said, realizing that he probably had indeed told me. "All I could think about that night was how badly I wanted you to kiss me."

He grinned, set his fork down. "Well, now that's just too cute." He got up, and in one fluid movement, which was his way—always smooth and confident—slid over to my side of the table and kissed me, tasting of wine and steak and him. We might have gone on kissing like a couple of kids in the balcony of a dark movie theater had it not been for the waiter clearing his throat before clearing the table.

Moments later, Edward was back on his side of the table and our waiter had returned with a slice of sour cream raisin pie and two coffees. There were a million other things we could have talked about, but I steered us back to the danger zone.

"So do you like it?" I asked, resting my fork on the lip of the plate.

"It's delicious. I've never had it before."

"Not the pie, silly. Your work. With the D.A."

"Oh, that." He nodded. "Yeah, yeah, I do. I just wish it paid a little better. I could make more money working for a law firm, but I like the type of cases I'm involved with now. They're rewarding."

That right there was music to my ears. Unlike my father, Edward was not driven by money and greed. And as I would come to learn, Edward Clifford was quite frugal, which would have made some women crazy, but not me. I laughed when he confessed that he'd almost had a heart attack when he realized how much that bottle of Chanel perfume cost. His apartment was even smaller than mine—a third-floor walk-up with modest furnishings. What he didn't mind spending money on, however, were his Brooks Brothers suits and his two-toned broguing shoes. In fact, he'd bought a new pair at Saks Fifth Avenue that same day he spotted me behind the counter. He also enjoyed fine restaurants once, sometimes twice, a week and good wine. Always good wine.

With such humble material cravings, I knew he would not be tempted to do anything unethical. Just the opposite. Here was a man who was devoted to cleaning up society. He lived by a strict moral code. All the more reason for me to fall in love with him.

I SKIPPED THE Millers' open house on Christmas Day and instead lingered in bed with Edward until hunger drove us out from under the covers. Bundled up in hats and scarfs wrapped about our necks, arms about each other, we went out in search of food. It had begun to snow, tiny little flakes like a saltshaker sprinkling down. The streets were empty, the storefronts dark, ribbons of smoke billowing up from chimneys. The air was scented with a hint of hickory. We finally found a deli open, and sitting near the front window we watched the snow coming down outside while we ate overstuffed corned beef sandwiches and potato pancakes slathered with sour cream and applesauce.

"This is the most untraditional Christmas dinner I've ever had," said Edward, setting his sandwich down before he leaned over to lick a dollop of mustard off my lower lip.

"I knew I should have bought a goose."

"I thought you said you don't cook."

"I don't. You could have made it." I winked.

"We'll break in that kitchen of yours one of these days." Even as he smiled, I saw a sudden sadness pass over his face. "I keep thinking, if I were in Kansas City right now, I'd be at my parents' house—along with my sisters, their husbands and kids, all our other relatives."

"Big family?"

"Sometimes too big." He laughed. "I guarantee you one of the kids has already broken a toy they just got and my uncle Burton and his son are probably drunk and arm-wrestling. My mom's already given up on getting everyone to sing Christmas carols. She tries, though—every year. They make it through the first verse of 'Silent Night' before it peters out. And that's when my father takes over, telling us about how he was so poor growing up they didn't even have one present to open. 'Not one single present, I tell you.'" He laughed, shaking his head. "Jesus—I don't mean to bore you with all this. I guess I'm just feeling a little sentimental. This is the first year I haven't gone home for Christmas."

"Same here." *Why did I say that? Shut up, just shut up!*

"Where is your family?" he asked.

I knew this question was going to surface sooner or later, but I wasn't prepared. My usual one-word explanation—*gone*—wasn't going to be enough this time. It got stuck in my throat. "I—ah . . ."

I shook my head. "C'mon, it's Christmas, I don't want to talk about my family, if you don't mind."

"Well, now you've got me curious."

"Don't be."

"You're not very comfortable with intimacy, are you?"

"What are you talking about? We just had sex. Twice, in fact."

He laughed. "You think sex is intimacy?"

"What do you think it is?"

"I think sex is sex—and it's great, don't get me wrong. But intimacy is something else completely. Intimacy is much more personal than sex."

"More personal than sex?" I rolled my eyes.

"Absolutely. It's a matter of trust. It means you're willing to let someone *really* know you, inside and out. I'd like to be more intimate with you, Gloria. I really would."

He might as well have said he wanted to boil me in oil. "Wow." I dabbed my mouth with my napkin. "I'm so full, I could burst."

"You're really good at changing the subject, aren't you?"

"And you're really good at prying."

"What can I say?" He shrugged. "I'm a prosecutor."

I smiled and reached for a cigarette. "Well, I'm stuffed."

He leaned over, offering me a light. "I guess you'll open up when you're ready."

I inhaled. I exhaled. I picked a fleck of tobacco off my tongue. I was ready to jump out of my skin. Outrunning my past, staying ahead of the lies, produced a frazzled sensation inside my body.

"You okay?" he asked, his eyes grabbing hold of mine, making me want to squirm and twist away.

"Yeah. I think I need some fresh air." My huge secret, lodged inside my chest, was squeezing the life out of me. Things were going so well with us. I didn't want to spoil it. If only I'd told Edward the truth when we first met. If only I'd done the same with Estée and everyone else, I wouldn't have felt so trapped. I'd needed my lie when my father was first arrested. Everywhere I went someone shunned me, saying my father had ruined their life. I'd heard about the death threats my mother received and saw firsthand what my brother's co-workers had done to him. Initially I had to hide behind a lie to protect myself. But now too much time had passed. I was in too deep. I hated myself for lying but didn't know how to get out of it.

After leaving the restaurant, Edward and I walked through Central Park, gloved fingers laced together, shoulders touching. We were talking about the silliness of making New Year's resolutions and I felt the earlier tension at the deli gradually begin to vaporize, replaced by a winter wonderland. The pathways in the park were tamped down with fresh footprints, the tree branches etched with an inch of white. It was all so beautiful and reminded me of a post-card that Leonard might have collected.

When I couldn't take the cold any longer, we went home, built a fire and exchanged gifts that had been waiting for us beneath our sorry little tree. We had agreed ahead of time to buy each other only token gifts. Shaving balm, a tortoiseshell comb and a couple of records for him. And for me, some bath salts, dusting powder and a large beautifully gift-wrapped box that turned out to be a slinky black satin negligee.

I went into the bedroom and slipped it on. "Hey, mister," I said, modeling it for him in the living room, "I thought we had a $10 limit for gifts."

"Yeah, well"—he stood next to me, running his fingers along one of my shoulder straps—"but selfishly, this is sort of a present for me, too."

THE FOLLOWING EVENING was the first time Edward hadn't slept over at my place. We were both exhausted and agreed that we could each use a good night's sleep. So, after dinner, he walked me home and went back to his apartment. I was sound asleep when my downstairs buzzer went off at half past one in the morning.

It was Waller. He'd recently stopped seeing the leggy actress and it was only natural that he'd want to pick up where we'd left off. That had always been our unspoken agreement, but now things were different.

"Not tonight, pal," I said, groggy and gravelly-sounding, speaking into the box next to the door.

"Ah, c'mon. Just let me up. It's freezing out here."

I sighed. After all, Waller was my friend and sooner or later I'd have to tell him that our little sexual arrangement was over. "Oh, okay. Come up. But just for a little bit."

Despite Waller having seen me buck naked dozens of times, I found myself shyly pinching my bathrobe closed at my neck as I let him inside. His overcoat and scarf were damp with snow, and he carried the smell of winter in with him, along with his aftershave. I draped his things over the radiator to dry, and before anything had a chance to get started, I broke the news to him about Edward.

"So, you see, I'm afraid I won't be bedding down with you anymore."

"If I didn't know better," he said, "I'd say you're in love." He had a queer look on his face. Not disappointed exactly, mostly surprised.

"I don't think so—no." I shook my head. "Oh God, actually, I *think* I am. No, I *am. I am* in love."

"Well, good for you." He laughed softly, rubbing his hands together as if trying to warm them.

I felt a little sorry for Waller just then and didn't want to turn him back out into the cold. I knew how he felt. When Waller fell head over heels for the actress, he had turned me away. And it stung.

"Want a beer?" I asked.

"Since when do you keep beer in the house?"

"It's his." I didn't want to say Edward's name. I felt like I was rubbing Waller's nose in it. I got up and went to the icebox. "It's Ballantine." I held up the bottle. "Is that okay?"

"Works for me."

I offered him a glass but he said no, the bottle was fine, and I settled in next to him on the sofa. My feet were cold so I tucked them underneath my bottom. We got to talking about all kinds of things, like the holidays, and he said how the Millers missed me yesterday. We talked about Bobbi and what the odds were of her ever selling her banana art.

"Probably about as good as my landing the part I just auditioned for." He shook his head, giving off a self-deprecating laugh. "I highly doubt I'm getting a callback."

"Be positive."

"Yeah, right. Sure." He changed the subject and asked how things were going at Saks, and after we'd exhausted that topic, he brought up what was happening over in Europe. "I just keep thinking," he said, picking at the label on his second beer, "what if I was over there? They'd slap an armband on me. They'd make me wear a star."

I looked at him a bit astonished. "Wait a minute—you're Jewish?"

"Of course I'm Jewish."

"Well, how would I know?"

He raised an eyebrow.

"You never said anything."

"Why would I? Did you ever tell me what you are—Catholic? Episcopalian? Presbyterian?"

I shrugged, acknowledging his point, and he continued. "You read about what's going on in England and France, all over Europe," he said, peeling off a piece of the label, dropping it on the coffee table. "I know everyone thinks we should stay out of it, but I don't think the U.S. should just sit back and do nothing. I really don't."

We continued to talk about it while he finished his beer. "It's getting late," he said, yawning. "I should probably get going."

I wasn't sure but thought his *probably* carried an enormous question mark with it. "Yeah," I said. "It's late."

"Well"—he shrugged on his coat—"I can't lie, I'm gonna miss you, kid, but I'm happy for you. Really, I am."

"It's not like I'm going away," I said, tugging his scarf off the radiator and looping it around his neck. "I'll still see you."

"I know. But it won't be the same." He pulled me in close and kissed the crown of my head.

I closed the door behind him, flooded with a bittersweet rush.

24

1941

ESTÉE CAME BACK from Palm Beach right after New Year's. She told me all about her trip over coffee at a café off Columbus Circle, simply called the Circle. It was a cozy little place with colorful plates from Portugal mounted along a brick wall. Like the Onyx Club, the Circle had become our place: a retreat on bad days, a place to celebrate on good ones. Whatever drove us there, the cheerful atmosphere and their fresh-brewed coffees were always welcoming. Estée and I were crowded into our usual corner table, next to a radiator that ticked and clacked as it toasted our toes. The window behind us was streaked with condensation.

"You know, there's something not quite right about Christmas in seventy-five-degree weather," she said. Her arms and the backs of her hands were tawny, but her face remained alabaster. I could almost picture her sunbathing with a wide-brimmed hat shielding her from the neck up. "I missed the snow. And I missed Leonard. I even missed Joe."

"Didn't you two talk every day?" I asked, stirring my coffee, remembering what Harriet had said. Poor Harriet. She was so completely threatened by Estée, and with good reason.

"We did," Estée said. "We talked all the time. But those were just quick calls. I tried to keep them under three minutes. So expensive to talk long distance." She tsk-tsked.

Mostly she'd called Joe, needing him to go to her apartment and ship more creams, more lotions, and send her more labels. And Joe, being Joe, did it without complaint. He managed to fit in Estée's requests around his new job, having left the zipper business to sell women's shoes—wholesale.

"We're going to celebrate a belated Christmas," said Estée. "And Joe's birthday. I think Leonard would like that. Joe would, too, I'm sure." She smiled, scooted her coffee cup aside and asked, "How is this thing going with Harriet?" Before I could answer, she tacked on, "And don't tell him I asked about her. Okay? Promise?"

"The two of you." I shook my head at the irony.

"What?"

"Oh, c'mon. He's always asking about Van and you're always asking about Harriet. Isn't it obvious?"

"Isn't *what* obvious?"

"You *know* what." I was frustrated with both of them. Joe didn't belong with Harriet any more than Estée belonged with Van.

And speaking of Van, I found it curious that Estée hadn't mentioned him. Not once. Finally, I couldn't help myself. "And so," I ventured, "how were the holidays with Van?"

She sighed, poured a dollop of cream in her coffee. "You were right about Christmas. He spent it with *her.* But he made it up to me." She held out her arm, displaying a gorgeous gold bracelet with a single charm shaped like a heart and engraved: *E & V.*

"That's spectacular," I said. And it was, although I couldn't believe that shiny bauble had been enough to pacify her.

"Now when are you going to tell me about this new fella you met?"

I was taken aback. "How do you know about that?"

"Joe told me. He said *Harriet* told him you'd met someone. Someone *special*."

I felt my cheeks warming, all of me warming. "Oh, Estée, I did. I did meet someone and I'm crazy about him."

"You have to introduce me to him. Pronto!"

THAT SUNDAY, SHE invited Edward and me over to her house for dinner. We rang the buzzer, expecting Estée, but instead it was Joe who answered the door.

"I didn't know you'd be here," I said, hugging him. "Joe, this is Edward. Edward, this is Joe, Estée's—" I paused, not sure how to label him.

"Estée's ex-husband," Joe volunteered, shaking Edward's hand.

"I'll be right out," Estée called from the kitchen. "Make yourselves at home."

While Joe took our coats, hung them in the front closet, I introduced Edward to Leonard, who was seated in the corner with a fresh pile of postcards to add to his collection. I noticed a photograph on the fireplace mantel of Estée and Van, their arms tight about each other, both of them smiling. And next to that was Joe and Estée's wedding picture. It was odd to see her two lives side by side like that. Unlike me, she wasn't hiding a thing.

Estée appeared a few minutes later, radiant in a rose-colored knit jersey dress, balancing a platter of sauerkraut balls on the palm of her hand like a waitress. As soon as she put the appetizers down and set her eyes on Edward, I knew she approved. She hugged him, kissing both his cheeks even before she said hello to me.

Estée was a natural hostess. She made it look so easy but I could tell she'd gone to a great deal of trouble that night. The table had been meticulously set with her good china, and marvelous scents were coming from the kitchen, which usually smelled of face cream and lotions. For dinner she served some sort of smoked meat with an egg on top along with cheese dumplings.

"This is one of my grandmother's recipes. It's a very popular dish back in Austria," she said, straightening her cuff so that Van's bracelet slid down to her wrist, catching the light.

"Gloria mentioned you were born there," said Edward, cutting into one of the dumplings, releasing a burst of steam.

"Oh yes, well— Oops!" Estée sprang up from her chair. "I almost forgot the rolls. Would you get the serving platter down for me, sweetheart?" she said to Joe.

Sweetheart? What was going on with the two of them? I thought maybe they'd ditched Harriet and Van and had gotten back together when I wasn't looking. But later when I went to the powder room, I saw all of Estée's products displayed on a glass shelf, along with a man's gold razor and a bottle of Van's aftershave. Hanging off the back of the door was a terry cloth robe with a *V* on the breast pocket, embroidered in gold stitching. I felt bad for Joe and wondered what all Van's leave-behinds were doing to him. But he didn't appear to mind. He and Estée seemed so natural, so at ease. There wasn't an awkward glance or a strained moment between them.

On our way home that night, Edward turned to me. "The two of them—they're divorced, right?"

"They sure are."

"Well, that's the happiest divorced couple I've ever seen. They act like they're still in love."

"That's because they are. I just wish they'd hurry up and realize it."

BY MID-JANUARY I achieved a new milestone. I—formerly Gloria Dowaziac, now Gloria Downing—was the number one salesgirl in the cosmetic department. Unlike most of the girls who had been hired directly by the cosmetic companies and then approved by Saks Fifth Avenue, I had been promoted from within the department store, and that allowed me to sell across all the lines—Arden, Rubinstein, Revlon, Dorothy Gray, Germaine Monteil. It gave me a slight advantage, but still, I was proclaimed the best among all the shopgirls at Saks. They gave me a gold ribbon for my name tag. None of the other girls could begin to touch my numbers, which I'm sure they weren't happy about. Especially Vivian.

This validation appealed to the tiger in me and I began breaking my own sales records. I couldn't say what the other girls did on break, but I used that free time to study the marketing materials for various products. I was especially intrigued by Revlon's new line of lipsticks and matching nail lacquer colors. What a stroke of genius. I polished my nails and coated my lips in their newest Berry Red shade and took great pleasure in showing it off to each of my customers. They also thought it was brilliant and I ended up selling matching lipsticks and nail polishes so quickly I could barely keep up with the demand.

One afternoon a rather attractive dark-haired man in an expensive-looking suit came up to the counter as I was finishing up with another customer. He drummed his fingers impatiently, making no attempt to hide the fact that he was watching me. His gaze sent a prickly rush down my spine.

As soon as I closed the sale, he stepped forward and removed a little notebook from his breast pocket. "What's your name, young lady?" He produced a fountain pen, poised, waiting for me.

"Gloria," I said, my eardrums filling with the pounding of my heartbeats.

"Gloria what?"

Oh God. I wasn't sure I could get another word out.

"Miss?"

"Downing," I managed to eke out.

"Downing. Gloria Downing." He nodded, capped his pen, stuffed the notebook back into his pocket and disappeared.

Once he was out of view, the real panic kicked in. Maybe he was with the police. Undercover security for the store. Maybe someone from my past had reported me, I thought, remembering the day Jennifer and Joan wandered into the lingerie department. I knew it was all so illogical, but I wasn't thinking clearly. I was convinced that one way or another, I was going to be found out. It didn't matter how many times I tried to comfort myself, repeating over and over again that it was my father—not me. I hadn't done anything wrong. Still, I feared Saks Fifth Avenue would never keep a Dowaziac on their payroll.

"WHAT'S BOTHERING YOU?" Edward asked, kneading my shoulders. "You've been uptight all night."

We were at my place, eating the one dish I had mastered, grilled cheese with bacon and tomato. He'd brought over a good bottle of Barbera d'Alba. I was on my second glass, having barely touched my sandwich. I kept thinking about that man who'd approached me at work earlier that day. My conscience was getting the better of me and I feared that my secret was about to unravel.

I was in love with Edward. I had no doubt about that, but I was withholding an enormous part of myself from him. He was withholding a secret handshake while I had a father in prison, a mother with a fairly serious drinking problem and two siblings whom I barely spoke to. And after that man had approached me at work, I didn't want Edward finding out who I was from anyone other than me.

"I have something to tell you," I ventured, my voice edgy as I took another sip of wine.

I felt his hands stiffen on my shoulders. "I thought we were being careful."

"Oh God, no. It's not that."

"Oh, okay." He exhaled, his breath warm against my neck. "Well, then what is it?"

I twisted around, letting my eyes meet his, terrified that he'd never look at me this way again.

"Gloria? You're starting to scare me. What is it? Are you sick?"

"No, no. It's nothing like that. It's—it's about me. It's about my past."

"Oh-kay." He took a sip of wine, more like a glug. "Go on."

"I don't even know where to begin." I rubbed my temples till they hurt. "It's just that I think you should know that my last name isn't really Downing." I paused, watching the confusion gather on his face. I'd made it this far. I was right at the edge. All I had to do was tumble forward and let the words out. "I had it changed. It was . . . Dowaziac."

It took a moment for that to register and then he pursed his lips, contemplating. "Any relation to Gustaw Dowaziac?"

The walls around me went soft, everything falling out of focus as the rest spilled out. "Gus Dowaziac—he's, well, he's my father."

"I see." He nodded and refilled both our glasses.

"No one else knows. But I had to tell you."

"Wow . . ." The full impact seemed to have just hit him. He nodded some more and dragged a hand across his face. "Wow," he said again, followed by a long stretch of silence. "How— I mean, did you know what was going on?"

"No. God, no! I swear I didn't."

"How did you find out about it?"

"Pretty much the same way everyone else did. These men came to the house and arrested him. I didn't even know what for." I pictured my father's hands behind his back, the sleeves on his suit jacket straining as the metal cuffs clashed against the leather band of his Waltham wristwatch. I shook my head to clear the image.

"I don't know what to say." He sighed, contemplated the wine bottle.

His silence was unbearable and I began babbling. "I feel like my entire childhood was one big giant lie. I'm so angry with him. And maybe this makes me a horrible daughter, but I can't go see him in prison. I can't even write to him." My voice was cracking, the tears building up behind my eyes. "And because of that, my mother and I don't talk. At all. I feel like I've been orphaned." I blinked, letting loose a string of tears that were coming fast and hard. I'd never cried in front of Edward before and didn't want to do it then, either, but I couldn't stop myself. I was so ashamed, so humiliated. My heart was in my lungs. I could barely breathe. I dropped my face to my hands, my shoulders shaking.

He reached over and tried to put his arms around me, but I pushed him away when all I wanted was for him to hold me. "Now do you understand why I didn't want to tell you about my family?"

"So why are you telling me now?" he asked, his voice so reasonable, so sincerely wanting to understand.

All I could do was mumble through my tears, telling him about the man who'd been asking questions at my counter. "I figured if the truth is going to come out, you should hear it from me, not from anyone else."

"Oh." He sounded disappointed and hurt.

This started me sobbing all over again because I knew I'd given him the wrong answer. He'd wanted me to tell him the truth because I trusted him, because I wanted us to be closer, and not because I felt backed into a corner, forced into a confession. This made me no different from my father, who would have gone on running his Ponzi scheme had he not been caught.

When I was all cried out, I dared to look at him and immediately wished I hadn't. "Oh God, say something. Please?"

He drew a deep breath. "This is a lot to take in," he said. "It's not some small insignificant thing you're telling me."

That was pretty much what Tommy had said just moments before he dumped me. I couldn't handle that again. My wall was going up. "You know what—don't say anything. I don't want to hear it. Just"—I shot up off the couch and opened the front door—"just go. Leave."

He stepped in front of me and closed the door. "Would you give me a chance here?"

"Why? So you can say I'm just like my father—just another liar?" I tried yanking the door back open but couldn't budge it past him.

"Gloria, I didn't say that—"

"You didn't have to. I can see it on your face. You're gonna leave me anyway, so just go now." I made another fruitless attempt to open the door.

"Gloria"—he offered a faint laugh—"can I just point out here that I never said anything about leaving you? You're the one trying to throw me out."

He was being logical, and I was being me. I slunk back over to the sofa, feeling foolish and confused. "I shouldn't have said anything. I should have just kept my mouth shut."

"Listen, I'm not happy about this. I'm not going to pretend this is great news." He came and sat down beside me. "And I'm not going to pretend that I know how you're feeling or what you've been through—"

"Oh God, I never wanted you to see this side of me. It's so ugly and I'm so embarrassed. And I'm no better than he is. I've been lying to you all this time. Ever since I met you."

"Are we done here?"

"You are leaving, aren't you?"

"I meant, are you done flogging yourself? You're still Gloria to me. You weren't the one running the Ponzi scheme."

His compassion just then shattered me. I hung my head in my hands, my heart gaping open. "I don't want to lose you over this, but I just don't know how to make it right."

After a long pause, he sighed. "Well, maybe you need to change your name again?"

I stared through splayed fingers at the hardwood floor. "What good would that do?" Changing my name again wasn't going to change the facts. Inventing Gloria Downing had been exhausting. "What am I supposed to change it to this time?"

"I don't know. You tell me—how does Gloria Clifford sound?"

"What?" I lifted my head and looked at him.

He brushed the hair from my face, which fell back in place, strands sticking to my tear-streaked cheeks. "Mrs. Edward Clifford." He broke into a smile for the first time that night.

"What are you saying?" I shook my head. "Edward? Did you just ask me to marry you?"

He lifted me off the sofa and placed me on his lap, wrapping his arms about me. "I believe I did, yes."

25

SO IN SPITE of it all, I was engaged. Unbelievable. Bobbi was ecstatic when I told her. So was Estée, who reached for my hand and carefully appraised my engagement ring. It had originally belonged to Edward's great-grandmother: an old European cut, just a shade over one and a half carats, set in a lovely gold band.

Estée whistled through her teeth. "He did good," she said. "Just make sure you get those prongs checked regularly."

"Prongs?"

"Oh my, yes. That's the only thing holding the stone in the setting. When I was married to Joe, my diamond came loose. One of the prongs was bent. The stone fell right out. Thank God we heard it hit the floor. But can you imagine losing that diamond?"

Now Estée had given me something new to worry about. I never thought such a thing was possible although it made perfect sense. Still, I'd never heard of this *prong checking* before. I never remembered my mother or sister or any of my married and engaged friends ever mentioning prongs. "Where do you get them checked?"

"Any jewelry store can do it," said Estée. "I'm sure the jewelry department at Saks would do it for you."

I looked at my ring, at the six prongs. The prospect of losing Edward's great-grandmother's stone—a diamond that had been in his family for generations—made me nervous.

But knowing that Edward wanted to marry me, even after hearing the truth, filled me with such a sense of relief. It seemed there was nothing I couldn't share with him, and now I felt an urgent need to come clean about everything. I wanted to prove to him that I had nothing more to hide. I reached way back into my earliest memories, trying to recall every bad, dishonest thing I'd ever done.

One night as we sat on opposite ends of the sofa, his hands gently massaging my feet, I once again unburdened myself to him, my father confessor.

". . . I did that," I said. "I actually paid the girl to write my book report."

"How much did you pay her?" He laughed.

I gave his hands a shove with my foot. "I'm serious. I read the book. I could have written the report myself, but I didn't want to."

"C'mon now," he said, "what kid didn't cheat on a test or book report?"

"And then—then there was this drugstore right on the corner of Sixty-Fifth and Fifth. They had this big rack of candy bars—Sugar Babies and Red Hots, Mallo Cups and Moon Pies—you name it. Anyway, I'd go in there after school, and when the clerk wasn't looking, I'd fill my pockets with whatever I could grab."

He laughed again. "I think stealing candy from the corner store is a rite of passage."

"But that's not the worst of it. I didn't even want the candy. I wouldn't even eat it. Instead, I'd hide it in Gail's bedroom so she'd get in trouble for it."

"Well, from what you've told me, Gail had it coming." He laughed and went back to massaging my toes.

I pulled my feet free and sat up. "And don't forget I fabricated a couple of dead parents, erased my sister's existence altogether, and I only acknowledge my brother when I need money. What kind of vile person does those sorts of things?"

"A person with a shitty family who's trying to distance herself from them."

"And I feel guilty about doing that. I feel like I *should* go see my father. I *should* go see my mother. I *should* try to make peace with my sister. I *should*—"

"You have a lot of *should*s in there." He leaned over and playfully tapped my temple. "Someday your feelings about your family may change."

I gave him a skeptical look.

"Or maybe not." He smiled. "Look, I know part of you wants me to tell you what a horrible person you are but I'm sorry"—he shrugged—"I can't do it. Won't do it." He kissed me on my forehead. "Do you feel better now that you got all that *terrible* stuff off your chest?"

I nodded, though there was more to atone for. Always more. Which was not to say that talking to Edward didn't help. It did, temporarily. He had a way of convincing me that I was a good, decent person despite my family. But I couldn't sustain that for very long. It always slipped away, replaced by some residual guilt that crept in, settling into my bones like a fever. When I looked in the mirror, I still saw my father's daughter. True, I didn't steal anything beyond candy, but I was manipulative, just like him. I learned from the best. He taught me how to charm people, how to get what I wanted.

I smiled at Edward now, fiddling with the radio dial, searching for the *Lux Radio Theatre*, which was our favorite program. Sometimes I wondered why he still wanted to marry me. He knew I was a slob, knew I couldn't cook, knew I wasn't a virgin, knew about my father in Sing Sing—not exactly wife material. He also knew that I was capable of lying to those closest to me: Estée, Bobbi, the Millers—even to him.

Edward had his flaws, too, but they were minor in comparison. My handsome, sexy prince was forever misplacing his keys, his cigarettes and lighter. Since I'd known him, he had misplaced half a dozen of those little plastic dime-store combs. It was only a matter of time before he'd lose the beautiful tortoiseshell comb I gave him for Christmas, too. Edward was also a dreadfully poor manager of his time, not doing anything until the absolute last minute. He was always running late. We regularly lost dinner reservations, missed the opening credits at the picture show, walked in late on the first act of plays.

And what if the man who put off everything to the last minute realized he'd rushed into this marriage proposal? What if he decided he couldn't get past the Ponzi scheme after all? That was what gnawed at me, keeping me up at night.

ONE DAY, AFTER a colleague at the jewelry counter had assured me that my prongs were fine and that my stone was secure, I went to the cosmetic department and wiped down the glass showcase. I was transfixed by the sparkle of my ring, endlessly fascinated by how it caught the light every time I moved my hand. I was lost in all this when Mrs. Coopers came up to me.

"Miss Downing?"

It was the way she said my name that told me I was in trouble. Up until that point, I had almost forgotten about the man who'd taken down my name the week before. But now he was all I could think about and I realized my time had come.

"Mr. Bates would like to see you in his office."

"Mr. Bates?" He was one of the big bosses, second-in-command next to Adam Gimbel, president of all of Saks Fifth Avenue. I'd never met Mr. Bates before, wasn't even sure I'd ever set eyes on him. I closed the cash register drawer with both my hands. I glanced down at my engagement ring and wondered if maybe this wasn't about my being a Dowaziac at all. Maybe they wanted to know if I was planning to quit after I got married, which honestly wasn't something I'd even thought about—especially since Edward and I hadn't set a date yet.

I don't remember if I said anything more to Mrs. Coopers as we headed for the bank of elevators that led to the executive offices. I remember only the clacking of her thick heels against the marble floor as we drew closer and closer to my demise.

Mrs. Coopers showed me in and then left me on my own, closing the door behind her. Mr. Bates's secretary told me to have a seat, asked if I'd like coffee. She was quite nice considering I was about to be fired. I thanked her anyway and sat down next to a stack of fashion magazines: *Vogue*, *Harper's Bazaar*, *Town & Country*. I kept my eyes planted on the floor, taking in the shiny black lace-up shoes that came and went while I listened to the ticking of the wall clock, the murmur of voices, telephones ringing, the burbling of the water cooler in the corner.

At last I was called into Mr. Bates's office. From the doorway it reminded me of my father's old office down on Wall Street with the high-back chair, the leather blotter and a matching pen set on that big desk, the credenza with crystal liquor decanters on top.

As I stepped inside I saw there were two other men seated opposite the desk. I swallowed hard. The one was the man who'd approached me at the counter that day, asking for my name. The other man had a long handsome face and deep-set gray eyes.

Mr. Bates stood up and shook my hand, which surprised me.

"Have a seat, Miss Downing." He gestured to the third chair. Mr. Bates began making introductions, starting with the long-faced man. "This is Bob Fiske. Mr. Fiske is the head cosmetic buyer here at Saks Fifth Avenue." He also stood up and shook my hand. "And this is Charles Revson. Mr. Revson is the president of Revlon. Turns out you made quite an impression on him."

I sidestepped my way to the vacant chair and sat down. I still hadn't really said much of anything, but it was obvious that nothing bad was going to happen. They weren't going to fire me.

Mr. Revson smiled as he produced a pipe from his pocket. "I told Bob here, I said, 'Bob, what the hell are you doing, keeping that gal behind the counter down there? She's obviously got some brains to go along with her looks.'"

If I'd found Charles Revson disconcerting before, he was especially perplexing just then.

"Mr. Revson seems to think that we're underutilizing your talents," said Mr. Bates. "And after speaking with Mrs. Coopers, I happen to think he's right."

"So, ah—" I stumbled, backed up and started over again. "So, what are you saying?"

"We're saying"—Mr. Bates smiled—"that you can thank Mr. Revson here for your new promotion."

"Promotion?"

"Congratulations, Miss Downing, I'm pleased to tell you that you'll now be an assistant cosmetic buyer here at Saks Fifth Avenue, reporting directly to Mr. Fiske."

26

WHEN I LEFT Mr. Bates's office that day, I found it curious that they never asked if I wanted the promotion. They'd just assumed—and rightfully so—that I would accept it. Along with a nice raise.

Estée was thrilled and insisted on taking me to our trusted table at the Onyx Club to celebrate. "Didn't I tell you?" she said. "Didn't I say you could do anything you set your mind to?"

I didn't have the heart to tell her that I had never set my mind on becoming an assistant cosmetic buyer. Something that lofty would have never occurred to me. Still, I was tickled and a bit anxious. Things were going well for me. Maybe a little too well. First my engagement and now this promotion? I kept waiting for something to come along and foul everything up.

"I'm so proud of you!" Estée reached across and squeezed my fingers so tight she crushed my pinky against my engagement ring.

Of course, we both knew that having me in such a pivotal position could only help her chances of getting her products into Saks. Even before our gimlets had arrived, she asked if I could get her a meeting with Mr. Fiske.

"I will if I can," I told her, and I meant it. "But he only meets with sales reps twice a week, so I can't promise anything. But I will try."

Every week, on Wednesdays and Fridays, Mr. Fiske listened to sales pitches from morning until the end of the day. On those days, the reception area would be full of men waiting outside Mr. Fiske's office. They came bearing lotions, potions and elixirs. Some worked for Revlon; others were with Max Factor or Coty or some new company we'd never heard of. Anyone—with the exception of Helena Rubinstein and Elizabeth Arden—who wanted to see their cosmetic products sold in Saks Fifth Avenue had to endure this process.

It wasn't unusual for Mr. Fiske to sit through fifty or sixty pitches a week. And not everyone who arrived got in to see him, either. Week after week, it was the same faces there again, hoping that it would be their lucky day. Part of my job involved screening this eager lot and keeping a log of new products they were pitching. Ultimately, though, it was Mr. Fiske who decided who was worthy of meeting with him. For the most part, I did little more than fetch coffee, take notes, schedule follow-up appointments. Really, I was a glorified secretary, which was part of the reason why I couldn't be of much help to Estée.

Another part of my job and by far the trickiest role I had to play was that of peacekeeper among the cosmetic moguls. And they were some strong flavors, to say the least. I remember the day Mr. Fiske told Madame Rubinstein that Saks Fifth Avenue would not allow her to drop bottles of her new perfume off the rooftop. "It's a safety hazard," he'd explained. "They're afraid someone will get hit on the head and sue us."

"What they should be afraid of is not me dropping bottles but me dropping my account. That's what the real risk is."

It took almost an hour of pleading and another two feet of counter space to convince Madame Rubinstein to keep her business at Saks.

But that was nothing compared to the day I'd made a dreadful mistake that almost cost me this new fancy job of mine. I had inadvertently scheduled Charles Revson and Elizabeth Arden so closely together that their comings and goings overlapped in the waiting room. Elizabeth Arden was already in with Mr. Fiske when Charles Revson arrived some thirty minutes later, touting a pink leather case that he called his Baroness Manicure Kit. His fingernails were also advertising Revlon's latest shade of Cherry Coke lacquer. Only Charles Revson could get away with walking around with red nails and a pink case. He was clearly interested in women and that day, it became apparent that he was interested in me.

Tracing the length of my arm with his polished nails, he said, "I liked you right away. As soon as I saw you. But"—he smiled—"I'd like you even more if you'll have dinner with me. And"—he raised one red nail—"if you give me six more inches of counter space downstairs, I'll give you nine inches of me."

I was appalled. Thankfully I didn't have to acknowledge any of this because at that very moment, the door to Mr. Fiske's office opened and out walked Miss Arden. A petite five feet, two inches tall, with icy blue eyes and lustrous brown hair. She was *très chic.* In her early sixties, she was old enough to have been Revson's mother.

She took one look at him and said, "What is that man doing here?"

"Please inform her royal bitchiness," said Revson, "that *that man* has a name."

"Tell *that man* I have nothing to say to him. Now if you'll excuse me." She stormed out of the waiting room.

What I found fascinating about all these cosmetic magnates, including Charles Revson, was that even though they detested each other, they were all exactly alike. They'd all grown up poor, most were Jewish immigrants, they had enormous egos and they were all competitive workaholics.

I made sure to never again schedule them so closely together or even on the same day. So aside from that initial hiccup, I'm pleased to report that I approached each assignment like the tiger Mrs. Coopers had groomed me to be, often being praised for my initiative, my attention to detail, my professional demeaner. And after nearly two years of working on the floor, standing on my feet for eight hours a day, sitting upstairs in the buying department was a welcome oasis.

Mr. Fiske had the big corner office. He was an energetic boss and had all kinds of little sayings and theories. He reminded me of a male version of Mrs. Coopers. Right after I started, Mr. Fiske called me into his office. He drew a triangle on a sheet of paper. On one side he wrote *Exclusive*, on another side *Good* and on the third side *Cheap*. "Pick any two," he said.

"Pardon me?"

"When it comes to buying cosmetics and dealing with sales reps, you can only have two. They'll try to sell you products that are *exclusive* and *good* but they won't be *cheap*. Or they have something that's *exclusive* and *cheap* but it won't be any *good*. Or you can get it *good* and *cheap* but it won't be *exclusive*. You only get two, never all three. Remember that, Miss Downing."

I actually thought this was a brilliant piece of advice. The answer to all of life's questions. Applicable to any and all situations. Take men for example. *Handsome. Rich. Faithful.* You could have a man who was *handsome* and *faithful* but he wouldn't be *rich*. Or he'd be *rich* and *faithful* but not *handsome*. Or you could get *handsome* and *rich* but forget about him being *faithful*. I glanced at my engagement ring, double-checking the prongs. I had *handsome* and *faithful*. I'd take that combo over the others any day.

The office next to Mr. Fiske belonged to Mr. Belfort, who had a variety of titles. I'd heard him referred to as the department manager, the deputy buying chief and, most commonly, Mr. Fiske's right-hand man. You could smell Mr. Belfort's sweet aromatic pipe tobacco as soon as you stepped off the elevator. He was a quirky gentleman with thick-framed glasses that spent most of their time pushed up onto his forehead. He had a dented wastepaper basket, the result of temper tantrums where he'd kicked it across the room.

I shared an office with the other assistant buyer, Marion Combs. We had a much smaller space than the men, with one tiny window. When I first got the job, Bobbi made me a piece of banana art—a lipstick and compact mirror reflecting a woman's face made entirely out of genuine Chiquita banana peels. The frame was worth more than the artwork, but I loved it. It was highly detailed and so unique, with a splash of color on the background. I hung it on my office wall and nearly everyone passing by commented on it.

Marion, my co-worker, was a beautiful girl in her late twenties with a tumble of auburn hair, enormous blue eyes and alabaster skin that rivaled Estée's in its flawlessness. I sat opposite her at a partner's desk in the office next to Mr. Belfort's.

I remember one morning, while reviewing the sale materials that had just arrived for some new display cases, Mr. Belfort called me into his office.

"What's the status on that Dorothy Gray order, Miss Downing?"

"It's scheduled to arrive at the end of business today."

"Hmmm. Better double-check to make sure enough stock boys are on hand to unload the freight," he said, clamping his back teeth down on his pipe. "The devil is in the details. Always better to be safe than sorry, right?"

"I've already doubled-checked and we should be fine, Mr. Belfort."

He nodded. "You are sharp as a tack, Miss Downing, you know that. Always going the extra mile. You play your cards right and you'll be at the top of your game in no time. It all comes down to how you slice the bologna."

Another thing about Mr. Belfort: he never met a cliché he didn't like, including a few that I swore he invented on the spot. Early on,

Marion warned me about this, saying, "Half the time I have no idea what he's talking about. But don't worry, he's harmless. His bark is worse than his bite, and remember, you can't judge a book by its cover." She winked, making me laugh.

The cosmetic buying department was a fast-paced office. Located on the eighth floor, it was at the end of a long corridor shared with other various buying departments: sportswear, haberdashery, fine dresses, jewelry, shoes and so on. Cosmetics had a private reception area and we had half a dozen secretaries, each one so beautifully dressed and coiffed they looked like they belonged in the Saks Fifth Avenue catalog. There was never a shortage of lipstick-kissed coffee cups resting on the various desks. You always heard telephones ringing, typewriters clacking, adding machines tallying up totals. And the deliveries never stopped. Mail, boxes, telegrams. It kept Soda Pop, our mail boy, busy.

Soda Pop was just a kid, couldn't have been more than sixteen, with shaggy brown hair and peach fuzz on his upper lip. He should have been in school, but instead, he was delivering mail and running packages all around the store. In the mornings he went from office to office with a cart of danish, bagels, coffee and tea. In the afternoon he brought us sandwiches, coffee and bottles of Coca-Cola that rattled as he went from desk to desk.

Soda Pop had a bit of a crush on me. He was forever buzzing around my office, looking for some excuse to talk to me, run an errand for me. He was sweet and only slightly annoying. Soda Pop seemed especially interested in my upcoming nuptials. He'd give me a free doughnut or bagel, perch himself on the edge of my desk and ask the sort of questions I would have expected to come from the office girls: When was I getting married? Was it going to be a big wedding? Where were we going on our honeymoon? I supposed the fact that I had no answers for him—not a single one—said something about me as a bride.

But just the same, I was ever vigilant about my engagement ring's prongs. Every time I accidentally knocked the ring against a door or it got caught on my sleeve, I would run to a jeweler. And always a different one. My colleague in the jewelry department here at Saks said, "Gloria, this is the second time you've asked me about this. If the ring makes you *that* nervous, just put it away and only wear it on special occasions." After that I couldn't go back to him, so I sought out different jewelers in Lower Manhattan. I remember one looked at the ring and said, "This stone is older than both of us combined."

Each time I left a jewelry store, I'd twist the ring around so no one would see the diamond and be tempted to rob me. Much as I didn't want to admit it, I knew I'd inherited this neurosis from my mother. She was a belt-and-suspenders type if ever there was one. The woman ran matches under tap water to make sure they were really out. She brought her own silverware to restaurants, not trusting the kitchen staff to properly sanitize theirs. She never sat beneath light fixtures just in case they came crashing down. *Just in case* ruled my mother's world. It fed right into her hypochondria. She was forever taking precautions—endless unnecessary doctor's appointments, never letting her gas tank dip below the halfway point, taking a cardigan with her in ninety-degree weather.

I could see now that my mother was really just a scared little creature and her fears had bled into me. Maybe it was in our DNA or it had gotten into my system by osmosis, but whatever the case, I could not shake the fact that underneath it all, I was still my mother's daughter as much as I was my father's. Through and through, I was still a Dowaziac.

27

IT WAS THE end of February and Edward's parents were coming to New York to meet me, their future daughter-in-law. They were arriving the following day and the four of us were having dinner at Café Rouge in the Hotel Pennsylvania.

The restaurant had been my idea. I thought his parents would enjoy a big night out on the town and had reserved a table on the terrace level near the giant fountain with a great view of the stage. The big band remote at Café Rouge was broadcasting Woody Herman live that night.

I was nervous about the evening. The last time I'd met someone's parents it hadn't gone well. Tommy's mother had decided she didn't like me even before she'd set eyes on me.

"They're going to love you," Edward assured me as I debated which dress to wear. He was sitting on the side of the bed while I stood before my closet, scooting hangers back and forth. Edward was practically living at my place by then and the closet was getting crowded with his suits and button-down shirts.

"You just have to promise me you won't tell them about, you know"—I looked at him from over my shoulder—"about my father."

"Don't worry. They already know."

"What!" My entire body went into shock, like someone had doused me with ice water.

"I told them." He said this so casually, as if he'd told them I was allergic to anchovies.

I slammed the closet door. "Why did you do that?" I held my head as if it might explode.

"Gloria, relax."

"Relax? You promised. You promised me you'd never tell anyone."

"These aren't *anyone.* These are my parents. They're entitled to know about the woman I'm marrying. I couldn't lie to them."

Stars swirled in my vision. I was sure a vertigo bout was coming on. "What exactly did you tell them? Tell me everything you said."

"I told them about your father," he said, again with such nonchalance I wanted to smack him.

"What specifically? Did you tell them he's in prison?"

"Well, yes. I had to."

"Oh Jesus God." I clasped the sides of my head again, tighter this time. "And?"

"And what?"

"What was their reaction?"

"I don't know. I mean, yeah, they were surprised. It's not exactly what they were expecting. But I assured them it has nothing to do with you."

"It has *everything* to do with me. How am I supposed to meet them now? How am I supposed to look them in the eye?"

"Listen to me. You have to understand, what happened to your father wasn't a big deal outside of New York. Maybe in New Jersey. And Connecticut. I honestly don't even think it made the papers in Kansas City, and if it did, like I said, it wasn't a big deal there. I promise."

He spent the rest of the evening trying, unconvincingly, to reassure me.

The next night, in an appropriate blue dress, I met the Cliffords in the lobby of their hotel, the Plaza—another suggestion of mine. I thought they'd enjoy staying there.

Mr. Clifford, also a lawyer and also a Freemason, wore a similar insignia ring on his little finger. He was distinguished, with a full head of salt-and-pepper hair, the same square jaw as his son. Mrs. Clifford had a nice Midwestern wholesomeness about her. She wore a string of pearls and a fur stole and clasped her clutch with both hands as if she feared someone was going to snatch it.

It didn't take long to realize that Mr. Clifford was not a fan of the big city. The hotel room was too small; everything was too crowded; Café Rouge was too noisy, too expensive.

"If you two plan on staying here in New York after you get married," he said, closing his menu, "you're going to have to leave the D.A.'s office."

Edward laughed.

"I'm serious, son. You've handled some very high-profile cases. Working there's been a wonderful experience for you. A good way to get started, but now it's time to buckle down and make some real money."

"I'm doing okay, Pops."

Pops. He called his father Pops—I had no idea.

"How are you going to support a wife and a family on that salary of yours?"

I watched his father's words settle in on Edward's face. It hit him hard, like it was something he hadn't considered before. "But I love my work," he said.

"Yeah, well, I love golfing, too, but nobody's going to pay me to do it."

There was an uncomfortable moment of silence broken only when the waiter came by to take our drink orders. I asked for a gin martini, same as Edward and his father. Mrs. Clifford requested a dry sherry.

"Let's talk about the wedding plans, shall we?" Mrs. Clifford said, steering the conversation toward me. "Have you picked a date?"

"Actually, we haven't really discussed it yet," I said. "We figure there's no rush, right?"

"Well, I know back home people are already reserving the country club now for June weddings. Have you started putting together the guest list?"

"Ah, no. Honestly, we haven't really gotten that far into the planning," I said. "We've both been so busy."

"Well, you should really get started now. At least finalize your guest list. I know on our side, we have, let's see." Mrs. Clifford began calculating. "There's eighteen, right in our immediate family alone. We have probably another dozen or so couples that would come in for the wedding. Steven—" she said to her husband. "Steven, do you think the Fletchers would come in for the wedding? What about the Bartons?"

"They better come in," Mr. Clifford said. "We went to Detroit for their kid's wedding. And to Cleveland when Marvin and Kate's son got married. And don't forgot about my cousin Wayne and his family. That's another six right there."

"Oh, that's right. My cousin Martha and her family, too. You see how quickly the list grows." Mrs. Clifford laughed.

My head was spinning. A burst of applause erupted at the opening notes of Woody Herman's "Woodchopper's Ball."

"And what about you, Gloria?" She turned to me again. "Do you have a large family?"

My family. I didn't know what to say. I looked at Edward for a rescue, feeling the screws beginning to tighten. The burbling fountain over my shoulder seemed to be growing louder. Mr. Clifford was right. It was too noisy in there.

Mrs. Clifford must have sensed that I was wrestling with this because she reached for my hand under the table and gave me a reassuring squeeze. "You know, all families have skeletons in their closets, dear. Even ours. Did Edward tell you about his uncle Montgomery?"

"Oh God, Montgomery," said Mr. Clifford, finishing off his martini. "At least we don't have to worry about that loon coming to the wedding."

"Such an odd, odd man he was." Mrs. Clifford shook her head. "He never wore leather. No belts, not even leather shoes. And he didn't eat meat or fish or even chicken. He said he wouldn't eat anything that had a mother. That's what he always said. And when he died—well, you'll never guess what they found in his icebox." She winced. "It was filled with dead birds. Hundreds of them," she whispered, saying this like Uncle Montgomery's dead birds were even in the same league with my father's Ponzi scheme. God love her, the woman was trying.

"So, where'd you grow up, Gloria?" Mr. Clifford asked. It was the first time he'd addressed me directly all evening.

"Right here. In New York City."

"Ah, a big-city girl," his father said. "A big-city girl with big-city tastes." He turned to Edward and said, "If I were you, I'd start putting feelers out with some of the firms here. One of my old classmates from law school is a partner with Mason, Smith and Schultz . . ."

I couldn't listen anymore. I ordered a second martini, knowing that I shouldn't have, and scooted my steak and baked potato about my plate.

LATER THAT NIGHT, after dropping his parents off at their hotel, Edward lay across the bed, which he'd made that morning. If left to me—surprise, surprise—the bed rarely got made. And when I did attempt the task, the bedspread ended up hanging half-cocked, the sheets and blankets underneath lumped together in the center. My lackluster housekeeping skills were sort of a running joke between us.

With his tie undone, loafers off and ankles crossed, he stared at the ceiling and said, "Do you think my father's right?"

"About what?" I shimmied out of my dress and lay down beside him in my slip, my head on his chest, my feet resting atop his.

"The D.A.'s office. Maybe he's right. Maybe I should go with a law firm, start making some decent money."

"Oh, c'mon, don't pay any attention to what your father said. You love your job."

He ran his fingertips through my hair in soft, easy strokes. "Yes, but he has a point. I mean, you're going to be my wife soon and I want to be able to take care of you."

"I'm not worried about that."

"Well, I am. You grew up with a lot of money—"

"Other people's money," I corrected him, and pulled away, my legs reflexively moving into a fetal position.

"Don't get upset. I just—I want to make you happy. I want to give you all the things you deserve, but we both know I can't do it on my salary."

"I'm not asking for anything. I'm fine with us just the way we are."

"At some point we have to be practical. This way you could quit your job and—"

"But I don't want to quit. I *want* to work." I closed my eyes, my body curling tighter.

"Okay, that's fine, but you can't say it wouldn't be nice having a little more money to live on."

"But you love your job," I said again. "Don't leave it because of me. I honestly don't care about the money." I sat up, propped my elbows on my knees and held my head in my hands.

"You're telling me you don't want a bigger apartment? Beautiful clothes? What about a maid, since we both know how much you love doing housework?"

"I don't need a maid as long as you don't mind a messy house."

He laughed and playfully tackled me onto the bed, both of us tumbling into each other. We were so perfectly happy, so well matched, so easy together. I wanted to freeze this moment, bottle it and savor it forever.

28

ESTÉE AND I were standing shoulder to shoulder, our gloved hands sharing the metal pole as our packed subway train shimmied along the tracks. It was my day off and we were heading to Gimbels. Estée was leading the charge, insisting it was time to shop for my wedding dress. She thought Gimbels was the best place to start since I couldn't afford any of the gowns in the Saks Fifth Avenue bridal department, even with my employee discount.

"Did you remember?" Estée asked.

"Remember what?"

"To ask Mr. Fiske if he'll meet with me?"

"Oh, that." My fingers tightened around the pole. "I haven't had a chance yet. Sorry."

Her red lips sagged into a pout.

"I'll ask him. I promise. But honestly, I doubt he'll agree to a meeting just because you're my friend." Her pout blossomed. "And don't look at me like that. He's a very busy man. He'll tell you to get in line just like everyone else."

"Oh, but I'm not like everyone else."

"*I* know that, and *you* know that. But Mr. Fiske"—I shook my head—"he doesn't know that."

"Not yet he doesn't."

We came to our stop at Herald Square and shuffled our way through the crowd and up the stairs that led us right into the housewares department. Gimbels was no Saks Fifth Avenue, that was for certain. You felt it the moment you stepped inside: glaring overhead lights, customers rifling through merchandise piled up on tables, shopgirls shouting across the floor to each other for price checks.

We were approaching a wire bin of pillows, tossed inside all willy-nilly. A big sign was hanging off the side: 75% KAPOK FILLING. $2.59 EA.

"Say, that's not a bad price." Estée pulled me over to the bin. "I should really get some new pillows while we're here. I'm past due." She reached inside the bin, scrunching, squeezing, discarding one that was too soft and pulling out another one. "When was the last time you replaced your pillows?"

"What? I don't know. Why?"

"They say you need to get new pillows every two years," she told me. "Pillows are breeding grounds for dust mites. Did you know that the average person sheds eight pounds of skin cells a year, and that lands in your pillow and breeds dust mites? They actually feed on your dead skin cells."

"That's disgusting."

"But it's true. And that's why you have to replace your pillows on a regular basis."

Only Estée knew this sort of thing. She was an encyclopedia of little-known domestic facts and cure-alls. She cleaned her coffee percolator with vinegar and seasoned cast iron skillets with vegetable oil. She had a million and one uses for baking soda and lemon juice and knew which stains to blot and which ones required scrubbing.

Estée eventually found the pillows she liked but didn't want to carry them around the store. She said she'd get them on the way out, which she didn't end up doing because by then, we were caught up in the business of my being a bride.

I must have tried on a dozen different gowns. Too poofy, too plain, too high waisted, too low-cut, the fabric either too rough or too slippery.

"I just don't know what you're waiting for," Estée said when I came out of the dressing room to model yet another reject. She was asking why Edward and I hadn't set a date for the wedding.

"We've been busy. He's got a big case. There's no rush."

"No rush?" Estée laughed. She was down on her knees, fluffing out the train of my dress. "You sure were in a rush to get engaged."

"Help me with these buttons, will you?" I asked, starting with the ones I could reach.

She straightened to her full five feet, four inches. "Well, believe me, if Van asked me to get married, I wouldn't drag my heels. I wouldn't give him a chance to get away."

"What's going on with his divorce?" I said, trying to shift the subject, and as soon as I did, I felt Estée's hands stiffen on my buttons.

"*She's* the one holding everything up. Not Van. If it was up to him, he would have been divorced ages ago and we'd be out shopping for *my* wedding gown."

We left Gimbels empty-handed and Estée suggested we go to Bonwit Teller. "You know," she said, "just to look. Let's see what they have."

It was an unseasonably warm day for March, and it felt good to walk with our coats open, the sun shining through the buildings. We were heading down Fifth and at 56th Street we came upon a cluster of women. They were pointing to the cloudless sky, all of them looking up, shielding their eyes.

I thought someone was about to jump until I, too, looked up and saw a flurry of balloons—pink and blue—floating feather-like through the air. On second glance, I saw that they were coming from the rooftop of Bonwit Teller. The balloons were attached to little baskets, drifting lazily through the breeze. No one knew what they were until one woman grabbed hold of a basket and squealed, "Look, everyone. It's perfume! It's perfume from heaven!"

That was all it took for Estée to charge the sidewalk like a quarterback. She got hold of a basket and sure enough, nestled inside like a stork-delivered newborn was a tiny vial of perfume: Heaven Sent by Helena Rubinstein.

I THOUGHT EDWARD and I had come to an agreement about his career, but I was wrong. In the spring of that year he left the D.A.'s office and accepted a position at Sperry, Wilson & Briggs. He was made partner with a starting salary of $575 a month.

It wasn't as if money were no object, but suddenly there was talk of a bigger apartment and a honeymoon to either Niagara Falls or the Poconos. We'd heard that the latter had double beds and heart-shaped bathtubs. We dined out more often and in better restaurants, we drank better bottles of wine. But there was a price to pay for all that because Edward's new salary came with a hefty moral burden.

One night we were having dinner at Beefsteak Charlie's and I could see that something was bothering him. He looked tired, distracted; his mind was far away. After our cocktails arrived, I asked what was wrong.

"Nothing."

"You can tell me," I pressed.

"You know I can't talk about this case. It's confidential information."

I knew what case he was referring to. It was a high-profile homicide case. The client—a rich, well-known Manhattan real estate developer—had been accused of not only cooking the books but also murdering his wife. News of the man's arrest had sent shock waves up and down New York's café society. As more facts were released to the press—the deceased wife's having taken a lover, the deceased wife's threatening to divorce him and take her considerable family fortune with her, the husband's having taken out a life insurance policy on the now deceased wife—it became obvious that, yes indeed, the man had murdered his wife.

"You don't have to say a word," I told him. "I can see it all over your face. You know he's guilty. You know he did it and—"

"I don't *know* that he did it."

"Oh, c'mon, *everybody* knows he did it."

"The man is entitled to a defense, Gloria. A person is presumed innocent until proven guilty." He rubbed his forehead, squeezed his eyes shut.

"I hate seeing you like this." I set my drink aside and reached for his hand. He tilted his head, pleading with me to drop it. But I couldn't. "Let's face it, Edward, you don't have the stomach for this kind of work. It goes against everything you stand for. I think you should resign. Just quit—just walk away. The money's not worth it."

But I could tell he was getting used to the better wine, the restaurants. It was hard to go backward once you'd had a taste of the finer things. No one understood that better than me.

"I'll tell you what," I said, perking up. "I just got that nice raise and who knows—I could get another promotion. My salary's only going to go up from here."

"What are you suggesting?"

"I'm saying why don't you quit the law firm, go back to the D.A.'s office and—"

"And what? Let *you* be the breadwinner?"

"Well, why not? It's nothing to be ashamed of."

"Great. Why don't you just slice my balls off now."

"Edward, good God, that's not what I'm trying to do."

He blew out a deep sigh that made his shoulders rise and fall. "I know that. I didn't mean to take it out on you. I'm sorry."

And I knew he was. It wasn't his style to snap at me and I should have accepted his apology and let it go, but that wasn't *my* style. "I'm trying to help you," I said. "You know when they were married, Estée always made more money than Joe."

"Yeah, and look where that got them."

"So what, you're going to suffer through a job you hate? Why? Just so you can flaunt your worth? Show everyone what a big man you are?"

"Hey—I'm not that guy and you know it. Why are you getting mad at me?"

Now that was an excellent question, and though I couldn't pinpoint the answer just then, I knew I was furious. I pounded my fist to the table, making the plates and glasses jump, drawing attention to my outburst. "I'm mad because I don't want our life to change." But what I meant was, *I don't want* you *to change.*

"Who in the hell said anything about our lives changing?"

Despite being a prosecutor turned defender, Edward wasn't confrontational. At least not with me, he wasn't. We weren't big arguers, although now that he'd changed jobs, we seemed to be doing a lot more bickering and outright fighting.

"Since when do you care so much about material things anyway?" I asked.

"Gloria, I live in a dump. You live in a slightly better dump. I don't think wanting to find a halfway decent apartment makes me materialistic."

And it was precisely *because* Edward was a prosecutor turned defender that when we did argue—he was infuriatingly cool, so logical it set my teeth on edge. He had a way of reducing my positions to those of an emotionally dim-witted adolescent. It was humiliating.

Now he'd flustered me completely, shot enough holes in my defense that all I could do was fire back with a flimsy, unsubstantiated claim: "Why does this damn job mean more to you than I do?"

"What the hell? Do you hear yourself?" He was incredulous. "You know what"—he threw his napkin on the table and signaled the waiter—"I'm not having this conversation with you. Not here. Not right now."

We weren't speaking when he got the check and paid the bill. We got into a taxicab and rode home in silence, each of us staying on our side of the seat. When I told the driver there were going to be two stops, Edward looked at me, a streetlight revealing his surprise.

"I'm tired," I said. "I need a good night's sleep."

"No."

"No?"

"It's going to be just the one stop," he called to the driver.

"Fine." I folded my arms in a huff. "Suit yourself."

I didn't even get the apartment door shut when he grabbed me by the shoulders and made me look at him. His eyes were shimmering, bluer than normal. "What is going on with you? This isn't just about my job and you know it."

He was right. I had conflated Edward and my father. I had advanced through time and saw Edward going down a path of corruption, cashing in his integrity for a paycheck. I saw him changing, becoming a person I no longer recognized, just like my father.

"I don't want to fight with you about this, Gloria."

"I don't want to fight with you, either," I said, clutching his lapel. "I just want you to be happy. I want *us* to be happy."

"That's all I want, too." He leaned forward, pressing his forehead to mine. "So, what are we arguing about, huh? Can we put this behind us and start looking for an apartment that isn't on the verge of collapse?"

I wrapped my arms around his waist and nodded. I knew if I spoke, I'd only say something stupid and reignite the tension.

From that night on, Edward continued working to free a guilty man while I found new jewelers to check the prongs on my engagement ring.

29

AND SO, IT was over with Estée and Van. She telephoned me on a Saturday afternoon and, in a fragile voice, asked if I could come over.

"I had to end it," she sobbed, breaking down in my embrace when I arrived at her apartment. She was dead weight in my arms and it took some maneuvering to walk her over to the sofa. She had that heavy-lidded, pasty-skinned look of someone who wasn't sleeping, wasn't eating. It was one of the only times I'd ever seen her without a trace of makeup. She was a wreck, and it was a good thing that Leonard was with Joe that weekend. He didn't need to see his mother like this.

"You did the right thing," I said.

"If I did the right thing, why do I feel so awful?"

"Aw, sweetie, that's the price you have to pay for your dignity and self-respect."

"He left me no choice," Estée said, struggling to get a cigarette lit. Her hands were shaking so badly that I finally reached over and lit it for her.

"I had to give him an ultimatum. I said, 'Leave your wife or we're through.' And now he's gone. I've lost him. In the end, he just couldn't do it. He couldn't walk out on her." She drew down on her cigarette and took a sip of coffee, the cup clattering in the saucer as her hands trembled.

"What have you got in this place besides coffee?" I asked. "Caffeine is not going to cut it."

She pointed to the liquor cabinet, and I got busy making gin martinis while she continued to lament over Van.

"I still love him, Gloria. I really do."

Honestly, I didn't believe that. She loved his power, his prestige, and the promise that he'd provide her with the lifestyle she'd been raised with, the lifestyle she so desperately wanted to reclaim. It was the idea of Van that she was in love with. Not Van himself.

"Oh," said Estée with a sigh, "but he could be so charming."

My father could be charming, too.

"Remember what a wonderful storyteller Van was? And his magic tricks. He could hold the whole room spellbound."

My father knew how to hold court, too.

"Van was smart and worldly and sophisticated."

"And rich," I said, handing her a drink. "You forgot rich."

"Don't," she said, wincing, taking a sip.

I raised my hands. "I'm sorry. I'm not going to kick you when you're down."

"And thank you for not saying 'I told you so.' I know you never liked him." She reached inside her pocketbook and plucked out her compact. "God, I look a fright. Can you tell I've been crying?"

"Well, yes, but—"

"I need to put my face on," she said, getting up, heading toward her bedroom.

I knew that would probably make her feel better, maybe more so than the gin, though I could tell the martini was helping, too. I followed her into the bedroom and leaned against the dresser while she sat at her vanity, the top populated with bottles and jars of her lotions and cold creams.

"I feel like such a fool. I'm so tired," Estée said, saturating a wad of cotton with her Cleansing Oil. Watching her at work with her beauty routine was a bit like watching an artist. Her teacup hands moved with such precision, and after the cleanser came the moisturizer, the rouge, eyeshadow and face powder.

"I thought Van was going to introduce me to the right people. Help me get my business off the ground," she said, uncapping her red lipstick and adding that final touch. In under five minutes—which had always been her sales pitch promise—she looked like Estée again. "Now what am I going to do?"

"You're going to do what you've always done. You're going to pick yourself up and move forward. That's exactly what you would tell me to do. You don't need Van's help. Look at all that you've done already, and all by yourself. Look at how far you've come. You are Estée Lauder, and as you've told me over and over again, 'You can do anything you set your mind to.'"

She looked at me through the mirror, her eyes still dewy. "Van was never the answer, was he?"

I shook my head. "Estée, *you're* the answer. You have been all along." As I said those words, I caught my reflection in the mirror, and something sparked inside me. It was as if I'd been speaking to myself. *I am the answer. I have been all along.*

Estée smiled. "Do I look okay? I don't want Joe to know I've been crying."

"Joe?"

"We're having dinner tonight."

I tried to hide my surprise, but according to Harriet, Joe was supposed to be having dinner with her that night.

"I need him now," Estée said. "I just need to keep busy, keep my mind off Van."

I LEFT ESTÉE'S place and decided to walk through Central Park. It was the end of April. A perfect spring day. And I enjoyed taking in the crocuses and tulips, the fresh green leaves just beginning to sprout all around. As I headed down a pathway, I saw a young boy, maybe six or seven years old. He was on the grass with a man I assumed was his father. The father was on his knees, palms facing out, while the little boy stood before him, throwing punches.

It reminded me of my father teaching Glenn to box. Glenn had always been a gentle soul, not terribly coordinated or athletic, much to my Hemingwayesque father's chagrin. I remember after Glenn came home from school one day with a black eye, my father had been determined to make a fighter out of his son. Just like that man in the park, my father instructed Glenn to punch him. *Harder. Harder,* he'd yelled at Glenn. *You call that a punch,* Glenda*? Your little sister can hit harder than that.* My father wanted Glenn to *make mincemeat out of that punk*. Glenn was terrified to fight, but even more terrified of disappointing my father. So, Glenn marched back to school the next day and slugged the boy, returning home with not one but two black eyes. Poor Glenn, he'd been trying all his life to prove to my father—and yet failing miserably—that he was a tough guy after all.

I realized I'd been staring at the little boy and his father and swiftly moved on.

It was almost five when I got home. I couldn't put off cleaning the kitchen any longer. Dishes from the night before were stacked on the counter, waiting for me to get to them. Edward offered his assistance, drying while I washed. I was filling the sink with soapy water when the telephone rang. It was Harriet.

"I can't believe it." She sounded like she'd been crying. "Joe just canceled on me for tonight."

"I'm sorry," I said, cradling the phone between my ear and shoulder as I handed Edward a plate.

"He waited until the last minute, too," she said. "That's what really aggravates me . . ."

Edward frowned, handing me back the plate, pointing out some stuck-on food that I'd missed. I dunked it back into the sink and tried again.

"Joe said something came up with Estée. He has to have dinner with her tonight instead. Do you believe it? He just dumps me for her every single time. It's always Estée, Estée, Estée."

Edward also rejected a coffee cup with my lipstick on the rim. He was laughing, shaking his head at my inept dishwashing abilities. I yanked the towel off his shoulder and swatted him with it.

". . . and I'm already dressed and— Gloria? Hello? Are you still there?"

"Yes, yes." I swallowed my laughter. "I'm still here. Go on, I'm listening."

"What I really resent is that Estée says 'jump' and Joe says 'how high.' I'm always going to be second-best, aren't I?"

"Oh, Harriet, you knew he wasn't over Estée." Edward gestured for me to step aside and let him take over. I dried my hands and fetched a cigarette. "I tried to warn you about him. He's not ready for anything serious."

She broke down and cried for a moment before saying, "Why does this always happen? Why is the timing always wrong for me? Why can't it just work out, just once? Someone's either getting over someone or else someone loves someone else more. It shouldn't be this hard— It's not fair."

After Harriet and I hung up, I looked at Edward, an apron tied about his waist, his hands submerged in a sink full of soapy water.

Given what Estée had gone through with Van and now Harriet with Joe, it made me appreciate how rare it was that in this great big world, two people could find each other, their hearts aligning so perfectly as to let them fall in love with each other in the same way at the exact same time.

30

AFTER ESTÉE STOPPED seeing Van, she threw herself into her work, focusing on growing her business and making money. Each day she forced herself to make the rounds, going from one beauty shop to the next, checking on her salesgirls, making deliveries and giving facials out of her apartment. She also made some halfhearted attempts to meet with the buyers at Bonwit Teller, Gimbels and Macy's, but all to no avail. The sparkle in her eyes had dulled, the determination had weakened, the optimism I'd always envied in her had clouded over.

She cried about being so exhausted all the time. She cried about always being broke. She cried about being lonely. She was dragging and depressed. She needed something to go right in her world. It was around this time that she begged me to ask Mr. Fiske if he'd be willing to meet with her. Over lunch. Her treat.

Honestly, I didn't think her products were up to Saks Fifth Avenue's standards. Maybe it was because I knew she made them in her kitchen or because her labels were a little shoddy, her bottles and jars didn't always match and they didn't have that elegant feel about them. Still, I went to bat for her.

Standing in the doorway of Mr. Fiske's office, I explained to him that Estée was a friend of mine. "She's really starting to build a following here in the city. Her skincare products are just terrific. Here"—I inched forward and placed a sample jar of her Super Rich All-Purpose Creme on the edge of his desk—"you can see for yourself. She uses all the best ingredients. Women love her products. She's selling them in beauty shops all around the Upper West Side and the Upper East Side, too."

He darted his pen to the blotter on his desk and ran a hand over his face. "Miss Downing, this shouldn't come as a surprise to you, but this is Saks Fifth Avenue. We are not in the business of competing with beauty parlors. I'm not looking to sell anything that can be obtained in a beauty shop."

"But Helena Rubinstein and Elizabeth Arden both have—" He stopped me with just a look. I knew I shouldn't have challenged him, but I couldn't help myself. "I realize it's a little different," I said. "I understand that Rubinstein's and Arden's products are in spas."

"Not just spas, Miss Downing. Madame Rubinstein and Miss Arden both happen to *own* those spas. It's their names on the doors. Can you not see the difference between that and selling products out of a beauty parlor?"

"I'm sorry. I meant no disrespect—"

"You should be sorry. And you tell your friend that I can't be bought with a corned beef sandwich." With that, he reached for the jar of Super Rich All-Purpose Creme and dramatically dropped it into his wastebasket.

Estée hadn't taken the news particularly well. And I watered down the version I told her to spare her feelings. Still, it was just one more disappointment on top of a heap of others.

It pained me to see her like this, especially since the things that were going so poorly for her were the very same things that were working in my favor. I took no pleasure in having switched places with her. So accustomed to being the underdog, I didn't trust that my good fortune would last. Or that it should last.

I HELD THE pink bottle of Pepto-Bismol up to the light. Nearly empty. Edward was going through that stuff like water. That and Rolaids. I found foiled spools on the nightstand, the coffee table, in the pockets of his suit pants. There weren't enough remedies to ease what ailed him. His job was making him sick. Moral as he was, he wouldn't discuss the case specifics, but he was at odds with himself, working to get a murderer off the hook.

And running in the background of all this, Edward and I finally set a date for the wedding, in August. We were finalizing wedding plans and looking at apartments. Expensive apartments. Expensive apartments that were going to need expensive furniture. I knew Edward was doing this for me, and as much as I protested, telling him I didn't need the doorman building, didn't need that new sofa, he pushed on.

With the wedding less than four months away, I was getting anxious. I had more vertigo bouts than I could ever remember having. Sometimes two and three a week. I blamed it on the change in the weather, a rash of thunderstorms we'd been having that spring, but I knew better. Something inside my head wanted to explode.

"You're not getting cold feet, are you?" Estée asked.

We were in the bridal department at Lord & Taylor. I was standing on a little platform while the seamstress kneeled on the ground, fixing the hem. I caught a glimpse of myself in the three-way mirror and I swear I had never before seen myself with such clarity. There I was—all three sides of me: Gloria Dowaziac turned Gloria Downing about to turn Gloria Clifford.

"I think Tommy expects me to quit my job after we're married."

"Tommy?" Estée gave me a look.

I clamped a hand over my mouth. "Where did that come from?" I shook my head. "I meant Edward. Edward! Oh my God. What is wrong with me?"

As the days stretched on, I grew clumsy and careless. I burned my wrist on the handle of the teapot, nearly sliced my finger off with a paring knife. I rolled my ankle while rushing to catch a bus. I gave myself a minor eruption of food poisoning, eating leftovers that I knew had sat two days too long in my icebox. And on a whim, knowing how much Edward loved my red hair, I decided to go back to being a brunette. Dark Cocoa #5.

When he met me for dinner that night, I saw his eyes roving over my hair but he didn't say a word. I could tell he didn't like it and we were halfway through our cocktails when he reached over, running a few strands of my hair between his fingers.

"So, what made you do this?" he asked.

Honestly, I didn't have a good reason, and I knew he wasn't going to like this new color. *Why would I do something like that? What was wrong with me?* I shrugged. "I just needed a change. Besides, I wasn't a natural redhead anyway."

He didn't say another word about it, but later that night, I reached for him across the bed only to find his side empty. He was sitting out in the living room, his head in his hands, a bottle of bromo at his side.

ONE NIGHT, JUST so Estée wouldn't feel like a third wheel, I invited Waller to join us for cocktails at Jimmy Ryan's, a jazz club tucked away in the basement of a brownstone on 52nd and Sixth Avenue. You could hear the band playing "Muskrat Ramble" at street level, growing louder with each step down.

Edward had never met Waller before that night—something I hadn't really thought through ahead of time. It wasn't until I saw them shake hands, sizing each other up like two prizefighters, that I began to feel uneasy.

After we'd taken our seats and settled in, Edward wagged his index finger between Waller and me, asking, "Now how is it that you two know each other again?"

"Oh, when I was living at the Millers'. We were roommates. Well, housemates. Waller's room was down the hall." Admittedly it didn't sound good. I watched Edward's jaw clench, a steady pulsing beneath his skin.

"They were asking about you, the Millers were," said Waller, lighting a cigarette and snapping his Zippo shut.

Edward grew unusually quiet after that.

Our drinks arrived and I saw the way Estée was looking at Waller while he propped his cigarette in the corner of his mouth, applauding as the band played the last chords of "Lazy River." I shouldn't have been surprised that she would have been so taken with him. After all, Waller was a devastatingly handsome man. Even Edward—as I would come to learn later on—had been intimidated by Waller's looks. I felt a bit guilty, given that I hadn't shared any details with Edward about my past with Waller—another lie by omission, I supposed.

"So Gloria tells me you're an actor," Estée said, leaning in suggestively while he lit her cigarette. "I've always loved the theater. I just saw *That Rib of Adam* at the Cherry Lane Theatre . . ."

Twenty minutes later she cornered me in the ladies' room, a long narrow space that you had to sidestep down to reach the stalls at the very end. The mirror above the tiny sink had a diagonal crack running through it.

"Where have you been hiding him? Waller is perfect for me."

"Oh, Estée, no."

"No? Why *no*?" She twisted up her lipstick, vivid red and shiny.

"I'm telling you it'll never work."

"Why not?" She swiped the lipstick over her bottom lip, then her top. "He's charming and very handsome and—"

"Estée, he's broke."

She looked at me through the cracked mirror, her frown fractured in two.

"Waller is the epitome of a starving actor. He tends bar just to get by. He's been living at the Millers' house *forever*."

"Oh no. Really?"

"Really."

"What a shame. He's just so handsome." Estée blotted her lips with a tissue, and when we returned to the table, she announced that it was getting late, she was tired and was ready to go home.

I'd barely had the key in the door of my apartment when Edward said, "So, how come you never told me that you and Waller were roommates?"

"Housemates," I corrected him. "I never said anything because I didn't think it was a big deal."

"It's not a big deal. I was just surprised that you never mentioned that particular detail before."

Something sparked inside me, and before I could rein myself in, I fired back with, "Are you suggesting that I purposely hid that from you?"

"I didn't say that."

"You didn't have to."

"Oh-kay. Wow. That touched a nerve. What's bugging you?"

"Nothing's bugging me. I just don't appreciate being called a liar."

"Whoa—" His hands flew up in surrender. "I did not say you were lying. What are you doing here—why are you trying to start a fight?"

"I'm not trying to start a fight." But it was clear that I was. I told myself to back down, but something inside wouldn't allow it. I was hell-bent on creating a problem where there was none. I was setting Edward up to lose this battle no matter what he said, no matter what he did.

"If you're feeling guilty about something, Gloria, that's your problem. Not mine." He shrugged off his suit jacket and tossed it onto the sofa.

"So now you're saying I'm feeling guilty because I lied to you." It was suddenly hot in my apartment. I went over and threw the window above the radiator wide open. Edward knew all about Tommy. We had talked that one through from top to bottom. He knew I had a friend named Waller, but that was all I'd ever said—he was a friend. Just a friend. I should have let it go, but I took it one step too far. "Besides, it was a long time ago, Edward. Before I even met you."

"Wait a minute. What—" I could hear it in his voice. I'd just delivered a body blow. "So you *were* with him?"

"It's not like what you think."

"Have you slept with him?" He jammed two fingers inside his collar and loosened his tie.

I turned and looked at him as I drew a deep breath. "Yes."

"Jesus, Gloria." He dropped his hands to his sides, slapping his thighs. "And you still see him? All the time? You let me sit across the table from him all night without knowing any of this?"

"Because it doesn't matter. We're just friends. It's all we've ever been."

"Do you have sex with all your friends?"

"Oh, good God, Edward, so what, now I'm a whore?"

"I never said that. Quit twisting my words."

"I'm sure you're thinking I didn't waste any time jumping into the sack with you, either, so why don't you just come out and say it? You think I'm a whore."

He stared at me, stunned disbelief clouding his eyes. "What the hell are you doing?"

I couldn't look at him. Just the sense of him was too much. I couldn't breathe; I wanted to throw up. "What are we doing, Edward? You're not happy. I'm not happy. You took that job because of me. I know you did, and you hate it. You hate going in there every single day. And you won't walk away and it's because of me. It's all my fault."

"Stop it. Just stop. That's not true and you—"

"I'm just . . . This isn't going to work. I've known it for a long time, but I didn't want to face it. I'm not good for you. I've got too much in my past. It's not fair. I can't go on doing this to you."

"Why don't you let me be the judge of that?"

"Because you won't see the truth." I went over and held his face in my hands. "I'm telling you, I'm not good for you. I'm sorry, but I can't—I just can't . . ."

"You can't *what*?"

My God, he was going to make me say it out loud. I couldn't get the words out so instead I took my hands away from his face, closed my eyes and started slipping his ring off my finger.

"Are you kidding me? What the hell are you doing?"

"I—I can't marry you."

"You're not serious." He looked sucker punched. "What the hell is wrong with you? You've got a real problem with being happy, you know that? I love you, Gloria, I do. But this is getting exhausting. Maybe you're right—maybe we should just call this whole thing off. You're set on being miserable—and that's your choice—but I can't live that way . . ."

I don't remember the specifics of what either of us said after that, but I do remember that we talked for too long, going round and round but getting nowhere. The sun was coming up by the time he finally left. Before closing the door, he said he'd send for his things later.

I balled myself up on the floor and cried myself dry. Edward was right, I couldn't handle being happy. I was just more comfortable in my state of purgatory. And in my anguish, at the most excruciating point of the ache, there came relief. A masochist's pleasure. In the name of self-sabotage and of the purest, most selfless love I'd ever known, I had found a way to set my darling Edward free.

I stayed on the floor until my tears subsided and my limbs went numb, having fallen asleep in a twisted mess. An early-morning spring rain came in through the open window. I couldn't even get up to close it.

31

SO I WAS single again and Estée had sworn off men. At least she had for the summer of 1941. After Van, and a handful of other ill-fated romances, she was done, disillusioned and depressed. As was I. Between the two of us, we were wearing out our Cole Porter, Gershwin and Irving Berlin records.

I was drinking more than I should have and had started playing games with myself—vowing every morning that I would have only one glass of wine with dinner and then I'd cave when five o'clock rolled around and the gin was already splashing against the ice cubes. I couldn't help myself. I was gutted over Edward, empty to the core. There wasn't enough booze to fill the void and yet I kept trying.

I'd started sleeping with Waller again, but he wasn't Edward and I sobbed into my pillowcase every time I heard the front door close behind him. I'm not sure how I managed to function at work, and when I walked out of Saks at the end of the day, I didn't know which way to turn. On particularly tough days, stepping into on-coming traffic seemed tempting. I felt so alone. Bobbi was dating an avant-garde sculptor who monopolized all her free time, so I rarely saw her. I'd made some new friends at Saks, but Marion didn't need to hear about my personal problems and all Harriet ever wanted to talk about was Joe. He wasn't seeing much of her anymore, trying to let her down easy, but Harriet refused to give up on him in much the same way Joe couldn't give up on Estée. It was a chain, a conga line of unrequited love.

Every now and again I went over to the Millers' just so I wouldn't have to be by myself. They'd recently taken in some new borders—a Jewish family from France. Friends of friends or something like that. Waller had complained about it being so crowded over there now.

"There's never any hot water."

"Why don't you move out?" I'd asked him. "I'm sure you can find another room to rent somewhere."

"I can't move out," he'd said. "It's my home."

Home. Family. I had neither. And yes, I was living under a self-inflicted exile from the Dowaziacs, but I couldn't do the one thing that would have let me back in: forgive my father. That's all my mother wanted, all she was waiting for, but I wasn't ready and I wasn't sure if I ever would be. So in the meantime, I drank and sulked.

In Estée's case, she had handled her breakup with Van much more constructively and concentrated on her work. Since Memorial Day, she'd begun splitting her time between Grossinger's in the Catskills and Lido Beach in Nassau County. I sometimes joined her on the weekends to keep her company and escape the city.

"You need to take some time off and relax," I said to her one afternoon as we sat in a tiny cabin-like cabana at the Lido Club in Nickerson Beach Park. "All you ever do is work."

"It's all I have left."

"It's not *all* you have left," I corrected her.

"Well, that's true." Estée offered a crooked smile as she propped the door open with a chair. "I still have you."

"And Leonard."

"And Joe," she said. "Did you see the flowers he sent?"

"They're beautiful." I glanced over at the bouquet of red roses that had been delivered just after we'd arrived earlier that day.

"He shouldn't have done that," Estée said. "He really can't afford it." She pulled out a long stem, brought the rose to her nose and inhaled deeply. "I'll never understand men as long as I live." She set the flower back in the vase and rearranged a few stems. "Do you still think about Edward?"

"Constantly," I said. I knew I'd hurt him, had broken his heart. In time, he'd get over it. He'd meet someone new, and when he did, the knife would be plunged even deeper into my heart.

"I still don't understand why you broke it off. You were so good together."

How could I begin to explain that I'd done it *for* Edward? And to punish myself. Two birds with one engagement stone. Thankfully, I didn't have to get into any of that because just then a perky woman knocked on the cabana door and stepped inside. She was wearing a white pleated tennis skirt and lightweight top, with her racket propped against her shoulder.

"Oh, Muriel," said Estée. "Come in. Come in. I'll be with you in just a minute."

Estée was giving free facials and makeup demonstrations right inside the cabana to wealthy vacationers on the beach. When each customer came in, she'd have them change into a plush terry cloth robe and lie down on a clean white beach towel that she'd spread out on the masseuse table. After Estée finished up with the tennis lady, she gave her some free samples to take with her.

"How are you ever going to make any money if you keep giving everything away?" I asked.

"Trust me. I know these women down here. They aren't afraid to pay for quality. Believe me, she'll be back and she'll buy. Eventually. Besides, Muriel knows everyone down here. She just better tell all her rich friends about me."

Two more facials and Estée closed up the cabana for the day and we headed down to the beach. Estée wore a loose flowing wrap and kept her face hidden from the sun beneath a floppy wide-brimmed hat. We walked, letting the surf wash over our bare feet, our sandals in hand, beach bags banging against our hips. A group of women were stretched out on their chaises, sunning themselves, and before I could stop her, Estée marched over and introduced herself.

"I don't mean to intrude," she said, "but I have something that would be absolutely perfect for your skin—especially after you've been out in the sun all day. May I tell you about it?"

The women propped their sunglasses up on their heads and sat up while Estée dug into her beach bag for samples of her Super Rich All-Purpose Creme and launched into her spiel. I stood off to the side, watching, while she slathered up the backs of their hands.

"You have beautiful eyes," Estée said to one of the women. "But that shadow you're wearing is not doing you justice." She reached inside the beach bag again and took out a tiny compact of turquoise eyeshadow. "Here," she said. "Take this home and try it. I know you're going to love it."

I couldn't tell if the woman was offended or delighted but she kept the eyeshadow just the same.

"And please—all of you—come see me for a free facial. I'm right over there in Cabana #9."

As we walked away, Estée waved goodbye to them with a flutter of her teacup fingers. "Those Jewish ladies," she said, laughing, "they just love me."

I stopped walking.

She turned back and saw my expression. "What? I didn't say anything wrong. They *are* Jewish, you know."

I bristled when she said that, feeling protective of Waller and the Millers. And even Joe.

"I don't have anything against Jewish people," she said.

"I should hope not—your husband's Jewish."

"Yes, but he's not observant. We don't go to the synagogue or church. Can we drop it now?"

And we did. The subject of religion vanished just like our footprints disappearing into the surf.

32

IT WAS A Sunday morning and I was sound asleep when my telephone rang. I looked at the alarm clock. It was half past eight. I threw off the covers and shrugged on my bathrobe. The shrill of the ringing seemed to grow louder when I reached the telephone.

"Oh, Gloria, I'm sorry to be calling so early. And on your day off."

"Estée? Is everything okay?"

"Oh yes. Yes. It's just that, well, I need a favor."

"What kind of favor?" I'd been covering for Marion, who was on vacation. I was working ten- and twelve-hour days, weekends, too. It was my first day off in almost two weeks. I was looking forward to doing nothing but staying in my bathrobe all day and reading an Agatha Christie novel.

"I need to pick up some supplies from my uncle John and, well, Joe's busy today and I'm too afraid to drive myself over the Queensboro Bridge. There's just no one else I can ask. I'd take the train but I'm afraid I'll have too much to carry back with me. So could you be a dear and drive me? We can take Joe's car."

She must have been desperate because in all the years I'd known her, Estée had never introduced me to her uncle, or to any other members of her family. If anything, she'd gone to great lengths to keep us apart. I'd assumed it was because I didn't have the proper pedigree. And yet she'd told me all about them. So many stories. Estée loved to reminisce about her childhood, about all the dukes and duchesses, the other nobility her parents had entertained. She'd told me about her older sister and her brothers. She'd told me so much about her famous uncle John that in a way, I felt like I already knew him.

"Will you help me, Gloria? Please?"

So later that morning, Estée and I headed out in Joe's 1936 Buick Century. It was forest green with a matching leather interior. The engine hummed along with the radio. I hadn't driven in almost three years, ever since my Cord 812 was sold at auction. I loved that car of mine, and though Joe's Buick didn't have the same pickup, the same comfy seats, I had to admit it felt good to drive again. Being behind the wheel of an automobile gave me a sense of power and freedom.

"It really is true," Estée said, adjusting the visor to block the autumn sun coming in from the east.

"What's true?"

"You know how they say, 'You don't know what you've got till it's gone.'"

"Ain't that the truth." I nodded. "But I still think you're better off without him. Van wasn't right for you."

"Oh, I wasn't talking about Van. I was thinking about Joe—and don't laugh, but I've been thinking about Joe *a lot* lately."

"No foolin'?" I perked up.

"I always knew he was a great guy, but I never realized just how lucky I was when we were together."

"I kept trying to tell you."

"Oh, I know." She sighed. "If he could just get his business going . . ."

I'd seen what a high-priced job had done to Edward. She didn't want to put Joe through that.

"I used to think it was because of the Depression," Estée was saying now. "Everyone was struggling, barely making ends meet. But now—now things are getting better. The economy's picking up and Joe *still* can't make a go of things. He shouldn't be in sales. His job with the shoe company is straight commission. Last week he made $179. That was it. And that was a *good* week for him."

"Not everyone can be successful in business," I reminded her, thinking about the time Joe told me he could make a million dollars and it wouldn't have been enough for Estée. She wanted to be famous, not just rich. "Let's face it," I said, "you're just more driven than he is."

She twisted up her mouth and went quiet, looking out the window. The leaves were changing colors and it was a beautiful fall day, crisp and picturesque.

We drove in silence for a few miles and then Estée let out a gasp, pointing to the sign that read, QUEENSBORO BRIDGE. "Just tell me when we're over it," she said. "Tell me when we get to the other side."

I glanced at her and saw that her eyes were squeezed tight, her hands gripping the dashboard as beads of perspiration clung to her upper lip. She really wasn't kidding about her fear of heights. Even when we were over the bridge, even though it was chilly outside and the temperature was in the low forties, she rolled down the window, needing fresh air.

I thought we were heading to Flushing—that's where her family lived—but Estée instead directed me to Corona. I'd never been there before, and let me tell you, I was fine with never going back. Corona was not a pretty town, and thanks to the Brooklyn Ash Removal Company, there was a rancid smell in the air, made all the worse by the garbage dumps and huge mounds of charcoal ash near the railroad yard. Judging by the signs up and down the main avenue, for MAMA LUIGI'S and PETROCELLI'S BAKERY, HOROWITZ'S GROCERY and PLAFKER & ROSENTHAL DEPARTMENT STORE, I figured it was primarily an Italian neighborhood, sprinkled with a few Jewish businesses.

"Didn't you say your family lived in Flushing?" I asked as we drove past a stretch of boarded-up buildings.

"They do," she said matter-of-factly. "We're going to Uncle John's."

I was confused. I thought he lived in Flushing, too. I didn't say anything, even as we arrived at a tiny house with crooked shutters, shingles missing from the roof and a chicken coop adjacent to a small abandoned horse stable. All I could think was, *This is where a leading European skincare specialist lives?*

Then there was John Schotz himself. I'd been expecting someone with a thick Austrian accent but his English was nearly perfect. Uncle John was a soft-spoken, charming man, warm and welcoming. He was lean and attractive, and Estée bore a strong resemblance to him. Uncle John's wife, Flora Anna, was a sweet congenial woman who wore a plaid hunting jacket and oversize rubber boots. She crunched her way through the sea of fallen leaves, bringing mugs of hot coffee to us in the horse stable, which now served as Uncle John's laboratory. This was also not what I'd been expecting.

There was a sign on the sliding barn door that read: NEW WAY LABORATORIES, SPECIALIZING IN WONDERFUL FACIALS AND PIGEON REMEDIES. Inside I noticed a bulletin board with a piece of paper in the middle: *Six-in-One Cold Cream* underscored along with a formula that I couldn't make heads or tails of, like it was written in code. Next to the vats of cold cream were vials of liquid and boxes marked INSECT KILLER, DOG RASH CURE, LAXATIVES, ARTERIAL FLUID, MASSAGE CREAM, FRECKLE FIXER and HUNGARIAN FACE POMADE. There was an old dentist chair in the corner that he used for giving facials to women from the neighborhood.

While Estée and Uncle John huddled together, I followed Flora Anna into their house, passing a mezuzah tacked to the doorway. The inside of the house was in worse shape than the outside. Threadbare upholstery, old worn-out carpets and moth-eaten drapes. Sitting in the middle of it all were two young boys from a nearby orphanage and a young woman, Janice, also originally from the orphanage. Aunt Flora Anna and Uncle John were her foster parents. Janice was eighteen and had dull reddish-brown hair and a face full of freckles, even on her eyelids. I wondered if she'd ever tried Uncle John's freckle-fixer cream. Janice was finishing her last year of high school, hoping for a scholarship so she could go on to college. She seemed older and wiser than her years, and perhaps that was what came of abandoned girls, forced to grow up quickly. I'd been just the opposite, stunted in my maturity until I had no choice but to either ripen or perish.

Before we left, I was introduced to Flora Anna's mother, Mrs. Greenstein, who also lived with them. There were a lot of people staying in that tiny house and I found it terribly depressing, stifling with a musty dank smell in the air. I couldn't wait to get on the road and back to Manhattan.

After Uncle John had loaded boxes of mysterious potions and powders into the trunk of the Buick, I glanced out the rearview mirror, watching the dilapidated house fade in the cloud of dust kicking up beneath the tires.

"What is all that stuff you're hauling back home anyway?" I asked.

"Just ingredients," she said.

"Well, yeah, I figured that much. But what *is* it?"

"Do you understand chemistry?"

"About as well as I understand trigonometry." I laughed.

"Exactly my point. It's just ingredients."

That had been Estée's way of saying, *It's none of your business.*

33

BY NOVEMBER OF that year Estée had begun spending more and more time with Joe. The two of them went to movies and plays, they took Leonard to the park and for butterscotch sundaes at the Tip Toe Inn. Poor Harriet. She knew Joe was slipping away, their dates few and far between, and there was nothing I could do to console her.

As for myself, I remained single. And gutted. My only salvation was the occasional romp with Waller. And my work. That, I could lose myself in. But at the end of the day, as soon as I'd come down from the executive offices and walk the main floor of Saks, I'd catch myself looking for Edward. Every handsome man, every fedora, made me do a double take.

Back upstairs in our office, Marion and I were busy, coordinating with Mr. Fiske and Mr. Belfort, who were already making purchasing decisions for spring. We'd sat through a string of long, tedious presentations made by nervous salesmen. One man's hands were so sweaty he could barely uncap his jar of night cream. All the while, Marion and I were off to the side with steno pads in our laps, taking copious notes that were later discussed at length during a separate meeting.

Recently, at one of those secondary meetings, Marion and I joined Mr. Belfort and Mr. Fiske in the conference room, the table covered in pamphlets and flyers touting the latest in rouge, mascara, eye-shadows, liners and face creams. Every vendor claimed to have some secret ingredient, some magic potion—everything from bee glue to carminic acid and snail slime—that would transform a woman's complexion. I wanted to include samples of Estée's products—just one or two—but Mr. Fiske still thought of her as the beauty shop line, and no amount of pitching on my part could change his opinion.

"Guanine?" he asked, holding up a bottle of burnt orange nail lacquer. "Is that the fish scales stuff?"

"Fish scales and bat excrement," said Marion, consulting her notes. "They say it makes the polish shinier after it dries."

"Hmmm." Mr. Fiske pushed it aside and moved on to the next item. "And what's the deal with this one?" He pointed to a sell sheet on a new product called Shimmer Cream.

"They claim it has gold compound particles mixed in," I said, recalling the sales pitch.

Mr. Fiske finished the last of his coffee, fisted up the paper cup and pitched it into the nearby trash can. "Who wants gold compound all over their face?" he asked.

"Not me," said Marion.

"Can't say it sounds very appealing to me, either," I added.

"Apparently all that glitters is not gold," said Mr. Belfort, packing his pipe with tobacco.

I looked down at my product sheet and next to Shimmer Cream I wrote *NG: No Good.*

We took a quick break, and when I came back from the ladies' room, Mr. Belfort teasingly said, "Your boyfriend was just in here asking for you."

I thought he meant Edward, and my heart leaped until I saw the cart of fresh coffee and danish that Soda Pop must have wheeled in. I'd set myself up, should have known better. It had been almost seven months since I'd seen Edward. There hadn't been a telephone call, a letter, not even a sighting on the street. Not that I didn't look for him or deliberately try to put myself in his path. I'd sit in his favorite coffee shop pretending to read a magazine, or browse the bookshop and used-record stores in his neighborhood. Nothing.

Deflated, I poured myself a cup of coffee and took my seat at the table. The wall clock ticked as more papers were shuffled, more notes were jotted down, more purchase orders completed. Mr. Fiske and Mr. Belfort were engaged in a long debate over whether or not to restock Revlon's Cheek Stick, a cream rouge that hadn't performed as well as expected. An hour later, our coffee cups were empty, our ashtrays full and the shadows along the wall were growing longer with the setting sun. The real dilemma came down to lipsticks.

"Six of one, half a dozen of the other," said Mr. Belfort, going back and forth between two shades of red that looked identical to me. "What do you think, Bob?"

"Did you see this one?" Mr. Fiske picked up a tube of Revlon's Windsor Red and gave it a smell before replacing the cap and rolling it across the table to Mr. Belfort.

"Well." Mr. Belfort pushed his eyeglasses onto his forehead. "We're damned if we do and damned if we don't."

"I don't want to end up with a surplus of merchandise," said Mr. Fiske. "But we can't take the Rubinstein red and not carry the Arden red. That'll set off another war. And if we don't take Revlon's new shade, I'm going to get an earful from Charles and frankly, I get enough grief from that man as it is."

"That's the price you pay," said Mr. Belfort before adding in, "You know what they say, 'Sometimes you're the dog and sometimes you're the hydrant.'"

Marion and I exchanged looks, trying not to laugh. We came out of that meeting with a new cliché and the insiders' knowledge that red was definitely going to be in again for spring.

THE FOLLOWING AFTERNOON, I got a frantic telephone call from Joe, asking if I knew where Estée was. "I can't find her anywhere and I need to get in touch with her right away."

"Whoa—slow down. What's wrong?"

"It's Leonard. He's running a fever. It's high—over a hundred and three. It started early this morning. I can't tie up the telephone line right now—I'm waiting for the doctor to call me back. But I need Estée. Can you help me find her?"

I hung up with Joe and went through the telephone book, calling all the beauty shops where she had concessions, finally tracking her down at House of the Ash Blondes. As soon as I told her about Leonard, she raced over to Joe's apartment. The fever was relentless. They moved Leonard back over to Estée's, thinking he'd be more comfortable in his own bed.

I arrived at her place later that day after work. As I stepped off the elevator, I could smell cabbage and onions coming from the Hungarian restaurant on the main floor, could even hear the ruckus and rumblings of conversations from the diners down below. I'd brought over chicken soup from the deli around the corner, a bottle of baby aspirin, orange juice and some other things she needed.

"What'd the doctor say?" I asked, standing in Estée's kitchen, the countertops cluttered with jars and stacks of labels.

"He thinks it's mumps." She eased the lid off the chicken soup. "I don't know if I can get him to eat this or not. He keeps saying he's not hungry." Estée shook her head. "Thank God Joe's here."

I took that as my cue to leave, and as I was buttoning my coat, I peered in through Leonard's open bedroom door. Joe was perched on the edge of the bed. Leonard looked so tiny and pale. I thought about the time we spent together in Miami, the two of us swimming and playing endless games of checkers. Part of me wanted to go sit with him, but he called for his mother and I showed myself out of the apartment.

For three days and three nights, Estée and Joe kept watch over Leonard, changing compresses, placing him in ice baths, forcing him to sip hot broth. By the fourth day, his fever finally broke.

I stopped by with more groceries, and as soon as Estée answered the door, I saw the dark circles beneath her eyes.

"Joe was here with me, every day, every night," she said. "Neither one of us got hardly any sleep."

While I put the milk and eggs into the icebox and stacked cans of creamed corn, carrots and fruit cocktail in the pantry, Estée told me what a big help Joe had been through all this.

"I don't know what I would have done without him," she said, folding the grocery bag in half before tucking it behind the kitchen door, where a slew of others were stored. "He was my rock. Really and truly he was. I know this may sound nuts," she said, "but having Joe here, having him with me in our old bed, well, it just felt right."

"Do tell." I raised an eyebrow.

"It's just that I realized something over these past few days. Even after everything we've been through—the divorce, the Harriets and Vans of the world—I realized Joe and I still belong together. I know it sounds insane, but oh, Gloria, I want him back."

"Estée, this is wonderful. I've been waiting to hear you say this for a long, long time."

"But is it crazy?"

"It's only crazy if you hurt him again."

"Leaving him, divorcing him, was a mistake. A terrible mistake. I was so young. Too young to have married him in the first place. I couldn't see it clearly before, but now I get it. When Joe and I first got together, I threw myself into my business and I left him behind. I was working twelve- and fourteen-hour days. Poor Joe couldn't get anything off the ground. He resented me because he didn't have anything of his own. And I didn't have any time for him."

"I think it's good that you recognize that now."

"But do you think Joe would be willing to give us another chance?"

"Oh, come on, I think you already know the answer to that. But the real question is, what would be different this time around?"

She took a moment, untied her apron and hung it off a hook on the wall. "This time I want to bring Joe into my world. I want to bring him into my business. We can work together. I don't know why I never thought of this before. I know Joe isn't as ambitious as I am, but I have enough drive for the two of us. And this way it would be ours. Both of ours. It's something we could both take pride in. We could both have a stake in."

I'd been learning to keep my mouth shut and not just blurt out every little thought that popped into my head, but as Estée continued to talk, I wanted to warn her. I was afraid that even a man like Joe would not be happy standing in his wife's shadow.

SHORTLY AFTER LEONARD had made a full recovery, Estée telephoned on a Saturday morning and asked if I could watch him for a few hours that night. "Joe's coming over for dinner," she whispered, giddy as a schoolgirl.

"I'll do better than that," I said. "Pack an overnight bag for him. I'll swing by and pick him up later." She squealed so that I had to pull the receiver away from my ear.

I knew Estée thought it would be a huge imposition, but I was looking forward to Leonard's visit. Saturdays were usually torture for me. I'd go into the office and get caught up on work just to get out of the apartment and keep myself busy. Other than an occasional movie with Bobbi or popping in for a drink while Waller was tending bar, I was home alone with the radio and a book. Leonard would probably bring his latest collection of postcards and I knew he liked to play checkers and work jigsaw puzzles. I'd make up the sofa for him with extra blankets and a set of pillows that Mrs. Miller had given me, which were certainly past Estée's two-year expiration date. After Estée and I hung up, I went around the corner and picked up some milk, Hershey's Kisses and a package of Mallomars for my house guest.

It was about five o'clock when I stopped by Estée's apartment to get Leonard. The hallway that usually smelled of cabbage and stew meat from the restaurant below now carried the aromatic scent of garlic, butter, onions and rich spices, all of it coming from Estée's kitchen. She answered the door in a blue chiffon dress that showed off her eyes. It had a plunging neckline that did the same for her décolletage.

"Wow," I said. "You look spectacular."

"Oh, do you really think so? It's not too much, is it?" she asked, pivoting in a circle.

"Oh, it's exactly the right amount of too much," I said with a laugh.

"I just want everything to be perfect tonight."

She hadn't missed a trick. She used her best china, silver and crystal on the table, along with two long tapered candles and a centerpiece of roses. She had a bottle of champagne chilling in an ice bucket.

"Looks very romantic to me," I said. "And whatever you're cooking smells delicious."

"It's chicken paprika. One of Joe's favorites. My grandmother's recipe." She rushed me into the kitchen, wanting me to taste it, making sure I thought it was okay.

"It's wonderful," I said, handing her back the wooden spoon. "Relax. Everything's going to be fine."

"I can't believe how nervous I am. I feel like this is our first date."

"Well, in a way it is."

Leonard came charging out of his bedroom and plowed into me for a big hug. He grabbed his little suitcase and off we went.

Estée said she'd call first thing in the morning and I was delighted when I didn't hear from her until noon the next day. Her voice sounded velvety, like she was still in a dream.

34

I WAS NOT SURPRISED that Joe took Estée back and without too many questions asked. He had never stopped loving her, stopped praying and hoping that she'd come back to him. And I believed that Estée had never truly stopped loving Joe, either.

I was happy that they were back together but also a bit mystified by the seamlessness of it all. Joe wasted no time moving into Estée's apartment on West End Avenue, and in some ways, it was as if they'd never been apart. Just like old times, Estée invited me over for our Sunday-night dinners. Occasionally, under the guise of needing a fourth for bridge or pinochle, they'd try to set me up with one of Joe's friends. Why was it that happy couples always wanted to make other happy couples?

Joe's pals were nice fellas, but I wasn't at my best. Estée would pull me into the kitchen, ask me what was wrong. "You're not even trying," she'd say, meaning I wasn't flirting, I wasn't engaging. I just wasn't interested. My life needed *something*. But one of Joe's friends wasn't the answer.

I didn't know how to fix what was wrong with me. I wasn't like Estée. No matter how big a mess she'd made of her life, she never suffered any lasting consequences. Things always seemed to work out for her in the long run. Always. I had no idea how she did it, but oh, how I wished I knew her secret. My existence had turned to still water, barely a current running through my veins. I was living a nonlife, going through the motions, marking time. Not too different, I imagined, from what my father was doing in Sing Sing.

I'd been thinking about my father a lot lately. Thanksgiving was right around the corner, and that day always reminded me of him. Thanksgiving was his favorite holiday, and every year, he would take us to a broken part of the city, to a mission lined with mint green subway tiles and thick rubber mats running crisscross along the floor. We would stand behind a long table and serve turkey dinners with all the trimmings to needy families waiting in snaking lines, plastic trays and silverware in hand. My father would carve the bird while my brother, sister and I used ice cream scoopers to measure the precise amount of mashed potatoes, dressing, yams and cranberry sauce allotted per plate, along with one slice of pumpkin pie. My mother never came with us. Not even once. She claimed it was too depressing, which it was.

One time Gail complained, saying she didn't want to go. It was the only time I'd ever seen my father slap her. *Not everyone has the kind of life you have, young lady. Some people are hungry, cold and in need of help.* The print of his meaty fingers was instantly blooming on her face. *All of you*—his accusatory finger moved from her to Glenn to me—*better learn to do what you can for those less fortunate.*

I never forgot those words, and how ironic that they should have come from him, of all people. My father may have spoiled me, but I was not a spoiled brat. And yes, there is a difference. Early on, he instilled in me an appreciation for what I had. And where did that leave me now? How was I to reconcile memories of that father with the man sitting in prison who'd robbed his best friends and relatives and so many other people who could very well end up in a food line this Thanksgiving?

THE NEXT DAY a co-worker came by my office and announced that the store's Christmas tree had arrived. Used to be the ornaments and wreaths didn't even come out of the box until after Thanksgiving, but nowadays Saks and every other store couldn't wait to gear up for holiday sales.

I'd volunteered along with half a dozen others to stick around and help supervise with the decorations. One team pulled crates of garlands and big red bows from the storage room. Another team retrieved the lights and ornaments. Someone had already replaced the regular piped-in music with Christmas carols, filling me with dread. All those songs reminded me of things I'd lost: my family, my childhood, all my friends and Edward. Especially Edward. I'd met him about a year ago, right here at Saks, just before Christmas, and less than twelve months later, I'd ruined everything that we had.

It was getting late, time to head home. I grabbed my pocketbook, my hat and gloves and rode down the escalator. As I was buttoning my overcoat, Soda Pop came up to me.

"What are you still doing here so late?" I asked.

"Just cleaning up the storage room. Thought I'd make some extra money. Mind if I walk with you?" he asked, holding the door for me.

"Not at all." He was sweet and I didn't mind the company.

A brisk shot of icy cold air blasted us as we stepped outside. About a block into our journey, I asked him about something I'd always found curious: "So tell me, how'd you get the nickname Soda Pop anyway?"

"Well, when I was just a kid," he said, despite the fact that he was still just a kid, "I worked in a bottling factory in Brooklyn. The guys there started calling me Soda and then my grandpa tacked on the Pop. And before I knew it everyone started calling me Soda Pop."

"And what's your real name?"

"Howard." He groaned. "It's boring. I don't really like it. I think Soda Pop's got more pizzazz."

"That it does." And Soda Pop did have a certain pizzazz. He was self-possessed, good-humored and hopefully had a bright future ahead of him. "So why aren't you in school, Soda Pop?"

"Dropped out," he said, sounding proud of the fact. "My dad lost his job and my mom's sewing business slowed down, so I dropped out and went to work to help bring in some money."

"That's a big sacrifice you made," I said. "Do you think you'll go back? Finish up high school?"

"Nah"—he shoved his hands into his deep coat pockets—"I don't much see the point. I feel like I'm getting more of an education out here in the working world. My grandpa says I'm going to the school of hard knocks." He chuckled and asked me about Thanksgiving. "Do you have big plans?"

"Big plans? No, I wouldn't exactly call them big plans. Just dinner with some friends." I'd been invited to the Millers' house. "What about you? Are you going to your family's?"

"Nah, my grandpa lives too far away and my mom's working tomorrow, washing dishes for some rich lady who's throwing a party. My dad's driving her over there. It's in Connecticut so he's gonna wait for her out in the car till she's done."

"So what are you going to do?"

"I make real good beans and toast," he said, which made my heart sink. "And I'll probably finish this—" He reached into his coat pocket and pulled out a paperback edition of *For Whom the Bell Tolls*. "You can borrow it when I'm done if you want?"

"No, thanks. I'm more of an Agatha Christie fan."

"Ah, you should give Hemingway a try. He's darn good."

"Well," I said, as we turned onto 79th Street. "This is me. Thank you for the walk home."

"No, thank you, ma'am."

"Ma'am? Oh God, no. That makes me sound ancient. Call me Gloria."

"Okay, then." He laughed. "Gloria."

"Happy Thanksgiving, Soda Pop."

"Happy Thanksgiving, Gloria."

When I reached the top step, I looked back and saw him lingering beneath the streetlight like he wasn't sure where to go next. I knew Mrs. Miller was serving a big buffet for some friends and the new tenants they'd taken in. She wouldn't mind one more mouth to feed.

"Hey, Soda Pop—"

"Yes, ma'—I mean, Gloria?"

"Why don't you come with me to my friends' house tomorrow?"

"You mean it?"

"Sure. Why not? It'll be fun."

He grinned like it was Christmas morning instead of the night before Thanksgiving.

35

I'D BEEN INVITED to Estée and Joe's for brunch one Sunday to help trim their Christmas tree. It was still early in December, but Estée wanted to put the tree up now because she was going to be traveling in the coming weeks. Joe was planning to stay back in New York with Leonard. So much for things changing between them.

Estée still wanted Joe working by her side, but he wasn't quite as eager. I could almost see the tug-of-war going on inside him. He was still a man, after all, and had already been called Mr. Estée Lauder one time too many. Now she was asking him to embrace that role full-time.

As he'd once said to me: "What kind of man goes to work for his wife?"

"But you'd be working *with* me, not *for* me," had always been Estée's argument.

That day I stood in their living room looking at their bare tree with a slight ache pulling at me. It reminded me of the last tree I'd decorated with Edward. *Edward.* I still couldn't get him out of my head. I searched for his name in the newspaper whenever I saw a headline about the murder trial he was working on, but I never found even a mention.

Leonard was in the kitchen with Estée, decorating holiday cookies. The buttery, sugary scents coming from the kitchen were mingling with the cabbage smells wafting up from the Hungarian restaurant below. Every now and again I'd hear a clatter of pots and pans rising up from the floorboards as the restaurant scrambled to serve their Sunday-brunch crowd. The New York Philharmonic had been playing in the background and Joe got up and switched the radio dial to the Giants-Dodgers game on WOR.

"What do I know about makeup?" Joe was saying to me as he handed over a box of ornaments wrapped in yellowing tissue paper from years gone by.

"I've told you a thousand times, I'll teach you everything you need to know," Estée called out from the kitchen.

"She wants me with her," Joe said, lifting a lid on another box and peeking inside. "And I suppose it makes sense, but I don't know if it's such a good move."

"It's a wonderful move," Estée said as she brought out a fresh pot of coffee.

Joe poured himself a cup, shaking his head. "But the lawyers, the accountant—everyone we've talked to, they all think it's a terrible idea."

"And what do they know?" Estée leaned over and turned the radio dial back to the Philharmonic on CBS.

Joe looked like he was about to protest but thought better of it. "They know more than we do," he said. "They think it's a big mistake for us to get into the beauty business. It's too competitive. The failure rate is too great. The odds are stacked against us."

"We just need to catch a break," said Estée, ignoring Joe's argument. "We need to get into those damn department stores." She looked at me, as if I were the one keeping her out of Saks Fifth Avenue.

"I'll do what I can to help you," I said, "but—"

"Just introduce me to your boss. That's all I need. Just to get my foot in the door."

I unwrapped another ornament, listening to the radio. I was stalling. I'd already tried to get her into Saks. Every chance I had, I mentioned her to Mr. Fiske, but he didn't take her seriously and thought it was a waste of his time.

"Why?" Estée pressed. "Why won't you do this one thing for me?"

I looked up and the truth came rushing out. "Because you're not ready."

"What is *that* supposed to mean?"

"Estée," Joe said in his *calm down* tone.

"Well?" She wasn't calming down and she wasn't going to let this go, either.

A torrent of truth that had been building up inside me finally let loose. "You look like an amateur," I blurted out. "Your jars and bottles look like they're full of castor oil, not luxury creams and lotions. Your labels look like you typed them yourself. The ink is smeared and they're always coming unglued at the edges. I can't present you to my boss like that."

"But my products are better than—"

"It doesn't matter what's inside if it doesn't look professional on the outside."

"Well," said Estée, "leave it to you to burst my bubble. Again."

"You asked and I'm telling you the truth. If you really want to get into Saks Fifth Avenue—you have to look like you *belong* in Saks Fifth Avenue."

Estée was pouting, her arms folded across her chest.

"Don't blame me," I said to her. "They only have so much space allotted for cosmetics and look who you're up against. Helena Rubinstein, Elizabeth Arden, Max Factor, Revlon, Germaine Monteil. Shall I go on? These are corporations. They have laboratories. You make your products in your kitchen and frankly, it looks like it."

"So what am I supposed to do now? Do you see all that?" Estée pointed to the hallway lined with boxes of her Creme Packs and other products. "What am I going to do with all that?"

"You'll sell them somewhere else," Joe offered.

"No," she snapped. "I need to get them into Saks." She paced for a moment, kicking some tissue paper out of her path before she turned around, exasperated. "I'm just going to have to start over again with new packaging. That's all there is to it."

"That costs money," said Joe. "Why do you think it's so vital that you get into Saks?"

"Because if I can get into Saks, we'll be on our way. Every other store will come knocking. Saks Fifth Avenue is the finest department store in the city. We have to be in there if we're ever going to be taken seriously."

Joe ran his fingers through his hair. "But didn't you hear what the accountant said? 'Don't throw good money after bad.' Those were his exact words."

"I'm not asking for the accountant's permission, Joe." Estée threaded a hook through one of the ornaments. "You're good with numbers—better at numbers than that accountant is," she told him. "And I'm good at sales. No, I'm *great* at sales." Estée hung a blue and silver ornament on the tree. "And don't forget, when it comes to cosmetics, women will do whatever it takes to get their hands on the newest face cream or, better yet, the latest shade of lipstick."

"She's right about that," I said, untangling a vine of lights. "Which reminds me, it wouldn't be a bad idea for you to raise your prices."

"What?" Joe looked at me in disbelief. "That's crazy."

"No," I said. "It's a game. Women want to feel like they're paying top dollar for a product. The more expensive it is, the better they think it is."

He shook his head, bewildered. "I will never understand this business."

"Oh, Joe, I can feel it in my bones," said Estée. "I just know it's going to work. And Gloria here is going to get me into Saks Fifth Avenue."

I was about to correct her on that when the radio announcer broke into the Philharmonic: *"We interrupt this program to bring you this important news bulletin. The White House has just confirmed that the Japanese have attacked Pearl Harbor, a U.S. naval base near Honolulu."* Silence. Crackling static. Silence. More crackling, more static. *"We are unable at this time to reach Honolulu or Manila, the capital of the Philippine Commonwealth."* Crackle. Scratch, scratch. Static. *"We are awaiting updates from our newsroom and will now return to the Philharmonic orchestra in New York."*

We all looked at one another, stunned. The United States was attacked? By Japan? None of us could fully grasp this. Another newsbreak cut in: *"We interrupt once again with this update on the Pearl Harbor attack from our newsroom. A United States Army transport carrying lumber was torpedoed 1,300 miles west of San Francisco. We are awaiting further details and will continue to update you as our newsroom receives more information. And now we return to today's performance of the New York Philharmonic Orchestra . . ."*

The three of us sat in a stupor while Shostakovich played on, the morose music of Symphony no. 1 in F Minor filling the apartment. Leonard came in from the kitchen, green and red icing all over his hands, down the front of his shirt. Over the sound of muffled applause from the oblivious concertgoers came more updates on the

Japanese attacking the American naval base at Pearl Harbor, Hawaii, and our defense facilities in Manila.

The radio cut in with more details all day. I sat at Estée's dining room table, too afraid to go back home, to even step outside. Were more attacks coming? Were they heading for Washington? For New York City? I stayed with Estée and Joe, all of us paralyzed. We drank coffee first and then switched over to whiskey, the ashtray before me filled with cigarettes smoked down within a quarter inch of their lives.

ELEANOR ROOSEVELT URGED us all to *go about our daily business* . . . but the Monday following the attack, Saks Fifth Avenue was nearly empty. No one was interested in shopping. No one wanted to leave their radios. The newsboys on the street corners had sold out of every paper they had in record time.

Upstairs in the executive offices, the secretaries hadn't even bothered to remove the covers from their typewriters. Mr. Belfort had kicked his wastebasket across the room while Mr. Fiske sat with his head in his hands. Marion and I had barely exchanged more than a somber greeting while we drank our coffees from paper cups. We were all so deep within our own thoughts, so perplexed by how much our lives had changed overnight. The telephone lines rang in the background, people calling to cancel appointments and meetings. Who could concentrate at a time like this? At half past noon, we all huddled together in the conference room, listening to President Roosevelt address the nation, making a declaration of war.

War? We were at war? What did that even mean? What did it look like? I saw what the past two years had done to Europe. I'd read all about the bombings in London, the invasion of France and so many other countries. Could the Germans hit the East Coast? I knew their submarines could torpedo California. Was all that heading our way? Would Fifth Avenue be lined with army tanks? Would soldiers be keeping guard in Washington? In every major city in America?

It was almost five o'clock when Soda Pop came rushing into my office, announcing that he'd joined the army. I glanced up from my newspaper and rolled my eyes, thinking he was making some sort of ill-timed joke. After all, Soda Pop was barely sixteen.

"I'm gonna kill every last Nazi," he said, shoulders back and square.

"Oh, shush," I said, my index finger marking my place in the article. "You're not even old enough to enlist."

"I am now. I lied about my age."

"And they believed you?"

"They did after I showed them this." He reached into his pocket and handed me a doctored birth certificate: *Howard Stanley Reid. Date of Birth: June 15, 1923.*

I brought my hand to my mouth. He wasn't kidding. This was really happening. "Oh God, Soda Pop, no. Why did you go and do that? Do your parents know?"

He nodded, proud and foolish. "I report for boot camp first thing tomorrow morning."

My heart dropped in my chest.

"I'll write to you when I know where I'm stationed. Will you write me back?"

All I could do was nod.

"You promise?"

And with that, I got up from my desk and kissed that little boy right on the lips and sent him off to war. I was beating back tears because I had a feeling deep in my gut that I would never see dear sweet Soda Pop again.

AFTER WORK, I didn't want to go back to my empty apartment, so I went down to the Automat for a coffee and sat by myself, picking up snippets of conversations at nearby tables. Already men were talking about enlisting, or wishing they were young enough to enlist.

I was numb with fear and disbelief. It was half past six. My coffee had long since turned cold. I'd been sitting there for over an hour. The Automat had all but emptied out and it was time for me to leave, too, but where would I go?

I started walking. The streets were deserted and the chill in the air penetrated my bones. When I reached 59th Street, I thought I was heading toward the Millers' house, but at 62nd, I changed course. Soon I was at Lexington and 69th, standing in the lobby of Edward's building. When I buzzed 3C a woman's voice answered.

I froze.

"Hello? Who's there?"

"Ah—is Edward in?" I asked, speaking into the box, checking to make sure I'd buzzed the correct apartment.

"Nobody here by that name."

"What? No, I'm looking for Ed-ward Clif-ford. Can I speak to him?"

"You got the wrong apartment, lady."

I stood there, heart pounding, my head pressed to the metal intercom.

"You're looking for Mr. Clifford?"

I turned around and saw Edward's landlady, a stoop-shouldered elderly woman. She was standing in a darkened vestibule, sweeping the floor. "He moved out."

"What? When?"

"Hmmm." She sucked her teeth, thinking. "I'd say he's been gone since summer. June, maybe July."

"Do you have his new address?" I was wondering if he'd gone ahead and moved into one of those fancy doorman buildings we'd looked at.

"Nope. No address. All I know is he went back home. St. Louis or maybe Kansas City—I can't remember which."

I gulped a mouthful of dry air, the wind knocked out of me. Edward was gone. Really gone. And he'd been gone. For months. He'd never even said goodbye.

I had no idea how I made it back to my apartment that night, but I did remember waking up the next morning, my coat still on, my mascara cried off onto my pillow and my body curled in the fetal position. Just when I needed Edward the most, I'd lost him again—this time, for good.

36

1942

SPRING ARRIVED, BUT I hardly recognized New York City anymore. I got off the subway one night at the 42nd Street stop and walked through the station, the tiled walls lined with posters imploring me to buy war bonds, to become a nurse, to volunteer. When I reached street level, nearly every store window had Uncle Sam pointing at me, mailboxes and telephone booths were plastered with instructions for conducting air raid drills. The streets were peppered with men in uniform, sailors and soldiers on liberty leave. They all made me think of Soda Pop.

I'd already received two letters from him. He was stationed in London but aside from that, he didn't say much about the war or what he was doing over there. Instead, he wanted to make sure *I* was okay and wanted to know how everyone at Saks was doing and if the new mail boy remembered that I took two creams in my coffee. He asked if I could send him a picture of myself, which I did: a photograph of the two of us, Soda Pop and me, taken at the Millers' house during Thanksgiving.

Dusk was setting in and I could barely make out the lettering on the giant Pepsi-Cola sign or the Camel cigarette billboard. Normally

Times Square would have been all ablaze in lights but not while we were at war. When I cut over to Broadway, not a single bulb on any of the marquees was turned on, only dull smaller lights near the entranceways to guide the theatergoers, who still attended night after night. Traffic lights had been turned way down, the same with streetlamps. Restaurants and bars were open if you could spot the faint glows coming from their doorways. Everything was reduced to low voltage. The surrounding buildings created an optical illusion, as if cut in half; anyone fifteen stories up or higher was required to kill all lights. In every direction there was evidence of the dimout, designed to keep us from coming under attack. On a clear night I could look into the inky blackness and see the Little Dipper, Orion's Belt, possibly the Milky Way.

Last December, when we first entered the war, I'd been terrified to even step outside. Now I had developed nerves of steel, walking down the darkened streets, not even a lamppost to guide my way. It was an acquired numbness that had set in, a reluctant acceptance that *this* was the new normal.

Marion had forgotten some paperwork back at the office that day and I dropped it off at her place on 49th and Seventh, leaving the packet with her doorman. It hadn't been a great day at work and so I continued walking to clear my head. I'd gotten into an argument earlier with a sales rep over his brand of liquid stockings. Because nylons were being rationed for the war effort, Saks had started selling Nu-Natural Leg Make-Up. Technically it was makeup, so it landed in our department rather than in hosieries where it belonged. The brand's slogan was *Stockings You Pour On* but customers complained of the mess, of the uneven coverage, that the product stained their hands orange. I had to tell the sales rep that we were canceling our future orders. He didn't take the news well and had some choice words for me. I had a few words of my own. Perhaps calling him an imbecile was a bit unprofessional. He threatened to report me to Mr. Fiske, which didn't faze me a bit. We were at war; what difference did it make?

I was getting tired of walking and eventually took another subway up to 81st Street. When I got home that night, Waller was waiting for me on my front stoop. He stood up, brushing something off his hands as I approached.

"To what do I owe this pleasant surprise?" I asked, feeling inside my pocketbook for my keys.

"I came to see you. To say goodbye."

"Goodbye?" I stopped. My key was in the door and I looked at him from over my shoulder. "What are you talking about?"

"I enlisted."

I heard myself gasp. First Soda Pop, now Waller. I wondered if my brother was next. What about Edward? When we entered my apartment, I drew the curtains and flipped on the overhead light so I could look into his eyes.

"I'm 1-A," he said, holding up his Notice of Classification, looking like a movie star delivering a line in a Hollywood script. "I report for basic training in two days."

"But Waller, why?"

"It's the right thing to do," he said. "And besides, let's face it, the acting thing isn't really working out. What am I gonna do, stick around here and be a bartender until I'm old and gray? At least this way I'll know I've done something worthwhile with my life. And don't worry, I'll be back soon."

"You sure will look handsome in a uniform," I said as my eyes glassed over.

He smiled and stroked my cheek.

"So what are you doing now? Just making the rounds, saying goodbye to your lovers?"

"I saved the best for last, kid."

A tear slid down my face.

"Well, don't just stand there blubbering," he said. "Aren't you going to at least kiss this soldier goodbye?"

"Oh, I'll do better than that." I smiled sadly, grabbed the front of his shirt and pulled him into my bedroom.

We held each other till dawn, and I was a puddle of tears by the time he climbed out of my bed.

Stepping into his trousers, he said, "Will you do me a favor?"

"Anything."

"Will you look in on the Millers for me while I'm gone? Take care of them? They took my enlisting kinda hard."

"Of course."

I stayed in bed, and when I heard the front door close, I broke down and sobbed all over again.

37

ESTÉE HAD FINALLY worn Joe down and that winter he officially went to work *for* her, *with* her, whatever you wanted to call it. He even enrolled in the Brooklyn College of Pharmacy. He figured that was the closest a man could get to attending beauty school. But more than that, not only were they in business together but on December 7, 1942, in a no-frills ceremony at city hall, Estée and Joe remarried.

Not that I was looking for romance, but every eligible man I knew was off fighting the war, while almost every woman I knew was doing something back home to help them. Bobbi and Mrs. Miller boarded a bus every morning that took them to the Brooklyn Navy Yard, where they assisted with the shipbuilding mission. Bobbi worked on the construction and painting crew, repairing ships and aircrafts, while Mrs. Miller was on the sewing committee, making flags and uniforms. Pieces of their hearts and souls were on board every ship that left New York Harbor filled with thousands of men ready to fight.

Estée and I stayed closer to home, volunteering our free time to work at the Red Cross. Three days a week and on every other weekend, we reported for our shifts at P.S. 145 on West 105th Street between Amsterdam and Columbus. We were part of the Production Corps, there to assemble Comfort Kits for the troops.

They had converted the gymnasium for the cause, bringing in long tables and makeshift workstations. The wooden bleachers were stacked four and five feet high with boxes of sterilized gauze, aspirin and laxatives, tubes of antifungal ointment, powdered milk, D ration chocolate bars and K ration biscuits. "Yankee Doodle Dandy" and other patriotic songs blasted over the loudspeaker, trying to boost everybody's can-do spirit.

Estée and I were part of an assembly line, putting together the kits, working shoulder to shoulder on the basketball court along with a group of other women. Everyone added an item to the kit: packages of sugar cubes, cans of Spam and tuna, bars of soap and cigarettes. We each loaded our item into the kit and passed the box down to the next woman for her contribution.

The women ranged in age from their teens to their golden years, and oh my, what a sorry lot they were. In comparison, Estée and I had waltzed in like a couple of fashion models. To look at those women, you'd think the war had been lost. Defeated and joyless, they had already surrendered. None of those women seemed to own a stitch of clothing that wasn't black, brown or gray. They dressed the way Estée had when I'd first met her. It was as if they were all in mourning. They had no sense of style, didn't wear makeup, not even a little lipstick. It seemed they'd forgotten how to dress like women.

Estée took one look at them and saw opportunity. The next time we went back to P.S. 145, Estée brought along a box of her own, filled with samples of face creams, lotions, rouge, powder and red lipsticks. After two and a half hours of packing canned goods and cheese into boxes, while the rest of us took our first break, Estée went to work.

She turned to our fellow volunteers, who were sitting on the bleachers with their coffees and cigarettes, and said, "I have something that would be just perfect for all your complexions. It will make your skin glow. May I show it to you? It'll only take a minute."

"Lady," said one woman with a fairly substantial mustache, "our men are at war. No one's worried about their complexions at a time like this."

"But it's exactly because our men are at war that you need to try this." Estée pulled out a jar of her Super Rich All-Purpose Creme. "We ladies need to do our part back home to keep up morale."

"How so?" Another woman challenged her, pitching her empty pack of Pall Malls into a wastebasket. "She's right," the woman said, gesturing toward her friend with the mustache. "Our men are at war. This isn't a time to be worried about our looks."

I held my breath. This argument was a popular one. Recently there had been a scathing article in the *New York Times* about how superficial it was for women to be concerned with their appearance during wartime. Estée certainly didn't agree with that sentiment.

"Well," said Estée, "I'm doing my part to help keep our women looking like women. If you ask me, it's vital that we look our best for our men in uniform. And it's not just for the men. It's something you need to do for yourselves—to keep your spirits up, too. Think of your lipstick as your shield of armor. Wearing bright red lipstick is a fearless move. It's empowering. It says you're not afraid to fight for what you believe in. Besides, do you honestly think it would help morale for anyone if I walked around like the rest of you—meek as a lamb and not caring what I looked like?"

"Estée," I said beneath my breath, "easy does it."

But she wasn't listening to me. "This is precisely the time we women should be even more concerned about our appearance. Do not be afraid to show the world what you've got. You have just as much strength and guts as the men on the front lines, but if you don't show it, what good is it? And what about all those men on liberty leave—they come to New York City to escape for a few days. We need to show them that we're keeping their homeland preserved. That we have faith in them. Seeing a woman put together will do more for their spirits—and ours—than us walking around looking broken. When was the last time any of you combed your hair? Washed your faces?"

Several of the women set down coffee cups and ground out their cigarettes. I thought it was going to come to blows until one of the younger girls spoke up. "I'll take a look at what you've got in there," she said, pointing to the box of jars.

And right there on the bleachers, Estée gave this girl a facial while the others, despite themselves, looked on. When Estée was finished, the girl looked terrific, especially after a hint of rouge and a dusting of face powder, topped off with an application of bright red lipstick.

"I'll just leave these samples here, ladies," Estée said. "Help yourselves."

Sure enough, by the end of the day, every one of Estée's samples had been scooped up. The next time we went to volunteer, a few more women were wearing lipstick, and the time after that, some of the other volunteers joined them. During breaks, Estée continued to give facials and beauty advice. She even convinced the woman with the mustache to try a depilatory cream.

I don't know that Estée actually sold enough to break even on the amount of products she gave away at P.S. 145, but she got those women caring about themselves again. And shortly after that, Estée was further vindicated when *Vogue* magazine encouraged women to do their patriotic part and keep up their beauty routines. Coty even started up a new advertising campaign—*Beauty Is Your Duty.*

AS AN ASSISTANT cosmetic buyer for Saks Fifth Avenue, I was Estée's window, her portal into the world she so desperately wanted to enter. She constantly pumped me for information, hoping I'd tell her what was going on at the store and, more pointedly, with the other cosmetic lines. I couldn't say a thing. I'd given my word and had signed half a dozen confidentiality forms. I knew Estée resented me for that, but my hands were tied. I wanted to help her, I did, but I wasn't willing to lose my job in the process.

My position at Saks gave me a new sense of power. For once in our complicated friendship, I had the upper hand. My opinion held a great deal of weight, and that wasn't a bad thing for my ego. Estée and Joe ran everything by me. *What did I think of the name Clearer Cleanser Creme? Or her idea for skin toner? Did I like the white lids better than the black ones?*

I may have known the industry, but Joe knew numbers. He could split a dinner bill down to the penny, and when Estée brought him into the business, his primary job was to keep the books, keep an eye on the money and keep Estée from spending like a drunken sailor.

"I can't believe it," said Joe. "$50. For jars!" He was incredulous one evening as the three of us sat around their dining room table, the site of so many wonderful Sunday-night dinners. Now it was strewn with paperwork, sample boxes and sheets of labels.

"They're from T. C. Wheaton," Estée said defensively.

"I don't care who they're from." Joe looked up, conversing with God. "She wants to spend $50! For one lousy box of jars."

"Oh, Gloria"—Estée gripped my wrist—"what am I going to do with him?"

"Not to mention $10 on labels," he added. "They're labels, for God's sake."

"Gloria—help! Maybe you can explain it to him."

I looked at Joe, offering an acquiescing shrug. "Packaging *is* important."

"See?" Estée nodded triumphantly. "What did I tell you?"

"And what about these?" Joe sifted through a stack of invoices. "They've already billed us and we haven't even gotten the jars yet."

"I've told you, Joe. We're in a CBD industry—*cash before delivery.* Everyone expects to be paid up front."

"Look at this!" Joe held up another invoice. "Dorfman's Shipping—$20. *Due now.*"

"I need special boxes."

"What for?"

"That's my fault," I said sheepishly. Estée had four products and I'd suggested she sell them all together in a box set. *Like a beauty kit.* She loved the idea and turned around and ordered glossy white boxes, die-cut to snugly fit the bottles, jars and a powder compact.

"And here's another invoice. $7.50 for cottonseed oil."

"I need ingredients."

"Can't you find cheaper boxes? Cheaper ingredients?" he asked.

"I can't and I won't. I'm not going to skimp on the quality of my products. Or the packaging. The packaging is almost as important as the creams and lotions. Tell him, Gloria."

"She's right, Joe," I said. "Women get seduced by the jars and bottles, even the little boxes they come in. They'll buy one item over another simply because they like the color of the box better. It sounds nuts but it's true."

"See?" Estée shot him a grin. "Sure, I could find cheaper jars but just look at these!" She held one up to the light, marveling at it like a precious bauble before handing it to me.

I held the jar. It had a nice heft to it. The cap was shiny black.

Much better than the white lids she'd been considering. I set the jar aside and glanced at the mock-up of the new labels.

"And I'm sorry," said Joe, "but you have to stop giving away all your products. People ask me, they say, 'Joe, what business are you in?' and I say, 'The giveaway business. It does very well.'"

38

1943

I WAS A TERRIBLE housekeeper—that was a given—but every now and again, I got inspired to clean my apartment. That's what happened one day in late June when the sunlight coming through my living room window revealed the cobwebs clinging to the crown molding, the streaks of dust on my coffee table, and the crumbs on the area rug. God only knew what was growing in the back of the icebox and I didn't dare think about what awaited me in the bathroom.

I started in the living room, and when I pulled apart the sofa cushions, I found not only a few popcorn kernels and a paper clip but something so unexpected and jarring, it squeezed my heart. There it was, buried between the cushions—one of Edward's combs.

That stupid black plastic dime-store comb just about did me in, reminding me of how he'd pull it from his pocket, pause before the hallway mirror, the coffee percolator—anything he could catch his reflection in—and comb that amazing hair of his. In that instant I conjured up his smell, his taste, the way his lip curled just a hint before he smiled, the feel of his arms around me on a Sunday morning when we had the luxury of lingering in bed, our bodies intertwined.

I missed sitting on the edge of the tub, watching him shave in the mornings. I missed his scrambled eggs with Parmesan cheese and hot sauce. I missed working crossword puzzles with him. He made better coffee than I did and built better fires . . . I sat there, clutching that comb, reminiscing until I had to force myself to stop. *Just stop it!*

I was suffocating and fled my apartment, finally ending up at a little diner on the corner of 59th and Fifth. Seated at a long counter by the front window, I sipped my coffee and chain-smoked cigarettes and tried not to think about Edward.

The man sitting next to me provided a little distraction. He was feeding cracker crumbs to something brown and furry hiding in his pocket. It could have been a gerbil or a kitten. I wasn't sure. I made the mistake of making eye contact with him and he shot me a big gap-toothed smile. I turned away.

At one point I happened to look up and did a double take. There was Estée with her head down, her hair as I'd never seen it before, all in disarray. She was walking very fast, her pocketbook swinging wildly from her wrist. I crushed my cigarette out in the ashtray, abandoned my coffee and pushed through the front door.

The sidewalk was crowded and it took a moment to spot her nearly half a block away. She was moving at a quick clip, a woman with a purpose. I called to her but my voice was drowned out by the horns honking, an ambulance whining, clogged in traffic. I broke into a jog, weaving in and out of people until I finally caught up to her at a red light. Up close I saw that her hair wasn't just a mess. It was sopping wet.

"Estée? Are you okay? What are you doing?"

She refused to look at me, but I saw she was crying. "I have never been so humiliated in all my life."

"Wait a minute. Calm down. What happened to your hair?"

She just shook her head. "Never in my life . . ." Someone bumped into her and I pulled her aside to save her from the onslaught of pedestrians. "Oh God," she wailed, "get me out of here, please. I need to go home before someone sees me like this."

I grabbed hold of her arm and flagged down a taxicab on the corner. I gave the driver her address and asked her again what happened.

"I went to the Elizabeth Arden spa," she whimpered, plucking a handkerchief from her pocketbook. "I just wanted to get my hair done. That's all."

"And?"

"And I was in the middle of my shampoo when that bitch—Elizabeth Arden—ordered me out of her shop."

"That's insane. Why would she do a thing like that?"

"I have no idea. I was minding my own business."

"Well, something must have provoked her."

Estée shrugged. "All I did was give some samples of my moisturizer to a few of the women in there and—"

"Oh, Estée, you didn't."

"It was no big deal."

"No big deal? You were peddling *your* products inside Miss Arden's spa? What did you think was going to happen?"

She broke down into a fresh round of tears. I paid the driver as he pulled up to Estée's building and I helped her inside.

"I just wanted to get my hair done and—" She caught a glimpse of herself in the mirror above the fireplace and sank down on the sofa. "Oh, just look at me," she shrieked, and folded nearly in half, her chest in her lap.

"It's okay. I'll help you do your hair. You'll look perfect. Good as new."

She groaned from deep inside. "I can't do this."

"Of course you can. You do your own hair all the time."

"No, I'm not talking about my hair." She straightened up and shook her head. "I can't do *this* anymore"—she held out her hands—"this business."

"What are you talking about?" I laughed when I shouldn't have.

"I'm serious. I've tried and it's just too damn hard. It's wearing me out. I've never been so tired in all my life. The grind is killing me."

"You've been pushing yourself too hard. Maybe you just need to ease up a bit. Take a rest. Why don't you and Joe get away—go upstate? I can look after Leonard while you're gone."

She didn't acknowledge my offer. She was too frustrated and discouraged. I could see it on her face. In the past when things got tough, she'd always been able to pick herself back up, but this time I sensed it was going to be my job. So I reminded her of how much she'd already accomplished, how she'd overcome every hurdle, every obstacle in her path.

"When was the last time you did something nice for yourself?" I asked. "How about taking a little time just for you?"

"That's what I tried to do today at Elizabeth Arden and look what happened!"

I didn't dare say she'd instigated it and instead handed her a fresh tissue.

"I've been turned down by every department store in this city. Gimbels, Macy's, Bloomingdale's, Bonwit's, Lord & Taylor. And do you know what B. Altman's said? They said I don't have enough products in my line."

"Estée, we've talked about this. You do need to expand if you're going to compete with the rest of the market. Not all women want to wear turquoise eyeshadow."

"But it makes their eyes brighter. It does."

"And what about lipstick? You insist on selling only that one shade of lipstick."

"But that shade of red is flattering on every complexion, every kind of skin tone."

"That very well may be true, but women want options."

"Oh, why do they need options when what I have is already the best? I tell you, I can't take any more rejection from those people. And as you well know, I can't even get a meeting with Saks Fifth Avenue. I'm through wasting my time."

"Maybe you don't need to be in the big department stores. Maybe you should just stick with the concession stands in the beauty parlors. You're making decent money now."

She looked as though I'd said something insulting. "That's not what I've been working toward all these years. If I can't be at the top, I don't want to be in this game at all. No, I'm getting out. Today was the last straw. I can't compete with women like Elizabeth Arden." She turned to me with tears leaking down her face. "I never thought I'd say this. I've never been a quitter, not in all my life, but I know when I'm beaten. I'm closing up my beauty parlor business. To hell with all of it. I'm done."

39

1984

IT'S A BLUSTERY, snowy February afternoon and no sooner do I return home from the bodega around the corner than my downstairs buzzer sounds. I open the door and there she is: Lee Israel. It's been almost a month since we'd met at the Pierre hotel bar. I never gave her my address and yet here she is. Reluctantly, I let her inside. She smells like wet dog, her woolen coat soaked with melting snow, her eyeglasses fogged up. I ask if she wants a towel, but she waves it off and I guide her away from my velvet sofa and over to a leather club chair in the family room.

"You're a hard lady to get ahold of," she says disapprovingly. "I've left half a dozen messages for you. But"—she sighs—"if the mountain won't come to Muhammad . . ."

She takes out all her accoutrements and slaps them on the coffee table: the spiral notebook, ballpoint pen, cigarettes and a red Cricket lighter that looks like she's chewed on it. Even though I bummed that cigarette off her the last time we met, I hope she's not planning to smoke in the house.

"So, I've been calling you because I want to ask you about the uncle."

"The uncle?"

"Estée's uncle. John Schotz. The one in Corona. You've met him, right?"

"Listen"—I pause, searching for the best way to phrase it—"I appreciate what you're trying to do, but, well, this whole book thing . . . it makes me very uncomfortable."

"Apparently, it's making your friend uncomfortable, too." She reaches for a cigarette.

"Do you mind not . . ." I gesture toward her Marlboros.

She makes a face, like she's put out, and tucks the cigarette back in its pack. "Did you know Estée Lauder's writing her own book now?"

"Really?" I do my best to look surprised.

"Yes, really." Her gaze is accusatory. "Random House is on board to publish it and they're determined to release it before mine comes out. Macmillan's already moved up my pub date. So now it's a race to publication. I have to deliver my manuscript almost six months early. I'm in a real crunch here, Gloria. I need your help. Now I know the two of you had a falling-out and—"

"Whoa—whoever's feeding you this information got their facts wrong," I say a bit too sharply.

"How so? I know you two had some kind of rift. All I'm asking for are the details." She studies me for a moment. "What really happened between the two of you?"

I make a point of checking my watch. "You know, I have to be somewhere soon. You really should have told me you were coming ahead of time and I would have cleared my—"

"I tried. Remember? You've been avoiding me and I'm more than a little curious as to why that is."

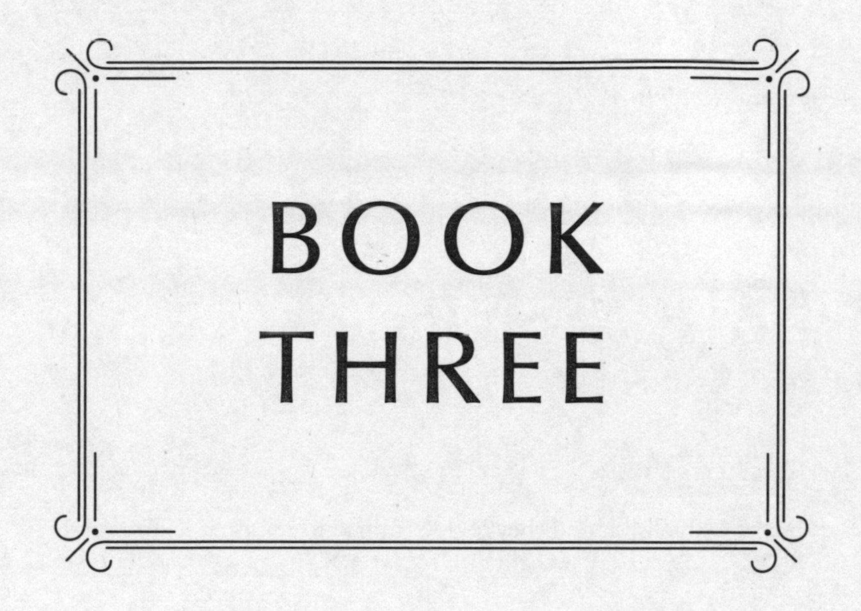

BOOK THREE

40

1944

ESTÉE DID EVENTUALLY close all her concession stands in those beauty parlors throughout the city, but she didn't do it back in 1943 when she'd threatened to give up on her business. If memory serves me correctly, the day after she got thrown out of Elizabeth Arden's spa, she had a good cry, whined and sulked for a whole twenty-four hours before she was done with her pity party. Maybe it was her sheer exhaustion coupled with the humiliation, but once she'd gotten all that out of her system, Estée was back. All the way back.

She continued working, even after she learned she was pregnant again. Joe wanted her to take time off, let him run things, but she wouldn't hear of it. Instead, she was busy expanding her line, creating two additional shades of eyeshadow and lipstick. She even toyed with a perfume but refused to release it until she felt it was perfect. She was putting in twelve- and fourteen-hour days right up till February 26, when she went into labor and welcomed Ronald Steven Lauder into the world.

Two weeks later I stopped by their apartment with a baby gift: a monogrammed cashmere blanket wrapped in heavy blue paper with yellow ducks all around. I hadn't planned on staying long, assuming that Estée would be weary, sleep-deprived and overwhelmed. I expected to find her in a housecoat, taking it easy on the sofa. Instead, she was fully dressed with her face on, holding a swaddled Ronald in her arms while she stood in the kitchen amid boxes and sacks of beeswax, lanolin and other ingredients. Two stockpots were boiling away—one was sterilizing baby bottles; the other was cooking a batch of face cream. The counters were lined with nipples and the new glass jars she'd ordered. Joe and Leonard were in there helping, too. Estée had set up a mini assembly line for producing her skincare creams and lotions. It reminded me of our days at the Red Cross, putting together those Comfort Kits.

The only thing I could do to help was hold the baby, and when I took him in my arms, I was overcome by a deep ache, a longing I didn't know was there. I gently pressed my lips to the downy fuzz of his hair and breathed in his baby scent. I was happy for Estée and Joe. Truly I was, but at the same time, I was feeling sorry for myself. If I hadn't broken off my engagement with Edward, we would have been married by now and possibly had a child of our own. I would have had a real family.

I was turning twenty-eight that summer, and at times like these, I had to stop and ask myself how long I was going to put off living—really living. What was I waiting for? My father had been in prison for five and a half years, and in a way, I'd been serving my own sentence right along with him. And for what? Intellectually, I knew I hadn't done anything wrong. I was not responsible for the things my father did. I understood that, but I still couldn't get past the embarrassment, the shame.

When he was first arrested, I'd had to consciously fight the urge to contact my mother and even Gail. I'd often contemplated picking up the telephone or sending cards on birthdays and holidays or just because I was feeling lonely. I was riddled with guilt for abandoning them, especially my father. It had all been such a struggle back then, but as time passed, I realized that there'd been long stretches—weeks and months—where I'd forgotten to even think about them. They had all but vanished and yet I was still stuck, and I had no idea what it would take to set myself free.

I felt selfish lamenting over things that seemed so trivial compared to the war. I thought about the men who were right there, prepared to face the ultimate sacrifice. I worried endlessly about Waller and Soda Pop. I hadn't received a letter from either one of them in months. I prayed for them and I was not one to pray.

I thought of all the shattered families those soldiers had left behind. My family was broken, too—not because of some patriotic duty but because my father was a crook and my brother was a coward. Glenn—fully capable of defending his country—had found a loophole to get himself out of the army. And to think I thought he was the honorable one. But he'd stepped over to the dark side along with my mother and sister. I wondered what my fearless doughboy father who'd fought during WWI would have to say about his son worming his way out of enlisting? Not that I wanted my brother fighting, but part of me sensed I'd already lost him just the same.

I'd never felt more alone, and after three years, there seemed to be no end in sight to the war. Sometimes, for sanity's sake, you had to try to block it out and trick yourself into feeling normal. That's what Bobbi and I were doing one Saturday night when we decided to go to the picture show. While waiting in line at the concession stand, she told me about her latest piece of artwork: a soldier going off to fight, rifle over his shoulder—all done in those leather-like banana slivers.

"I thought I had a taker for it," she said. "But I blew it."

The buttery smell and light *pop, pop, pop* sound filled the air.

"What happened?" I asked.

"The guy wanted to know what it was made of and I told him. As soon as he heard the word 'banana' he changed his mind. His wife was sure they'd get fruit flies. I should have told him it was string or silk rope."

"No," I said. "You did the right thing." Such a hypocrite I was, the guardian of honesty, even as I lied to my closest friends about who I really was. This was the contradiction of my life that I kept butting up against. Over and over again.

The truth was always right there, waiting to rise up inside me, looking for a way out. The effort it took to keep the lid sealed tight was intensifying. For a brief time, I had Edward as my outlet, a place to unload my secrets, but now he was long gone and I had no release. The same old lies were stacking up inside me, one on top of another. It was a physical sensation that pulled my skin taunt, making me feel like I might split open. How many times had I been on the verge of coming clean? But I couldn't go that extra distance, so I rode out the anxiety, knowing it would pass. It always did. Until the next time.

Bobbi and I got our popcorn and went into the theater. The lights were already going down as we sidestepped our way to two vacant seats. Their hinges squeaked as we sat down and the newsreel burst to life before us on the screen. It was all bouncy music, jet propellers, explosions, clouds of smoke and that authoritative voice telling us that America and Uncle Sam were defending our liberties. I squinted, looking at the men as if I might catch a glimpse of a familiar face.

ESTÉE WAS NOT one of those mothers content to stay home with her newborn. No, she went back to work six weeks after giving birth, and if she could have gone back sooner, I believe she would have. And it wasn't that Estée didn't treasure being with baby Ronald, but I think she believed she'd lost some valuable ground due to her pregnancy and now she wanted to make up for lost time. While Joe took care of the boys and ran the financial side of their business, Estée was trying, to no avail, to get her products into the department stores. And when she wasn't knocking on their doors, she was going from beauty parlor to beauty parlor, keeping a close watch on a dozen different concessions and a team of salesgirls.

Once again, she asked me to orchestrate a meeting with Mr. Fiske. "Just tell him all I need is twelve inches of counter space. That's all I'm asking for."

"Twelve inches?" I laughed. "Estée, you might as well be asking for twelve feet. Besides, you can't just make an appointment with him. I've already told you, Mr. Fiske only listens to sales pitches twice a week. Wednesdays and Fridays. That's it."

The following Friday Estée was in the buying department's waiting room, sitting among a sea of men with a box of her products resting on her lap. Shortly after she arrived, Helena Rubinstein unexpectedly swept into the office. In her floor-length mink coat and ladies' black homburg hat, her many necklaces and rings, she looked like a Gypsy or maybe a sweet Jewish grandmother. I couldn't decide which. But she was cosmetic royalty and, like Miss Arden, she didn't require an appointment.

"I'll let Mr. Fiske know you're here, Madame Rubinstein." As soon as I said her name aloud, I regretted not being more discreet, for Estée's head turned like a whirling dervish, her eyes wide.

I rushed to Mr. Fiske's office, interrupting his meeting to alert him of Madame's arrival, and by the time I returned to the waiting room, Estée had already cornered the great Helena Rubinstein. Thrusting one of her business cards into Madame's jeweled hand, Estée was talking rapidly. Madame Rubinstein narrowed her eyes, raised her chin. And it wasn't that Estée couldn't read the situation—she was better at that than anyone I knew—but she was choosing to ignore the obvious. Instead, she pressed on, as if with enough persistence, she could win anyone over. Estée was still talking to the cosmetic queen—rambling, actually. I had to cut her off so I could rescue Madame Rubinstein and whisk her into Mr. Fiske's office.

When I came back out, I motioned to Estée and pulled her aside. "You can't do that," I said.

"Do what?"

"That was Helena Rubinstein." I said this as if the rest were implied.

"I know! I wish you'd given me a few more minutes with her."

"No one does what you just did to her. No one," I said.

"Well, at least she has my business card now. Maybe she'll contact me."

"Estée—" I was exasperated.

Madame Rubinstein was in with Mr. Fiske for a good thirty minutes. All the while, Estée was doing her best to engage in conversation with the other sales reps, asking about their products and the other stores they were in. Each time I went out to the waiting room, she was talking to someone new. I watched her occasionally remove various bottles and jars from her box. She'd hold them up to the light and examine them like they had something magical inside.

I was still out in the waiting room when Mr. Fiske's door opened and he escorted Helena Rubinstein out of his office. Madame had her mink draped over one arm, and much to my surprise, she walked over to where Estée was seated.

"Estée Lauder?" Madame said in her thick Polish accent. "I believe this belongs to you." And with that she crumpled up Estée's business card and deposited it into Estée's hand.

"YOUR FRIEND HAD better watch her step," Marion said to me later that day. We were at our partner's desk, nibbling egg salad sandwiches at four in the afternoon, having been too busy earlier to take our usual lunch break at the Automat.

"I already talked to her about that," I said, peeling back the top slice of bread to remove a wilted lettuce leaf.

"I still can't get over how she ambushed Madame Rubinstein. I've never seen anyone approach her like that, let alone try and stuff their business card in her hand." Marion laughed, still in disbelief.

"I told her that, too."

"You know," said Marion, "if you really want to be a good friend, you need to show Estée the ropes around here or she'll never get a meeting with Mr. Fiske, let alone counter space in Saks."

"God knows I've tried. She doesn't listen." In fact, I'd had many conversations with Estée about the best approach to take with Mr. Fiske. And others in the industry, too. The whole time I'd talk she'd nod, acting like she understood what I was saying, but then she'd turn around and do whatever she wanted anyway. "She gets something in her head and that's it."

At the end of the day, Mr. Fiske called me into his office. I knew he was going to reprimand me about Estée. I could hear it now—she had offended Madame Rubinstein and was no longer welcome to pitch her wares. I dreaded having to deliver that message to Estée.

Out of habit, I grabbed my steno pad and pen and went in to see him. I sat in my usual seat across from his desk and was stunned to see that he was smiling.

"Is everything okay?" I asked.

"I hope you'll think it's better than okay." He reached into his drawer for an envelope and slid it across to me. "That's your paycheck. You'll see it's quite a bit larger than your previous ones. Congratulations."

I looked inside and my jaw about dropped. It wasn't until I was back at my desk and armed with an adding machine that I was able to figure out that I'd received an extra $18.75. That meant I'd be earning an additional $75 a month, $900 a year—on top of what I was already making. I felt suddenly flush.

I needed a moment to let that sink in, and when it finally did, I exploded with starbursts of pride. Me—*starburst*—I, Gloria, did this—*starburst*—I earned this myself—*starburst*—no one gave it to me. And there it was, the grand finale that had me nearly giggling as possibilities bloomed before my eyes. I could open a savings account. I could afford a better apartment now. Maybe one in a doorman building. Overlooking the park. I could get those patent leather shoes I'd been eyeing all season. There was so much I could do with this windfall. Everything that most women expected a man to bring into their lives, I could now go out and buy for myself.

41

1945

SAKS FIFTH AVENUE held an annual luncheon for its cosmetic vendors every spring. It was the who's who of the industry. Invitations were coveted and the event took months of preparation. We were holding it in the ballroom at the Plaza Hotel that year. Marion and I had arrived ahead of time to ensure the centerpieces, nameplates and other details were in order.

Because Madame Rubinstein and Elizabeth Arden refused to be in the same room at the same time, we alternated inviting them from one year to the next. This year was Miss Arden's turn. She agreed to attend as long as Mr. Fiske promised to keep *that man*—which was how she referred to Charles Revson—as far away from her as possible. We assured her that would not be a problem. She was the most important guest on our list and would be seated at the head table next to Mr. Fiske.

I knew Estée wanted an invitation. Frankly, getting a meeting with President Truman would have been easier. But at the last minute, we had a few guests drop out because of a nasty stomach bug that was going around and there was an opening at my table. I wanted to surprise her with a ticket and asked Mr. Fiske, who was too preoccupied with other matters to have really weighed my request. I think the thought of having empty seats was more concerning than letting an interloper like Estée join the luncheon.

"Yes, yes." He'd waved his hand impatiently. "Go ahead. Invite her."

Estée was seated next to me toward the back of the room along with a very cranky Charles Revson. I remember thinking his table manners were appalling as I watched his ruby red fingernails rip a roll in half and toss the rest back into the breadbasket. He was also two martinis ahead of the rest of us. Estée paid him little attention at first. She was too busy eyeing the room, sizing up her competition, unaware that her greatest future rival was right there at her table.

It was a considerably inebriated Revson who had initiated a conversation with Estée. "So, you're Estée Lauder, huh?" he said, resting an elbow on the table.

The way he said *huh* rubbed me the wrong way, but not Estée. I could tell by how her face opened wide with surprise, by the way she turned toward him, that she was thrilled he'd even heard of her.

"My people tell me you're trying to get into Saks." He had such a snide laugh. "Good luck, toots—'cause you're gonna need it."

And suddenly Estée wasn't so thrilled. I watched the change come over her face. "You're a man, Mr. Revson. What could you possibly know about cosmetics and what women want?"

"It's *because* I'm a man that I know what men want women to look like."

"Well, that's just insulting," she said. "And absurd. Do you even hear yourself?"

"I sure do and you better be listening. You're a novice. You got a lot to learn, girly."

Estée delicately dabbed the corners of her mouth with her napkin. "Why, Mr. Revson, if I didn't know better, I'd say you're afraid of the competition."

"Afraid?" He laughed again. "Hardly."

"Well, look out because I'm going to get my line into Saks Fifth Avenue. And that's a promise."

"I'll tell you what"—he waved his red fingernails through the air—"if you *ever* get into Saks, I'll buy out your company." He laughed and added a hand flourish. "I'll become the Cadillac of the cosmetic industry."

"Well, that's very flattering," Estée said, her voice amazingly controlled, "but I think I'd rather buy out *your* company and be the Rolls Royce of the industry."

Everyone at the table laughed. Except for Charles Revson. His face turned as red as his fingernails. Without a word he threw his napkin down, pushed away from the table and stormed out of the ballroom. I rushed after him, hoping to smooth things over.

When I finally caught up to him, he leaned into a potted plant for balance and said, "You mark my words—I will destroy that woman!"

When I returned to Saks later that afternoon, Mr. Fiske wasted no time calling me into his office. "What on earth happened today with Charles Revson and that friend of yours?"

THANKFULLY MY HAIR—Maple Sugar Brown—was again long enough to pin up, but still tendrils clung to the nape of my neck. It was unseasonably hot that day, a record breaker for May. The air-conditioning at work hadn't been turned on yet for the season and it was sweltering inside. Fans oscillated back and forth, fluttering the papers on our partner's desk, which were being held in place by adding machines, staplers and sweating bottles of Coca-Cola. The windows were all thrown open but even eight stories up it was hard to block the sirens and horns filtering up from street level.

I reached for a cigarette but realized the pack was empty. I pitched the crumpled wrapper in my wastebasket and dragged the back of my hand across my forehead, damp with perspiration. I was having a hard enough time concentrating even before Marion came into our office.

"Your friend Bobbi's here to see you," she said.

"Bobbi's here?" Bobbi would sometimes meet me at work, but it was always downstairs by the main entrance. She'd never been up to the buying offices before. I glanced at her artwork on my wall, thinking how pleased she'd be to see it hanging there. That's what I was thinking when Marion showed her in.

As soon as I saw Bobbi's face, I felt a chill despite the stifling heat. I could tell she'd been crying. "What's wrong? What happened?"

Bobbi came over and wrapped her arms around me, her long heavy hair draped over my shoulder like a blanket. "Oh, Gloria, it's Waller."

Waller! I heard myself gasp and my skin turned to ice even before she'd said the words *killed in action.* Waller was dead? I went limp in Bobbi's embrace, and even as the tears streamed down my face, as those words ricocheted inside my head, it seemed unreal. My hands were shaking so, I struggled with the clasp of my pocketbook for a fresh pack of cigarettes. It took me three tries to get the lighter working and I sat back, drawing the smoke in deep. It did nothing to calm me. For years I'd been reading about the war, listening to radio reports, seeing life-size clips on newsreels, but the horrors hadn't hit home until just then. *Waller—gone. Forever.* How was it possible that I'd never see him again? Ever.

I eventually pulled myself together and clutched a damp handkerchief in my hand. "We should probably go tell the Millers. They'll want to know."

Bobbi gave me such a puzzled look, I feared she had more bad news. "The Millers know," she said.

"They do?" I dabbed my eyes and wiped my nose.

"They got the telegram this morning."

Now I was truly confused. *Why would the Millers have received the telegram?*

"They're the ones who called and told me. Mr. Miller asked me to let you know, too."

"But how—I still don't get why—"

"What do you mean why? Waller is—*was*—their son and—"

"What?" I blinked. "What are you talking about?"

Now it was Bobbi who looked confused or, more accurately, surprised. "I thought you knew. I thought for sure he told you."

"Waller is Richard and Sylvia Miller's son?" I said it aloud, in disbelief. It sounded so obscure, like I was speaking a foreign language. "Waller never said a word. Why wouldn't he have told me?"

"I think he was embarrassed. Ashamed—you know, a grown man, still living at home with his parents, not being able to make it as an actor. Especially growing up in a showbiz family."

I gave it another moment to register with me. "How long have you known?"

Bobbi shrugged as if to say, *What difference does it make now?*

"When did you find out?" I asked.

"I don't remember exactly. It's been a while, though. Mrs. Miller mentioned it one day. Maybe she let it slip—I can't really remember."

As Bobbi and I made our way over to the Millers', I was still trying to get my mind wrapped around all this, including the fact that Waller was dead. The closer we got to the Millers' home, the more the pieces started to fit. Waller had refused to tell me his real name, he'd said he'd lived at the Millers' *forever*, and even told me he'd once lived in the room I'd rented from them. The baseball pennants and decals . . . the photos of the little boy on the stairwell . . . how handsome Mr. and Mrs. Miller had been in their youth—it all made sense. Even down to the acting—Waller had gotten it all from his parents, Richard and Sylvia Miller.

With a stab of guilt, I remembered how Waller had asked me to keep an eye on the Millers for him while he was gone—something I hadn't done a very good job of lately. A telephone call here and there, dropping in on holidays, but that was about it. The last time I went to one of their parties, Mrs. Miller didn't dance, complaining that her varicose veins were acting up. Mr. Miller told his jokes, kept glasses filled, but there was a heaviness about him, the way he moved, the way he spoke. At the time, I thought maybe it was the war or just that they were getting on in years. I knew something was different about them and now I realized it was because their son, Waller, was overseas, fighting in the war. They hadn't received a letter from him in weeks. None of us had.

I was holding back a fresh wave of tears when Mrs. Miller answered the door.

"Hello, hello," she said, and before she could say anything more, I rushed in and hugged her harder than I should have.

"I'm so sorry. So very, very sorry."

She patted my back in silence and though it was wrong—that she was the one consoling me—I couldn't help myself. As soon as I released her, I went over to Mr. Miller and did the same to him.

Fifteen minutes later, after we'd dried another round of tears, out came the old photo albums and scrapbooks. A stack of red and green leather-bound volumes filled with photographs, flyers from school plays, grammar school report cards. Mrs. Miller had documented everything in her son's short life.

"Look at this," she said, handing me a photograph. "That was his high school graduation."

I studied the picture. Waller in a cap and gown, one arm around Richard, the other around Sylvia. He definitely had his mother's good looks and his father's solid chin.

"And here he is on his second birthday," Mr. Miller said, handing me another picture, this one of Waller mugging for the camera.

"Even then, we knew he was destined to be an actor. A real ham, he was, right from the start. Singing and dancing as soon as he could walk, as soon as he could talk."

"He always wanted a little brother or sister," said Mrs. Miller. "But Richard and I were so busy working all the time that we didn't get around to starting a family until later on. I was already thirty-eight when I had Moische. Named after his grandfather on Richard's side," she explained. "He always hated that name. Wouldn't even let us call him Moe for short." She smiled like she was replaying some memory of her son protesting.

I almost wished she hadn't told me so Waller could have taken that part of his secret to the grave.

42

THOUGH MR. FISKE still wasn't interested in bringing the Estée Lauder line to Saks Fifth Avenue, even he couldn't deny that her name was floating around the store. Marion and I heard more and more of the salesgirls saying their customers were asking if we carried the Lauder Creme Packs or the Super Rich All-Purpose Creme.

Estée was well aware of this, too. She would come into Saks and stand near the cosmetic counters and watch—just watch—the customers coming and going. She knew all the Saks shopgirls by name and had even become quite chummy with Vivian, which I found annoying. Estée was constantly digging for information: Who were their top customers? What was selling that week?

One day, when I happened to be down on the floor, Estée made the mistake of approaching Harriet at the perfume counter. Before Estée even opened her mouth, Harriet reached for a bottle of Shalimar. "Go away!" Harriet began spritzing Estée with the bottle like it was bug repellent. "Just get out of here. Just go!"

After that Estée did her best to steer clear of Harriet but it soon became obvious that it wasn't only the customers and salesgirls who were aware of Estée Lauder. I had sat in on meetings with the giants in the industry, like Elizabeth Arden, as well as the top executives from Max Factor, Maybelline and Coty, all asking about her. They wanted a list of the products in her line. Her price points, a look at her packaging.

The one person who seemed most concerned about the encroaching Estée Lauder threat was Helena Rubinstein, of all people. Madame was in her seventies, though she didn't look it. Ironically, she didn't follow her own prescribed beauty regimen, confessing that she was too tired at the end of the day to be bothered with the whole routine. Fortunately for her, she had good genes and the supple complexion of a woman who'd devoted her life to skincare.

One day she came up to the offices unannounced. She was wearing a smart hat, pearl-drop earrings, her hair pulled back in a bun, and her makeup was flawless. She breezed in past the receptionist and went looking for Mr. Fiske.

"Where is he?" she asked, poking her head inside my office.

"I'm sorry," I said, getting up from the desk, "he stepped out. Is there something I can help you with, Madame?"

She tapped her fingernails on the doorjamb, contemplating. "Tell me something—what do you know about those Lauder Packs? Those Creme Packs? What do you know about *her*?"

Frankly I was surprised that it had taken Mrs. Rubinstein this long to ask me about Estée. I knew Mr. Fiske had told her that Estée was my friend and I wondered if she'd even remembered meeting her over a year ago in the waiting room, the day Estée had accosted her with a business card. I was dealing with an ego about as delicate as a snowflake and knew I had to tread lightly.

"Some people like her line," I said with great trepidation. Anything shy of claiming Estée's products caused warts would not have been welcome news.

"I see." She nodded and asked where Estée had received her

training, who was backing her financially, if she was working on a fragrance.

These were all questions that I did my best to dodge while Madame studied my office and inched farther and farther inside. It wasn't until she went to the wall by the window that I realized what had drawn her in—it was Bobbi's banana art.

"This is quite interesting," she said. "Very unusual."

"Oh, that." I laughed, grateful that the focus had shifted away from Estée. "My friend made it for me."

"So the artist—the artist is your friend?"

Artist? I had never thought of Bobbi as an actual artist. "Uh, yes. Yes, she is."

"Hmmm." Madame nodded. "I'm a collector, you know."

Actually, I didn't know this at the time, but as it turned out, Madame Rubinstein had over 300 pieces of coveted artwork in her possession. She was personal friends with Picasso, Dalí and a host of other celebrated artists.

"This is a very unusual piece indeed," she said, nodding again.

I was contemplating whether or not to tell her it was made of banana peels but it sounded so absurd to say something like that to Madame Rubinstein.

"Arrange a meeting, will you?" she said.

"What? You mean with Bobbi?"

She scrutinized the signature in the lower corner of the piece. "Yes, with Bobbi, the artist."

I WAS WITH Bobbi the day she met Helena Rubinstein. Or more accurately I should say that I had escorted Madame Rubinstein to Bobbi's run-down apartment on Amsterdam and 95th Street. Bobbi had a full-time job back then, doing illustrations for a greeting card company. Judging from her apartment, it didn't seem to pay very well. Sometimes I thought she would have been better off staying at the Millers'.

Bobbi had yet to sell any of her pieces, but still she kept going, said she couldn't give up on her artwork even if she wanted to. She just had this thing about the bananas, even though they presented an enormous stumbling block to her career. She met with gallery owners, collectors, appraisers, and hung out with other artists, all of whom were far more successful than she. The gallery owners and potential buyers were always intrigued with her work. Some might have even considered buying a piece or two, or including her in an exhibit, until they realized that her medium was banana peels. That killed every opportunity. They couldn't take her work seriously. But she wasn't going to let that stop her. Bobbi pursued her art with as much vigor as Estée pursued her cosmetic business. In that respect, my two best friends were surprisingly similar.

The August air was stagnant with heat and humidity; the curtains by the open window barely stirred. Madame Rubinstein didn't say a word about the clutter, the rickety furnishings, the dark, gloomy hallway. Instead, she seemed to find the humble hovel of an artist quaint and endearing. Looking at Bobbi in her bohemian garb and Madame in her Gypsy-like getup, the long flowing skirt, the billowy sleeves, the heaps of necklaces and bracelets, I saw the two of them as kindred spirits.

I stood back, keeping to myself, while Bobbi showed her several pieces, some framed, some not. I noticed a bunch of bruising bananas on the countertop in the kitchenette, strings of slivered peels hanging in the bathroom on a lingerie-drying rack. I'd been wrestling with myself about whether or not to warn Madame about the bananas but decided it was Bobbi's place to do that, not mine.

But when Madame Rubinstein asked about the medium she worked in, Bobbi said, "It's a special type of string made from silk."

Made from silk! I glared at Bobbi, my eyes bulging from my skull.

"My driver is downstairs. I have a meeting," said Madame. "I must go now. But you," she said to Bobbi, "you will create for me—a portrait, yes?"

"Ah yes." Bobbi sounded like she did after three cocktails.

So not only had Helena Rubinstein commissioned Bobbi to do a piece but she wanted it to be a portrait. Madame Rubinstein made out of rotted banana peels. I was mortified.

"Oh, and I'm having a salon next Sunday," Madame Rubinstein said as she adjusted her hat. "At my home. You will both come, yes?"

"Ah yes," Bobbi said again. "Sure. Thanks."

I turned to Bobbi after Helena Rubinstein left. "How could you do that?"

"Do what?" Bobbi was downright giddy. It was her first sale. And to the great Helena Rubinstein, no less, who was intricately connected to the art world, to other collectors, and who had just invited her to a salon.

"You're selling her banana peels."

"No, I'm selling her *artwork*," Bobbi said defensively.

"It's not silk string. It's goddamn banana peels!" I raised my hands and let them drop to my hips. "How could you do this?"

"Why are you getting so upset?"

"Because you just put me in the position of deceiving Helena Rubinstein."

"You didn't deceive her. I did—and you know as well as I do that if she knew what it was, she wouldn't buy it."

"But you have to tell her the truth. You just have to."

"No, I don't." She tweaked the scarf about her head. "And quit trying to make me feel like I've done something wrong."

"But you have."

"Says who? Do you have any idea how long I've been working toward this moment? Listen"—her voice softened some—"I'm grateful that you brought her here, but honestly, this isn't your problem. This is between Helena Rubinstein and me."

She was right about that, but still, I was not prepared to be as disappointed as I was. I wanted to warn Bobbi that she didn't know how to play the game of deception. Unlike me, it wasn't in her nature. But even more upsetting was the fact that Bobbi had just sold out and I thought she'd never do that. I'd always admired her for being so genuine, for pursuing her crazy art for the love of it, regardless of her ability to sell it. She'd never done it for the money. Up until now.

Money truly was the root of all evil. Sooner or later, it got to everyone—my father, who had put himself through college, who had started out as an honest, hardworking stockbroker only to be destroyed by greed. Even Edward had traded in a job he was passionate about for a bigger paycheck. Bobbi had no idea what she'd just set in motion or the price she'd pay for the sake of selling one piece of art. She'd falsely represented herself and now she was going to waltz into Madame Rubinstein's salon and perpetuate her lie.

43

AUGUST 14, 1945. Three minutes past seven o'clock. Bobbi and I were standing in Times Square, shoulder to shoulder with about two million of our fellow New Yorkers, all eyes trained on the zipper news running along Times Tower. So quiet, no one shouting, even speaking. We were at a standstill, all of us holding our breath, braced and waiting, waiting and—there it was:

OFFICIAL—TRUMAN ANNOUNCES JAPANESE SURRENDER.

The exhale of a thunderous cheer rose up from the crowd as horns blasted, music began blaring and people started dancing amid confetti floating through the air like snowflakes. The war was over and the collective joy in Times Square was impossible to contain. Even the ground beneath our feet seemed to breathe anew, a fresh start. The streets were full of men in uniform, couples jitterbugging, strangers hugging strangers. We were all so blissfully happy. And suddenly acutely aware of how beat-up and weary we were from it all. But mostly, we were so damn relieved.

Out of nowhere a young soldier grabbed me, threw his arms around me and whirled me in a dizzying circle. It wasn't until my feet landed back on the ground that I looked into his face and saw a familiar twinkle in his eyes.

"Soda Pop! Oh my God—Soda Pop!" I cried, and hugged him all the harder. He was a good four inches taller than I'd remembered and he'd filled out, his shoulders broad, his stance firm. He was a young man now. A handsome young man. "Oh, Soda Pop, you're back. And you're okay?"

"Fit as a fiddle," he said, slapping his flat stomach.

While Soda Pop and I stood there talking, I lost Bobbi in the crowd. I ended up spending the rest of the night with Soda Pop, drinking in the corner of a crowded bar and listening to his stories from the front. He had been a private in the 11th Armored Division, stationed mostly in France, and had traveled throughout Europe in an armored tank. He started to tell me about Omaha Beach but changed the subject, asking instead if I'd ever gotten married.

Married. The word about clobbered me. "No, never married," I said, explaining in vague terms that I'd just never met the right person.

"Well, I'm sorry about that but I can't imagine you spending too many Saturday nights home alone."

I smiled and had to laugh. That was actually true. While I'd managed to keep myself unattached, I did gallivant about town with two eligible bachelors who hadn't gone off to fight, both of whom I'd met at Madame Rubinstein's salons. But none of them were Edward. It had been four years and he was still constantly on my mind. I thought about him, dreamed about him, waking up with tears running down my face. Knowing Edward's sense of honor and duty, I was sure he'd enlisted and now I only hoped that he was safe and whole.

"And what about you?" I asked, noticing how many women in the bar were stealing glances at him. "You got yourself a girl?"

"Ah, you know you're the only girl for me." He winked. "You're still just as pretty as I remembered."

I laughed. "Well, you didn't turn out half bad yourself."

Soda Pop and I drank some more and it was almost four in the morning when we finally stumbled out of the bar. The streets were still packed with drunken men and women, everyone celebrating. The sidewalks were freckled with streamers and confetti, empty beer and whiskey bottles, an abandoned sailor's cap. A couple nearby were leaning against a lamppost, slur-singing a song I couldn't recognize.

I hugged Soda Pop goodbye and watched as he disappeared into the crowd, a regular hero home safe from the war. It made me think of Waller and I teared up on the spot.

A WEEK LATER, I, along with everyone else, was still celebrating the end of the war. I attended a dinner party on the Upper East Side thrown by a playwright I'd met at one of Helena Rubinstein's salons. There were twelve of us gathered around a long mahogany table. To my left was a theater director, to my right was an actress and seated directly across from me was Vicki Baum, whom I would not have recognized from the photo in the back of her book. She had a long face with a sharp chin and dirty blonde marcelled hair that rested upon her shoulders.

What I found most fascinating about Vicki Baum was not that she was the novelist who'd written *Grand Hotel*, or that she was also a Hollywood screenwriter, and an actress as well as a harpist. No, what I found most compelling about her was that she was a boxer.

"Oh, there's nothing like a high-spirited brawl to get your blood pumping," she said, laughing.

"My father was a boxer." *Oh crap!* I couldn't believe I'd just let that slip. The words had tumbled out of me like I had nothing to hide, like I was a normal girl with a normal father.

"A professional fighter?" Vicki asked, intrigued.

"No, no." I shook my head as an old photograph flashed through my mind: my father in his early twenties, dressed in trunks, a trophy in his gloved hands held high above his head. "He was an amateur. Put himself through college winning local matches." *Shut up! What the hell are you doing?* What was happening to the wall I'd built up? Why was I weakening, so casually letting these details ooze out after years of guarding my past so closely? I wasn't sure if I should set my drink aside or guzzle what was left of it and have another. I opted for the latter.

"I got an idea." Vicki struck the tabletop and laughed. "You really ought to jump in the ring, give it a try sometime."

"Ah no." I forced a laugh to match hers. "I don't think I'm the boxing type."

"You kidding me?" She cracked a cunning smile. "You're a fighter, kiddo. I can tell. It's in your blood."

Me? A fighter? I'd never thought of myself that way before, but I supposed in some ways that was true, seeing as how I'd scraped together this new life of mine. Now I just had to put a lid on it, harden myself up again. I couldn't afford to go soft and let anything else leak out.

"You should come with me to Nelson's," she said, referring to a gym in Brooklyn. "Marlene and I do some sparring up there from time to time."

I was pretty sure she was referring to Marlene Dietrich.

"But don't tell anyone"—she pressed a finger to her lips—"they're not supposed to let women in the ring."

"My lips are sealed."

The two of us spent the rest of the evening chattering away, pretty much ignoring the other guests. We drank ourselves into a frenzy that resulted in arm-in-arm declarations of love and promises to get together next time she was in New York.

VICKI AND I did correspond regularly over the next few weeks. When I learned that my new friend was from Austria, born in Vienna, I couldn't wait to introduce her to my other Austrian friend.

Not long after that, Vicki was back in New York and the three of us—Estée, Vicki and I—met at the Onyx Club. Estée seemed more excited about meeting a famous writer than a fellow countryman. Vicki had just come from a meeting to discuss the film adaptation for another one of her novels. She was such a lovable gossip and told us tales about Rita Hayworth, John Wayne, and Hedy Lamarr. Estée was spellbound.

"You know Hedy's from Austria, too," said Vicki. "Studied acting in Vienna."

"Really?" Estée propped her elbow on the table, resting her chin upon the back of her hand. "I didn't know that."

"Oh yes." Vicki held her glass in the air like a dinner bell, summoning the bartender for another. "Gloria here tells me you're also from Austria. Whereabouts?"

"Oh, just in Vienna." In a very un-Estée-like graceless movement, her elbow slipped off the table.

"Not *just in Vienna*," I explained, deciding to do Estée's bragging for her. I thought Vicki would find her background fascinating. "She's an aristocrat. Born into a very prominent Austrian family."

"Oh, Gloria," Estée said with a flick of her wrist, like suddenly the very thing she seemed most proud of was no big deal. "Just family lore. Let's not bore Vicki with all that." Estée shot me a strange look.

"I'm not bored at all," said Vicki, tilting her pointy chin in Estée's direction. "Go on."

"Oh"—Estée shook her head—"my family . . . well, I was just a baby and . . ." She laughed in an odd, queer way that didn't sound like her at all. I wondered if she'd maybe had too much to drink. "Come on now, I don't want to monopolize the conversation with all that family talk."

Since when did Estée not want to monopolize a conversation? I gave her an inquisitive look but her entire focus had shifted to Vicki.

Reaching across the table for her hand, Estée said, "Let's talk about your marvelous complexion. You must tell me what your secret is."

And from there Estée did indeed proceed to monopolize the conversation with talk about her line of beauty products.

44

1946

NEW YORK GOT hit with a blizzard late one afternoon, and in the middle of the night, the temperature had warmed just enough to change the snow over to sleet and freezing rain. The city was now one enormous slush puddle. At each intersection I was greeted with a sea of dark sludgy water; it was impossible to detect if it was three inches or three feet deep. There was a lot of taking the long way around to get me to Saks Fifth Avenue that day.

I finally arrived at the executive offices, and as I stomped the slush from my boots and hung my coat, hat and scarf on the rack, I looked up and immediately knew that something was wrong. No one said good morning. Radios were turned down low or off altogether. If anyone was talking, it was done in hushed tones. I hadn't seen such gloom and doom hanging in the air since the days of the war. With great caution I peered into Mr. Belfort's office. He was staring out the window, his fingers steepled beneath his chin. Next door, Mr. Fiske sat with his elbows squared on his desk, his head hung low, eyes closed.

Carla, the receptionist, hesitated for a moment before approaching me. "Did you hear?" she asked, shaking her head. "Poor Marion."

"Marion? What happened to Marion?" I rushed to our office. It was dark and Marion was always the first one in.

"She was in a car accident last night," Carla said. "She's in the hospital. They said she went through the windshield. She's been in surgery for hours. We're waiting to hear if she's going to make it."

I was in a stupor the rest of the day. Message slips and paperwork piled up on my desk; there were telephone calls I couldn't bring myself to return and forms I couldn't comprehend enough to complete. I couldn't tell you how many times I went to ask Marion something and then remembered she wasn't there. Finally, we got word that she was out of surgery and expected to pull through, although the next forty-eight hours were going to be critical.

The rest was a bit of a blur. It seemed like Marion was in the hospital forever. While she was out, I covered for her at the office, taking on her workload in addition to my own. The hours were long, the days jam-packed. I was so tired I ended up forgoing parties, invites to luncheons, even taking a pass on watching Vicki spar with one of her boxing pals. What little free time I had was spent with the Millers, with Estée and Bobbi.

Apparently, Bobbi had been deeply troubled by the discussion we'd had about her selling banana peels to Helena Rubinstein. For the first time in her life, Bobbi's creative juices had dried up. One of Madame Rubinstein's friends, a famous art dealer at M. Knoedler & Company, had commissioned her for a piece. So had several of Madame's other salon-goers. Bobbi had commissioned work piling up and she was positively stymied.

"What am I going to do?" We were in her new apartment down in the Village. It was a lovely place with a wall of windows that flooded the main room with natural light. After all this time, she was finally making enough money off her artwork to afford such a place, but she was buckling under the guilt. She showed me an interview that ran in *Art in America* with the headline BUDDING ARTIST TURNING SILK INTO GOLD.

"I feel like a total fraud," she said. "You were right. I should have just told Madame from the start what it was. Now when I look at my artwork, all I see are goddamn banana peels." She shoved aside a pile of discarded canvases lying in a heap on the floor. "And I'm in too deep now. I can't say anything. If I do, I'll never sell another piece. I'd have to pay back all the commissions, and that money's already been spent."

I knew this was all because of me. I had planted those seeds of doubt in her head. And now Bobbi appeared to be having as hard a time justifying her banana peels as I was coping with a father in prison.

MARION WAS OUT for a month, and when she did return to Saks, the evidence of what she'd been through was visible on her face. There was a terrible scar along her chin and another one on her forehead that she tried fruitlessly to cover with a sprig of hair.

While we were having lunch one day at the Automat, we ran into Estée and I invited her to join us.

"I'm so glad you've recovered," Estée said, squeezing Marion's hand. "Have the doctors given you anything for your scars?"

Marion's face froze.

Mortified, I kicked Estée under the table but that didn't stop her.

"I've got just the thing for you. It's a very simple treatment. May I show it to you?"

I kicked her again as she snapped open her pocketbook and set a little jar of her Super Rich All-Purpose Creme on the table. "Did you know that massage is an effective way to reduce scarring?"

Marion shook her head, speechless but curious.

"Here, let me show you a simple technique." She grabbed hold of Marion's hand and began rubbing the cream into her pale skin in tight circles, its sheen visible in the overhead lights. "And if you'd like," Estée continued, "I can give you a Creme Pack treatment. Frankly, that's what you really need. It will reduce the redness and bring down the inflammation, too." She pulled out her appointment book and began leafing through the pages with her little teacup hands. "Let's see . . . I could give you a treatment—oh yes. I could give you one tomorrow evening. Right after work. Would six o'clock be convenient for you?"

I apologized to Marion on the way back to the office. She'd been gracious about Estée's offer and, apparently, also desperate enough to have kept the appointment with her. Maybe a week or two later, I kid you not, I noticed that Marion's skin was improving. And it kept improving. And what the Super Rich All-Purpose Creme and Creme Pack treatments couldn't correct, Estée could with the magic of makeup. She taught Marion to camouflage the scars with pancake foundation, face powder and other techniques.

Estée had made a believer out of Marion, and after that, both of us were championing Estée, trying to get her products into the hallowed halls of Saks Fifth Avenue.

With Marion's encouragement, Mr. Fiske and Mr. Belfort made a rare exception and agreed to meet with Estée. The three of us—Estée, Marion and I—were sitting across from them in the conference room when Mr. Fiske leaned forward and in no uncertain terms said, "No. The answer is still no. No one here is interested in your Lauder products."

"But that's not true," Estée protested even as I shot her a *Would you just shut up* look. She ignored me and kept pushing, as was her nature. "Did you see my latest sales figures?" She flipped open a manila folder and shoved a sheet of paper under his nose. "You can see that I'm up significantly. And we just opened another concession at a beauty parlor on—"

Mr. Fiske raised his hand to stop her. "I've heard enough. My decision has been made."

Mr. Belfort reached over, took the paper and eyed it. "Remember, my dear," he said to Estée, "patience is a virtue and it's all about the journey, not the destination."

After Mr. Belfort had strung two cliches together, Mr. Fiske cleared his throat. "Mrs. Lauder," he said, "if ever you can prove to me that there's a real market for your products here at Saks Fifth Avenue, we'll reconsider the matter, but for now, the subject is closed."

"You want me to prove it to you, is that it?"

Oh God, Estée, don't challenge him. I wanted to smack her.

"All right then," she said, "you're on."

I imagined smoke coming out of Mr. Fiske's ears. He slapped his hands down on the conference table and said, "This meeting is over. Done."

Marion and I ushered Estée out of the conference room and over to the elevator banks.

"Madame Rubinstein is probably the only person who could get away with talking to him like that," said Marion as she pushed the call button, summoning the elevator girl.

"Well, I just did it. And you wait and see, I'm going to prove it to him. He'll have no choice but to take my line."

Estée seemed so confident and oblivious to the fact that she'd just shot herself in the foot. Or so I thought.

THE FOLLOWING MONTH Estée had been invited to speak at a women's luncheon at the Waldorf Astoria. Lately she'd been doing that sort of thing, giving talks and makeup demonstrations for various women's charity groups, but this was definitely the most upscale, prestigious event Estée had ever participated in. They were expecting 500 women and at $12 a plate, this was no ordinary gathering. In her excitement, Estée had shown me the guest list. Half a dozen names jumped out at me. Including Alexandria Spencer and my boss, Mr. Fiske.

Two days later, he called me into his office. He had Estée's vellum invite in his hand. "I want you to attend on my behalf and report back to me."

And that was how I found myself on the nineteenth floor at the Waldorf Astoria, in the Starlight Roof room. Never before had my two worlds—past and present—come this close to colliding. It was unnerving, like a meteor hurtling straight toward me. There was no place to hide, no way to dodge it. Thankfully I hadn't seen Alexandria yet and hoped that she was a no-show.

I was seated at a table with a group of New York socialites: Babe Cushing, Slim Keith, Pamela Churchill, C.Z. Guest and three of their friends. Other familiar faces, which I was avoiding, were peppered around the room. I'd been sitting there, among them, for nearly forty minutes and so far nothing catastrophic had happened.

At this stage in my reinvention, I had restored my wardrobe—maybe not entirely to its former glory, but I had nothing to apologize for. Especially since I'd paid for every stitch of it myself, thanks in part to my employee discount. It was really quite astonishing for me to realize just how far I'd come in the past eight years. And I'd done it all on my own.

Unlike my luncheon companions, I wasn't independently wealthy. I *had* to work. But I made a good living and had a bright, cheery apartment with a view of the Chrysler Building. I loved every minute of my job. I loved being on the front line of the cosmetic industry. I knew all the key players and, what's more, they knew me. I'd had lunches with Charles Revson, who was still trying to bed me down. I'd been to dinner parties with writers and poets, artists and musicians. I palled around town with Vicki Baum and her theater friends. So being an assistant cosmetic buyer at Saks Fifth Avenue wasn't just a job for me. It was a lifestyle, allowing me to hold my head up high, to stand tall, dressed head to toe in the latest fashions. I fancied myself a modern free-spirited career woman and for that I would not apologize to anyone.

Yes, I was still single and inching toward my thirtieth birthday, but I was rarely lonely for male companionship. I never had to look too hard to find a handsome man to escort me to a gala or an opening. Even if I never felt that elusive spark with any of them that I'd had with Edward, I had still made a life for myself, and a damn fine one at that.

With these thoughts running through my mind, I began to relax and take in the room. And what a lovely room it was. In the summertime the retractable roof opened, letting in the moonlight and calming breezes. But it was early March now, and when I looked up there were only patches of gray sky, the color of a dull nickel, as far as the eye could see. As I nibbled my watercress and crabmeat salad, sipping iced tea, thinking how proud I was of myself, a familiar voice called to me.

"Gloria?"

I turned around and there she was. My nemesis, Alexandria Spencer.

"Well, if it isn't Gloria Dowaziac. What on earth are you doing here? Shouldn't you be visiting your father in prison . . ."

I couldn't listen to another thing after she said that. To my ears, it had been broadcast over a loudspeaker. Her lips were still moving but all I heard was the sound of my own heartbeats. I gripped the lip of the table, praying I wouldn't have a vertigo attack. I dared to move my eyes, taking a look around the table. Slim was talking to Babe. Pamela was adjusting her necklace while trying to get the waiter's attention for more lemon.

"Hello, Alexandria," I managed to say. "It's certainly a surprise to see you here."

"I'll bet you're not nearly as surprised as I am. I ran into Tommy the other day. He and Lana had another baby. A little girl or little boy," she said as if there were any other options. "I heard you have a job—you're a shopgirl or something like that at a department store. Such a pity." She tsk-tsked. "And look—you've changed your hair color. Again." She tacked on an irritating laugh.

"If you don't mind"—I gestured toward Estée, who was taking her place at the podium—"the speaker is about to begin."

Alexandria moved on but my nerves were so rattled I missed Estée's opening lines. It took a few minutes and half a cigarette to calm me down. And by then, while the waiters served coffee and dessert, I could see that Estée had enchanted the room, as only she could.

She talked about the importance of caring for one's skin. "Just five minutes is all it takes." She promised to share her favorite tips and said that one jar of her Super Rich All-Purpose Creme would do the work of three different creams. "After all, what exactly *is* night cream anyway? Do you honestly think your skin knows when it's dark outside?" The room gave off a delightful chuckle and there wasn't a woman at that luncheon who wasn't held captive, eager to hear what the latest makeup secret might be. Estée had already won them over.

"In closing," she said, "as a token of my appreciation for having me here today, I'd like to give each of you a free sample of one of my products."

In great dramatic fashion, "A Pretty Girl Is Like a Melody" played over the speaker system as half a dozen beautiful young ladies—whom Estée had hired and adorned in full-length gowns, tiaras and sashes inscribed with *Estée Lauder*—made their way around the room. They went table to table, giving each woman a little box containing a sample of an Estée Lauder product. Some women got a red lipstick or a turquoise eyeshadow; others got a Creme Pack treatment, a jar of Super Rich All-Purpose Creme or a small bottle of Cleansing Oil or Skin Lotion. They were like children on Christmas morning, taking out their samples, smelling them, dabbing some onto the backs of their hands.

It was quite a sensation, and when the luncheon was over, I went to congratulate Estée but the cluster of women surrounding her was too thick to penetrate. I figured I'd talk to her later and began making my way back to the office. As I started down Park Avenue, I recognized several women from the luncheon all heading in the same direction, and as I turned onto 49th Street, I saw more of these women, clutching their pocketbooks in one hand and Estée's little gift box in the other. It soon became obvious that they were all heading to the closest department store and, not so coincidentally, that store was Saks Fifth Avenue.

Someone who received a lipstick also wanted the eyeshadow her friend got. Another one wanted the Cleansing Oil to go along with the Skin Lotion she'd received. They had taken over the first-floor aisles, lining up at the cosmetic counters asking for Estée Lauder products. But, alas, we had none to sell.

I saw Mr. Fiske coming down the escalator. "What the devil is going on down here?" he asked when I caught up to him.

"They all just came from the luncheon at the Waldorf Astoria. Estée was a smash hit. It looks like everybody wants her products."

Adjusting his glasses as if not believing his eyes, he said with great exasperation, "Okay, very well. She wins. Tell your friend I'm ready to talk. Set up a meeting."

45

TWO DAYS LATER, I sat next to Estée during her meeting with Mr. Fiske and Mr. Belfort.

"Well, Mrs. Lauder," Mr. Fiske said, "you've convinced me. We're going to start out slow, though. We'd like to place an initial order for $800 and we'll see how it goes from there."

I thought Estée's eyes were going to pop out of her head.

"We're primarily interested in the four skincare products." He paused to consult the notes I'd provided for him. "The, ah, the Super Rich All-Purpose Creme. We'll take the Cleansing Oil, the Creme Pack treatments and the, ah, the Skin Lotion."

"But what about the lipsticks and eyeshadows?" she asked, leaning forward, inching closer to his desk.

"We'll include *some* of the lipsticks and perhaps the eyeshadows, too," said Mr. Belfort, fiddling with his glasses.

"And what about my face powder?"

I could have strangled her for not being more gracious, but Mr. Belfort beat me to it. "Don't look a gift horse in the mouth, Mrs. Lauder."

"Yes, we'll include your face powder, too," said Mr. Fiske. "Now there's a few things I need from you in exchange."

"Such as?"

"Such as your packaging, for starters." He held up a white jar with a black lid.

"What's wrong with my packaging?"

"This could be a bottle of aspirin," said Mr. Fiske. "It looks like it belongs in Woolworth's, not in Saks Fifth Avenue."

"You want me to change my packaging?" She was incredulous. "But I've already changed it once." She looked at me, as if I'd failed her somehow, led her down the wrong path. And perhaps I had. Her new packaging was certainly an improvement, but it still wasn't good enough.

"Change it again," said Mr. Fiske.

"All of it?"

"All of it." He nodded. "We're selling an image as much as anything else. Think luxury. Think elegance. That's what our customers come to Saks Fifth Avenue for."

She drew a deep breath and nodded. "Fine. All right. I'll do it."

"Next is your distribution. We pride ourselves on exclusivity, so your beauty parlor sideline business must go and—"

"Oh no," she said before he'd finished his thought. "I won't give up my concessions in the beauty parlors."

"Don't bite the hand that feeds you," Mr. Belfort warned.

"C'mon now, Estée," I said. "Be reasonable." She was gambling here, taking a real chance. Mr. Fiske could have pulled the whole deal. "We're offering you Saks Fifth Avenue."

Finally, Estée let out a heavy sigh that brought her shoulders to her ears before dropping back in place. "Oh, all right. Very well." She sighed again. "I'll close them down."

"Immediately," Mr. Fiske said.

She nodded. "Immediately."

So a deal was made between Estée Lauder and Saks Fifth Avenue.

THE HARD PART for Estée was over. She'd done it. She was in Saks. Now all she had to do was fill the order. And even more importantly, she wanted to ensure that her products would not only sell but fly off the shelves.

"Who handles Revlon's advertising?" she asked as we walked out of Mr. Fiske's office and headed toward the elevator banks. Knowing how she felt about heights, I wanted to ride down with her.

"They're with McCann Erickson," I said after instructing the elevator girl to take us to the main floor. "John McCarthy handles their account."

"Can you get me a meeting with him—with this John McCarthy?"

"Trust me, Estée, you don't want to be at the same ad agency. They've got their hands full with Revlon. They won't give you the time of day."

"Then where should I go? I've got a chance now with Saks but it won't do any good if no one knows my products are for sale here. I need to start advertising."

I thought for a moment as we stepped out of the elevator. I knew I was probably going to regret it, but I said it just the same: "Why don't you try Ben Duffy at BBDO? Use my name."

There's truth in that old saying *No good deed goes unpunished.* Estée and Joe dropped my name and got a meeting right away with Batten, Barton, Durstine & Osborn. Fifteen minutes into it, Ben Duffy flat out told them, *Thanks but no thanks.*

I met Estée and Joe at the Oyster Bar in Grand Central after they left Ben Duffy's office. It was the end of the workday and the restaurant was already crowded for dinner. All the tables were taken so we ate at the bar, sitting three in a row with Estée in the middle. BBDO's cut was still fresh.

"Your Mr. Duffy said we didn't have a big enough budget." Estée set her martini down and picked it right back up again. "We told him we have $50,000 to spend on advertising. And if that's not enough, well, I don't know what it's going to take."

"It's our entire savings," Joe added, leaning forward to look at me. "It took us years to save up that much."

"Yeah," I said, forking a bluepoint oyster to loosen the meat from its briny bath. "I know it seems like a lot of money, but honestly, it's not enough."

"Oh God"—Estée turned to me—"now you're starting to sound like Duffy. He said $50,000 wouldn't come close to launching the type of advertising campaign we need to make a splash, to make it worth our while. Or his."

"Well, he knows what he's talking about," I said, slurping down the oyster.

"So what do we do now?" Joe asked, looking at me as if I had the answer.

I had nothing to offer, but Estée, well, she was always two steps ahead of everyone else.

"We don't need BBDO," she said boldly. "To hell with them." I could see the wheels turning inside her head. She was working on her next move. "I'll tell you what we're going to do. We're going to take that $50,000 and put it all—every last cent—into samples to give away at my Saks counter."

Joe immediately protested. "No way, Estée." He set his cocktail aside. "That's insane. We can't do that. You're always giving the store away."

"I know what I'm doing here, Joe." She turned to me. "Can you get me a copy of the Saks Fifth Avenue mailing list?" She asked this like she was asking me to pass the salt.

"What? What do you want with our mailing list?" I felt a knot beginning to form in my gut.

"I'm going to write to every Saks Fifth Avenue customer and tell them I have a free gift waiting for them at my new counter."

I coughed, choking on the very thought of this. "Estée, are you kidding me? I can't do that."

"Why on earth not?"

"For one thing, I could get fired."

"Why would you get fired? This would bring more women into Saks. It would boost sales. There's absolutely no downside to this. Don't you want me to succeed?"

"Of course I do." I picked up another oyster but found that I'd lost my appetite.

"Please, Gloria? I need this. I need that list."

The next morning I went into work, set my coffee down on the desk, closed our office door and told Marion what Estée wanted me to do.

"Is this crazy?" I asked. "I mean, it really could bring more business into the store. What do you think?"

Marion took it in for a moment, her elbows squared on the desk. I couldn't read her expression and it dawned on me that she might very well report me to Mr. Fiske. With a rush of panic I feared that I'd just gotten myself fired anyway. Marion sat back, lacing her fingers behind her neck. The scars from her accident were barely visible, even with the sunlight pouring in from the window.

At last she smiled and said, "What Mr. Fiske doesn't know won't hurt him."

With Marion as my accomplice, we gave Estée the mailing list for Saks Fifth Avenue. Estée took those names and commenced working on her own direct mail advertising campaign. She ordered special cream vellum cards with gold script printed across the front that read: *Estée Lauder Cosmetics Are Now Available at Saks Fifth*

Avenue New York. She stayed up until all hours of the night, night after night, writing to each woman on that list. In her own hand, she personalized each card, letting them know that she had a gift for them and that she'd be glad to give them a free makeup demonstration.

Joe addressed each one while Leonard licked stamps and envelopes, sealing them before riding his bike to the post office to drop them in the mail. Even back then it was a family-run business.

I LET MYSELF into Estée's apartment. No one answered when I knocked and the front door was unlocked. I followed the cries of baby Ron and found him in the kitchen with Estée. She was on the telephone, on hold, the receiver cradled between her ear and shoulder. Ron was fussing, squirming to get out of his high chair and into his mother's arms. I lifted him up, bouncing him on my hip trying to pacify him.

The kitchen was cluttered with boxes of ingredients. There were jars and bottles, droppers, lipstick molds and cases piled up everywhere. You could barely move in there. Estée was overwhelmed and faced with the daunting task of fulfilling the production of the Saks order. She was working out the logistics of mass-producing her entire line. Even before this, every inch of her apartment had been devoted to making products for her existing clients and now she was going to have to quadruple her output.

"Well, it's about time," she said to the person on the other end of the telephone. "I need one case of lanolin, twenty-five pounds of paraffin . . ." She cupped her hand over the mouthpiece and whispered something. One of her secret essential oils or other mysterious ingredients. I didn't take it personally. I had to laugh. That's just how protective she was of her formulas.

When she hung up the telephone, she looked frazzled. "How am

I going to do this?" she asked, taking the baby from me and hoisting him on her hip.

"You need a bigger kitchen," I said. "That's all there is to it."

When I said that, I didn't realize I'd given her an idea. But Estée was one of those people who could problem-solve in her sleep, see the faintest crack of opportunity where others saw dead ends. She really possessed an extraordinary mindset and her thoughts traveled in only one direction, onward and upward. So I should not have been surprised when she recognized that the answer to her problems was right beneath her feet.

"The restaurant downstairs," she said.

"What about it?"

"I'll rent out their kitchen. After hours."

And that was exactly what she did. Estée paid them a small fee in exchange for the use of the kitchen. I don't exactly remember volunteering to help, but somehow I'd gotten pulled into the operation.

Since we couldn't get into the kitchen until midnight, I mostly helped out on the weekends. When I first entered the massive kitchen, the smell was overwhelming: a mixture of fried foods, garlic, cabbage and ammonia. Despite the restaurant's best efforts to mop the floor, the tiles remained slick and greasy. As much as I hated to do it, I eventually had to kick off my heels to keep from slipping and I was still sliding around in my stockings as it was. With no windows in that kitchen and all the burners fired up, the blue and orange flames licking up the sides of the pots, it was stifling hot in there.

Joe was standing over a giant stockpot, sterilizing bottles and jars in boiling water. His curls were plastered against his forehead with sweat as he reached in with a pair of tongs and set the containers on pristine white towels to dry. I was assigned labels and Leonard applied them and stacked the finished products into boxes.

Two-year-old baby Ron was in his high chair, doing his best to amuse himself, while Estée sorted through a box of glass vials and canisters of various powders.

There was a lot of murmuring and whispering going back and forth between Estée and Joe. She would signal to him and he'd bring her a box of this or a gallon of that. I knew the basic ingredients she used because they were common to all face creams and beauty products in general, but Estée had other secrets—a total of twenty-six ingredients—and only she and Joe knew what they were.

46

I HEADED TO THE store early one morning in May. I wanted to get organized for what I knew would be a hectic day. I had back-to-back appointments, a slew of telephone calls to return and orders to place, not to mention a mountain of paperwork awaiting me. It was only about half past seven. With not a cloud in the sky, the sun was everywhere, glinting off the skyscraper windows, flooding light down between the buildings. I shaded my eyes from the glare and stopped for a coffee and the newspaper before heading into work.

At the side entrance, the doorman offered a tip of his hat and let me inside. It was always a little eerie to be in Saks before all the lights were turned up, before the music started playing and the shop-girls were in place. I rode up the elevator to the executive offices, thinking of the busy day ahead. The buying department was empty when I entered the lobby. No scent of Mr. Belfort's pipe tobacco to greet me. Even Marion hadn't arrived yet. I was the first one in. After settling in at my desk, I eased the lid off my coffee and opened my newspaper. I had just taken a sip and turned the page when my heart about stopped.

It was a small article, buried among all the other news, but the headline jumped out. DOWAZIAC PAROLE BOARD HEARING IS SET. *Parole? My father was up for parole?* My body began to fill with lead. It was hard to raise my arms, let alone stand up and walk the five steps it would take to close my office door. I drew a deep breath, sat back down and forced myself to read:

> Gustaw Dowaziac, the notorious fraudster who in 1938 pleaded guilty to running a Ponzi scheme that robbed his investment clients of in excess of one million dollars, originally sentenced to twenty-five years in prison, is expected to appear for a parole board hearing sometime later this year. The outcome of the hearing will determine whether or not the fifty-nine-year-old Dowaziac will be released from prison . . .

That was enough. I couldn't take any more. I never imagined my father could have been released early. I assumed I had time—years, even decades—to prepare for something like this. The part of me that remained his daughter didn't want him rotting away in prison, but I didn't know that eight years was punishment enough for what he'd done. Had he learned his lesson, or was he capable of setting up another con? My father's early release would surely stir the public's anger.

Just when I was starting to realize that the only way I could move forward in my life was to put my past behind me, my past was about to resurface. I'd have to walk in fear again, terrified of being recognized, forced to dodge my father's victims and those people who knew the truth about who I was and where I'd come from.

My head began to throb. I felt the ping in my ear and my face going numb. Before vertigo sent the room whirling, I crinkled up the newspaper and was about to stuff it into the wastepaper basket when everything tilted, and just like my first day at Darlene's, I passed out cold.

OTHER THAN MY brother begging me to write a letter of support to the parole board, I didn't hear another word about my father's possible release. Like the tide receding toward the sea, my fears and anxieties slipped away. I concentrated on work and selecting the perfect wallpaper for my powder room. I hosted my first-ever dinner party—catered by Nom Wah Tea Parlor, since I would have surely poisoned my guests if I'd done the cooking myself.

Life, by all measures, was good, and as long as I kept busy, I could put the parole hearing out of my thoughts. It was only at night, after the world stilled and quieted, that my mind took off. Would my father get out? Would I want to see him? Would he and my mother stay in Poughkeepsie or move back to the city? How would he support himself? If the only kind of job an ex-con could get was bagging groceries or pumping gasoline, I feared my father would revert to doing something illegal. All of this circled in my mind like water around a drain. By daylight, though, the phantoms went into hiding and I got back on with my life.

One day, however, about a month after the newspaper article appeared, I heard my telephone ringing as I was keying into my apartment. I tossed my pocketbook on the sofa and ran, picking up on the sixth or seventh ring.

"Hello?" I sounded a little winded as I kicked off my heels, savoring the coolness of the hardwood floor against the balls of my feet.

I heard a gruff but familiar voice say, "Finally."

"Glenn?"

"Jesus, where the hell have you been?"

"What's wrong?"

"I've been trying to reach you for days. I left messages for you at work. Didn't you get them?"

"I did," I confessed, thinking about those pink message slips I'd been ignoring:

Glenn called. Said he must speak to you about the hearing.

I was annoyed because I had specifically asked Glenn not to leave any personal information with the receptionist at work. *Ever.*

"I've been really busy," I said. "I'm just now getting home from work and it's almost—"

"We're still waiting on your letter for Dad." My father's lawyers wanted all of us to write letters of support to strengthen his case for early release. "We need it by the end of the week. And remember, you have to write: 'Dear Honorable Members of the Parole Board,' and remember to use a colon, not a comma, and sign your full name."

"But I changed my name, remember? A letter from me won't mean anything anyway."

"That's bullshit. He's still your father. It's bad enough that you've never—not once—gone to see him." I could picture Glenn jabbing his index finger in my direction. "Everyone else in this family has done their letters. We're all going to speak at the hearing, too, in case you're interested."

"In speaking? On his behalf? I—I can't." I wasn't sure my father deserved to be released early. How could I convincingly help sway the parole board's decision?

"I should have known better. How do you sleep at night?"

"What makes you think I do?" I couldn't remember the last time I'd had a decent night's sleep.

"Don't be glib with me."

I swallowed hard and reached for my Chesterfields, stretching as far as the telephone cord would allow. Holding my hair back, I leaned over the pilot light on the stove and lit my cigarette.

"Hel-lo? Are you there?" He sounded truly annoyed.

"Yes, I'm still here." I exhaled.

"What the hell is wrong with you?" His voice had teeth. Sharp teeth. "I swear, sometimes you have nothing but ice water running through your veins. Dad's hearing is in two weeks, and if he's not released, it's on you."

"That's not fair."

"Just because the Cavendishes lost their investment—"

"They didn't *lose* their investment. Dad stole it from them."

"You can't blame Dad because your boyfriend dumped you. Dad needs our support and you need to get your priorities straight." There was that finger again, jabbing away. "You're nothing but a selfish, spoiled, lazy, pathetic . . ."

Glenn continued with my character assassination for a full minute, maybe longer. Why I didn't hang up right then and there was another matter altogether. Crazy as it sounds, I didn't think I had the right to do that. Glenn could have hung up on me, but the water didn't run both ways. I was the youngest and felt like I had to stand there and take it. Like he was allowed to speak to me that way.

I took a final drag off my cigarette and noticed a slight tremor in my hand as I tossed the butt into the sink, hearing it hiss when it landed beneath the dripping faucet. I stayed like that, standing at the counter, shaking, while Glenn verbally accosted me. In his eyes, I was the bigger family disgrace, not my father. There was a time when Glenn and I had been buddies, but this business with my father had driven a wedge between us. I no longer felt the closeness I'd once had with my big brother. And that made me sad.

Naturally, I didn't sleep that night, or the night after. I was too busy wrestling with myself over that letter of support. At one point I even attempted it:

Dear Honorable Members of the Parole Board:

I'm writing on behalf of Gustaw Dowaziac . . .

But two pages in I realized that the letter to the parole board had turned into a letter to my father. And rather than vouching for his character I was ranting about how I was so bitterly disappointed in him and how I found him disgusting, disgraceful, dishonest and disrespectful until I ran out of words with that particular prefix. I tore the letter up and started another one:

Dear Honorable Members of the Parole Board:

I'm writing to tell you that Gustaw Dowaziac is ~~an honorable~~ a wonderful man. ~~I am the woman I am today because of him.~~

Scratch. That made me sound terrible, like I was just as corrupt as he was. I tore that one up as well and tried another approach. I wrote about his generosity, his kindheartedness, his sense of loyalty . . . And then I got stuck because for every attribute, a liability reared its ugly head: his cruelty, his arrogance, his utter lack of remorse. I took out another clean sheet of paper and stared at the blank page until it was time to get up and go to work.

THE BIG DAY had arrived. Estée Lauder products were officially on sale at Saks Fifth Avenue. After checking into the office upstairs and depositing my pocketbook in the bottom drawer of my desk, I went down to the main floor to say hello to Estée and see how things were going.

We'd given her three feet of counter space, which nicely showcased her newly designed blue-green boxes. I saw that Estée had pulled the stool out from behind the register and already had a customer sitting there while she stood at her side, tucking a sheet of tissue paper inside the woman's collar.

"We don't want any makeup to get on your pretty blouse, now do we?" Estée said as she proceeded to pin back the woman's hair while launching into her sales pitch. "Five minutes is all it takes . . . Now first you need to start with a clean, fresh face." She had a little dish of water and dabbed the woman's cheeks and forehead with her Cleansing Oil, all the while talking about how effective oil was in breaking down skin residue. "See how easy Estée Lauder products are to use? Did you know that Elizabeth Arden can't even put on her own face? And Helena Rubinstein doesn't even bother to wash her skin properly. It's true. That's how laborious both their routines are . . ."

Now I'd seen Estée give facials and makeup lessons all the time inside the beauty parlors, but I never would have dreamed she'd attempt the same thing in the middle of a department store—especially not in the middle of Saks Fifth Avenue.

"Are you sure you should be doing this?" I asked Estée after the woman left—having purchased a Creme Pack and a bottle of Cleansing Oil. "Does Mr. Fiske even *know* you're doing this?"

"Doing what?" She looked at me, clearly not understanding.

"I mean, you're basically giving a makeup demonstration right here on the floor."

"That's *exactly* what I'm doing."

"But—"

"Gloria"—she sounded a bit piqued—"this is the only way I can sell. I demonstrate and they buy." She said this as if I should have realized that by now. "And you know I've always said that 'Once you touch a customer, you're halfway there.' My goal is to touch fifty faces a day."

Another customer approached the counter, looking for her free gift, and after Estée wiggled back into her pumps, she came around from behind the counter, dragging the stool with her. She had the woman sit down and proceeded to give another makeup demonstration.

I thought Estée was making a huge mistake. Applying makeup in public was tacky, right up there with putting your lipstick on at the table. I thought she was going to blow it. Vivian, Harriet and the other shopgirls were watching with knitted brows and whispers going back and forth.

Mrs. Coopers wasn't pleased with Estée's technique, either. She wasted no time moving the stool back behind the counter. "The floor must appear uniform at all times," she said to Estée. "We can't have stools cluttering the aisles. And let me just remind you, Mrs. Lauder, we do not allow people to *test* our products in the store here at Saks Fifth Avenue."

Estée accepted Mrs. Coopers's reprimand and agreed to leave the stool behind the counter. But that didn't stop her from giving makeup demonstrations on the floor. Estée was barely five foot four, and if she had to, she went up on her tiptoes to reach the taller customers. Soon the women were lining up at Estée's counter. Customers would come in looking for a red lipstick. They had their choice of buying it from the Revlon counter or the Arden or Rubinstein counters but at Estée's counter, they could actually try it on, plus they'd get a free sample of another product. Word soon got out that there were free samples at the Estée Lauder display, free makeup demonstrations, too. Estée had taken her beauty parlor technique and brought it to Fifth Avenue. She ended up selling out her first order in just two days.

47

IT WAS STILL hot outside when I left work at half past six. I was at the corner of Madison and 69th, waiting for the light to change, when I glanced over at the man next to me and did a double take.

"Edward?"

He nearly dropped his cigarette and gave me one of the world's most awkward half-hug-cheek-kiss combos.

"This is certainly a surprise." My heart was thrumming, and I assure you that what they say about going weak in the knees is a very real thing. I asked if he was back in New York on business.

"No, I—I actually moved back."

"What? You did?" This floored me. How could he have moved back and not told me? But then again, how could he have left in the first place without telling me? Acquaintances did that sort of thing. Acquaintances and, I guess, ex-fiancés. I tried not to let my disappointment show as we stood there, exchanging pleasantries and making stupid small talk. When I couldn't take it a second longer, I just came out and asked if he had time for a drink.

He checked his watch, which was a bad sign. My heart had already plummeted when he looked up and said, "Hey, sure. Why not?"

We ducked into a little place around the corner called The Shaker. Edward and I used to stop in there from time to time after work. And now, here we were again. We were seated opposite each other in a leather tufted booth that produced embarrassing responses each time one of us moved our rear ends. His suit jacket was hanging off a coat-tree nearby. He looked sexy, leaning back, his shirtsleeves rolled, one arm stretched out, resting atop the seat back. We ordered manhattans and a couple of burgers, which came with your choice of french fries or coleslaw. I knew he preferred the fries and so I ordered those, assuming he'd end up eating them off my plate after they'd turned cold. Just like old times.

We were catching up and he was explaining that he hadn't gone overseas during the war.

"Really? You didn't enlist? I thought for sure you would have gone off to fight," I said.

"I wanted to. But"—he smiled, a little bashfully—"I'm 4-F."

"You?" *Edward Clifford, the perfect specimen of a man, was 4-F?*

"Flat feet," he said, lifting his shoe. "I tried to get myself reclassified. Tried everything I could think of, but they still wouldn't take me."

"Well, thank God for that."

"What about your brother?"

"He weaseled his way out of serving." I rolled my eyes. "Turns out he's just as bad as the rest of my family."

"Well, I see you've made peace with them." Though he smiled, Edward was no good at sarcasm and I saw the look of pity in his eyes, like he felt sorry for me. "Tell me how you're doing," he said.

"Oh, you know me." I laughed.

"Yeah, I *do* know you," he said a little too seriously. "That's why I'm asking. I saw that your father's up for parole. How are you dealing with all that?"

"I've decided *not* to deal with it. Everyone wants me to write a letter of support for him, but I can't do it."

"Well, I happen to know the folks on the parole board. They're only interested in facts. Emotional family pleas won't sway them. It won't change the outcome."

"Tell that to my brother. And my mother. They both hate me. I'm sure my sister does, too."

"You're not still punishing yourself over all this, are you?"

"No." I slumped back in my seat. "Not really."

He shot me a skeptical glance. "Don't be so hard on yourself. *You* didn't steal from anyone. *You* didn't cheat anyone."

"I know all that. I'm fine. No, really I am." I was looking at Edward through a haze of tears.

He reached into his pocket and handed me his handkerchief. "The thing about families—especially *your* family—is that just because you love them doesn't mean you have to like them."

"I'll have to remember that."

"What about Estée?"

"What about her?" I dabbed the corners of my eyes.

"Did you finally tell her and Joe about your dad? About the rest of your family?"

My eyes welled up again. "I can't. I've wanted to so many times but it's too late. I can't tell them I've been lying to them all these years."

"So, I'm assuming this means Bobbi doesn't know, either? Or the Millers?"

I shook my head. "I can't tell them *now*. I just can't."

"That's your choice, but it's a heavy burden to carry. Personally, I think you need to have more faith in them. In yourself. Those people love you—why not give them a chance to really know who you are?"

The waiter came by and set two plates down before us. I blinked to clear my vision and slid his handkerchief back across the table to him. He let it sit there, as if I might need it again. I took a bite of my burger, juices dripping out the other end. We ate in silence, either like complete strangers or like two people so utterly comfortable with each other, the quiet demanded no attention.

"So what made you decide to move back to New York?" I asked.

"I couldn't handle Kansas City. Not after living in New York for three years. It just didn't feel like home anymore. I was bored so I came back."

"How long ago was that?"

He seemed a little sheepish and looked away. "About a year ago."

A year? I'd been expecting a week or two, maybe even a month. *He'd been back in New York for an entire year and hadn't bothered to contact me.* Now I felt foolish and embarrassed for even asking. Suddenly there was a stack of bricks on my chest. I wrapped my hands so tightly around my glass I wanted to shatter it.

"What are you doing now?" I asked, trying to sound casual, but my voice was strained.

"Believe it or not, I went back to my old job."

"With the law firm?"

"God no. I went back to the D.A.'s office. I stayed in touch with my old boss, and when I mentioned I was moving back to New York, he made me an offer."

"So, you're through defending the bad guys, huh?"

He dropped his head, bobbing a couple slow-paced nods. "You were right about that. I wasn't cut out for that kind of work. I never did have the stomach for it." He helped himself to the fries on my plate like I knew he would.

By the time our second round of drinks arrived, the mood had lightened considerably. We'd both relaxed and were laughing, reminiscing about old times. I pulled out a cigarette, and as I leaned into the flame he produced, I looked at his signet ring while the match continued to burn.

"God," I said as I exhaled, "I almost forgot how much I hate that thing." I tapped his finger, barely touching his skin, but it was enough to set off an electric charge.

He laughed, blew out the match, dropped it into the ashtray.

"Show me the secret handshake," I said.

"Never. Not a chance."

We locked eyes and I felt that familiar longing for him begin to stir. I was still in love with him, as if I'd ever doubted it.

When we couldn't possibly have had any more to drink and had run out of ways to prolong the evening, he paid the bill and we stepped outside. We were both heading uptown and ended up sharing a taxicab. Each time his leg pressed against mine it sent a rush of heat coursing through my body. When we pulled up to my building, I was surprised that Edward got out with me. We stood on the sidewalk for a moment beneath the streetlamp, looking at each other. My heart was pounding. I couldn't wait to kiss him again, to feel his arms around me.

I was sure he was coming upstairs with me—not a doubt in my mind—until he gestured over his shoulder and said, "I'm—I'm gonna walk the rest of the way. Need to clear my head and—"

"Wait." I reached for his hand. "Don't go yet."

"I have to. I can't . . ." He let his words fade out, like there was nothing more to say.

I willed myself not to cry. I was still holding his hand. I couldn't let him get away. "Just tell me something—if we hadn't bumped into each other tonight, would you have ever contacted me?"

"Ah, c'mon." He winced a little.

"Just tell me. I need to know."

"It was good to see you tonight. Can't we just leave it at that?"

"Didn't you at least think about calling me?" My eyes were glassing up; my voice was frail.

"Yeah. All right?" He glanced off, somewhere over my shoulder. "I thought about it. I thought about it a lot."

"But?"

"Do you really want to dredge all this up?"

"I—I don't understand. If you thought about it . . ." I ran out of words myself then and waited, expecting him to say something. When he didn't, a fresh wave of panic shot through me and I blurted out something that had been formulating inside me all night: "Give me another chance—give us another chance."

He looked away and I saw his jaw was clenched. "It'll never work."

"But why? Why can't it work?" My heart fisted up tight. It was crushed yet still beating hard.

"Because you have a real problem with being happy, Gloria. It's just that simple. You sabotage yourself at every turn. There's something inside you that wants to be miserable. You want to feel bad about yourself, and I'm sorry, but I can't sit back and watch you do that to yourself." He let go of my hand and reached up to stroke my cheek. "I loved you, I wanted to spend the rest of my life with you, and you pushed me away. You broke my heart when you did that. I would give anything for you to be able to see what *I see* when I look at you."

There was so much I wanted to say but I couldn't get a sound past the lump in my throat.

"I wish you would just let yourself be happy, but I know you— you're not there yet and I don't know if you ever will be. And I can't put my heart on the line again."

"So, what?" I asked, letting the tears spill loose. "This is it? Goodbye? Forever?"

"It's getting late." He pulled his hand back, stuffed it into his pocket. "Go upstairs. I'm gonna—I'm gonna head home."

But I didn't go upstairs. I couldn't. I stood there on the sidewalk and watched him walk away. When he reached the corner, he turned back and said, "Hey, Gloria—if you ever find a way to forgive yourself, let me know."

And then he was gone, and that all-too-familiar sense of being abandoned, being left behind, opened wide inside me, wide enough to swallow me whole.

ABOUT A WEEK later I had just returned from lunch. It was still too painful to think about Edward, so I shifted all thoughts to my father's pending parole hearing. I was still struggling to justify my not writing that letter. It was a pestering thought that kept coming at me like a gnat I'd already swatted away. It was exhausting.

But when I entered Saks Fifth Avenue, something almost magical happened. I left my troubles along with the grime and grit of the city outside and found myself swept up in the glamour of it all. The store had a way of doing that to you, just whisking you away into a world of luxury where everything sparkled, everything had a welcoming softness, an allure unmatched by Macy's, Bloomingdale's, even Bergdorf Goodman.

Although I worked at Saks, it never ceased to provide a delightful distraction. I couldn't resist strolling through the various departments, taking in the latest arrivals of new pocketbooks, hats, the earrings and baubles. There was a lovely lime green summer shift that I planned to try on later, when I had more time.

I was drifting toward the escalators when I heard two women arguing. I turned around and spotted one of the new salesgirls grabbing hold of Mrs. Hutt.

"Let go of me this instant!" Mrs. Hutt demanded as I rushed over. She had a pair of white sunglasses in her hand.

"Let her go," I said, practically prying the salesgirl's fingers off Mrs. Hutt's arm. "Mrs. Hutt, I'm so sorry. I apologize."

"Apologize?" the salesgirl shrieked. "She's trying to steal those sunglasses. She was about to put them in her pocketbook and—"

"Just be quiet." I turned back to Mrs. Hutt. "Are you all right? I am so sorry."

"Would you please tell this girl who I am? Who my husband is?"

By now Mrs. Coopers had joined us, showering Mrs. Hutt with apologies.

The salesgirl was baffled. "But she—"

"Shush." I glared at her.

"I have news for all of you," said Mrs. Hutt as she brushed some imaginary dirt off her sleeve. "I will never step foot inside Saks Fifth Avenue again. From now on I shall take my business elsewhere."

And with that, Mrs. Hutt placed the stolen sunglasses back into her pocketbook and strolled out of Saks Fifth Avenue for the last time. That day we lost one of our best customers and that salesgirl lost her job.

Mrs. Hutt had always charmed me in her own quirky way, but just then I saw all too clearly how someone with enough money had carte blanche to do as they pleased. My father had done that for years until he'd been caught. Well, Mrs. Hutt had been caught but there were no consequences to her aside from moving her shoplifting to a new location. It was all twisted inside out and now the shopgirl had been punished for Mrs. Hutt's crimes.

The whole thing nagged at me for days. I couldn't let it go. I asked around on the girl's behalf and finally got her a job waiting tables at the Hungarian restaurant below Estée's apartment. It wasn't ideal and I didn't know how long she'd last there, but it was my small way of trying to set things right.

Back over at Saks, cosmetic sales were up. Almost six percent, according to our latest tally. Part of that was thanks to Estée. She was a rising star at Saks Fifth Avenue, and just six weeks after her debut, we expanded and gave her another two feet of counter space.

Estée was working twelve-hour shifts and insisting that no one could sell her products like she could. And this was true. Estée could always get a woman to splurge for an extra lipstick or a box of face powder. And she still gave them free samples on top of that. But even Estée had her limits. She was exhausted and needed to hire sales help.

But as she said to Mrs. Coopers, "I want to train them myself and I won't tolerate any of those T&T Girls. Telephone and toilet. If they're not on one, they're on the other."

NOT LONG AFTER hiring on two shopgirls, Estée received some wonderful news. Another luxury department store, based in Dallas, had begun courting her.

She stood in my office, wringing her hands. "Is that in breach of my contract?" she asked. "Can I open in another department store?"

It wasn't just another department store. It was Neiman Marcus.

Marion already had Estée's contract out and was reading through the fine print. Shaking her head, she said, "Doesn't say anything about operations outside of New York City." She slid the contract over to me. "We'll have to double-check with Mr. Fiske, but I don't see anything in there that says you can't do it."

Estée nodded but she didn't seem very happy about this.

"What's wrong?" I scanned through the contract in case Marion had missed anything. "Neiman Marcus is a big deal." Just the year before, *Life* magazine had featured them, claiming they were *the most luxurious store in America*, something which hadn't gone over too well at Saks. "This is incredible news, Estée."

"But they want to have a meeting. Next week."

"So?"

"So, it takes two and a half days by train to get there. That's two and a half days getting there and two and a half days getting back. I can't afford to waste that kind of time on a train. I'm going to have to fly and I'm terrified."

"Oh, people fly every day," said Marion. "They say you have a better chance of being killed on your way to the airport than on your flight." She laughed. "You'll be fine."

"No, you don't understand." Estée turned to me. "I'm petrified." And she was. Those hazel eyes were panic-stricken. "Will you come with me, Gloria? Hold my hand?"

"Isn't that what husbands are for?" I asked, setting her contract aside.

"Joe has to stay here and take care of the boys. Oh, please, Gloria. I'm begging you."

"It might be good for you to get away," said Marion. "You've got all that vacation time piling up."

This was true. Even Mr. Fiske had been asking when I was going to take some time off.

"Please?" Estée gripped onto my hand. "I'll pay for everything. I just can't get on that plane by myself."

What made me think I would ever be able to say no to her? I'd never been able to before. So after Estée left, I went into Mr. Fiske's office with her contract in hand. I explained the situation brewing down in Dallas with Neiman Marcus.

"Dammit," he grumbled, and scrubbed a hand over his face.

"Do you want to review the contract?" I asked, offering it up.

"I don't need to review the contract," he said, shaking his head. "Saks Fifth Avenue has no exclusivity claim on Estée Lauder outside of New York."

And now I had to drop the second bomb. "I have some vacation days coming and, well, Estée wants me to go down there with her. It'll only be for two days." She didn't want to be away from Joe and the boys a minute longer than needed.

He looked up at me, brows pulled together. "Go—go! And," he added, "you're not taking two days off. I want you to take a full week off. For God's sake, Gloria, your vacation is long overdue. Go out there and live a little."

So there you have it. Like it or not, I was flying down to Dallas with Estée on her maiden voyage.

48

THE DAY BEFORE our trip to Dallas, I was down on the main floor at Saks, checking in with all the shopgirls on their inventory, trying to get a feel for what products were moving and what wasn't. I wanted to write up a report and get it to Marion. I wanted to make sure I had everything buttoned up for Mr. Belfort and Mr. Fiske before I left town.

I had just returned to my desk when the receptionist buzzed me. There was someone here to see me. I double-checked my appointment book. I didn't have any meetings scheduled for that afternoon, and when I went out to the waiting room, I saw a young woman with reddish-brown hair, a face full of freckles. She looked vaguely familiar but I couldn't place her.

"Gloria? It's me, Janice." She stood up, held out her hand to me. "We met when you came out to the house to see John Schotz. My foster father."

"Oh yes. Of course." I clasped my hand over top of hers. "So nice to see you again. Did you see Estée's counter downstairs? Isn't it wonderful?"

"She's not here right now, is she?"

"Afraid not. Estée's getting ready for a business trip down to Dallas tomorrow, so she stepped out to run a few errands. I know she's going to be disappointed she missed you."

Janice didn't acknowledge that. Instead, she lowered her voice and said, "Could we, ah, could we go somewhere private and talk?"

The hairs on the back of my neck prickled at this. Something was wrong. Maybe Uncle John was sick. Maybe another member of Estée's family? I grabbed my pocketbook, and while we headed toward the Automat, Janice talked about the weather and how she'd gotten that scholarship after all. She was at Barnard here in the city, studying chemistry. She wanted to go into skincare, like her foster father.

After we got our coffees, I leaned in conspiratorially and said, "So what's going on? Is everyone all right?"

"Well." Janice tapped her spoon against the lip of her cup. "I'm not sure exactly where to start. My father—my *foster* father—doesn't even know I'm here. He'd be furious if he knew, but I just had to do something."

"About what?"

Fixated on her coffee, she took a moment, as if gathering her thoughts, before she gazed up. "You know he taught Estée everything she knows, right?"

"Yes. I do know that."

"So you know those formulas she's selling are *his*."

"Well, she may have *started* with his formulas, but—"

"But the point is, they're still *his* formulas."

"I'm not sure I understand what you're getting at."

"She's making a small fortune at Saks and she hasn't paid my father a dime. Not one dime. Don't you think he deserves some compensation for the use of his formulas?"

"I, ah—" I didn't know what to say. Estée would never have done anything like that to anyone. Especially not her own uncle. No,

Janice was mistaken. "I think this is something you should talk to Estée about. It's not my place to get involved."

She sat back in her chair, exasperated. "Well, I think you and Saks at least deserve to know who you're *really* doing business with."

"What exactly does that mean?" There was a bit of an edge to my voice. I couldn't help it. I was feeling protective of Estée.

"Let's just say Estée Lauder isn't all she's cracked up to be. For starters, her name isn't really Estée."

That shot a current through my body. *Your name isn't really Downing, either.* All the activity in the Automat—the conversations at other tables, the sound of vending machine doors sliding open and shut, the dishes rattling—came to a halt. I reached for a cigarette, struck the match so hard I nearly tore it in two.

"Her real name is Josephine. Josephine Esther. We used to call her Esther. Sometimes Estelle. But never Estée. Oh, and the way she uses that ridiculous accent mark over the *e*. Like she's European. It just kills me."

"But she *is* European. She was born in Austria."

"Oh boy." Janice laughed. "Did she tell you that bit about the aristocratic family?" She laughed again. "She's a big phony, is what she is. All that talk about Europe and growing up in a big house in Flushing. The chauffeurs, the servants—it's all a big lie. Esther was born in Queens. She grew up in a run-down apartment above her father's hardware store in Corona. Mentzer Hardware. Yeah, *Mentzer*," she said pointedly. "She's Jewish and she won't admit it. How do you like that?"

The more Janice talked, the more confused I became. My mind was shuffling back through time, remembering the Christmas trees at her house, the comments she'd drop from time to time about other Jewish women . . . "But what about her uncle—your foster father? He's a world-renowned skincare specialist, a highly regarded dermatologist from Vienna."

Janice shook her head. "He's not from Vienna. Try a small town in Hungary. And he is brilliant, and yes, he did study chemistry, but he isn't exactly a skincare specialist. He's not even a doctor."

"What?" I recalled our visit to Corona to see him. That shack where he produced everything from cold cream to bird feed. I thought about that dilapidated house. All the foster children. I started to feel a little sick. "Well . . ." I stubbed out my cigarette. The tightness in my throat made it hard to get the words out. "This is really between Estée and her uncle. There's nothing I can do about it." My voice remained calm, but I was rattled.

I felt all my guideposts moving. Some of Janice's claims were adding up. They explained things that had always puzzled me—Estée never introducing me to her family, the mezuzah on John Schotz's doorpost, her strange behavior when she met Vicki Baum, Estée's fascination with celebrities and socialites, why she had a million uses for toothpaste, vinegar, and lemon juice—it was all starting to make sense now. It was the tablecloth trick—everything I thought I knew about my best friend was pulled out from under me.

Or was it?

I couldn't jump to conclusions. Maybe Janice had an ax to grind. Estée was my friend and I was willing to give her the benefit of the doubt.

"You can at least let Saks know they've been duped," she said. "I mean, why should John Schotz be penniless while Esther's making money hand over fist off his hard work?"

Those were the words that put me over the edge. Wasn't that exactly what my father had done—made money off other people's hard work? This all hit too close to home. I couldn't believe that Estée would have done such a thing to her own uncle. I'd put so much faith in her. I admired and respected her drive, her determination. To me she'd been a self-made woman and it would crush me if all her success had been built on a lie. Just like my father. *Just like my father.*

WHEN I GOT home that night, I stared at the blue Pan Am globe on my ticket sticking out from the mail on the kitchen counter. Estée and I were supposed to leave in the morning, but I had too many questions running through my mind. If what Janice said was true, I didn't know how I'd hold Estée's hand all the way to Dallas and back. I hadn't packed yet, my suitcase still stowed away in the back of my closet, waiting for me.

Janice's words rang out inside my head, vibrating inside my chest. *Why should John Schotz be penniless while Esther's making money hand over fist off his hard work? Her name isn't really Estée.* I paused, swallowed hard. *Your name isn't really Downing, either.*

Yes, I had been lying to Estée, too, but I had no choice. My father was a criminal, and it had been so raw when Estée and I first met. My family's name was all over the news. I saw what people had done to my brother—spitting on him, punching him—just because he was a Dowaziac. I'd had to protect myself as best I could. But if Janice was right, then what Estée did was outright deceit. And if true, then she'd tricked me, too, made me one of her biggest champions. How many times had I tried to arrange meetings for her with Mr. Fiske? And what about that mailing list that I gave her? I could have gotten fired for doing that. I couldn't even write a letter of support for my own father because he was a cheat and a liar and yet I'd put my neck on the line for Estée. I couldn't handle thinking that my best friend was no better than Gus Dowaziac, betraying her own uncle and lying to me and everyone else.

After working my way to that edge, my thoughts came back to the center, and I was torn. Estée was my friend. Yes, she might have started with her uncle's formulas, but she'd improved upon them. Hadn't she? I told myself she'd have a perfectly good explanation for all this.

It was almost one in the morning when I finally got my suitcase out. I packed, rolling my skirts and dresses the way Estée had taught me, turning my blouses inside out before I placed them on top and snapped the latches shut.

The next morning Estée picked me up in a taxicab. "I'm a nervous wreck," she said when I got inside. "I didn't sleep a wink last night."

"That makes two of us."

"Are you okay?" she asked.

I didn't answer, but she was too preoccupied to have noticed, her hands clutching the seat cushion, her window cracked for air. I was still working up the nerve to ask her about my visit with Janice, but she seemed so anxious about the flight, I couldn't quite get there.

When we arrived at Idlewild, we entered the terminal with our suitcases in hand. There were boarding announcements over the loudspeaker, the clacking of rushing heels against the tiled floor, people hugging hellos and goodbyes. Estée was wearing a new Chanel suit along with a hat and pocketbook I'd never seen before. She'd spent more on her traveling outfit than her poor uncle made in a year.

We were working our way to the ticket counter but each step became harder to take, my suitcase growing heavier in my hand. Three feet from the counter I couldn't take another step. I had to know the truth. I dropped my luggage, letting it land with a loud thud.

"What's wrong? Do you not feel well?" Estée turned back toward me.

"Actually, no." I drew a deep breath. "Janice came to see me at work yesterday."

"Janice?" She walked over to me. She had no idea who I was referring to.

"Your uncle John's daughter."

"Oh. Is everything okay?"

"No one's sick or hurt or anything like that, but she told me all these things about you—she said your real name is Josephine or Esther. She said you grew up in Corona and—"

"Oh." The change on her face was unmistakable. I could tell by the way the color in her cheeks blanched out and the way her hand shot up to cover her mouth that everything Janice had told me was true.

That's when my own fury began to build. I'd been trying to give her the benefit of the doubt, but now everything I'd been holding back came rushing forward. "I can't believe you've been lying to me this whole time. Born in goddamn Vienna? Austrian aristocracy? John Schotz is some world-renowned skincare doctor? You're nothing but a liar. A fake."

Estée's nostrils flared and in an instant her cheeks went from white to dark red. Then she growled in a way I didn't think possible. "You little hypocrite. I know *all* about you, too, Gloria *Dow-az-iac*." Her voice boomed, making my stomach drop.

My mouth opened but no words came out.

"I've known about *you* for a very, very long time."

A ping went off in my ear, followed by the rush of pulsing blood. It wasn't the start of vertigo. No, this was raw adrenaline.

"Your little friend Alexandria Spencer had quite a lot to say about you—rich little girl from Fifth Avenue. Your father's in federal prison, your—"

"When did you two—"

"The night of Arlene's party."

"Arlene? Who's Arlene?"

"Arlene Forester. Don't you remember her party in Palm Beach?"

Palm Beach—but that was ages ago. Good Lord—had Estée known all this time?

"Alexandria told me everything. So don't you dare talk to me about being a liar. Being a fake. You told me your parents were dead. You had my heart breaking for you. *Poor Gloria all alone with no family.* Every time you opened your mouth you were lying to me." She'd gone from growling to screeching now. People were staring. "Your father's a con man and a felon and—"

"Don't you start with that." Now I was mortified and ashamed, caught in my own lie. The mature thing would have been to fess up and back down, but instead, to cover my embarrassment, I lashed out even more, determined to prove that what she'd done had been far worse. "Let's see, you lied about your ancestry, lied about being Jewish, lied about the big house in Flushing. You lied about *everything.* And you want to know what really galls me? It's that you pulled me in on the whole thing. I went to bat for you. I vouched for you to Mr. Fiske and the rest of the buying department. I believed in you. Do you have any idea how foolish that makes me feel? I was duped right along with everyone else. You used your uncle's formulas. You cut him out of the business he helped you start. You'd be nothing without John Schotz."

"Talk about nothing. When I met you, you were a miserable, helpless little girl. You were pathetic."

"And you were nothing but a huckster. You were obnoxious—"

Estée stomped her foot. I should have stopped but I kept going, aware that a cluster of people had gathered around us.

A gentleman came forward. "Ladies, is—"

"Stay out of it," I snapped, and fired off another round. "That's right, Estée. You were *ob-nox-ious.* Every time you pulled out your little jars at parties, on the bus, walking up to perfect strangers, I'd cringe. You couldn't even see the way they'd roll their eyes, the way they'd laugh at you as soon as you walked away. I was embarrassed to even be seen with you."

I could tell by the look on her face that I'd just wounded her badly. "Well," she said, "you won't have to be *embarrassed* by me anymore, Gloria Dowaziac."

"You're damn right about that." And at that moment, I leveled the biggest blow imaginable. I glared at her and said, "Have a good flight, Estée."

Her eyes went wide, her mouth gaped open. She was going to have to get on the plane and make that flight all by herself. I thought she might pass out, or else back out of the whole thing, but she wanted Neiman Marcus and she wasn't about to let me or her fear of flying stand in her way. "To hell with you, Gloria. You and me—we're done."

"That's just fine by me." I picked up my suitcase, turned and walked away from her and never looked back.

49

BY THE TIME I made it home that day, everything inside me had shifted like items in the plane's overhead compartments. Now that the truth was out there, I felt vulnerable and utterly exposed. I'd never seen Estée so angry and though she'd kept my secret all these years, now she had every reason to blow my cover. She could tell everyone at Saks about my father. But then again, I knew all about her, too, and could tell everyone that she was the bigger fraud. We both had the goods on each other and maybe that was enough to keep us in check. Or was it smarter to swallow my pride and make up with her in an attempt to *keep your friends close and your enemies closer*?

Later that day, when I should have been in Dallas, I found myself sitting with Bobbi at Mr. Foster's Tavern, its mangy hound keeping his eye on us. The man to my left at the bar was reading the newspaper while he downed a beer and a shot of whiskey.

Over cocktails, I told Bobbi about the scene Estée and I made at the airport.

"Wow," Bobbi mused, "I didn't think she had it in her."

"Actually, neither did I."

"Gotta give her credit for still getting on that plane," Bobbi said, flicking the cigarette between her fingers, which were tinged green and purple. With her banana art halted, she'd recently taken up painting though she said she wasn't any good it.

The man next to me got up and left, leaving his newspaper behind, and that's when I saw something that made me flinch.

Bobbi saw my reaction. "What?"

There it was, on the financial page of the *New York Times*: DOWAZIAC PAROLE DENIED.

In a rash move, I grabbed the paper for a closer look. My cheeks were burning red as a whoosh of heat came over me. It was a short article, hardly more than a mention, but in my mind, it might as well have been front-page news, above the fold.

"What is it? What's wrong?"

I felt cornered—the newspaper was still in my hand. What choice did I have? I surrendered and showed Bobbi the article.

"What is this?" she asked. "What am I looking at?"

"Ever heard of Gus Dowaziac?"

She thought for a minute. "Sounds familiar. Isn't he some politician or something?"

I laughed sadly and polished off the last dregs of my martini. "Do you remember that big Ponzi scheme about eight years ago?"

"What's a Ponzi scheme?"

"It's a financial fraud. Hundreds and hundreds of people got wiped out—they lost their life savings. And that man right there"—I pointed to the headline—"Gus Dowaziac, is the one who swindled everyone."

"Yeah, so what?"

"Well, he's my father."

"Huh? What?" She looked at the newspaper and back at me. "But wait, your name isn't—"

"I changed it. Right after he got arrested."

Bobbi was still looking at me, a blank expression on her face. I had no idea what was running through her mind.

I barreled on, unable to stop my rambling confession. "My whole childhood, my whole life was nothing but a big lie. I have a father in prison, a mother, a sister—I don't speak to either of them."

Silence. More empty staring.

"And I have a brother, too, who's probably never going to speak to me again."

"Well," Bobbi said eventually with a shrug, her bottom lip turned down, "I don't speak to my brother and, believe me, I prefer it that way." She looked again at the newspaper. "So, your dad's in prison, huh?"

I nodded.

"Wow, I'm sorry." She shook her head and tweaked her scarf. "That's really rough. I had no idea."

"You had *no idea* because I *lied* to you. I never told you who I really was."

She cocked her head and smiled. "Changing your name doesn't change who you really are. So technically, it's not really a lie." She called over to the bartender. "Marty, we need another round."

"No one knows that con artist is my father. I never told the Millers or Estée or anyone at work, either. The only person I ever told was Edward."

"Well"—Bobbi glanced at the headline again—"if it makes you feel any better, I wouldn't want people knowing my father was in prison, either."

"I'm sorry I never told you. Can you ever forgive me?"

She surprised me with a laugh. "Silly—there's nothing to forgive.

You certainly don't have to apologize to me. I probably would have done the same thing in your position. And at least you didn't do anything wrong," she added, setting the newspaper aside. "What I did—now *that* was wrong. And believe me, God is punishing me for it."

Our drinks arrived, and after the bartender left, she said, "I wish I'd never sold that first piece to Madame Rubinstein. I really do. I just can't do my art anymore." I noticed she couldn't even bring herself to say the word *banana*. Her voice tightened. "It's killing me. I feel like part of me died."

We both went quiet for a moment. She was lost in her world, and I was left on the edge, looking in, baffled by Bobbi's reaction to the news about my father. Did she not understand, or did she truly not care? All I knew was that the sky hadn't fallen in. Nothing awful had happened. My friend was still my friend. I had a moment's relief, a breath taken after years of holding it all inside. But that was just Bobbi. How would the Millers react? What about everyone else? Telling Bobbi may have been a start, but the tug back under was still there; the roots were still attached.

With a searing stab of guilt, I realized that Estée had known the truth for years and it hadn't changed the way she felt about me. But I'd blown all that at the airport because I was a hypocrite. It had been okay for me to lie, but not her.

Eventually Bobbi turned her focus back to me. "We're like two girls in white suits."

"Excuse me?"

"You've never heard the story about the white suit and the bird shit?"

"Ah no. Can't say that I have."

"Okay, well, you see there's two guys standing on the street corner. One's dressed in an all-white suit and the guy next to him is covered in shit. Just covered from head to toe. Then a bird comes along and it takes a crap on both of them. Nobody even notices it on the guy already covered in crap. I mean, what's another piece of shit on top of all the other shit, right? But for the guy dressed in white, that one tiny speck of bird shit is the first thing everybody sees when they look at him."

I shot her an amused-but-puzzled look in return.

"Don't you get it? We're like the guy in the white suit."

I had to laugh. Only my Bobbi would see the world this way.

"We're basically good people—you and me," she went on to say, "but we did something we're not too proud of and that's left a speck of bird shit on us. We're worried that it's the only thing people would see if they knew the truth."

"And so, what are we supposed to do about it?"

"We have to remove the stain. Scrub it out, take it to the cleaners—do whatever it takes to get the speck of shit out." She pondered this for a moment as she lit a cigarette and toyed with the matchbox. "This might sound crazy," she said, "but maybe if I admit the truth to Madame Rubinstein and tell her she bought a bunch of banana peels, it could get rid of the bird crap on me. It might free me up so I could start making my art again. Is that crazy?"

I thought about what she'd just said. Was it a full moon or something? It seemed like everybody's deep dark secrets were coming to light. "Actually, no. I don't think that's crazy at all."

"Really? You don't?" She ran her fingers through her thick hair. "So then you think I *should* tell Madame Rubinstein the truth? Now, even after all this time? I mean, it could ruin my career. Probably will."

"Sounds to me like your guilt is already doing that for you as it is."

"So then, you *really* think I should do it. Just tell her the truth?"

She kept rephrasing her question, possibly hoping for a different answer. I considered this carefully and nodded. "Yes, I do think you should tell the truth." I heard the words leave my mouth and realized I could have been talking to myself. *Yes, the time had come to tell the truth.*

Bobbi's eyes glassed up. "Will you come with me?"

THE NEXT DAY we arrived at Helena Rubinstein's home on Park Avenue and 65th, a limestone triplex with grand terraces. Lately Madame had taken to conducting business from her bed and so we were led into her bedroom, where she was luxuriating in satin sheets. We stood before her, my hat in my hands, Bobbi's heart in her stomach. Madame Rubinstein was a serious collector with precious artwork by Raoul Dufy and Picasso. She had an entire wall devoted to portraits of herself created by Marie Laurencin, Christian Bérard, Dora Maar, Salvador Dalí and, yes, Bobbi Koerner.

"I have something to tell you," Bobbi said. "It's about the piece of artwork you bought. From me."

"Yes?" Madame raised her chin, lips pursed.

"I'm sorry to say—and I should have spoken up sooner—but, well, it's not what you think it is."

"Oh?" Her perfectly arched eyebrows hiked up.

Everything froze for a moment. The air in the room barely stirred. Bobbi went stiff; I felt nauseated and couldn't look at Madame Rubinstein, propped up against her pillows, waiting.

Finally, Bobbi spoke up. "It's just that, well, it's not constructed out of silk or string or whatever it was I told you."

"Oh." Madame's eyebrows rose again, a bit higher this time.

"The thing is, it's . . ." Bobbi's words trickled out before she swallowed and started over again. "It's actually—well, it's actually made out of peels. Banana peels."

Silence. More silence. I was dying inside. Dying for Bobbi and for me. Bobbi was turning herself inside out, hanging herself out as a liar and a fraud. I felt small and despicable just for being complicit in the whole thing.

Bobbi and I stood still, waiting for Madame to say something, and after another agonizing minute passed, Helena Rubinstein did something I never—not in a million years—would have expected. She laughed. And I mean, she laughed hard, her hand over her heart as she doubled over, tears escaping the corners of her eyes.

"Oh my goodness," she said, trying to catch her breath, "I thought you were going to tell me it was a forgery."

"But it's *bananas*," I said, as if maybe she hadn't understood.

She continued to howl, and when she did finally manage to compose herself, dabbing at her eyes with her silk sheets, she pointed to the banana portrait of herself hanging prominently on the wall. "I love this piece. Do you understand? It speaks to me. I wouldn't care if you'd made it out of dental floss."

"But—but you've introduced me to your friends, to other collectors," said Bobbi.

"They commissioned her for work, too," I added for emphasis.

"Because they, too, loved what they saw. Let me tell you both something about art. When I buy a piece, I'm not paying for the paint the artist used or the canvas they put it on. I'm paying for their imagination, their talent. Her imagination, her talent," she said, pointing to Bobbi. "I'm paying for the art that's been produced. I have a painting in my living room by an African artist. It's made out of berry juice."

"So you're not mad?" asked Bobbi.

"Maybe yes, just a wee bit." She laughed. "But now I want you to do another piece for me."

Bobbi's shoulders squared and I heard her sigh as she grabbed my hand.

The longer I stood before Madame Rubinstein, the more dumbfounded I was by her reaction to Bobbi's confession. I found it as bewildering as Bobbi's reaction had been to the news about my father. Madame didn't care that she'd been hoodwinked. In fact, she didn't see it that way at all. All she cared about was the finished product, the end result.

While Helena Rubinstein discussed the new piece she wanted Bobbi to create for her, I excused myself and said my goodbyes. Once outside, I drew in as much air as my lungs could hold. Madame had forgiven Bobbi. Bobbi had forgiven me. The obvious question now stared me in the face: Was it time for me to forgive my father? Everyone else in my family had managed to do that. Maybe I'd been so blind in my anger that I couldn't see the situation through the correct lens. Didn't all families have their secrets? Embarrassing relatives, old family feuds?

Seeing what happened between Bobbi and Helena Rubinstein, my own solution was becoming clearer. If I was going to move forward in my life, if I was ever going to be happy, let myself appreciate all that I'd accomplished and let myself have the love I deserved, I would have to make peace with my father. I imagined eight years in prison would change a man and maybe it was time to give him the benefit of the doubt.

I continued to walk with these thoughts seesawing back and forth, looking for a side to land on. I passed a series of uniformed doormen along Park Avenue, standing beneath the awnings at the ready. I turned at the corner and crossed Madison and Fifth until I was at the edge of Central Park. I hadn't eaten anything all day and my stomach was growling. I bought a bag of roasted nuts from a street vendor beneath a bright yellow umbrella.

With my bag of nuts, still warm in my hand, I went into the park and settled in on a bench. The leaves were rustling in the breeze, birds where chirping, squirrels were racing up and down the tree trunks. I ate a few nuts and tossed some to a group of pigeons pecking about. I sprinkled another handful, watching the nuts bounce on the pavement as more pigeons came to feast. In a city as crowded as New York, it was just me and the birds.

God, I was lonely. I was constantly missing Edward, that was nothing new, but now I was missing Estée, too, and most surprising of all, I was missing my miserable family. I was back to questioning my decision about not writing that letter for my father. I had let him down, and the rest of my family, too. Like Glenn said, if my father didn't make parole, it would be on me, and now it was.

I sat for some time, weighing all this before leaving the park. I was still wandering aimlessly, and when I reached 57th and Seventh Avenue, I found myself staring at an advertisement for Maybelline. It was a new campaign they were running. I'd seen it on the subway platform, in various magazines, and here it was again, plastered in a storefront window. It featured a model smiling radiantly with the caption, *What a Difference Maybelline Makes.* All anyone saw was the pretty face, covered in makeup. No one cared if there were freckles or blemishes or a birthmark hidden underneath. I knew that without makeup, none of those models looked like their stunning photographs. Some would say that the whole beauty industry was conceived to deceive, designed to create an illusion. But what about the Marions of the world who used makeup to camouflage scars? Or someone like me, with lashes so fair, I couldn't go without mascara? Everyone was guilty of a little embellishment, doing a little enhancing to what God had or hadn't given us. If it weren't for women's desire to look their best, we wouldn't have a billion-dollar cosmetic industry.

In that moment, something dawned on me; it was like a branch of lightning that illuminated the sky and disappeared just as quickly. But I had seen it in a flicker, and if there was one thing I knew for sure, it was that everybody lied—Waller, Bobbi, Estée, my father. Even Soda Pop had lied about his age so he could join the army. All lies had their motivations, some certainly more benign than others.

In a twist of irony to end all ironies, now that I realized that everyone else did it, too, I decided I was done. No more lying. It was time to be authentic. I started walking faster now and faster still. I knew what I had to do, and it propelled me forward until I was practically running.

By the time I made it to Darlene's Palace of Beauty, I was out of breath. I looked around the familiar shop, to where my journey began. The same old pink shampoo bowls were there, and the smells of setting lotion, hair spray and nail polish hung in the air. Bernice was still there rolling about on her stool and Darlene, predictably, had a cigarette parked in the corner of her mouth.

Still a little winded, I said, "I need you to dye my hair back, get me as close as you can to my original platinum blonde."

50

THE NEXT DAY, I boarded a train for Poughkeepsie. I used to think Poughkeepsie *sounded* like a happy place. Like it should have been the name of an amusement park. *Poo-kip-see*—it just had a fun ring to it. But when the conductor called the Duchess County stop, without warning I began beating back an onslaught of tears.

As the train pulled into the station, to my surprise I saw Glenn standing on the platform waiting for me, his hands stuffed inside his pockets, his light blond hair blowing in the wind. Although we'd spoken on the telephone several times, I hadn't seen Glenn since he left me at the Hermitage Hotel eight years ago. He looked a little stockier now and even from a distance I could see the shadows beneath his eyes, the overall weariness of who he'd become.

I'd telephoned Glenn when I'd returned home from Darlene's the day before and told him I was ready to see my father. And my mother, too. He must have hung up from me and hopped the next train to New York. I took the gesture as a reassuring sign. I was doing the right thing.

But then he gave me a half hug that seemed so perfunctory I

wondered why he'd even bothered. The first thing he said to me was, "Talk about a day late and a dollar short."

"Well, I'm here now, aren't I?" I wasn't ready to admit that maybe I'd been too hard on my parents, that lately I'd been consumed with regret. And guilt.

We walked in silence over to a dark blue Durant, rusted out on the passenger side.

"Where'd this old clunker come from?" I asked.

"It's Mom's. Gail and I bought it for her a few years ago. $165 bucks."

I slid my finger into a tear in the upholstery, nervously working it the whole way until we pulled up to a nondescript two-story red-brick building. It had eight windows, two up, four across, the black paint peeling off the shutters.

My mother greeted us at the door with a glass of wine in her hand. For a moment I wasn't sure she was going to invite me inside. Even when her lower lip began to crumble and her eyes turned glassy, I wasn't sure she was happy to see me. It wasn't until she set her wineglass down and wrapped herself around me that I felt somewhat welcome.

When she finally did let me in, I gulped audibly. And it wasn't just that the place was even worse on the inside. It was because Gail was there, slumped down on a worn-out sofa, looking up from a magazine and positively glaring at me. I shot Glenn a furious look for not having warned me.

"Well, well, well. Look who finally decided to grace us with her presence," Gail said, dramatically turning the pages of *Vogue*.

"All that matters is that she's with us now." My mother stroked my arm like I was made of chinchilla. She was drunk. It wasn't even noon.

My mother looked awful and ancient, shuffling about the room like a little old lady. She'd always been slender but now she was positively gaunt. Her enormous three-carat wedding ring was so loose on her finger it rode up against her knuckle. Gail, on the other hand, seemed to have gained every pound my mother lost and then some. She was starting to go gray, too, which shocked me. I could tell by her expression that she was wondering if I'd noticed how much she'd aged, but I'd shifted my focus to the room itself.

It was jarring to see my mother living in an efficiency, with a Murphy bed tucked away inside the wall, the carpet shot, stained and dimpled by the furniture of tenants past. The Chippendale armchairs and Tomaso Buzzi Venini vases she'd managed to hold on to from our penthouse looked out of place there.

"Mom, tell Gloria about how you ran into Thomas," Gail said, stretching her arms overhead, revealing the fleshy roll about her middle when her blouse came untucked.

I don't recall what my mother said. I'd tuned out the entire discussion. There was no point in sticking around my mother's gloomy apartment, so we opted for something even more depressing, and all piled into my mother's Durant and headed to Sing Sing.

Glenn drove while my mother chain-smoked in the passenger seat. Gail and I stayed on our respective sides in the back, just like when we were kids. Somehow, we began reminiscing about my father, rehashing old stories and family lore: the time he'd set live lobsters on the kitchen floor to see if they would race; how he'd dress as Santa Claus every year; the mangy lovable mutt he brought home from the pound . . . It made me sentimental because at one time we did seem like a regular family. We had our quirks, our holiday traditions, and in our own way, we had love, which made me feel all the more awful for having turned my back on them.

Finally, we arrived at Sing Sing, a cluster of buildings and a stone-walled tower set on a sprawling hillside near a stretch of railroad tracks. We parked and walked up a wooden staircase that led to the main entrance and visitors' room. After one of the guards—

stocky and red-nosed, straight out of central casting—laid down the rules, we were ushered into a cold, stark room with a long table, crowded with inmates and their visitors. Everything was steel, brick and concrete and smelled musty and sour.

Until that moment, I hadn't realized that I'd been expecting to find my father wearing black-and-white stripes and leg-irons. Instead, there he was, dressed in a blue work shirt and pants a few shades darker. His hair was unkempt and mostly gray and he had a couple days' worth of silvery whiskers on his cheeks and chin. And jowls. My father had jowls now, puffy and sagging. Prison had turned him into a frail old man, a paper tiger. My stomach roiled to see him waiting for us at the end of the table. I felt sorry for him and held my breath, not sure if he wanted me there or not. But then he smiled and thanked us for coming, like he was hosting a social gathering.

"You look good, Gus." My mother was in la-la land. "He looks good, doesn't he, kids?" She turned to us for confirmation.

Glenn and Gail agreed, nodding. I was frozen because we were sitting across from a man who most certainly did not look good. My father had always been immaculate about bathing, shaving. He wore Dunhill for Men and gave off that scent of woodsy spice. Now he looked like a thug. Like every other inmate. I feared he might smell wretched and was grateful there was no touching allowed—no hugging—between inmates and visitors.

I was working up my nerve to say something, but my father had already taken over, already beginning to chuckle as he launched into a story we'd heard him tell a gazillion times before. It was about the first job he ever had, working at a funeral home. The rear doorway, where they loaded up the hearses, was too narrow for the caskets to pass through, so when no one was looking, they'd turn the casket—body and all—onto its side and fit it through the doorway before sliding it right side up and into the hearse.

". . . just flip it. Flip it right on its side." My father slapped the table, his eyes tearing from laughter. Other inmates looked over to see what was so funny. And shame on me for laughing with him—and not because I thought it was amusing but because that was what my father expected of us, his adoring audience. Even here in prison he still had a magnetic pull on me. On all of us. Laughing at my father's stories and jokes had always been a competition among Gail, Glenn and me—who could laugh the hardest, the longest.

After the merriment died down, my father said, "I'll tell you what, Gwen, kids—give me a minute alone here with your sister." He pointed to me.

I felt a pinprick of heat coming off his fingertip. I was anointed. His favorite child once again, the one he adored, who could do no wrong. I imagined my siblings were jealous, wishing he'd wanted time alone with them.

After they left, I said, "I'm sorry about your parole." This could have been interpreted as *I'm sorry you've been denied* or *I'm sorry that I did absolutely nothing to help you get released.*

"Ah." He swatted a hand through the air—*No big deal.* "They were never gonna give me a fair hearing anyway. The system's broken. That's how I landed in this hellhole to begin with. The real shame is that, believe it or not, I was a damn good stockbroker. Everything would have been fine if the market hadn't crashed. Everyone would have made their money back in spades. I just needed more time to make the numbers work . . ."

I crossed my legs, fighting the impulse to roll my eyes. I'd heard this all before. It was the same speech he'd given to the judge, to the press, to anyone who would listen. But I was his daughter, and I hadn't come to Sing Sing to hear his monologue again.

". . . but then," my father was saying now, "one of my biggest investors started getting nervous. He wanted to take his money out and I had to find some way to cover that loss. The market was in trouble and another investor wanted out, and then another and another, and before I knew it, the money was draining like a sieve. But I swear I never set out to hurt anyone . . ."

By now my foot was jiggling uncontrollably, my patience wearing thin.

"You know me—I'm not a bad guy."

He paused, expecting me to confirm this, but I couldn't. For once I dared to challenge him. "But people trusted you. Even our housekeeper, the doorman—people you knew couldn't afford to lose a dime." Instead of a raise, he'd always say, *Let me do a little investing for you. I guarantee you'll come out way further ahead . . .* When my father didn't respond, I felt my courage mounting. "You tell me you're not a bad guy, but how could you have done that? What about all the lives you destroyed?"

He dropped his head in shame, his shoulders shaking. The crying seemed to go on for a minute or two before he finally managed to croak out, "You gotta believe me when I tell you I was going to take care of everybody." He looked up, and despite the sobbing, his cheeks were dry. There were no tears. It sent a chill through me. "Gloria, I swear on the Bible, if the market hadn't crashed, if time hadn't run out, I would—"

"Oh, stop it!" I slapped the table with my palms. "Just stop with the lies."

He looked stunned, as though with one punch I'd taken down the great boxer he'd once been. But after a moment's stammering, he got back up and now his entire demeanor had changed. I saw it happen right before my eyes—he dropped the mask and all I could think was, *My God, here it comes. My father's wrath.*

"What did you say, young lady?"

I started to shrink back into that little girl always seeking his approval, his love. Now it was my turn to hang my head, unable to let my eyes meet his.

"You got some nerve," he said. "Eight years"—his red-hot finger stabbed the table—"eight freakin' years I've been here, and not one visit from you. Not one letter, not even a goddamn phone call. And now, you come waltzing in here thinking you're gonna judge me, try to make me feel guilty, make me repent. Well, let me tell you something. The worst thing that could happen to a person has already happened to me. My die's been cast. There's no saving my reputation, no getting my life back. I can do whatever the hell I please now, 'cause it won't make a damn bit of difference, won't change the way people think of me. Or what people think of my wife or my children . . ."

There it was—Bobbi's parable about the man covered in bird crap.

"I feel bad for what this has done to your mother. Your sister and brother, too. That's the one thing I do feel bad about."

I looked up. "And what about me, Dad?"

"What about *you*?"

"Do you *not* feel any remorse for what you did to me? To my life?"

"You?" He laughed cruelly. "Why the hell should I show you any remorse? You turned your back on me. On your mother, too." He leaned in, his voice too controlled, tight and ominous. "You think you can change your name, pretend I don't exist? Well, you can't get rid of me that easily." He laughed so hard he started to cough.

When he said that, something inside me gave way, sparking a revolt. In all my life, I'd never had the guts to stand up to him. Until now. "I came here to make my peace with you, and you know what, I think I have. I thought I was coming here to forgive you, but it turns out, I came here to forgive myself. I did the right thing, cutting you out of my life. You deserve to be exactly where you are."

I could tell he was stunned and I kept going. I was growing stronger on the spot, the yolk separating from the egg. "Look at you," I said. "You're nothing. You're locked up in a federal prison where you belong. I'm glad you didn't get parole. I'm glad I never wrote that letter."

"Watch it, missy," he warned, coughing harder now.

"Or what? What are you gonna do to me?" I laughed back at him. "You're harmless now. You can't hurt me anymore. You can't ever hurt anyone else again." I pushed back from the table, the legs of the chair screeching as I stood up. "Have a nice life, Dad." I turned and walked away, the sound of his wet, phlegmy coughing fit following behind me.

I went out to the waiting room, passed my mother, Glenn and Gail. I kept going and walked out the main entrance, down the wooden staircase, over the footbridge and across the tracks, where I stood and waited for the next train to take me away from them all and back to my life in New York City.

I cried a little on the way home because I knew there was no going back. I hadn't just burned a bridge; I'd set it on fire and blown it up. But it was something I had to do. Edward once told me that just because you love your family doesn't mean you have to like them. Well, I didn't like the Dowaziacs and I knew they didn't like the new Gloria, either. They couldn't see me with fresh eyes, and I realized how much they had debilitated and limited me my whole life. No wonder Estée said I'd been pathetic when we first met. I'd been raised helpless, always expecting someone to rescue me. They were convinced that I couldn't take care of myself. But I'd proven them wrong and now they didn't know what to do with me. Well, I refused to shrink back down just to keep them comfortable.

It was all so clear now. If I'd stayed Gloria Dowaziac, if my father had never gone to prison, I never would have had a career with Saks Fifth Avenue. I never would have known the Millers, or Bobbi and Waller. I never would have met Edward or my lost friend, Estée.

51

IT WAS THE last day of my so-called vacation. I slept in, took my time at home and gave myself one of Estée's Creme Pack treatments, thinking it would help muster my courage. I put on my face along with a new dress that I'd just bought at Saks. It was emerald green and designed by Adrian, clean-lined and perfectly tailored. The fabric felt luxurious against my skin.

I took one last look in the mirror, smoothed down my blonde hair and swept it back off my shoulders. For the first time in over eight years, I saw a familiar face looking back at me. Familiar on the outside and yet I was someone altogether different inside. I drew a deep breath, grabbed my pocketbook, my jacket, and headed out, knowing it was now or never.

Edward was in a meeting when I arrived at the D.A.'s office in Lower Manhattan. I told the receptionist, a pert brunette with a beauty mark penciled in on her cheek, that I'd like to wait. I sat in the lobby for nearly half an hour, smoking cigarettes, my hands sweating as I leafed through the newspaper, unable to focus on any of the words.

When Edward came out to the lobby, my heart lurched forward. And to think I'd given this man up. The expression on his face was one of surprise. I realized he'd never seen me with my natural hair color.

"Can we go somewhere and talk?" I asked.

"Actually, I—I, ah, I have a meeting in about twenty minutes." He checked his watch. "Will my office do?"

We walked down the hallway in silence. I was so focused on not letting my arm brush against his or reaching for his hand or looking at him too longingly—all the things that had once seemed so natural to me.

After he closed the office door, we sat down and I began to babble, nervously telling him about Bobbi confessing to Madame Rubinstein and about my fight with Estée.

There was a long pause in the conversation and he was staring at me. Finally he said, "Sorry. I'm just still getting used to you as a blonde. It looks good. I like it."

That gave me the confidence to say what I'd wanted to tell him in the first place. With my heart pounding wildly, I said, "Do you remember saying to me that if I ever found a way to forgive myself . . ."

He shifted in his chair, rested his elbows on his desk. "Yeah, I remember."

"Well, I finally did it. I found a way to forgive myself. Look—See?" I pointed to my smile. "This is me—Gloria—all forgiven and ready to be happy." He grinned but didn't speak, so I pressed on. "I went to see my father. I did it."

"And?" He leaned forward, just a bit.

"And it was awful. I mean, he looks like a prisoner, like he's right where he belongs. But seeing him that way was also really liberating. And now I know he can't hurt me or anyone else ever again. It's over and I can't begin to tell you how relieved I feel."

"That's great news." Edward shook a cigarette free from the pack, cupped his hands about the match as he lit it. "I'm happy for you, I am—"

"I'm happy for *us*. We can start over again. I'm ready now."

He dropped the match into the ashtray, still burning. My pulse began jumping. The expression on his face was hard to read.

"Did you hear what I just said? I'm finally ready."

"Yeah, but you see"—he sighed, closed his eyes—"I'm not sure you really are."

"What—how can you say that?" My heart—it felt like someone had just hit me in the chest. "This is the first time since my father was arrested that I feel halfway normal."

"I think going to see your father and facing your past was a great start, but"—he raised his hands—"I'm sorry, I can't help it, I'm skeptical."

"Of what? Of me?"

"Well, actually, yes. You act like you're completely over this. And in my experience, epiphanies and huge revelations like this don't usually just appear, click and lock into place. They take time to sort through and—"

"Why are you playing armchair psychologist with me?"

"I just think it's going to take more than a visit to your father to undo all the damage. I think your issues with your father and your whole family run deeper than that." He looked at me and sighed. "Ah, come on, please don't cry."

I couldn't help myself.

He pushed away from his desk, came over and kneeled down in front of me. "Come on now. You know I still love you. I miss you, I do, but I don't think you're as ready as you think you are. I think you need more time."

"How much more time?"

He shrugged. "That depends on you, I guess."

We stayed like that, looking at each other but saying nothing more. His eyes were glassing up. Tears were steadily streaming down my cheeks. Another minute passed. His telephone buzzed and a staticky voice screeched over the intercom, announcing his next appointment.

I was in shock. I didn't remember him walking me out to the lobby and could only vaguely recall him kissing me on the cheek before heading back down the hallway. This hadn't gone the way I'd expected at all. I was leaving empty-handed. I wasn't angry or hurt, I was just sad. So very, very sad. I didn't know if we were completely over or not. But what I did know was that love alone was not enough. Not for us anyway.

If ever there was a time I'd needed Estée, it was just then. She would have found something to say that would have helped me make sense of this, helped me find an optimistic angle to hold on to, but she was gone now. And it was my fault, or at least as much mine as it was hers. I could see now that I'd overreacted, and if I could, I would have rewound the tape, taken back the things I'd said. But the damage was done and now I'd lost my two loves, Estée and Edward.

I willed myself not to break down and start crying all over again on the subway, telling myself that I could bawl my eyes out as soon as I made it safely inside my apartment. *Just hang on. Just two more blocks. One more block. One half block . . .*

I heard the telephone ringing from the hallway as I was keying in. I was sure it was Edward, calling to say he'd made a big mistake, that he was sorry, that I was ready after all, and he wanted me back. I grabbed the receiver on the fifth or sixth ring.

It was Joe, asking me to meet him for a drink. And boy, did I need one.

I told him I was on my way.

TWENTY MINUTES LATER when I arrived at the Onyx Club, I saw Joe sitting at that familiar table off to the side and—surprise,

surprise—he had Estée with him. She looked just as stunned to see me.

"Well," I said, pulling off my gloves, one finger at a time. "What's going on here, Joe?"

He stood up, a curious triumphant grin on his face. "You two are the most stubborn women I've ever known. I don't care who started it, who said what to who—all I know is that if you were men, I'd tell you to step outside and settle it. So, you do whatever it is you gals have to do to work this out because I'm tired of this one"—he pointed to Estée—"moping around like somebody died. And you"—he turned to me—"well, I happen to miss you." He pulled out his chair, offering it to me. "You sit. I'm going home to make dinner."

"I'm going to kill you later when I get back there," Estée called after him.

After Joe cleared the doorway, I sat but Estée refused to look at me. I was acting just as childish, especially when all I wanted to do was hug her.

Finally, I waved down the waiter and ordered a manhattan on the rocks. "You want another gimlet?" I asked Estée. "Or are you going to order a cup of coffee like you did the first time I brought you here?"

She snickered. "Another gimlet would be fine."

When the waiter came back with our drinks, Estée looked at me for the first time, her head cocked to the side, like she was studying me. "Your skin looks dry," she said. "I can tell you're dehydrated. Are you drinking enough?"

"Oh, I'd say I'm drinking plenty." I held up my glass, jiggled the ice cubes.

"I'm talking about water, not booze." I could tell she wanted to laugh but she wouldn't let herself. Instead she drummed her red-lacquered nails on the table.

"So, how was Dallas?" I asked.

"A lot of turbulence."

"Ha-ha. Very funny."

"I was terrified getting on that plane."

"I know you were. I'm sorry about that. Really, I am. I just—I was just so disappointed in you."

"I beg your—"

"Wait"—I held up my hand—"let me finish. I was disappointed because I'd always admired you so much. You showed me what a woman could do. All on her own. All that crazy nonsense about seeing it all in your head first. You made a believer out of me. And then Janice came along and disputed everything I thought I knew about you. I couldn't believe you made up all that stuff about Austria and your family."

"You're a fine one to talk. Look at what you—"

"Let me finish, will you?"

She sighed and acquiesced.

"Thank you." I took a sip of my drink for courage. "But then, the more I thought about it, the more I realized I may have overreacted. I mean, you still did all the work; you're the one who took all the risks. And, my God, look how far you've come." I couldn't help but smile. "True, I mean, you did base everything off your uncle's formulas. But you made them better. That's not a crime. What my father did—now *that* was a crime."

"Well, you'll be happy to know I'm making things right with my uncle."

"Actually, I *am* glad to hear that."

"I was always going to take care of him and his family. That had been my plan all along. It was just that I've been putting every penny I make back into the business."

I nodded, even though her strategy reminded me a little of my father's—his intention to pay everyone back. Eventually.

She shook her head. "What hurt me the most is that I knew—all those years—I knew about your father and I kept hoping you'd open up. But you never did. And then when you pulled that stunt on me in the airport, well, I felt so betrayed by you."

I nodded, unable to defend what I'd done. I took another sip from my cocktail. "You know what the real shame is? We didn't trust each other. We both lied about who we really were and where we came from. We did it for different reasons, but we still did it. Why didn't we have enough faith in our friendship to tell each other the truth? I keep thinking how much easier it would have been if I could have confided in you, talked to you about my father. My family."

"The reason I didn't tell you the truth about my family wasn't because I didn't trust you," she said. "It wasn't a matter of trust. I did it because I wanted to be a success. A huge success. And huge successes don't start out like I did. I was a poor little girl from Queens. Who was going to take me seriously in this industry of ours? I'm selling glamour and I needed a glamorous past if I was going to make it. You went to Corona with me that day—you saw firsthand what a dump it is. I was afraid that if people knew the truth, they'd discount me right off the bat. Plus, on top of everything, I'm a Jew."

"And why didn't you want me to know you were Jewish? Why would you hide something like that?"

"I wasn't *hiding* it," she said with an exasperated sigh. "I've never hidden it. I just didn't broadcast it is all. It was a business decision."

"But Helena Rubinstein's Jewish."

"She got lucky. She was a fluke. Plus, it was different when she was coming up."

"What about Charles Revson? He's Jewish, too. Practically the whole beauty industry is Jewish."

"Charles Revson is a man—and that's a whole different ball game. I don't expect you to understand this, but I saw what was happening in Europe. Even now, there's still antisemitism here in the

States." She paused. "Do you remember that time you came down to Palm Beach? And we were supposed to meet C.Z. at her country club?"

I searched for it. "Vaguely," I said.

"Well, do you want to know why she canceled at the last minute? It was because of me. I played golf there with her the week before and someone—I have no idea who it was or how they knew—found out I was Jewish and they threatened to revoke her membership if she ever brought me there again."

"Oh gosh, I'm sorry. That's lousy."

"I had to lie. I had to tell her it wasn't true, because I felt so dirty, so ashamed. Like there was something wrong with me. It's hard enough being a woman trying to get a business off the ground," she said. "I didn't need a second strike against me. It's a tough world out there. Sometimes the truth is just too painful or doesn't fit with where you're heading. If we're not allowed a little escape from our pasts, how else are we all supposed to get by?" Her eyes turned glassy and she went silent for a long time.

Thinking I could lighten the mood, I asked her about Neiman Marcus.

"It went well. Better than expected. I'm launching my line down there in the fall."

"See, you didn't need me with you after all. And, well, for whatever it's worth, I'm happy for you. I knew you could do it." I raised my glass to her. "Here's to Estée Lauder and Neiman Marcus."

With that she burst into tears. Elbows on the table, she cupped her eyes with both hands, her shoulder shaking. She was mumbling but the one thing I heard clearly, without mistake, was: "God, how I've missed you."

I can't remember who made the first move—if she got up and came over to me, or if I stood and went to her—but there we were, in the middle of the Onyx Club, gripping each other in a fierce hug, crying onto each other's shoulders.

When we pulled apart, I looked at her. My beautiful perfect Estée had two streaks of black running onto her cheeks. Sad little clown eyes. "You really need to make waterproof mascara," I said.

We burst out laughing, and then, as if we'd rehearsed it all a million times, at the exact same moment we both stuck out our hands and said, "Truce?"

Epilogue

1985

I CHECK MYSELF IN the mirror once more. The hair is still platinum and I'm well aware that I'm not fooling anyone, least of all myself. At sixty-nine, I see all too clearly every fine line, every battle that gravity has won in our endless tug-of-war. The expensive creams and lotions, the monthly facials, can only do so much, but I'm not going down without a fight. You can't when you're married to a younger man. Nine years younger, to be specific.

As I slip into my dress, the one I bought especially for tonight's event, my husband comes up to the bedroom and hands me a package. "Just arrived for you," he says. "Special delivery. The timing couldn't be more intentional, now could it?"

I check the return address: Macmillan Publishing Company. Even before I open it, I know what it is—an advance copy of Lee Israel's book. She made sure I got it today, the very day that Estée's book goes on sale. I open the package and the book slides out: a pale yellow cover, no picture, no illustration. Just all type: *Estée Lauder: Beyond the Magic* by Lee Israel. Estée's name is bigger than Lee Israel's. I warned Estée that I'd probably receive an early copy and I know she's going to want to see this, so I tuck it under my arm without even bothering to crack the spine.

"Take good care of the guest of honor," he says, giving me a peck on the cheek before I go.

Estée's friends Pat and William F. Buckley are throwing a big splashy bash for the release of her book at Mortimer's on 75th and Lexington. The guest list is long and impressive. Everyone from Jackie O to Debbie Reynolds, and even Wallis Simpson has RSVP'd. With Joe gone—having passed away more than two years ago—Estée doesn't want to walk in alone. I've volunteered to pick her up at her office and escort her to the party. My husband will meet me there later.

I still think about Edward from time to time. And I'm sure he still thinks of me. Big love like that doesn't disappear completely. But now when I think of him, I realize that he was not my destiny after all, but rather my catalyst. When it didn't work out with us for the second time—and yes, we did try it again—our breakup drove me into analysis. Turns out, he was right. I had more father issues to work on than I'd realized. But going down that rocky road paved the way for me and the man who turned out to be the true love of my life.

Even after thirty-five years of marriage, I still can't bring myself to call him Howard. To me, he'll always be Soda Pop, or S.P., as everyone else calls him. Years after I'd run into him in Times Square, he spotted me at a gala for the newly formed Fragrance Foundation. He was working for Coty at the time, the director of sales and marketing, before moving on to Dior, where he holds one of the top posts. Not bad for someone with an eighth-grade education. I already knew from seeing him years before that he'd grown up to be a handsome man, but when I saw him that night at the fragrance gala, I was surprised by how attracted I was to him. I wrestled with that and the age difference for a good long time, but he was patient, as he'd always been with me, and waited while I worked my way through it. Together we have two grown daughters, an English sheepdog and a quirky old brownstone on the Upper West Side. To this day, he carries that photograph of the two of us in his wallet, the one taken at the Millers' Thanksgiving dinner all those years ago.

Before I head over to the General Motors Building to get Estée—who, in typical Estée style, insists on working up to the last minute—I make a special stop that seems only befitting, given the day. Like most of my colleagues—Marion, Bob Fiske and Mrs. Coopers—I've retired from Saks Fifth Avenue, but that doesn't keep me from dropping by the store every now and again, just to check on things.

I use the 50th Street entrance, still marveling, after all these years, at that metal canopy and the decorative bronze detailing. For my money, this store is still the jewel of Fifth Avenue. They renovated the interior back in 1979 but I still prefer the original marble floors and the old chandeliers. But modern times call for modern touches. I also notice that various departments have been moved about. But the one thing that remains constant in Saks Fifth Avenue is its air of luxury. That is timeless.

I drift into the cosmetic department, which is much larger than it was in my day. It's so busy, it's almost dizzying, but not in that vertigo sense. Thank goodness those episodes are a thing of the past. I haven't had a bout in decades. But still, this store is a whirlwind of activity. You can't walk more than two feet without a salesgirl offering a spritz of perfume or a complimentary makeover. The salesgirls stand in front of their counters, hovering over customers, applying foundation, blush, eyeliner, and I'm reminded that Estée was the one who pioneered that type of selling. She was the first person to demonstrate her products on the floor. That was an Estée signature move. So were all the freebies and samples she gave away that used to drive Joe crazy. And yet now, there isn't one of her competitors that isn't offering some sort of gift with purchase, all lavishly displayed under glass.

As I glance at the department, I can't help but notice that just Estée's perfumes alone—Youth-Dew, White Linen and her newest creation, Beautiful—take up more real estate than her original counter space had. A bit of cosmetic folklore claims that back in 1953, after Bob Fiske rejected the idea of Estée launching a fragrance, she intentionally dropped a bottle of Youth-Dew in the middle of the store floor just so women could smell it and then ask for it at the counter. I can't verify that story, but it sure sounds like something Estée would do.

Not surprisingly I see a big stack of autographed red glossy-covered books at the Estée Lauder counter: *Estée: A Success Story.* Not that I'm taking credit for her accomplishments, but the book was my idea. Estée had been talking about writing a book for ages, but after my first meeting with Lee Israel, I told her to get going on it. *Now!* The finished product is beautiful, truly stunning, and I'm sure if it were up to Estée and not her publisher, she'd be giving a copy away with every purchase.

It's almost four o'clock and time to head over to Estée's office. She resides on the thirty-ninth floor of the General Motors Building, which some call the *General Odors Building*, given all the cosmetic and perfume industries headquartered there. How ironic that Estée would have anchored her company in the very same building that housed her rival, Revlon. Before Charles Revson passed away, the two of them used to glower at each other in the lobby and insisted on taking separate elevators. Charles has been gone since '75, but the competition between the brands is as fierce as ever, even after Estée drove Revlon out of Saks Fifth Avenue and into the drugstore market.

I push through the double doors—ESTÉE LAUDER COMPANIES etched in the frosted glass—and the receptionist shows me into Estée's corner office. She sits behind her Chippendale desk, still fast at work but already dressed for her party in a lovely red ruffled

Halston cocktail dress. Her office is elegant with plush carpeting, her view of the city framed within heavy, floor-to-ceiling drapes. Photographs are everywhere: Estée with Grace Kelly, Ann-Margret, with Nancy and Ronald Reagan. And of course there are photographs of Estée and Joe everywhere. I know how much I miss him and can't begin to imagine the void his passing has left for her.

"You'll never guess what turned up on my doorstep today." I hold up Lee Israel's book.

"Oh good Lord, let me see it."

"Only on one condition. You can't open it. Not yet. Not today. Today is your day. So you put this book away somewhere. There'll be plenty of time to read it later."

"But I need to see what she wrote about me."

"Listen to me." I sit down across from her, still holding the book at bay. "It doesn't matter what Lee Israel said in this book. You got out in front of her. Your book is out today. Hers won't be in bookstores for another three weeks."

"Just tell me what it says. What did she write about me?"

"I don't know, and I don't care. I haven't even opened it. I already know your story—better than most." I wink. "And more than that, I know how hard you worked to get where you are. I know the sacrifices you made. And I also know that tonight is a celebration of you."

She relaxes into her chair, shoulders easing back in place as a proud smile rises on her face.

"Now c'mon, let's go," I say. "Your adoring fans await you, because you, Estée Lauder, are truly a success story."

And that's the truth.

Author's Note

WRITING ABOUT THE iconic Estée Lauder was intimidating, to say the least. I wanted to tell her story and do justice to her accomplishments as well as her struggles. While she might not have been perfect—who among us is?—she was undeniably a trailblazer, and I have enormous respect for her chutzpah and drive. Prior to her death in 2004 at the age of ninety-seven, Estée Lauder had amassed a personal fortune in excess of $233 million. Not too shabby for a self-made girl from Queens.

As acknowledged in her autobiography, *Estée: A Success Story*, some of her past was less than flattering, but she had plausible explanations for the many discrepancies often attributed to her. The majority of those inconsistencies in Estée's past can be found in Lee Israel's unauthorized biography, *Estée Lauder: Beyond the Magic*, which served as one of my sources.

I did, however, try to paint a balanced portrait of a remarkable woman who revolutionized the cosmetic industry. That said, let me take this opportunity to separate fact from fiction and let you, the reader, know where I've taken some creative license.

Estée began selling her face creams and lotions at Florence Morris's House of the Ash Blondes. For purposes of this book, I have her starting her operation out of the fictional Darlene's Palace of Beauty. Also, please note that Estée prided herself on being very fashionable and stylish, and Gloria's references early in the book to the contrary were my own invention.

Leonard Lauder's book, *The Company I Keep: My Life in Beauty*, was an enormous help to me. I sought inspiration from Mr. Lauder in re-creating Estée's first trip to Miami—during which, by the way, Leonard was four rather than five years old, as I've stated in this novel. I also relied on Mr. Lauder's book to help convey Estée's attempts at getting her products into Saks Fifth Avenue as well as her speaking engagement at the Waldorf Astoria luncheon, which proved to be a pivotal moment in her career.

As an aside, the story of that luncheon at the Waldorf Astoria has been retold many times and has many different versions. Some say she gave away $3.00 tubes of lipstick, others say she gave away samples of face powder, others still say it was tiny bottles of lotions. For the sake of this book, I had her giving away a combination of all her products, but it's true that following that luncheon, the women formed a line at Saks Fifth Avenue, eager to purchase Estée Lauder products.

While conducting research, I came across various versions of Estée's rise. Some say that Estée's first department store was Bonwit Teller, others say it was Saks Fifth Avenue. No doubt that of the two, the latter would have been a far more significant account. My research indicated that Saks was the crucial account that launched Estée's career, and I do believe that was true and therefore have portrayed that here.

In the late 1940s, Estée and Joe approached BBDO to help advertise their budding brand. For the sake of the narrative, I've moved this up on the timeline. The same is true for Estée pioneering her direct mail campaign after BBDO said Lauder's $50,000 advertising budget was insufficient. That was when Estée took that money and put it all toward free samples, thereby establishing her long-standing tradition of "Gift with Purchase," a sales tactic perpetually mimicked by her competitors.

Estée was very outspoken about her rivalry with Charles Revson as well as her dislike of Elizabeth Arden. In her autobiography, she recalls the time Miss Arden threw her out of her Red Door Spa with her hair still in rollers. I took that nugget and did a bit of embellishing in the scene where I have Estée telling Gloria she'd been handing out free samples of her products at Arden's spa. According to Estée's autobiography, Arden's asking her to leave was completely unprovoked. Also, it appears that Estée was unruffled by the incident, whereas in my fictionalized retelling, Estée was quite upset by the event.

Helena Rubinstein was a competitor and fellow pioneer of the cosmetic industry. While it is true that she dropped bottles of Heaven Sent tied to balloons from Bonwit Teller's rooftop, there is no evidence to suggest that she ever approached Saks Fifth Avenue with this same promotional idea. Madame Rubinstein was an avid art collector; however, her purchase of banana art is purely fictional. Which is not to say that banana art is not a real thing. As touched upon in the Readers Guide, Bobbi Koerner was inspired by my friend Roy Koerner, who is the one and only Banana Boy Roy. We worked together at my brother's advertising agency, The Rosen Group, where Roy began tinkering with banana peels and creating his unique artwork.

While Estée was very forthcoming in her book about relationships and courtships with other men after her divorce from Joe, Lee Israel disclosed that Estée had an affair with a married man, Arnold Louis van Ameringen. Van, as he was known, went on to become the president and chairman of International Flavors and Fragrances. Estée never addressed their romantic relationship, insisting the two were merely friends and professional colleagues. Some say he was instrumental in the development of her first fragrance, Youth-Dew.

Something else that Lee Israel and others reported was the financial arrangement between Estée and her uncle John Schotz. As a young girl, Estée's uncle John served as her inspiration, and most of her initial products were based on his formulas, and yet some believe he was never fairly compensated for his contributions to the Estée Lauder brand. He died nearly penniless, despite his niece grossing over $14 million annually.

It has also been widely stated that though Estée was born in Queens as Josephine Esther, she reinvented herself as Estée, born in Austria, the daughter of a noble family, having been raised with servants in a large mansion. In truth, she and her family lived above the hardware store her father owned. She addressed this in her own book and offered an explanation for the popular misconceptions about her past, as well as her downplaying her Jewish heritage.

While it's true that Estée did divorce Joe Lauder on the grounds of mental cruelty, Harriet Allen, Joe's stand-in for Estée during their separation, was purely my creation. According to all accounts, Joe remained loyal and was hopelessly in love with Estée, his Blondie. The couple later remarried, in 1942 according to some sources and in 1943 according to others. Regardless of the date, Estée and Joe remained happily married and very much in love until Joe's death in 1983. Also, it should be noted that in the early days of World War II, Joe did operate a somewhat successful business venture of his own, selling lighters and other items to the military.

If you'd like to learn more about Estée Lauder, I highly recommend the following:

Estée: A Success Story by Estée Lauder

Estée Lauder: Beyond the Magic by Lee Israel

The Company I Keep: My Life in Beauty by Leonard Lauder

At the Top by Marylin Bender

Selling Dreams: Inside the Beauty Business by Margaret Allen

Estée Lauder: Businesswoman and Cosmetics Pioneer by Robert Grayson

Estée Lauder: Beauty Business Success by Rachel Epstein

Helena Rubinstein: The Woman who Invented Beauty by Michèle Fitoussi

The Powder and the Glory, a documentary produced, written, and directed by Ann Carol Grossman & Arnie Reisman

Acknowledgments

I am incapable of writing a novel all by myself and am grateful to many friends and colleagues who have helped me along the way. My heartfelt thanks to Julie Anderson, who first suggested I make Estée Lauder the subject of my next book. To Erika Robuck for helping me shape the concept along with Stephanie Thornton, Kerri Maher, Lauren Margolin and Andrea Rosen, who gave me early reads and provided crucial feedback. Thanks also to Patti and Stephen Nisenholz for insight into the cosmetic world and Roy Koerner, the one and only Banana Boy Roy.

I have always considered booksellers, librarians, bloggers and influencers to be my partners, and as the years go by, I'm grateful that so many of you have become my friends. Though the pandemic may have kept us apart, I am ever appreciative of your ongoing support of my work: Robin Allen, Melissa Amster, Nina Barrett, Cindy Burnette, Bobbi Dumas, Rebecca and Kimberly George, Kristin Gilbert, Alli Gilley, Daniel Goldin, Maxwell Gregory, Deborah Harpham, Ashley Hasty, Kym Havens, Stephanie Hochschild, Andrea Peskind Katz, Pamela Klinger-Horn, Courtney Marzilli,

Susan McBeth, Jill Miner, Sharlene Moore, Mary O'Malley, Gary Parkes, Denise Phillips, Dan Radovich, Javier Ramirez, Suzy Takacs and Eleanor Thorn.

Thanks also to my trusted friends and fellow authors: Tasha Alexander, Stacey Ballis, Lisa Barr, Melanie Benjamin, Jill Bernstein, Jamie Freveletti, Keir Graff, Andrew Grant, Sara Gruen, Alison Hammer, Abbott Kahler, Brenda Klem, Lisa Kotin, Mindy Mailman, Stephanie Nelson and Barbara Sapstein. Also, a big thanks to the Tall Poppies and the Lyonesses—I'm honored to know such talented women.

I am fortunate to have two of the smartest and hardest-working women in publishing in my corner: my agent, Kevan Lyon, and my editor, Amanda Bergeron. Kevan, you continue to amaze me with your wisdom, compassion and ability to multitask like nobody's business. Amanda, your patience and expert guidance are invaluable to me. Thank you for continuing to push me (ever so gently) to write the best books I have in me. To my Berkley team at Penguin Random House—especially Ivan Held, Christine Bell, Claire Zion, Craig Burke, Jeanne-Marie Hudson, Tara O'Connor, Tina Joell, Fareeda Bullert, Elisha Katz, Sareer Khader, Tawanna Sullivan, Michelle Kasper, Sarah Oberrender, Patricia Clark, Stefan Moorehead and, of course, Brian Wilson. I am forever grateful to all of you for your behind-the-scenes dedication and your support.

And lastly, to my family: Debbie Rosen, Pam Rosen, Jerry Rosen, Andrea Rosen, Joey Perilman, Devon Rosen and my one and only, John Dul. None of this would be possible without all of you.

Fifth Avenue Glamour Girl

RENÉE ROSEN

Behind the Scenes: A Conversation with Renée Rosen

Questions for Discussion

Further Reading: On Renée Rosen's Bookshelf

Behind the Scenes: A Conversation with Renée Rosen

Where did the idea for *Fifth Avenue Glamour Girl* come from?
I owe a great deal of thanks to my friend Julie Anderson. We were talking one day, and when I told her I hadn't a clue as to what I should write about next, without skipping a beat, she smiled and said, "What about Estée Lauder?" All it took was one five-minute Google search to realize I had the subject of my next book.

In your books, you tend to introduce fictional characters into the story with real-life figures. Is there a reason for that?
It's two pronged. One, I absolutely love the freedom of creating characters from scratch without any restrictions on their past or future. But I also introduce the fictional element in order to tell a story we haven't heard before. When you're writing about a real person, many readers already know their story, and therefore, there's no reason for me to fictionalize what's already out there. By bringing in the fictional element, I can explore new themes and new twists while still delivering the facts about a well-known figure.

When you're writing, do you rely on critique partners?

Years ago I had a writing mentor, Joe Esselin. His father was a prominent Yiddish poet and Joe himself was a playwright and writer. He was always the first to read every word of every draft I ever wrote. We devoted hours to reading the final drafts aloud and would argue over word choices, sentence structures, character arcs and so on. Sadly, I lost Joe at the age of ninety-three back in 2016 and I was terrified going it alone with my 2017 release, *Windy City Blues*.

The truth of the matter is that I don't think any one person ever truly writes a novel all on their own. It takes a village. I always have my agent and editor, both of whom I lean on quite a bit. And thankfully, I have the support of a number of very generous and talented readers and fellow authors who read early drafts, share their feedback and basically hold my hand through the process.

How much of yourself is in the pages of *Fifth Avenue Glamour Girl?*

This novel probably contains more of "me" tucked into the pages and between the lines than anything else I've written since my autobiographical debut, *Every Crooked Pot*. Usually I keep myself out of my work but for some reason, this book was different and I found I could make use of people and things pulled from my own life.

For example, like Gloria I have been known to suffer vertigo bouts. Bobbi is based on my friend and real-life banana artist, Roy Koerner, aka Banana Boy Roy. Roy and I worked together in an ad agency when he started fiddling with banana peels. I remember they were tacked up on his wall, drying out. The Millers grew out of a bit that John and I started doing, acting as if we were an elderly Jewish couple, Richard and Sylvia Miller. We even played around with starting a podcast, *Is It News or Is It Narishkeit?* (nonsense), but got cold feet and dropped it. Mr. Belfort is loosely based on a man I worked with who spoke only in clichés. Mrs. Hutt is loosely based on a woman with a well-known and accepted shoplifting habit, and like in the book, all the stores just tallied up the totals of whatever she'd taken and charged her husband for it each month. There are various other tidbits here and there throughout that people very close to me will pick up on.

I once heard you say that there's a difference between being a writer and being an author. Could you elaborate on that?

This is something that struck me after I published my first novel and frankly, it took me by surprise. When you're crafting a manuscript, you're a writer. That is very interior and solitary work. You spend hours a day alone, in your head. It's perfect for introverts. But once you sell your book and get published, you have to put on your author hat. Overnight you go from private to public—and usually without much warning. That's when you need to be an extrovert, comfortable standing up in front of people, going on radio and TV and being *out there*. It's a difficult switch for some of us to flip. I know I really struggled with the two sides of this coin early on and have gradually become more at ease with the author part. But truly, I feel most at home being a writer.

Questions for Discussion

1. Friendship is at the heart of this novel. However, in the beginning, Gloria says she never could have imagined that she and Estée would have become friends. What do you think drew these women to each other? Have you ever formed a friendship with someone you initially thought you had nothing in common with?

2. In the beginning of the novel, Gloria is the first to admit that she's helpless when it comes to taking care of herself. What do you think were the major turning points that allowed her to grow and become independent and self-sufficient? How much influence do you think Estée had on Gloria's transformation?

3. Because of Gus Dowaziac's crimes, Gloria was estranged from her father and other members of her family. Did you feel she was justified in keeping her past secret from those closest to her? Do you think their relationships would have changed if they'd known the truth earlier?

4. What did you think of Estée's relationship with Joe? How did you feel when she left him? Were you supportive of her decision to divorce him? What did you think about them reuniting and going into business together?

5. Gloria and Waller had an unspoken understanding about the nature of their relationship. Were you ever rooting for the two of them to become more involved or were you satisfied by the terms of their so-called arrangement?

6. For much of the book Gloria goes out of her way to avoid getting romantically involved with anyone. Why do you think that was and what was it about Edward that allowed her to lower her guard and let him in?

7. Estée was very determined to make a name for herself in the beauty industry. There were times when her drive could have been construed as brash and downright pushy. Did you find her sales tactics admirable or annoying?

8. Estée's public persona turned out to be very different from her humble beginnings. Did discovering the truth about her cause you to think less of her accomplishments? Did it change the way you think of her? Were you sympathetic or at least able to understand why she did what she did?

9. A theme in this book is reinvention, and one could say that makeup is another tool for just that. Many women use it to camouflage, embellish and otherwise alter what they were

born with. Do you think there's anything wrong with a woman using cosmetics to be her best? And with all that is available in terms of false eyelashes, hair extensions, plastic surgery and so on, where do you draw the line?

10. How did you feel about the way Gloria finally resolved her differences with her father and the rest of her family? Did you think she waited too long? Should she have forgiven her father for the crimes that he committed?

11. Family relationships can be complicated. Could you relate to any of what Gloria was going through? What do you think about the popularly held belief: *You like because of, and you love in spite of*?

12. Estée Lauder was a true pioneer in the cosmetic business and to this day her company remains one of the major brands worldwide. Certain concepts that are now commonplace practices within the cosmetic industry came from Estée's own ingenuity. Can you identify some of the ways in which she revolutionized the makeup counter as we know it today? Aside from her own Estée Lauder brand, can you name the other companies that are now under the Estée Lauder umbrella?

13. Lee Israel is best known for her memoir, *Can You Ever Forgive Me?*, based on her forgery of literary letters. Given this background, how do you feel about her working on an unauthorized biography of Estée Lauder?

Further Reading: On Renée Rosen's Bookshelf

GREAT HISTORICAL FICTION

The Women of Chateau Lafayette by Stephanie Dray

The Diamond Eye by Kate Quinn

A Most Clever Girl by Stephanie Marie Thornton

Lillian Boxfish Takes a Walk by Kathleen Rooney

The Mayfair Bookshop by Eliza Knight

A Gentleman in Moscow by Amor Towles

OTHER BOOKS I'VE LOVED

A Little Life by Hanya Yanagihara

The Secrets We Kept by Lara Prescott

Utopia Avenue by David Mitchell

Shuggie Bain by Douglas Stuart

Wahala by Nikki May

Lessons in Chemistry by Bonnie Garmus

The Fran Lebowitz Reader by Fran Lebowitz

Photo by Charles Osgood Photography

RENÉE ROSEN is the *USA Today* bestselling author of *The Social Graces*, *Park Avenue Summer*, *Windy City Blues*, *White Collar Girl*, *What the Lady Wants* and *Dollface*. She is also the author of *Every Crooked Pot*, a YA novel. Renée lives in Chicago and is working on a new historical novel about Ruth Handler, the woman who invented the Barbie doll.

CONNECT ONLINE

ReneeRosen.com

ReneeRosen1

ReneeRosenAuthor

ReneeRosen_